Acknowledgements

Deepest thanks

To Nicolas, for his incredible smile and charm,
To Carlie for her courage and all encompassing beauty,
To Erik for his sweet purity,
To David for his eternal love,
To God above, for my amazing family and friends

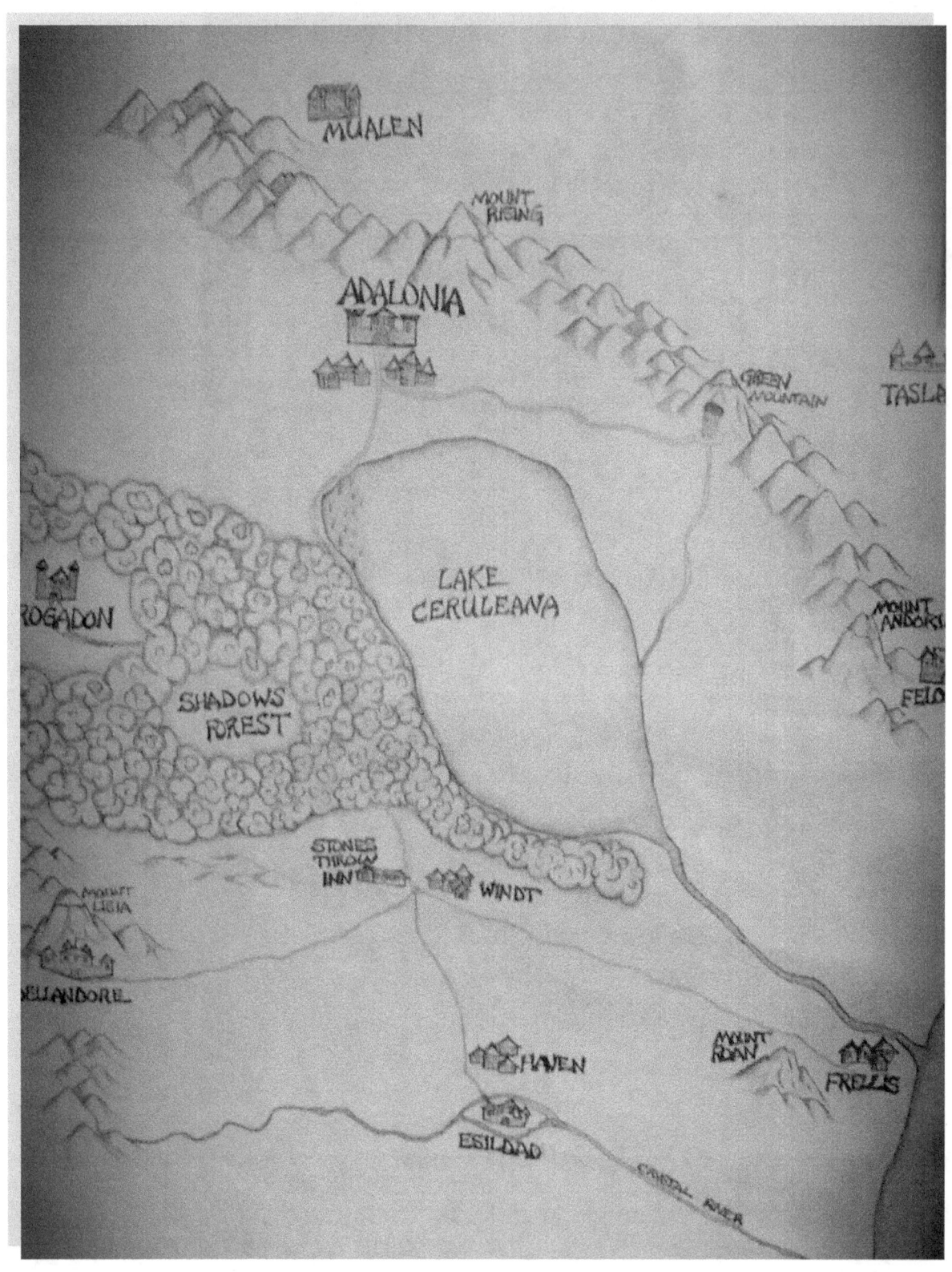

PROLOGE

DESPERATE BEGININGS

Renna forced her bewildered, weeping sister through the rapidly darkening woods. They had been running for hours now, and had found themselves thoroughly lost; entrenched in the myriad of identical pathways that carved through the Shadow's forest. Ralla finally fell; seizing muscles giving in to her exhaustion. Renna rushed to her sister, wrapping her free arm around her in a shaking attempt to comfort her.

"Why does he hunt us, sister?" Ralla shook with tearless sobs. Renna shivered against the chill that ran down her quivering spine.

"He *fears* your children, and *detests* mine," Renna turned sorrowful, dark brown eyes on her bundled infant; sleeping peacefully amidst their escape.

"But why *your* child? He has so many he will not even *claim*!" Ralla cried. Renna sighed before turning to face her frightened sister; a tear rolling down her dirty cheek as she spoke.

"Because his oblivious, *adoring* constituents would frown upon their juvenile king, owning a *slave*, let alone his conceiving an *heir* with one. He means to destroy the...*evidence*." Renna's hushed voice chilled as she answered causing Ralla to cringe.

"Why does he fear *Carr* and *Cai*? They are mere boys, not yet eight years old! Besides, my husband has no *royal* ties...he is of no threat to the throne of Dellandore. Why has he imprisoned *him*?"

"I only know that Kiera sent for me after Cassen was apprehended not yards from Triden's own court. He beseeched her to hide your sons but had no time to give explanation. He could not have chosen a better place to keep them. Ulei and his cowardly father would not dare enter *that* castle!" Renna smirked despite herself with the thought.

"I *need* to see my boys. They will be terrified without their father or I!" Ralla moaned, but Renna promptly snapped her quiet.

"They are safe in Adalonia! Kiera and Sarana will hide them, you mustn't fear for them now but for yourself!" Renna warned. Ralla paled with a frightening thought.

"Does he mean to...*kill* us, Renna? Is he so *evil* as to strike down two unarmed women and a *child?*" Ralla asked. Renna faced her slowly.

"Evil is *all* he is, sister," she answered coldly. Swallowed by the darkness of sunset and the dense cover of the forest, the sisters fled in vain towards a dawn and northern salvation they would never reach.

It was only a matter of time, her mother had warned. Callana was of age now, 16, and could no longer hide behind her adolescence to avoid the very adult duty expected of her. When her father had died, six years earlier, she had thought that the devastating loss would be the worst she would endure. She found out, as her mother had; life had far more grueling lessons to teach than bereavement. Her mother, Hellena knew life was cruel; being a widowed mother of five, but she was every bit as much of a soldier as her beloved husband. She would carry on, though her options were few.

In the Windt village, soldiers had no allowance, nor assistance for leftover destitute families in the event of death. Widows and young girls with no prospects in the village were sent to the Stone's throw tavern and inn looking for a means to help feed hungry families or simply secure enough coin to get out of Windt all together.
Her mother and four sisters had tried desperately to operate an inn. Travelers passed through their conveniently located village often en route to Della Verde to the North; Esildad to the far south; West towards Dellandore or East to Frellis and the sea. So, it seemed easy enough to supplant a lost soldier's income by housing and feeding said passers by. Hellena had named it Stone's throw because it was right in the middle and only yards from the cross section of the main roads running in each direction. But men coming from out of town were not interested in sleeping and eating alone. Hellena had given all of her girls the choice to leave or stay at the Inn. Soon Callana would have to decide. Her sister's loyalties had proved foremost to their dignities. They had chosen to stay and suffer drunken advances and love-less sex with faceless men who would ravage their bodies, then evaporate like mist come dawn. Callana didn't know if she could be as resilient. Each had one by one become of age and learned to serve more than stew and ale.

Attracting men had never been difficult for Hellena, even from a young age; she was a curvy, attractive woman of modest stature, with blazing red hair kept in a long braid down her back with porcelain milky white skin, a rounded, small nose, and light, brown eyes, the color of a deep orange sunset. Hellena's husband, Cai, had called her, carrot, for her red-orange hair and orange eyes. Her daughters were like mirror images of their striking mother, save for Callana, who had her father's dark brown eyes as well as his temper. Though Cai was enormous and Callana was small, the two were severely similar in many ways.

Hellena found that even though her money was ill earned, for the most part, she was well respected by most men as an enterprising woman in the market; however detested by most women; Callana and her sisters had never bowed their heads for what they did. It was simply a method of survival and they had no time for luxuries as vain as *shame*. The ladies were clean and dressed suitably; instructed on etiquette, household duties, cooking, writing and reading. As walking, talking merchandise, appearance was everything.

All of Hellena's girls were known for their beauty and charm; the word of the Inn spread far. Crystalline was oldest at twenty one, named for the Crystal river between Windt and the kingdom Esildad to the south. Then Cylan, twenty, Caran, nineteen, Cella, eighteen and Callana, just days into her sixteenth year, all named with their father's first letter, as was tradition.

Callana's time to decide had come and with it the end of her innocence. The sun would set for the last time on Callana the child. By morning, she would be a woman.

....

Callana lay, staring at the ceiling of her humble bed chamber, damp from the June humidity. Mother had assured her the first time would be horrid and only sufferable after that. She felt sick. Her stomach lurched at the sound of squeaking floor boards. Someone was coming, she had been chosen during dinner and he was on his way to take his use of her. She wanted to leap out of her window. Her heart was hammering in her chest so hard she was sure he would hear it. She flinched as the door swung open and was upright in a second, unsure of whether to stand, or sit, or lay or talk or smile or plunge a knife into her own throat!

"Eh girl," He breathed the words, in a voice much deeper than his tall thin frame suggested. Callana's air caught in her throat. She could smell the rancid odor of his alcohol soaked breath and the musk of old sweat. Blood drained from her face and she felt sweat beads start on her forehead, her knees wobbled. The room spun and she uncontrollably lurched forward as the anxious boiling in her stomach came up suddenly. She vomited violently, bathing black leather boots with her bright yellow stomach acid. Judging by his outrage, this was not the good time he had hoped for.

....

"Callana, you awake bird?" Hellena's singsong voice filled Callana's ears. Her mind was filled at once with the memory of her failure the night before.

"Oh mother, I feel absolutely ridiculous!" She dropped her head into her hands and fell sideways into her mother's ample bosom. Hellena was stroking her hair, being sure not to get her hands stuck in the tangled red ball at the end. She was shushing Callana.

"Come come, I could never be cross with you. That gentleman however, will not be a return visitor here at Stone's throw."

"Mother I will make it up to you; I promise!"

"What for? I could *hardly* imagine how, you're not my type at all, love!" Callana wiped her tears and peered up into the orange reassurance of her mother's twinkling eyes; for such a hardy woman she had such sweet eyes. Callana sagged in her mother's embrace; saddened all over again and wracked with guilt over the food money lost when her visitor had stormed out demanding a full refund after forcing a giggling Cylan to clean his boots thoroughly. Callana perked when she heard the shuffling and sniggering approaching her door. Her sisters burst in to tease her, pulling her hair and poking her ribs.

"*Eh, girl, time to show what you got right?*" Cella teased standing feet wide with her hands on her hips pretending to stagger into the room.

"You said a mouthful sir!" Caran bent over as she made the sound of vomiting. The playful harassment brought out the jovial side of Callana, in spite of herself and she jumped to her feet and began chasing them along the hall and outside with the threat of forcing all four to smell her retch covered hair and puke breath.

"Sire," Jiden sneered out the word. "I am afraid I cannot go through with this...this...." He dropped his glare to the floor searching for words, as if the cold stone would know what to say. The king impatiently groaned; dreading the impending argument he was no more interested in *hearing* than he was to have to *wait* to hear, postponing matters of actual importance.

"This, this bargain you've made; this abomination to, to love!" The young Prince stood tall; chain mail jingling as he lifted his chin and crossed his arms to punctuate his affirmation.

"I understand, your frustration my son, *as I have for the past two months*, but, as I have said before, marriage is not a matter of *love*."

"Thank you, husband," grinned Lena.

"My Queen, please, do not help him. This is his duty."

"So marriage is a duty now you say sire?" she snorted. Jiden jumped at his chance to tear his father's line of reasoning apart.

"You admit you don't love my mother than?" Jiden stabbed a finger at his father.

"Jiden!" roared the King. "My Queen," he turned apologetically to his wife. "We were *arranged* from birth by our parents to unite our kingdoms as Jiden has been *arranged* from birth to bond Adalonia and Rogadon in Peace." He took her tiny hand at that moment and kissed it. Her beautiful green eyes softened at the earnest look on his rugged face.

"But the morning you stepped out of that carriage holding your father's hand in that exceptionally taut scarlet dress..."

He flicked his thick brows over intensely dark indigo eyes and winked. "I knew love."

Lena laughed throatily.

"Do not pretend *love* is what came to your degenerate mind! That gown was a strategic push of my mother's doing and your resulting stupor was precisely what she intended to bring about!"

The two tittered like love birds and stared into each others eyes; the King kissing his beloved's hands, while Jiden battled revulsion and huffed.

"Mother!" Lena jumped back to attention and after pretending to straighten her garments she turned up her red cheeked oval face. Jiden's eyes were unrelenting.

"You can't have me go through with this." He slumped slightly and put a little whine on the end of his words for the benefit of his mother. She turned towards her husband to beseech on her son's behalf and flinched back at the King's slanting glare. He was no longer willing to listen; The Council of elders had started filing in, signaling Jiden's opportunity had passed. He may speak openly in front of Odin, his *father*, but not Odin the *King*. He stood at parade rest with arms crossed at the wrists behind his back awaiting the inevitable. "Prince Jiden, I will hear your morning report after council. That is all." Jiden bowed respectfully to his father as did Lena as she was usually a part of the council but today she had a neglected guest room to attend to. They left the Hall together in silence.

....

Despite his disappointing start, Jiden could always enjoy his morning patrol. To take in a vantage point view of this remarkable kingdom, from the rolling green lands climbing up the mountain bases sloping down to the silt Lake Ceruleana shore. He had a small guard of six accompanied by his squire, Nicholas. He was the same age as Jiden, 16, with the same six foot two inch broad frame, bronzed skin and unruly flaxen curls. But the difference was in the eyes. While Jiden's were an intense sea green, identical to his mother's, Nicholas had the same crystal blue eyes of his father; Rasden of Tasladad, cousin to Odin. Nicholas was named by Lena, as it was her baby sister, Lunette's first born son, and the final step into adult hood and out from under the grip of a very over bearing big sister. Both women were full of pride for their Valley, and Kingdom; raising equally proud boys, who would easily lay down their lives for the other. Nicholas was assigned squire duty by his Uncle as a formality as Nicholas had tagged along on every training circuit, each patrol, and nearly all events in Jiden's life since they were only children. They were indivisible, despite Odin's growing intolerance of their mischievous natures and ridiculously embellished tales. However, in spite of all, there was not a man alive in the whole Della Verde that would deny their generosity and sincere character. This was, more often than not, the only reason Odin did not throttle the twosome.

"Sir Galland split the guard; I will take the east." Jiden commanded. "Aye" rumbled Sir Galland, oldest at twenty nine and most trusted; he was a gargantuan man of very few words. He had served as first Knight under Odin, and trained Jiden when he turned ten, and was a masterful swordsman and archer. At over six and half feet tall with arms like tree trunks he was a good man to have at your flank. Jiden had hand selected six Knights from the royal guard that would remain his own personal detachment. It was the highest honored rank for a Knight to be in the royal guard and the most demanding. Prince Jiden was still too young to have battle tested his guard, but felt he was well safe from harm.

As Sir Galland nodded to the strategically gifted Sir Gracien to head north to the base of Mount Rising, the fearless Sir David and hot tempered Sir

Franklin would skirt the waters edge and the western rim of the Shadow's forest. The jabbering and stout Sir Senren and affable lanky youth Sir Laden were sent south east, around Ceruleana Lake, towards Mount Andoria's sprawling plains. The Prince, with cousin in tow, headed east where they would convene deep in the farmlands near Green Mountain's base, with the three detachments and collect a report for the King. Jiden could hear Sir Senren already prattling about an early summer this year and warily hushed his voice.

"Ey, Nicholas?" He whispered. Nicholas was standing in his stirrups, scratching his bottom with some vigor, Jiden noticed, and instantly started to regret the delicate inquiries he had planned for his trusted yet so regularly ghastly companion.
"Aye, Princess?" Nicholas exclaimed loud enough to catch a few quizzical glances from the departing guard as he jolted sideways and thwacked his cousin in the shoulder nearly knocking him off his mount. Jiden frowned as he straightened in the saddle. Nicholas had a smile from ear to ear like a jackal despite Jiden's burning red face.
"You done? Daft donkey." Jiden shook his head, crinkling his slightly turned up nose.
"I am trying to have an intelligent conversation with an ass," he sighed.
"All right all right, I am ready to be serious princess," Nicholas assured.
"Stop calling me princess for starters,"
"What's eating your grapes? You ve been acting like a *girl* all morning." Nicholas chided, guiding his mount east.
"Has it escaped you dolt? In a year I am to be married!" Jiden announced.
"Married!" Jiden repeated, waiting for some kind of response from his blinking cousin.
"Married!" Jiden barked.
"Married, yes, I know. Royally announced and all...And?" Nicholas shrugged.
"And there are... things I will be expected to do that I... well ...as a woman, I mean *she's* a woman," Jiden rambled.
"Let's hope so!" Nicholas snorted.
"And as, me being a man, she would expect ...certain proficiencies in the art of... well...bed chamber ... matters..." Jiden sputtered.
"Oh for the love of God in Heaven are you trying to make me toss Gillian's breakfast sausages?" Nicholas held his stomach and feigned sickness.
"Well what do you know about it than? Look who I am speaking to," Jiden motioned to Nicholas's slovenly unlaced boots and filthy tunic.
"Courageous is the woman who can tolerate the stench long enough to *endure* your shambling efforts."
"What ever are you talking about?" Nicholas looked over himself, raising an arm pit to smell it, revealing sweat stained circles.

"She will *assume* me to be an amazing lover, being a prince." Jiden raised his eyebrows.

"Well than she will begin the marriage with disappointment and won't be too surprised days to come when she uncovers the many other skills you do not possess. For example; dancing, whistling or simple addition." Nicholas simpered about. Jiden grinned in spite of his uneasy mood.

"I don't want to be married cousin. I am no *husband*; I have no interest in settling and spending my time raising an heir and gratifying some rotten adolescent princess!"

"Don't' worry, you wont be gratifying to *anyone*."

"Exactly!" Barked Jiden; spooking his young alabaster stallion.

"Why so obsessed cousin? Keep in mind, she will be as untried as you and will have no basis of comparison for your assuredly lame performance and doubtless utter lack of stamina." With that Jiden took his right foot out of his stirrup and kicked his cousin in the leg. The pair spurred their mounts into a full gallop, with Castle Adalonia's signature silver moon embellishment over vibrant jade velvet capes soaring out behind, up towards the basin of Green Mountain, still hours away, to rendezvous with the guard.

Callana kissed her mother, and each sister good bye. She brushed away tears
with the back of her hand .This was the hardest decision she had made yet in
her young life. Leaving home, leaving the only people she had ever known.
She felt the tearing of her very heart as she slowly looked from one beautiful,
familiar face to the next, committing to memory every nuance, every color
and detail of this day, these last moments in the only place she had ever
known. Callana strained to remember the brightness of the burning July sun
on the green grasses where she had ran as a child; the view of the ominous
forest to the north of Windt in the furthermost southern edge of Rogadon; and
the earthen crossroads; deep red in the summer sun; even the bright beaming
saffron dress her mother wore in honor of her daughter's favorite color.
Behind the fervent hurt climbing and consuming her inside out, destroying
what little composure she had conjured for this last farewell, however, there
was something else. Trembling hands shook with a tiny fire of anxious
excitement connected to the journey she would begin today. Callana had
watched from her windows as other people traveled these roads her entire
life, and had ached to do the same. For all her want for stability and sense of
home, Callana of Windt longed to be .....*more*.

Hellena's heart was breaking today. She loved her children tremendously,
more than she could bear at times. Although they were undeniably alike,
each wonderful girl had certain identifying personality traits that made the
physically almost indistinguishable girls very different. Crystalline was quiet
and polite, but devious in her own little way. She was not a person to cross
lightly. Cylan was spirited and jovial, always looking on the bright side of
every thing and quite possibly the happiest soul Hellena had ever met. Caran
was sweet, caring, like her mother in many ways but had in herself an
oversized love for others; a friend to the friendless. Cella was clever,
organized, wise beyond her years, and very dominant. She was the captain of
their household, never mind her age. Callana was her mother's youngest, and
the only one of Hellena's girls to inherit her father's personality faultlessly.
She had his low voice; deep and sultry, with his gentle ways with just a bit of
bite, but gallant and brave. Callana was every bit the lion heart her father
had been. Charming and solid, the best friend anyone could have. And just
like Cai, she needed to be *useful*, and vital to the world around her. She
longed to be a part of something much larger than herself. She was so much
more than this village could contain. Hellena knew Callana would not make

it here, and had saved enough coins to get her to Della Verde. Now all she had left to do was let her go.

Callana held each sister once more, than came to face her mother. Hellena combed her fingers through Callana's silky hair, fleeting back in her mind just for a moment of when her girls were young, tussling for father's lap or the seat beside him at supper; all five sitting cross-legged on the porch, smallest to tallest, each braiding the other's hair, save for Crystalline on the end who would always braid her own beforehand, as she was oldest and first to bathe; a circle of red heads around a return fire awaiting Cai from a hunting trip. Hellena wondered, where did all those moments go? Back when she had a husband who adored her and time on her side. The era of choices had long since passed for Hellena, now she had demands to meet and a family who depended on her and her alone.

Callana held her mother in a tight hug, never to let go. Mother and daughter wept into each other's hair.

"I will miss you every day," Callana sobbed quietly.

"And I you my daughter....my baby!" Hellena released her and grasped her hand pushing something into Callana's palm. Callana opened her fingers revealing a small leather satchel. Her forehead wrinkled as she met her mother's troubled eyes.

"Mother, where did you..." Hellena closed Callana's fist around the coins and clasped her hand around tight.

"Let me worry about whom and what I had to do ey? It should be enough to eat for a few weeks just long enough for you to find employment." Callana put her money in her saddle bag and turned to her family once more.

"I will send word as soon as I settle, I promise," four sisters nodded tear soaked faces.

"You had better!" Cella and her mother said in unison. Callana mounted her father's roan gelding and with one last look at her family, she turned and prodded him into a soft gallop. When last she looked back, her family was nothing more than five red specks silhouetted against the bright purple trees of the distant Mount Roan. Callana found herself fighting one last compulsion to hasten back to their waiting arms as the warm sunlight of this July morning gave way to the cool, heavy darkness of the Shadows forest.

....

Callana rode for what felt like an eternity until she decided that even though it was dim in the forest, it was probably only early afternoon. She marveled at the immense, rough barked, bristly pines, and twisted purple manzanita. There were blue oaks, full of fat leaves, and towering sleek barked furs, pushing for the canopy. The profound serenity of the landscape betrayed the forest's sinister reputation. She had no intention of stopping in this God forsaken gloom if she could help it and felt her stomach growling in protest. She patted the sturdy roan's thick arched neck.

"Don't be nervous George; it can't be too much further...I hope." George bobbed his head and whinnied quietly. Callana rode in silence, letting the clopping of the big horse's hoofs on the packed path lull her. It occurred to her suddenly that she could not remember the last time she had a moment to herself like this. She thought about her father, smiling at her mother, hand in hand on the log bench in front of their hearth. Her warm, cozy nights wedged between her sisters in their goose down childhood bed. Many nights when she was young, Callana had laid awake, imagining herself as a grown woman; married, blissfully in love, as her parents had been. Love must be wonderful. But her mother was beautiful and clever, and therefore worthy of such devotion. No man could find such a plain dull witted girl worthy of his affections. But in her imagination, she would grow to be brilliant and lovely! She day dreamed about a majestic kingdom, with open gates, where she would find her love and a modest cottage of her own in the lower city and set up her own seamstress shop. She felt at once a spreading tingling, and eagerness for her dream future and was so lost in her make believe she was surprised by a horse drawn, gleaming white carriage bouncing her way. Callana slowed her roan down and pulled off the path to give way. Without waiting for the carriage to come to a complete halt, a petite blonde dove out to the soft earth below, where she began vomiting. Her carriage man leaped off his perch, to hold her at the waist as she bent in evident agony. Callana swung from George's saddle to catch the reins of the exhausted bay horse, than quickly fell to the woman's side.

"Ey, is she alright?" Callana was holding the woman's long wavy locks back from her face. The man glanced at her only long enough for Callana to see he was genuinely concerned.

"What happened?" Callana pried as the woman heaved again. Callana patted her back sympathetically, remembering her own ordeal only weeks earlier.

"She ...does not like to travel, that's all." His voice betrayed him. Callana wondered briefly why a carriage man would be permitted to put his hands around a noble lady's waist in such a way or that a lady would travel with only one guard. The petite young woman's silk dress was staining in the deep red earth as she rocked back and forth on her knees. Callana and the dark man helped the woman stand, brushing her dress off and straightening her bouncy blonde waves. The small woman looked up at the man than to Callana.

"Who, who are *you*?" She slowly looked Callana up and down. When her gaze paused uncouthly on Callana's copious cleavage, her eyes widened as she exclaimed, "Oh my". Callana blushed brightly and the man cleared his throat, still holding the petite woman's waist.

"I am Callana of Windt my lady," Callana did a brief curtsy while maintaining a hold on one of the woman's delicate elbows.

"Oh, please, do *not* call me lady after that display," she motioned her head to the steaming retch mound on the roots of the large oak behind her.

"Please, do not mind my asking, but, your Knight bares the red horse of Rogadon." Callana paused at the guilty look that passed between the two. She continued slowly, with a furrowed brow; not sure what she had said wrong.

"I was just hoping you might tell me how much farther it is to the lake of Ceruleana". Callana decided not to permit her overwhelming curiosity to question the pair's evidently secretive journey.

"It will be half a day; at the rate you were traveling young Callana." After the man spoke, the woman elbowed his rib, motioning her head towards Callana. He cleared his throat again.

"We were about to make camp and as you have shown such concern for the Princess Rogala, I must persist you heed mine for you, as young ladies should not be alone in this forest at night. We insist you join us."

"*Princess Rogala! Of kingdom Rogadon*? Oh my Lady, I would be most grateful!" She kissed the Princesses hand as she kneeled in a gracious curtsey.

"Rise, for there is nothing noble in our quest, love." The two exchanged nods before the man released his hold slightly on the princess as she opened her royal red robe. This time it was Callana's turn to gawk.

....

Jiden ate in the great hall, opposite his parents, a sea of cedar between them. Lena sat to the right of her husband, her duck and potatoes going cold as she watched her son and husband devour their dinners like starving dogs. She beamed with pride in her family unit. She would trade her soul for either of her men. She often wondered if she was admirable enough to be surrounded with such honorable company.

It was already a few months after Jiden's birthday, but Lena could not help but dwell on the events of that tremendous day, sixteen years ago. If only she could have blessed her husband with more children. Jiden was a difficult birth, to say the least. Lena's water had broken but for all her pushing, Jiden would not come down her birthing canal without her surgeon's painful pushing down on her stomach. It was than the stunned man wrenched out a five pound boy to discover and retrieve an identical five pound girl after, blue with suffocation. A then, young Lustene had been unable to deliver Jiden with enough time to save the ill-fated twin. The Queen, in her grief, had sworn Lustene to secrecy, as to not despoil the happiest day in her beloved King's life; the birth of his first born son and heir to the throne. Lena loved Jiden immeasurably with all of her injured heart. Yet hardly a day passed without the remembrance of her beautiful baby girl she still ached to hold. She continued to have fantastic dreams of her daughter; with Jiden's curls and Odin's eyes. Lena heaved a mournful breath. She would not wish this pain on another soul. Jiden and Odin were never to know; the guilt would destroy them both. Her husband's low grumbling brought her back to present time.

"No wonder you are so thin my Queen. A pigeon could out eat you." He gestured towards her poultry, which she quickly waved away. He stabbed the dark meat and plopped it on his plate before continuing.

"You mustn't consume yourself with such trivial matters." He grumbled.

"*Trivial*, trivial you say father? Aye, how insignificant; the day a man rides out to meet his *unwelcome* bride to be. Mother, are you not insulted? Were you received so callously?" Jiden deepened his voice to imitate his father and furrowed his thick brows.

"*So trivial my Queen, your only son rides to meet perpetual sorrow! Fiddle de Dee... Are you going to finish that?*" Jiden grunted and poked his fork at an imaginary plate next to his than rubbed his belly and mocked flatulence.

"*Jiden!*" his mother piped stifling a snicker. Her husband glared from one to the other.

"Is this too much for you my son? Is your constitution so delicate that you cannot withstand something as simple as riding out to meet a beautiful woman? For Heavens sake I dream of such problems!" Lena and Jiden shamefully sobered. Jiden knew his father was right; it was the duty of every future king to uphold tradition and the continuance of peace. Although Odin was just as concerned as Lena about their son's angst over this marriage, first and foremost must be the kingdom.

"Please, forgive me father," Jiden straightened. His face distorted in humiliation for his selfish behavior.

"I should not slough off my duty so ignorantly. I would do anything for this Kingdom." With that, Jiden stood and bent to his parents.

"Please excuse me, I have to ready for the reception of Princess Rogala in the morning." When he had gone Odin covered his wife's petite hands with one of his gigantic ones and leaned to kiss her.

"I know you worry; you carry his burdens for him, my Queen. He has to grow up as I did; as you did. She may turn out to be as wonderful as you, and what better could you wish for your son?" Lena nodded in agreement and kissed him.

"Of course you are right my Lord." Lena rose to join the serving girl in clearing the table before joining her husband for evening council.

"Sire, your horse is ready," Nicholas announced stepping into his cousin's bed chamber. Prince Jiden was in full royal dress; jade tunic and cape with silver crescent moon, black trousers and leather knee high shoes, polished to a shine, and his silver crown. He was staring down at the cobblestone court; his eyes traveling the road through the main gates and down through the lower town where rounded stone gave way to hard dirt. Morning's sunlight had burst over Green Mountain upon the villagers , bustling about with mules and carts, loaded full on their way to market, being unburdened of linens, and wool blankets and cloths of various colors to be traded for vegetables or livestock, all raised right here in this great valley; *his* great valley, and home. Rambunctious Children were throwing stones in the green grass behind small houses or zig zagging through the market, joyously having never known the misery of starvation or depravity because of his father's life long dedication to his people and this city. Jiden would not take this arranged marriage as anything less than necessary from this moment on. He would rather die than jeopardize the happiness of these industrious and magnificent people. Jiden knew there were most likely those who envied his life although he would give every day he had left in this castle for one day as an ordinary man with *simple* problems. He turned gravely to his cousin and inhaled deeply.
"I am ready."

Renk, the dark skinned Knight took great pains to make camp far enough off the road as not to be spotted. He had to expect that the great friendships he had with his fellow Knights of Rogadon would not hold against their loyalty to their king and he did not expect that if asked, they would keep his secret. King Bromell was a vindictive man and would make an example of Renk for gross dereliction of duty; impregnating and kidnapping the Princess. If he was lucky, he would only be banished from Rogadon, and Renk didn't believe in luck. In the meantime, Rogala had apparently found a kindred spirit.
"*Four* sisters! My Kingdom for one!" Rogala pouted enviously.
"My sisters for your Kingdom!" Callana giggled.
"You do not mean that," Rogala rolled blue eyes.
"No," Callana admitted, solemnly. "I would do anything to save them the fate they've been given".
"I am truly sorry, I cannot empathize with poverty; I have never known it, but I *am* sorry." Rogala tried.

"Not your fault." Callana forced a smile as she lowered her eyes. Rogala's heart went out to her who had such a cruel rank in life while she, the spoiled princess herself, was running from an effortless life of nobility!

"So you've seen why Renk and I run young Callana of Windt;" Rogala patted her round tummy, "but why do you?" She pried, sitting backed against a fallen log next to a roaring fire. Callana snorted, ladling stew out in a wooden bowl to serve the pregnant princess.

"I am hardly running!" she lied.

"Not on that old nag!" Renk laughed, earning him a swift kick in the shin from Callana. Renk recovered than leaned against a young tree near the fire; bowing graciously when Callana handed him his bowl before she settled cross legged opposite the princess to engulf her own. Rogala smiled at Renk over the firelight.

"Has it been long since you've eaten or is there another person in you too?" Rogala asked, raising thin eyebrows and grinning.

"Or a goat?" Renk teased. Rogala nearly choked as she fell sideways cackling so hard she started crying.

"Ey, Ey! You had three bowls yourself *sir*!" Callana smiled with a stew mustache, throwing Rogala into hysterics again. Callana giggled and wiped the back of her hand across her lip.

"You're a pair! There's no doubt about that is there? Peas in a pod!" Callana laughed. Rogala righted herself and struggled to get up. Renk was immediately there, pulling her to a hunched standing position.

"I have got to pee!" The princess announced. Callana took her hand and led her towards the darkness out of the fire's light.

"I've got this sir Knight, you've got dish duty!" Renk released his princess and watched them disappear into the dark, snickering and stumbling about. He replaced the empty stew pot on the fire with another full of creek water he had filled upon making camp. Seeing Rogala laugh in the midst of their straining ordeal relaxed his spirit. He had no idea where they would hide once she failed to meet Prince Jiden midday tomorrow and word was sent to King Bromell of her disappearance, but knowing they would be together was enough for him for now. Sneaking around a castle guard and a King's watchful eye proved difficult, although exciting, but after a while it wore on both lovers. When she became pregnant, he had made the decision to steal her away before her engagement was made official, not too difficult with his knightly knowledge of the kingdom. All he knew to be true was he would give anything to see her smile every day. When she returned with her cohort, he filled his eyes with her; absently holding his hand over his heart. Yes, this feeling, this overwhelming consuming love, was worth running, or dying for that matter.

"I have found a true friend in this large breasted girl, my love," Rogala shouted to her suitor.

"Oh?" Renk winked at Callana's embarrassed reaction to the attention drawn to her chest.

"She held me while I urinated although I was sure I splashed!" Rogala giggled.

"That's revolting and noteworthy my love. We shall have to keep her." Renk decided.

"That's a marvelous idea! My new sister!" Rogala tittered as she collapsed back into her spot against the log.

"Hot tea my love?" Renk handed her and her comrade their tea he had made with the boiling water before washing the dishes during the girls' peeing adventure. Callana bowed her head gratefully to the gentleman. She looked thoughtful.

"What troubles someone so young enough to send her into the Shadows forest alone on a rickety purple horse?" Rogala pushed.

"Honestly my lady? I only had one option in Windt, and leaving was just … better." Callana seemed to sadden.

"Where do you want to go Callana?" Renk asked.

"I just want to live somewhere, wonderful." Callana sighed dreamily.

"Is that all?" posed Renk.

"Well it's not Rogadon for sure," Rogala huffed.

"It is terrible that you cannot be with the one you love in your own kingdom. Your uncle is really this unforgiving?" Callana asked, slightly incredulous. Rogala nodded solemnly.

"He is, but only because he is paranoid and believes that the *Kingdom of Kin* will neglect him because he is the only king in Della Verde not *blood* related to any other." Rogala looked pensively off towards her home.

"Kingdom of Kin?" Callana repeated. "That is the valley Della Verde? In all my time at the Stone's throw Inn I had never heard it called that before."

"That's because it is a *smear* my uncle uses only in front of his council." Rogala chided.

"Ahhhh, I see. So have you seen Della Verde?" Callana bubbled with curiosity.

"Oh my, many times; once a year the city of Adalonia holds a marvelous ball and extends all surrounding cities invitation." Rogala rolled her eyes.

"A ball? How glorious! Is Adalonia everything people say?" Callana asked, brown eyes sparkling in the fire light.

"Aye that it is. Beautiful and fair. Save for their rotten *Prince Jiden*." Rogala nearly spit out his name.

"You have seen him at these events?" Callana perked.

"Oh yes, seen, but never met. He is no different than any other Prince, to be sure; arrogant and bored little pratts! And has the audacity, the *gall* to actually protest marrying *me*! It should be me protesting marrying *him*!" Callana spit a mouthful of tea on the fire.

"You are to be *married* to the Prince of Adalonia?" She asked, wide eyed.

"*Was* to be married to the Prince of Adalonia! I have been carrying on this albeit clandestine, love affair with Renk for over two years and was only informed of this duty to my kingdom two short months ago! For the love of God, I was already pregnant!" Rogala threw her hands up.

"What will your uncle do when he finds you have neglected this arranged marriage?" asked Callana.

"He is not a complete tyrant, but he will banish my Renk for sure and keep me to this arrangement, baby or no baby". With this she caressed her protruding belly. Renk came to her side. Callana watched the two, completely in love, so much so, that they would risk all to be together. She must help them. How? How? She searched her mind. In a moment the thought dangling tantalizingly out of reach in the back of her mind suddenly slammed front.

"Yes!" She cried out, jolting the pair out of their embrace.

"Oh, that made me have to pee again!" moaned Rogala. As Renk tried to help the struggling blonde to her feet to relieve her painfully full bladder, Callana jumped to her feet and blocked their way.

"Wait, I have a plan!"

"I have a plan too and it's to pee my brains out!" the little blonde insisted.

"No I mean I know how to honorably relieve you of your duty to marry this Prince without you... *not* marrying this prince that is...I mean... I···"

"Hold!" The princess stepped over the log she been using as a back rest and squatted to urinate.

"Ohhh....that's heavenly! Go ahead, I am listening" she grinned.

"He has never seen you; is that right?" asked Callana. Rogala nodded.

"So he wouldn't know you if he met you or not you right?" Callana's eyes were wide with some kind of discovery. Rogala nodded again, slowly.

"I mean, if he met *me*, he wouldn't know it wasn't *you*, right?" Callana persisted.

"What are you saying Callana? You would go through with a *wedding* for me?" Rogala's face was sincerely stunned.

"No, not just for you and Renk. I will do it in the name of... love! What the two of you have is pure and honorable. Men fall in battle for less, my father did. And if all a meager village girl has to do is marry a *prince* to preserve that than so be it; so be this and call it fate for it came to me as if meant to be. Besides, we're sisters aren't we?" Callana stood straight and tall, chest filled with pride. Rogala had tears in her eyes as she slowly stood. Renk was faltering.

"Callana, how can you call yourself *meager*, when you are the most honorable person I have ever met? You are giving yourself to *my* duty? I don't know if I can permit you to do this...what if you are discovered?" Rogala worried.

"What if I *am* discovered? You said Adalonia is fair, if the worst I get is banished than I will go somewhere else and you and Renk will be long gone away where no one will find you. Say you will let me! It will be a dream come true, you understand? I have prayed for a royal life and save for changing my blood line this is my only chance to experience it. Please, I beg of you, just let me meet with him? He has nothing to suspect, he does not know you and so will not recognize he is being deceived. Please, at least sleep on the idea?"

"This is *my* duty, not yours! I cannot force this on you!" Rogala stomped her foot, as if this would end the argument.

"You can not *force* this, but you could *allow* it! Please? Please?" Callana was begging now, literally on her knees with hands clasped.

Reluctantly, the couple agreed to sleep on it, fully intending to refuse Callana with morning's light. With that the three huddled close to the fire, deep in thought. Callana slept, with a wistful grin painted on her porcelain face, dreaming of a handsome prince.

Princess Rogala woke to find an eager Callana leaning over her.
"Good! You're awake! So what did you, decide than?"
"Well," objected Rogala, but Callana was prepared.
"It's a fool proof plan! I knew you'd come round!" Callana was up and running down to the creek to wash up. Rogala rolled over slowly and got on all fours. Renk was there; doubtless up before dawn, on guard, dressed in his full armor and Red Rogadon cape with red lion embellishments on his sleeves. A weary and wan Rogala tipped an aching head back to look at Renk from her low position. Renk was beaming. Rogala's jaw dropped slack.
"*You have* decided *yes*?" She rebuked him.
"There was no decision to be made! Have you not heard? She has been blathering on about it for the last three hours! You snore like a dragon... by the way, love.... She has systematically devised a plan for every contingency. She has thought of little else all night. She wants this more than she has ever wanted for anything, including a unicorn! ....Ask her!" Renk pointed after the skipping Callana. Rogala let her head drop with tired resignation.
"Love, *she* is asking, you did not force this upon her. King Odin is a fair King. She will only be banished at worst. We will send word when we settle, so she will have somewhere to go. That's what she told me we will be doing, anyway.... He might fall in love with her, think of that? She could marry a prince! For God's sake she is an indigent villager who could marry a *prince*!"
"She *hand* over that argument did she? You are repeating what she said verbatim aren't you?" Renk, with dark eyes pleading, reached for Rogala's lifted arm. She allowed him to tug her gracelessly along to the river to drink and give Callana the approval she had already accepted.

....

Prince Jiden rode at the front of his royal guard with Nicholas to his right. By midday he was to meet the Princess at the northernmost tip of Lake Ceruleana. Jiden took a deep breath and stopped his tall white horse, Leviathan, at the rise in the sloping village path just beyond the last of the small cottages. The summer day was bright and warm. The yellow of the sun tinged the colors of the village, turning the brown roofs and buildings a dull copper and the green grass a tarnished bronze. With the bustling market place, now behind him on his stoop, Jiden absorbed the warmth of the sun, momentarily closing his eyes.
The hefty Sir David swapped leg knives with his robust training partner Sir Gracien, while Sir Franklin steamed in the hot sun, scowling in general resentment over the wasted training day. The thick Sir Senren leaned in,

whispering an evaluation of the Prince's detour to the uninterested Sir Galland and the blithe Sir Laden, who sat cringing slightly, at the cramp developing in his bent, lengthy limbs.

"It s like a death march isn't it? Like one of those burial processions for a king where you march real slow than stare at his body in respect for hours and pray for his soul... you know what I am sayin Laden, ? Galland? It's like what I said, like a death march only no one's dead are they? No, no they's not," Senren's words, completely disregarded by all in ear shot, were too low for Jiden to hear, although he was very well aware how awkward his moment of meditation was for the men. He opened his eyes towards the lake, dazzling azure blue, sparkling like a starry night. He wanted to take in his surroundings as a single young man, before he was to be tied to this *woman* he only knew 'makes up in brains what she lacks in size' from King Bromell's descriptive letters.

"Sire, it's still a few hours ride to the far north of the lake and nearly midmorning." Nicholas informed the Prince when he had lingered too long. Jiden huffed and glanced back at his impetuous Knights. After a nod of support from sir Galland, he spurred Leviathan, casting a malevolent look over his other shoulder at the smirk on his young squire's face.

....

"It s not going to fit right, you are far too tiny!" Callana squirmed uncomfortably in the tight linen tunic. Rogala tugged the Rogadon red velvet outer tunic down over Callana's breasts inch by inch.

"Can you not flatten them?" Rogala laughed at the muffled protests of her busty friend. When she was successfully dressed, Callana sat cross legged on her coarse blanket while Rogala braided and looped her silky lengths into a high pile on the top of her head, pinning it firmly in place and adorning it with wild daisies, beheaded from a charming bouquet a now abhorred Renk had picked for his lover that morning. Callana rose and turned to face her friends. Her scarlet hair twisted regally atop her head, deep brown eyes and soft pink lips sharply contrasting to creamy white skin, with her curvaceous body, wrapped in scarlet, accentuating her small waist. Rogala gasped and put a hand over her mouth.

"What? What is it? It's too tight?" Callana anxiously ran her hands over the taunt garments as if smoothing herself would change her shape.

"Actually," said Renk raising an eyebrow, "I think the prince will rather enjoy the fit!"

"Look at you," Rogala breathed. "Absolutely gorgeous!" Renk nodded his agreement.

"Me? Are you joking? I feel like a sausage!" Renk approached her and knelt, kissing her hand.

"My lady Callana, you are as beautiful in heart as you are in stature".
"You mean that. You believe we can pull this off?" Callana stared at Rogala, dark eyes searching hers for support.
"I will tell you this, Princess, if he doesn't fall in love with you he's not any kind of a Prince at all!" Rogala assured, and with that, the trio set out, Callana north and Rogala and her knight south. *This is it*, thought Callana; *this is the day I decide my own destiny; make my own future.*
George galloped smoothly towards the bright light of the awaiting day. She had to be on the northern shore of the lake by midday and was not sure how much further she had to go. She collected herself internally, going over her own strategy in her head as she bounced along. She must remember to remain regal, as not to appear unused to noble behaviors. Above all, Callana wanted to give the Princess of Rogadon a good first impression in honor of her newly acquired friends.

George had been holding a canter for almost three hours now and although she was thoroughly impressed, she felt sure he needed a break. With a much needed change of pace, George stretched his strides in a brisk walk. Finally, they broke from the cool, dark of the Shadows forest into the brilliant heat of a glorious afternoon. Callana was far too nervous to savor her magnificent surroundings however. There was the lake, maybe a half an hour away till the northernmost shore, she guessed. When they reached the nearest bank, Callana had to search for an opening in the enormous cat tail reeds so she and George could drink. She dismounted and let the gelding find his own way through the small gap. Callana knelt and filled her palm with the cool, clear water, over and over again until she felt quenched. George was half asleep already, bringing a smile to Callana's face. She loved the old boy. Her father had brought him back from a successful market trip to Haven, a village south of her own. The then only green broke stallion was thrown in as a bonus in the vendor's bliss over Cai purchasing his entire wagon full of potatoes he had planned would take at least a week to offload, seeing as how potatoes were the most plentiful crop that year. Callana patted George's great, purple neck softly, than climbed into the saddle. She was probably going to be late, though she had no known landmarks to ascertain how long it would take to reach the northern most shore, but from her vantage point, she had a fair bit left yet.
"Come George, we mustn't keep our prince waiting!" She urged him into a canter again. Her mind raced; what will he see when he first looks upon her? Her heart tingled with a cold fear…he is protesting the marriage. What if he is angry and turns her away? Her stomach started to knot over this consideration. She was lost in her anguish when she rounded a large bend, opening up into a huge expanse of wild lilacs and dandelions, swaying on the slight breeze on tall green stems to the west. The trail widened and took her away from the water's edge, where she could look east and see a densely

packed village, dotting an emerald countryside, spreading east and west of the far water's bank, opening wide to vast open farmlands. Winding down the hard packed trail towards her was a handful of knights, covered in rich jade green capes, lead by what she had to assume was ...Her Prince! She fidgeted at her dress, her hair, she felt sick, she felt giddy, and she should dismount, no! He'll notice her weight! She can't ride a horse forever just to appear thinner! She chose to sit tall and stay in the saddle, than quickly dismounted.

Jiden was jolting along down his destined path at a forced trot when he saw the woman in all red emerge from the shore line's tall reedy cover. His breath caught, the moment he had been simultaneously dreading, yet desperately wanting to put behind him for months was upon him. For her benefit, on cue the Knights moved into an arrow formation, the Prince as point, concurrently breaking into a canter. He kept his eyes focused on the red figure, watched it fidget, than dismount. His false politeness at the ready, he had accepted his fate, and would honor his duty for his kingdom if not for anyone else! *For Adalonia*! He cried to himself as he would have shouted to his men riding into a battle. As he neared her, he raised his fist and at once the formation slowed and halted, not ten feet from a trembling princess, peeking out from under the neck of a frothy roan horse. The prince descended and tossed his reins over his own stallion's neck. Callana stepped out from behind her lone companion, dropping her reins to the ground and slowly swaying towards the prince, covering half the distance between herself and the handsome stranger. When she pulled back her hood, there was an exchange of nods and sighs of approval among the Knights. Nicholas sat gawking, lost in this scarlet vision. Jiden couldn't help but gape. It seemed along with his standard welcome speech, he had forgotten his name and where he was. Her hair was a silky collection of glossy garnet braids on top of her head and her skin was a milky white. Her pink lips, slightly pursed, were full and soft. Jiden skimmed the curvy figure, causing a sudden spike in his blood pressure and sending heat rushing into his neck. He was caught short by the rich chocolate eyes that shimmered and glistened, so alive, so vivid! She was captivating.

Callana blushed slightly, not sure how to handle being *appreciated* this intently, although, she had too been admiring him. He had the most amazing green eyes, like priceless emeralds found in royal jewelry, accented further by the gold flecks around the enlarged pupil and the thick dark brows. He was breathing deeply, soft lips slightly parted, a muscular chest rising and falling under his tunic. He seemed to be carved from bronze, with his tan skin and hard features. His golden hair was shining in the sun, curling in all directions and around his crown. He was magnificent, standing before her, eyes locked on hers; her heart pounded in her ears and she felt her stomach tingle with an excitement she couldn't remember ever experiencing before.

"I am Prince Jiden!" Startled, she jumped at his sudden, booming announcement. There was a low rumble of guffaws through the guard at the thunderous volume of the noticeably nervous prince. He faltered, leather gloved hand reaching for hers, which she extended; her alabaster skin was radiant in the sun, as she allowed herself to be pulled closer to him.

"I am sorry my lady, I have forgotten my manners. I welcome you to Adalonia," and with that he knelt and kissed her hand. She bowed her head graciously.

"Please, Sire, do not apologize," She smiled warmly down at him, putting him instantly at ease. She didn't seem prissy or spoiled at all. She almost seemed flattered to meet *him*.

"Please, let me escort you and your, uh, steed, to the court. The King and Queen have been awaiting your arrival Princess Rogala--"

"Callana!" she blurted out. "Ah, I actually prefer the name my grandmother gave me, Callana, if you don't mind sire". She bowed again, as if the act would take the gracelessness out of her odd request.

"Of course, Princess, *Callana*, I will oblige you in any way I can... I mean in this, honoring this change of title, Of course," he stammered. The knights exchanged a puzzled glance; Sir Nicholas socked Sir David in the arm for his mumbled comment, offering to *oblige the princess* as well. The Prince led her back to George and off to the kingdom Adalonia. Once mounted, Callana sighed, relieved it seemed to go fairly well. Who was she kidding? She couldn't have hoped for a better reaction from a man. She may be a virgin, but she knew excitement when she saw it. She couldn't help but notice she had been drawn to him as well. He kept turning to watch her and found her already watching him. He liked the way she was assessing him, and couldn't help but notice her bouncing bosom when they trotted through the village, or how Sir Senren, David and Laden were noticing her bouncing bosom! When Sir Franklin turned to peek himself he caught the attention of the glaring Prince. The scrappy knight flushed and grinned sheepishly, shrinking back to the end of the formation. Callana wasn't conscious of any of this. She had started returning the waves of the villagers. One exuberant man was flailing wildly and got a cooking pan to the head for his efforts from a livid wife. The hard, earthen path of the village gave way to a cobblestone road passing through two enormous wooden doors and into a great open court yard. There was a fountain with a large, hand carved marble statue at its center.

"That is King Triden, my father's grandfather, the former sole ruler of the Della Verde valley before it was divided." Explained Jiden.

"Why would he want to divide his kingdom?" Callana asked, marveling at the size of the marble masterpiece.

"Actually, he had siblings, and being the benevolent sole he was, had split his inheritance to spare any ill will;" Jiden was beaming with pride for his family. Philanthropy was not usually attributed to Kings nowadays and he was proud to be part of a long standing tradition of such generosity. It was in that moment that Callana felt a pang of guilt for her trickery. Maybe he would understand if she just explained why she took Rogala's place. But she had to give her friends enough time to escape King Bromell's reach. A wave of cold fear washed over her. What would she do, seeing that warm, desire in his eyes turn to contempt? She couldn't bare it! She had to see this through.

Callana joined Jiden at the base of a huge limestone stair, where he helped her dismount. She tingled with the exhilaration his strong hands on her waist caused. He smiled down at her, leaving his hands about her. She blushed again when he suddenly realized he was still holding her and forced his hands to his sides. They turned together to face the mature couple coming down the stairs to meet them. As they neared, Callana could see the perfect blend of either parent in Jiden. They were both golden brown, but Jiden had his father's flaxen curls, height and build, while he had inherited his mother's gorgeous green eyes and small nose. His mother was so graceful and thin! Callana was suddenly aware of her size and absently crossed her hands in front of her stomach.

"King Odin and Queen Lena, father and mother, this is the Princess Callana, as named by her grandmother," he interjected in answer to their quizzical glance. Callana curtsied low and bowed her head respectfully.

"Your majesties, I am most humbled to meet you," she expressed sincerely, for she had never felt so unworthy in her life!

"Princess Callana, please rise, for you are *our* honored guest!" King Odin bellowed in a lion's voice. He took her hand and bowed his head to kiss it. She met his glance and found it warm and most forthcoming. She turned to the queen, and bowed her head.

"Your majesty," she said. The queen was most impressed with the great humility the princess possessed. She did not carry on like a woman being forced into marriage at any rate. Lena took both Callana's hands in her delicate ones, facing her eye to eye.

"Princess Callana, what a lovely name for such an enchanting girl. We are most pleased to meet you! You must come in, the dining hall is being decorated for the celebration of your engagement so you have just enough time to find your room and then Prince Jiden will escort you to dinner. You are hungry no doubt?" Suddenly Callana realized how hungry she really was.

"Oh yes your majesty, actually I am starving!" she admitted.

"Right this way," Jiden took her hand and led her towards the open front doors of the glorious limestone castle, being proceeded by a King, a Queen and a royal guard. She almost asked Jiden to pinch her for this was even better than her wildest dreams.

"I trust you have everything you need my lady?" A petite teenage chamber maid asked, courteously bowing her brunette curls. Callana gasped, captivated by her room! Candles lit every corner and table, their warm, yellow glow reflecting in the faceted crystal chandelier over the four post pine bed, oil rubbed to a soft shine, the massive down mattress layered in purple silks and velvet blankets, adorned by a varied purple mountain of feather stuffed pillows. The bed was on a raised wooden floor, show casing its enormousness. Callana felt guilty over the soft glamour of her surroundings. Her sisters deserved as much, as well as her mother. What made her so special? She had left, that's what, and she had chosen change. She sighed and turned towards the timid girl and bowed.

"Thank you, yes my dear…just one thing," Callana moved towards the open wardrobe and pulled out a magnificent ermine over tunic she had spied from across the room.
"Can I wear this?" Callana asked politely. The young girl looked puzzled, and allowed a smile to curl one side of her elfin mouth.
"Why of course, my lady, it is yours, sent ahead by your uncle."
"Oh yes, I remember now. Silly me… Just one *more* favor love."
"Anything my lady"
"Tell me *your* name?"
"Miala, my lady."
"Miala, good to meet you. Now help me get out of this filthy tunic! I smell like my horse!" The two giggled and set about prying Callana out of one tight tunic and into another.

....

"Ah, the harsh burden of duty," Odin goaded his son.
"She is that," Jiden smiled brightly at his father, walking in stride towards the princess's guest chambers.
"Perhaps in time, you could find it in your heart to forgive me for saddling you with such a heavily breasted yoke," The king cupped his hands out in front of his chest, taunting the prince.
"Her breasts, generously proportioned as they are, will not solely make her a good wife. She could snore, or snort when she laughs…"
"Easy enough to overlook if she has large breasts!" The king jabbed his son in the ribs with an elbow and Jiden thumped his father in his chest.

"You are an absolute adolescent, you know that? I could have this caliber of conversation with Nicholas!" Odin turned to cuff the young prince on the ear. They turned the corner to intercept Miala rushing to retrieve the prince. "Pardon, my Lord, but the Princess Callana is ready for you Prince Jiden,"

"Thank you, um..."

"Miala, Sire."

"*Miala*, I don't recognize you love," The King took her arm as he led her away.

"I started only a few days ago, Sire," Jiden shook his head at his father's playful flirting and turned to retrieve his princess to try some flirting of his own. Jiden knocked loudly on the door and stepped back. He had changed into a golden silk tunic with clean black trousers and boots. For weddings, funerals, balls, and tournaments he was to wear the vivid green of his kingdom; allowing himself a change of venue for this casual celebration. Callana cleared her throat.

"Yes, come," she announced. Jiden pushed the door open, letting it swing all the way into the room.

"I would like to escort you to the dining ha..."He froze as his gaze found Callana standing in the corner of the chamber. She stood before him, wearing a fitted velvet tunic dyed the softest lilac he had ever seen. She had a shimmering golden silk ribbon winding through a glossy braid, cascading over her left shoulder. Callana blushed, nervously twisting the loose ends of the ribbon in her fingers.

"I dressed to match; I was told you would wear gold. Does it not please you sire?" Her forehead wrinkled; worried he was disappointed in her choice.

"Forgive me; I was taken aback by your beauty Princess. You are most pleasing." He walked to her and held his arm out. She smiled up at him, linking her arm in his. After a few steps, he stopped short and turned her to him.

"And I princess, am I *pleasing* to you?" Jiden's eyes earnestly searching Callana's for praise. Callana tilted her head sideways, re-evaluating him as if she hadn't already memorized every detail. Jiden shifted under her gaze than cleared his throat.

"Well?" He demanded. Callana met his demanding stare with a smile and winked.

"You are a dream come true Sire," This time it was Jiden's turn to blush.

The couple met with the King and Queen in the receiving hall, lining up to file in two by two followed by their royal guard, wearing only their green tunics and black trousers, for tonight was an informal event, meant to be lighthearted and comfortable. Marching behind the queen, Callana took note of the delicate woman's exquisite poise. She was a beautiful woman, slender and fit, in a shimmering white satin tunic and soft velvet over tunic in the daintiest shade of pink. The King, massive and dashing, was wearing a cherry red silk tunic and black trousers. Aside from crowns, the royal party was clothed like everyone else in the room. When Jiden and Callana stepped into the tremendous hall, Jiden halted, allowing the room time to see his bride to be, and they eagerly strained to do so. There was an eruption of awes from the onlookers, causing Callana to blush. The couple made their way to their seats on either side of the King and Queen. At the king's nod, the honored guests lowered themselves in place around the table. Most guests were knights and wives of knights, and others were the council men and women and respective spouses, if any, along with selected vendors, elders and tradesmen. It was a celebration for Adalonia only. This was a matter for immediate family alone. The entire Della Verde Valley would be present for the wedding but for now there were less than one hundred fifty in attendance, present only for their amity to the king and queen.

"Ladies and gentlemen. Friends!" The King roared, silencing the busy room. "We are gathered tonight in honor of tradition. The Della Verde has long stood an example to its neighbors for its highest standard of peace, above all!" The room erupted in applause. The great man nodded, and then raised his hand for silence.

"It is in this tradition, that my son, Prince Jiden, has accepted the dutiful decision to be bound in matrimony, to the beautiful Princess Callana, permanently re-uniting the kingdom of Rogadon to our valley and our family!" Applause rang out, reverberating throughout the room. Jiden was marveling at his princess again. His eyes were glowing, warm and inviting. She returned his penetrating gaze with a tender smile. The implications of this marriage were of the most severe importance. She would not let Rogadon or Adalonia down, princess or not.

Odin was gesturing for Jiden to speak. Jiden stood, reluctantly. Callana watched as all the boyish qualities hardened on his young face. He stood tall, hands behind his back, chest raised. His adolescent charms replaced by a virile astuteness. He was the king he would one day be and Callana's heart filled with admiration for him.

"Ladies," he bowed to the women in the room and separately to his mother. "And gentlemen," he nodded.

"And Knights, apart, for I can classify you as neither!" There was a ripple of laughter up and down the table. The knights in unison booed their prince. He raised his hand for silence.

"As my father said, we are a valley steeped in the tradition of peace but I can tell you I have the added privilege of being born into a family that holds love in highest regard. And it is in *this* capacity that I offer my devotion to the enchanting Princess Callana, if she will have me," Jiden turned to her than. A blushing Callana rose to join her prince.

"For love, Prince Jiden," She bowed respectfully to him. The pair locked in a romantic stare and raised their goblets. Having scrutinized the princess from the moment of arrival, Lena had come to the conclusion that Callana was sincerely and utterly taken with Jiden. She sighed in relief, catching the eye of Sir Galland, who nodded to her and raised his chalice. Lena raised her's to the room.

"To love!" She toasted.

"To love!" The room echoed and seated themselves to begin the meal. Lena was thankful to see Jiden and Callana so close, ending months of protest and misery. He was smitten if not in love, and as his mother, Lena was ecstatic the girl appeared to return his feelings. What more could a mother hope for than her only child to find true love? Odin was delighted with the change that came over his son since the arrival of this princess. It was a good woman who brought out the best in a man; he had come to learn himself. He was looking at Lena throughout supper with an amorous gleam in his eye and she laughed out loud at her husband. He was, if nothing else, depraved!

Musicians played fluted pipes while minstrels sang joyous songs of mythical creatures, heroic men and true love. The tumblers held center court, one walking on hands with a hoop between his feet while another leapt through, landing with a somersault! There was a jester, juggling various items diners tossed at him, including a long stemmed fork, a potato, and a shoe! Callana clapped wildly for them, overwhelmed with their talent. The ample spread of roasted pigs, rabbits and deer, boiled potatoes, carrots, and dark breads was devoured shortly after the first song, and replaced by bottled red wines. Callana had never had wine, and found it bitter, but enjoyed the effect tremendously. She had lost all inhibitions by her fourth goblet and Jiden had certainly noticed. He saw a lustful glow in her eyes that hadn't been so blatant before. In his efforts to keep his spirits high and self-consciousness low, Jiden quickly found himself drunk. He longed to kiss her full lips, and fought it with his entire being. They had met today after all and the engagement was to last a *year*! The desire burning through him, ignited by wine, was sure to make this an achingly slow year indeed!

When dining had turned to dancing, a few single knights, young and old sought to hold the gracious princess with the jiggling bosom. Odin and Lena kept an eye on their young prince who had turned all but green with envy. By midnight Sir Franklin had cut in on Sir David at least six times and a young, hefty knight from the first battalion called Sir Jerrik had bumped out Sir Franklin twice and Sir Laden once!

When enough was enough, and the guests had bid farewell, Odin told Jiden to properly escort the princess to her room. Jiden did a mock bow, losing his balance and slumping into his father's chest. Odin pulled his son up to a standing position, as Lena gave him a quick slap to sober him up. Jiden shook his head to clear the ringing in his ears and composed himself; afraid he might earn another wallop. Jiden held an arm around Callana's waste to stable her down the long hall to her chambers. The inebriated couple staggered to her door, pinging back and forth between stone walls, cackling all the way.

"This is you, my lady." Jiden announced, standing tall, all humor draining from his face. The inappropriate images that had teased and tortured him all evening returned, having reached her bed chamber. The inescapable fact was she was to be virtuous on their wedding day. Jiden knew this, but her voluptuous body within arms reach, standing only feet away from a silken bed, had left him feeling *extremely* open to suggestion. Jiden opened the door and let Callana step in first. When she did, she turned to face him. Her exhilaration from an over active imagination had burned through most of her wine. She wanted him to touch her, but more than that, she wanted *everything* to be perfect when he touched her. The moment and surroundings were both romantic, but there was something missing. They hardly knew each other and if she relented, he would have no mysteries to pursue in her and a physical connection alone was not foundation enough for a marriage. She was far too nervous at the thought of acting on any of her ramped fantasies any how, not that she knew how to begin to act on them. She feared she would be a disappointing lover, and it petrified her. After all, the last time she saw that randy look on a man's face she threw up! She wasn't ready and would undoubtedly impair any lovemaking. Tradition was for her to be a virgin on her wedding day anyway. What if this was a test of her resolve; her royal morality? Yes, that's it. He is making sure she will be an appropriate addition to the imperial line! Her mind was made up. She straightened and cleared her throat to speak.

"I had a marvelous time," she said. Jiden tried to step through her door way, saying "As did I so why end so soon" Callana quickly interrupted his inevitable advance.

"Good night sire!" she curtsied quickly than shut the door as the prince stepped towards her. Jiden stumbled back, unsure of where his advances had gone wrong.

"Good night my lady." he told the door. He had been convinced she was as eager as he. He wilted and ambled to his own bed chamber on the other end of the castle, and although on fire with a lust that would not be slaked, he did have one small consolation. He knew a couple of shameless Knights who were sure to get double training duty in the morning. Maybe that would have them thinking twice about where they put there hands, or they eyes for that matter, from now on!

....

Rogala fell out of the carriage, vomiting in the road. It was turning into a regular morning, midday and evening routine for her. Renk held her as usual, until she could stand on her own.

"Thank you love, so sorry," Rogala apologized.

"Don't be sorry love. This is what pregnant women do, that's all;" Renk tried to straighten her muffled yellow hair but she waved him off.

"Renk, this is it! We made it! Oh Thank Heaven above I can get out of that Godforsaken carriage!" The couple stood before a long cottage with a wooden sign suspended by two short chains off a porch rafter. The Stone's Throw Inn it read. The stretching, narrow house sat at the crossroads running north, south, east and west, with what appeared to be five Callana duplicates of various ages eating at a large, candle lit dining table inside a great, west facing window. The pair glanced at each other and smiled. This was the right place for sure.

Renk knocked and grinned brightly at the middle aged friendly woman who threw open the door.

"Good evening my lady," Renk bowed low in respect while Rogala attempted a curtsy.

"Oh love! Do not trouble yourself! Come in, come in! And such a tiny thing you are!" Hellena grabbed the miniature blonde and pulled her in. Christopher, a long, lanky young man hired for stable duty, bowed awkwardly to the knight before stepping past to attend to the couples horse and carriage, blushing bashfully at Crystalline who followed outside to carry in the luggage. Caran and Cella were clearing dishes while Cylan set two heaping steaming hot wooden bowls of stew on the table. Hellena settled the pregnant girl down on the hard wooden bench and frowned. Crystalline returned with the luggage and immediately surmised the problem and dashed towards her room.

"Ooooh this won't do!" Hellena lifted the princess up to put the soft feather pillow Crystalline had hurried to retrieve, under the small rear end.

"So accommodating! Thank you very much, Hellena right?" Rogala searched the woman's sweet face. Helena looked puzzled.

"Have we met before? I usually remember faces, especially one as adorable as yours!" Helena squeezed and lifted Rogala's chin to inspect her closer.

"Oh, I am sorry, forgive me, you see; we happened upon your daughter Callana, in the Shadows forest, only a day ago." Helena's eyes sparked with the mention of her youngest child.

"My bird? You've seen her? Is she alright? Tell me everything!" Rogala looked at Renk, who had been ushered to the table by Cella. They exchanged nods, and Rogala began.

"Well...congratulations! Your daughter is the new princess of Rogadon!" Rogala and Renk watched as Helena stilled, than fell to the floor and four pairs of carrot colored eyes widened in disbelief.

"Well done, love," Renk winked.

....

Callana leaped out of her velvety soft bed early the next morning; her restless night of unspeakable fantasies thankfully over. She had so many things to set in motion if she was to keep up appearances. First things first, she needed to see George. Miala knocked and entered with a gleaming silver breakfast tray. "Ah, Miala!" Callana surprised the young girl into jerking violently, inadvertently sending sliced ham and pears flying across the room.

"Oh dear, so sorry my lady, please forgive my clumsiness... I did not expect you up... it is not yet dawn!" Miala set about her scavenger hunt for the strewn about pieces of breakfast. Callana laughed out loud.

"You're apologizing? My dear, I should have warned you I am an early riser. This is when George needs his morning romp!" Miala dropped the tray and covered her mouth with both hands; hazel eyes wide with apparent mortification.

"So sorry my lady, I will leave you and your gentleman to conduct your *business...*" Miala turned to leave, bright red and staring at her feet, stopping short at Callana's loud chuckle.

"You are too much Miala! Ha! Ha! Ha! My goodness, what do you take me for? George is my *horse*! I was on my way to the stables." Miala blushed even further and bowed her head shamefully.

"Oh princess Callana, you must forgive me, I was not judging, I mean to say, it is not my place...I am a servant, you will do who, I mean what! What you please! Oh my, I should just stop talking altogether!" Callana's laugh was contagious and soon Miala couldn't help but join in.

"Miala, no need to be so terrified. I am a person, just as you are." Callana patted Miala's shoulder and picked the maid's chin up to look her in the eye. "I am not above humor! You keep me in line and we will get along famously. So think of me as a friend, agreed?" Miala nodded exuberantly.

"Now," Callana stood in only her linen under tunic with her hands on her sweeping hips.

"A gold coin says you know where we can get some trousers!"

....

"Morning gentlemen!" The Prince called out to his training battalion, first battalion, the same battalion that just so happened to contain a *certain* group of knights who had danced with a *certain* princess only hours before.

"Good morning sire!" An ever cheerful Sir Laden answered. Nicholas kicked the back of Laden's stilt like legs, causing him to dip suddenly to one side.

Laden simply straightened himself, chuckling at his apparent ungainliness. Jiden rolled his eyes. Too bad, he thought, all the grueling training he had planned and Laden wouldn't have a clue it was a punishment.

"Seeing as how some of you were awfully light on your feet last night, I have come to the realization that training has not been *challenging* enough for you," with that, Sir Franklin, Laden, Jerrik and David all received a barrage of wallops from their nearest fellow knights of the first battalion, who had most of them, warned the drunkards not to get close to the, albeit tantalizing, off-limits princess. Jiden fought the urge to smile.

"The blame falls entirely on me. Training is not only my duty but your right, and I have failed you. Worry not, my good men, for I will not be making the same mistake twice!" Jiden heard another round of thumps throughout the royal guard, followed by an almost inaudible 'ouch'. With a pounding head and an empty stomach, Jiden led his men on an unplanned excruciating three hour jaunt in full armor. He couldn't help but grin with satisfaction at the sound of his two hundred closest Knights grunting in anguish behind him.

....

"Your hospitality has been most appreciated!" Rogala pulled Helena close in a generous hug, placing a sack of gold coins in her hand. Helena pushed them back towards the princess, but she was adamant.

"Please Princess, I can't...."

"It is the least I can do for inconveniencing you for a whole week! It's not like I can't spare it love!" Rogala shrugged. Helena held the coin purse to her chest and bowed gracefully for the princess. Rogala looked once more over this loveable band of girls she had become so attached to, for more than their likeness to her friend, but for the generosity and kindness that emanated from them all. It was like a year round sunshine, permeating their home. They were happy! For all their hard work, they were smiling always, and they were together in every aspect and every moment. This was a *real* home; loud, messy, and full. She would miss this dearly. She inhaled deeply, bursting into tears as she exhaled. Renk shook his head, as he loaded their carriage; he would also miss this busy little place. Visits to the daily markets with its eclectic collection of items as well as people; gatherings at night around the center fire pit, swapping fantastic stories, mostly true with magical embellishments, with the elders and youth alike. With the constant flow of newcomers from the road, it was possible to make a new comrade every day in Windt. Renk sighed and joined Rogala in time for another round of good byes.

"Make sure the messenger in town gets on the road today with our letter for Callana, as she will be sending a messenger with the letter I wrote my uncle out today from Adalonia. Remember, once a month she should be writing you. Once we settle I will send word. I promise." Rogala assured.

Helena hugged her tiny ally again. She placed a hand on the high, hard bump and closed her eyes. She gasped and turned towards her daughters excitedly! "Ten to one it's a boy, who's in?"

"I'll take that bet, what would you know anyway? All you know how to make are girls!" Crystalline sniped.

"That's *how* she would know it was a boy, not the same as us, right mum? I am for boy!" Caran hooked her arm in her mother's.

"Girl, all the way, girl! Sorry mum!" Cella poked Caran's shoulder and shook hands with her mother, sealing the bet.

"Put me in for boy as well!" Renk swung an arm around Helena's neck as he dropped a gold coin in her hand.

"We will hold you to it, than. I want a visit when you have junior here!"

"Deal!" Rogala jumped in the middle for a last group hug. Christopher brought their carriage around, and Rogala's four young escorts loaded her into her dusty carriage. Renk climbed up to his drivers perch in his red tunic and brown faded trousers as Helena blew him a kiss. Playfully, Renk pretended it smacked him, falling sideways in feigning surprise. Hellena had not known him long, but would care for him forever none the less. After all, they were all in this together now.

....

"Make sure this gets to my uncle soon, lest he worry I did not arrive!" Callana hurried the young messenger towards his horse. He eyed her awkwardly for her attire; lose fitting brown belted tunic top, over a borrowed and extremely tight fitting pair of matching trousers. He recognized her, but only just. Her hair was mussed, only mostly still braided from the night before, hanging over her left shoulder.

"Yes my lady, Rogadon is only a day's hard ride. King Bromell will be receiving me, and your letter, by morning!" The skinny youth, named Dakin, swiftly mounted his small appaloosa mare and spurred her into a loping canter out of the courtyard.

"So Miala, we have some riding to do. Have you a horse?" Callana spun to face her companion, who was dressed in a regular ankle length linen tunic, tied at the waist with her cleaning apron.

"Sorry my lady, I don't have a *horse*," Miala cringed at the word and lowered her head, dismayed she was ruining the princesses' morning fun.

"My lady, there is a great deal of chores I am expected to finish before dinner midday, and though I am far too terrified to ride a horse anyhow, I would love to spend the day with you, but cannot neglect my duties to do so. Forgive me?" She bowed, waiting for dismissal.

"I tell you what young servant. You may escape my morning escapades for now but I will return in a few hours and whatever is left to do we shall finish together so you can spend the rest of the day at my beckon call! Understood?" Callana put her hands on her hips and tapped her foot impatiently. Miala was in shock. A princess willing to help with menial chores just to spend time *playing* with her servant? It was outrageous, but, as Miala was learning, this princess was just that. She nodded eagerly and flew to her kitchen duty. Gillian would not be so affable if Miala was late!

Callana watched after her young friend until she had vanished into the kitchen's narrow servant's entrance than rushed to her purple steed and a much awaited chase through this new landscape. The stable was off the southern wall of the limestone steps through the overwhelming wooden gates of the court yard. Market vendors yet to wake, Callana rushed down the silent street and into the expansive royal barn. A young boy was mucking out the stalls when she burst in, sweating in the balmy heat of the upcoming day.
 "Good morning, young sir," She curtsied quickly to the dirty-faced pre-teen. He turned, a sneer twisting his face, apparently not thrilled about rising so early.
"Good morning, my lady. Did you need helping?" He asked, only slightly willing to actually oblige.
 "Thank you, no, I can take care of this old nag myself. The name's Callana and you are?" She stuck out her hand in introduction. His mouth fell open and he immediately dropped to a knee, plopping into wet manure.
 "Princess, forgive me. I did not recognize you! I am at your service!" Callana was growing tired of reverent gestures, and quickly pulled him to his feet.
 "You are at my service and now covered in poop! Pay me no mind, I just enjoy riding at dawn and George gets anxious if we don't. I asked you your name young sir." Callana took straw in her hand and tried to use it to knock some of the dung off the young boy's knees. He assured her she didn't need worry about it.
"That's all right Princess, it comes with the job, as it were. My mom calls me Paul, but my name is Edward." It was Edward's turn to stick his hand out this time. Callana indulged, shaking his arm as she asked.
"Why does your mother call you Paul if your name is Edward?" Edward shrugged his shoulders and shook his head.
"I have six brothers, all younger, so guessin' she just gets mixed is all".
"Oh, one of your brother's names is Paul," Callana assumed. Edward furrowed his brow,
"No, maam;" he said, confused. Callana nodded politely, raising her eyebrows and turning to swing her worn saddle over George's coffee colored saddle blanket. He was stomping, snorting and pawing in anticipation. Morning

rides had been their routine since she could saddle him on her own and she was sure he enjoyed it even more than she! Edward went on about his mucking as Callana put the bit in George's mouth, looping the bridle up around his ears and securing it under his rounded cheek. She mounted and waved farewell to the lanky lad as she rode out into the pink light of an early, new day.

Today felt different than any other in her life. Days ago she started something, and although she wasn't sure ordinary people had *destinies*, she felt as if her life was accidentally falling into place. Literally, she felt out of control, as if tumbling towards some hidden destination. She had been so eager to step in for Princess Rogala all the while terrified of the consequences if exposed. Although she had been anxious, something inside her *knew* it was meant to be; fated. She had a constant, gnawing fear of being discovered, as much as she tried to ignore it. She didn't know if she could live with herself if Jiden despised her. She found herself thinking about those smoldering green eyes that had only the night before looked upon her with so much want and affection. She was lost in fantasy, now gazing off into a blurry, far off dream, allowing George to take her down the cobblestone walk way and clopping through the hard packed road of the upper village. They would pick up pace after they had cleared the majority of the crowded, small houses. George was tossing his head up and down, snapping Callana back to her present surroundings. The delighted prancing of her oldest friend ignited the excitement of their morning rides all at once in Callana and she urged him into a canter. The giant roan leaped into stride, thundering east towards the grassy, vast undulating countryside of the Green mountain basin, dotted with sprawling farmlands and large wooden barns. The Sheppard's herding sheep and goats out to pasture to graze watched intently as the grand burgundy horse rushed by, raised tail fluttering out behind him like a billowing standard. Callana held the reins just tight enough to tug the horse in any chosen direction, leaving the speed entirely up to the gelding himself. The last of Callana's thick braid was loosening and setting free her glorious red hair to stream out behind her. She urged George up and over the green rises towards the shimmering granite walls behind the roaring Green Mountain falls. She would never reach them in the short time she had for riding today, but she made a mental note to explore later. They made a wide half circle to turn George towards home, a good day's ride before the rolling green gave way to a stepped plateau southeast between Adalonia and Mount Andoria's red base.
George was nearly vaulting forward, infecting Callana with his glee. She laughed out loud and stood in the stirrups, knees bent for stability. She rode like this for almost the entire hour back, with the wind resisting her, until her thighs burned and shook with exhaustion. The sun was just peaking over the pointed rocky tip of Green Mountain behind her, cascading a deep, golden

radiance over the glowing white limestone of the castle Adalonia up ahead. George loped slowly, taking the pair back to the dirt road of the upper village; George was exhaling, wet, hot air and huffing from his nostrils as he slowed to a walk. Callana's sweat was running down her neck like a salty river, making the warm morning air feel sticky and cool. Callana pulled the fatigued horse to a stop to watch as the sun leisurely made its full appearance, lighting up the white court, and spilling out through the wooden gates and into the market. A few of the vendors were staring at her, sitting atop her horse, motionless at the bottom of the sloping road, just smiling at the sun.

"Isn't it beautiful George?" she asked aloud. She pulled her eyes away from the sunrise to meet some of their curious glances. She wondered what she must look like, sweaty and pink with exertion, wearing rags. Princesses probably don't ever look like this; she realized and suddenly felt very self-aware.

"I can't tell who looks worse for wear, you or your mount?" Callana twisted in her saddle towards the familiar voice. It was the queen, looking lean, tidy, and most casual in a thin lined outer tunic in a pale brown. She was accompanied by only one guard; a large, blonde haired man named Sir Keitan. Callana dismounted, kneeling immediately in front of the striking woman.

"Your majesty, forgive my appearance!" Callana rose to face the queen, blushing in embarrassment for her grotesque attire.

"Oh please don't feel ashamed! I am just supremely envious, for I rarely get any time for pleasure riding." She tilted her head towards her unwitting guard and rolled her eyes.

"Seems going for a ride through the country just isn't on the schedule for a queen and time alone is limited to bathing, and even that is difficult with *my* wanton husband!" Her smile lit her sparkling eyes, identical to Jiden's. Callana let his face flash through her memory for a moment and felt the rush of blood hit her cheeks. The queen was running her hand over the coarse purple hair of George's mane. Paul, or Edward, Callana couldn't decide which, was heading towards her and her now sleeping mount.

"Pleasure to clean him for you my lady," He said bowing to the princess.

"Good morning, most beautiful Queen Lena." He sank graciously into a formal bow. Callana heard the immense respect in his young voice. Such a Queen she must be to demand reverence like this from a young boy. Callana watched Lena gently bow her head, smiling pleasantly, at the dirty stable boy.

"Rise and tell me, young Edward, how are those delightful brothers of yours?" Callana noted the genuine concern in the queen's voice.

"Well can't vouch for the delightful part mum, but..." he snorted "Mother's got her hands full for sure".

"You tell her again I *can* sneak away for an afternoon if she would like a bit of a day away," a despondent grumble growled out of Sir Keiton at the thought of having to accompany the queen to look after six kids! Edward nodded, grinning widely and turned to lead Callana's mount to the stable. Callana slapped George on the rump on his way by.

"So, I trust Jiden's old sleepwear fit?" Lena smiled. She spun Callana around to look her over.

"My it really does fit quite well doesn't it? I have always wanted one of those!" She tapped Callana's ample round buttock. Callana turned red and covered her backside with her hands. The Queen winked and turned towards the market street, gesturing for Callana to follow. Callana looked quizzically at the queen's knowing about the reconnaissance mission assigned to Miala. Lena noted the pale girl's confused expression and explained.

"*I* handle the laundry for the royal family. I can't bare the thought of someone having to wash *Odin's* clothes! How dreadful! Any how, Miala asked me if there was some riding wear for her princess….she is very taken with you!" Callana shook off her disbelief about a queen doing laundry and smiled brightly at the mention of Miala.

"She is a very likable girl, although timid, she and I are getting along famously! She reminds me of my…" Callana stopped short of saying sister, suddenly remembering she was supposed to be an only child from Rogadon. "My…own servant girl from home," The queen studied her for a moment than satisfied, she set about shopping again.

"Join me for a little buying trip?" Lena took Callana's hand and led her slowly, passed carts and tables, full of treasures. Callana tried to protest.

"I have no money with me my lady," Lena pulled her to a stop, than turned to the large guard. She nodded and he tossed a small leather pouch to the queen, who handed it to Callana.

"I am the queen aren't I? Come! You can help me spend my allowance!" She tugged Callana towards a table filled with stacks of different linens. Some thicker for cool spring weather, some with long sleeves and lined with rabbit fur, for harsh winter chills, and some thin and breezy for the humid summers. There was a rainbow of colors in each style.

"Ooooh, I love this one!" The queen nearly squealed, yanking a pink summer linen outer tunic out of a pile and unfurling it to test the length.

"It s perfect my lady! That color will complement your lovely brown hair," the woman behind the table commented. Callana noted. The vendor, a tall, unshaved man and his short friendly faced wife were bowing for Callana and the queen.

"My lady, we would be honored. Such a figure deserves such a dress!" the woman gestured towards the queen's small waist.

"Oh the things you'd say to sell a garment, shameful Dellora! Now, as you were saying?" The queen pretended to primp her hair, batting her eyes and posturing for the couple. The trio laughed as Lena glanced back at the

obviously bored Sir Keitan, who quickly produced another pouch of gold coins.
"Three gold coins, right love?" The queen retrieved the coins and dropped
them on the table. The couple shook their heads. The husband grabbed the
coins and held them out to the queen.

"None sense my lady! This is only linen, a gold coin alone buys *three* whole
tunics!" Lena shook her head and pushed his hand away.

"I recognize quality when I see it; I 'have paid my price!" She quickly walked
away, leaving the grateful couple to watch after her admiringly. Dellora
turned towards the departing princess and pleaded for her to take a tunic.
"Please, the queen has paid more than enough, do us the honor of picking any
linen, please Princess Callana. Your favorite color perhaps?" Callana sighed,
politely bowing to the gracious couple.

"Have anything in a sunny yellow?" She mused. The man quickly flipped
through a pile to his left, retrieving a soft linen tunic of the brightest yellow
Callana had ever seen.

"It's yours!" He said, eagerly handing it to her. She pulled out a gold coin and
put it in his hand. When he tried to protest, she insisted.
"The queen was right; this is of the greatest quality. Thank you very much."
Callana swished away in her dirty riding clothes and caught up with the
queen, who was eagerly throwing money at another protesting vendor. This
time it was for necklaces, and further up the market street it was a woman
selling blankets. Callana giggled to herself, watching the queen turn her nose
up and promptly refuse any refund. Callana was sure Lena had paid a gold
coin for a potato!

"My lady, you will bankrupt your kingdom!" Callana joked, handing her
remaining gold coins back to the closely following guard.

"None sense!" the queen leaned in to whisper to Callana.
"It is their tax money, paid for our army's armor. I just give back to them
what Adalonia does not spend on steel. Besides, I *love* pink!" She held out her
arms, displaying a pink stone necklace, pink tunic, pink ribbons for her hair,
a pink blanket, and a potato.

"So? It's not pink. I still love it!" The two laughed their way towards the open
court where the queen turned to face the young princess.

"My queen, you are the most gracious person I have met to date! How your
kingdom must adore you." The queen beamed with pride as she looked back
over her city.

"It is a mutual adoration," than glancing back at Callana, Lena continued.
"One day Callana, it will be your city full of admirers!" Callana blushed and
glanced back to the market.

At that moment, a mule, unleashed from his wagon, spooked at the flapping
of a red wool blanket being inspected by a buyer. A small boy, unaware of the
animal's distress, was using it's backside as cover for a game of hide and
seek. The large male's ears laid flat to his head, and he coiled his leg to boot

the invisible agitator. Callana dove at once thrusting the boy backwards, catching the full brunt of the animals rage in her hip bone.

"Callana!" The queen rushed to the injured girl's side. The mule's owner tied it quickly to a post and rushed to join the queen.

"My lady! I only glanced away for a moment! Please, forgive me!"

"I am alright," Callana gasped, trying desperately to sit up. The act caused her to yelp in pain. The queen held Callana's shoulders down to keep her still. Onlookers had gathered, and Sir Keitan promptly signaled the watch on the wall to send assistance.

"The boy, is he...?" Callana tried to roll on to her side to look for the boy, but the queen held her tight.

"Still princess, he has a scrape on his knee, he is safe." She promised.

"She saved that boy!" A voice cried out in the crowd.

"Princess Callana just saved a boy!" Another voice explained to a passing villager. Another guard arrived to carry Callana to the home of Lustene. The queen rushed ahead to alert the sleeping surgeon. Lustene was ready in moments.

"Lay her down on the table sir knight." The knight did as he was told and joined the queen's guard to stand watch by the door. The queen had sent the fortunate boy, Gant, out to the north shore where the prince would be conducting training. Jiden would want to know the princess was wounded.

"My dear, what on earth has happened to you?" asked a gentle, old voice. Callana was left side was on fire with pain.

"She pushed Gant out of the way of an angry mule and received a good knock to the hip for her gallantry!" Lena was distressed, Lustene could see. The queen rolled Callana gently over to her right hip and began cutting the tight leggings with a small, sharp blade she had strapped to her inner leg. She had to expose the length of the princess's thigh, unveiling a large, swollen greenish hump. The queen wrinkled her forehead in worry and looked to her long time friend.

"Do you think she has broken anything Lustene?" The aging surgeon bent to examine the swell.

"Hard to say without further examination my queen;" He raised his voice slightly and leaned over Callana

"Princess, this is going to hurt a little, but I need to assess whether or not you have broken your hip. Are you ready?" Callana nodded slowly and held her breath against the terrible burn. Lena held the princess's shoulder tight to stabilize her against any pain induced flailing. Lustene gently placed a hand on either side of the hip bone and pushed in, causing the pain to shoot up through Callana's chest and turn her stomach. Lustene went about feeling and poking for another moment before laying Callana on her back to examine her from the front. Callana kept quiet, though she felt as though she had a molten hot rock stuck under her skin. He turned to the anxious queen.

"It is not broken." Lena blew out the breath she had been holding. Callana sighed.

"But, the muscle tissue itself is deeply bruised; that's causing this tremendous swelling. She needs a soak in a hot salt bath first off. I will make a poultice and bring it up when she has salted the wound for infection."

"Thank you Lustene, I will make ready her bath." With that Lena vanished out the door, dashing towards the castle, a scrambling guard trailing her. Callana smiled up at the wise eyes staring kindly down at her.

"Princess Callana, how do you do?" She held her hand out to him.

"Charmed, I am Lustene, my lady," He bowed and kissed her hand delicately. Callana winced in pain. Lustene shushed her softly and pulled a sheet over her exposed side.

"You realize if that mule had kicked that lad as hard as he kicked you there would be a dead boy on my table instead of a battered princess...Are you always so fearless young lady?" Lustene scolded her. She smiled laboriously and shook her head.

"I did not have time to think, so I hardly had time to *fear*!" She laughed, holding her hand on her inflamed side.

"So you are a true hero; thoughtlessly brave, putting the lives of others ahead of your own! Sir Galland will be most grateful. Gant is his *only* child."

Rogala giggled as she lumbered around the soft bed, running, only pretending to be unwilling to be caught by her handsome Renk. It was their fist night together as man and wife. The ceremony was small, but lawful, no blue; however, to symbolize the obviously lacking purity, save for the swelling indigo ocean sighing in audience. Frellis was an incredible, beach front city, heavy into ocean fishing and imports. The amorous couple had settled in a small village named Sea Fair, in a cozy stilted cottage, and had found a priest willing to marry a vigilante pregnant woman to a fugitive knight. The aroused newlyweds finally gave in to their overwhelming passions, raucously thrashing, lost in soft linen sheets, completely consumed with need.

....

After a few days of uncontrollable passions, the couple decided to make a trip to the market. Renk was unable to keep his hands off of his bride, and being legally wed made it even more stimulating, not having to hide his love for this enchanting woman. The protruding belly was so becoming on her, illuminating her from the inside, as if their child was a being of light itself. Rogala kissed him on his generous, soft lips, pulling him to her and holding him tight.

"All right now love, we need food! Can you contain yourself long enough to gather sustenance? I don't think you need reminding how furious a pregnant woman gets when she's hungry!"

"No, Oooo, I don't!" Renk shook his head, holding his arms up in surrender, and resigned himself to merely holding her hand. A woman selling apples under a canopy called out to the couple.

"Apples are essential for a developing baby…you will try one?" Renk led his wife to the table and the petite woman. He returned her friendly smile, but couldn't help feel an intimacy to this woman. She reminded him of someone. He was studying her when she looked up from her fruit and caught his eye.

"I know we have met before love, remind me of your name," He stuck a hand out to her but she had locked eyes on his princess. Rogala was gnashing loudly into a crisp green apple and had not noticed the attention. Finally, Renk realized the two women had the exact same crystal blue eyes! The same build, even the same wavy golden hair! He had never met her, he realized, but felt a familiarity because she was an older version of his Rogala! The princess had stopped chewing long enough to see the color had drained from the woman's face, and turning towards her husband she saw he had grown still. The woman covered her mouth with her hands as tears welled in her eyes.

"How did you *know*?" She gasped. Rogala shook her head. She wasn't sure what she was supposed to know, but Renk had a notion.

"Who are you?" He demanded. The woman had tears streaming down her face now as Rogala scrutinized her.

"My name is Nia....I ... I ....was the woman who raised you, your mother's servant. I knew your parents, Kiera and Granlund, before they died." She stammered the words out through shaky lips. Renk felt something was awry with the woman's story.

"What are you hiding woman? Speak!" Renk barked, awarding him a few startled glances from other buyers.

"You don't know?" The woman was disappointed. "Than why did you come here?" Her eyes pleaded with Rogala.

"What don't we know?" asked Rogala, agitated she couldn't put her finger on a thought gnawing at the back of her mind. She knew something but couldn't pull it forward.

"Rogala, I am your *mother*," the woman breathed, collapsing into tears. Rogala's face opened wide in shock. She paled, reaching for Renk to stabilize her.

"My mother? How...how is this possible?"

"I don't know how it's possible Rogala but there is no other explanation! Look at her! You are identical in every way!" Renk said, gesturing from one delicate blonde to the other.

"I am sorry Rogala; I thought, seeing you here, that somehow you had sought me out, that you knew," Nia was crushed, having thought this would be a touching reunion, only to find it was just an accident.

"Wait, wait, just tell me why my mother... isn't my mother." Rogala begged. The woman nodded, giving a sidelong glance at Renk than began loading her cart. Renk folded up the canopy and helped her pack for the short walk to their cottage. He understood the ramifications of what this would mean if overheard. King Granlund, King Bromell's brother, was of no royal blood, but met and married Kiera, ward of King Leston, giving him a royal, if not blood, claim to leave to his brother who was awarded the kingdom in Granlund's will. If it was public knowledge that king Granlund had conceived a child with a servant, it would mean King Bromell had no legal heir or blood to the throne, than Rogadon would be literally, up for grabs. This discovery was best discussed in private.

Secure inside the cottage, Nia tried to explain. Rogala was trembling and pale.

"Your mother was my queen, I adored her! She had hired me when I was only a girl of thirteen, so I could support my ailing mother. My father had died when I was young and my mother had what the surgeon simply called a fever, but it was awful. Your parents were gracious and kind to me; I would have done anything for them. Your poor mother had suffered several miscarriages, and feared she could not provide the kingdom with an heir. She asked me if I would...help." Nia cringed; she did not want to admit to what had been done in desperation; to tell Rogala that her father had committed adultery. Renk had already put the pieces together but feared Rogala would deny the obvious because it was too heartbreaking. Rogala had adored her parents. She was a child when their carriage was robbed, and her parents brutally murdered. To learn they were anything other than honorable would be devastating. Nia tried to put it gently.

"Rogala, your father and I...*created* you, together....so Rogadon would have an heir...I *am* your mother," Nia said softly. Rogala finally collapsed.

....

"It's been days! I must see her!" The Prince was livid with Lustene for keeping him at bay yet again, outside Callana's quarters. Lustene put a finger to his mouth to shush the agitated young man.

"She is well, sire, but *indisposed* at the moment. She must soak every day."

"You mean, oh, she is n n naked?" Jiden crossed his arms and tried his best stern look.

"Yes, Sire, it is best when soaking to be unclothed."

"Of course, I will come back later. That is all." Lustene bowed and watched the prince's awkward departure. Lustene allowed himself a chuckle only after his Jiden had rounded the far corner.

"My lady, how does your hip feel today?" An overly concerned Miala asked. Callana shooed her away, determined to stand on her own.

"I feel magnificent!" She lied, shakily lifting herself to a standing position in her now lukewarm wooden tub with a red mop of wet hair stuck to her back.

"I intend to be riding by the end of today, you watch me!" Callana swore. Miala shook her head, handing her friend a soft sheep's wool towel.

"You know, a certain *prince* has been beside himself with worry..." Miala smiled wryly.

"Lustene has turned him away everyday for the last three days!" she giggled with this. Callana perked at the mention of Jiden.

"*Every* day?" She asked incredulously. Miala nodded. Callana grinned from ear to ear.

"Why wasn't he permitted to visit?" Callana suddenly frowned. Miala laughed out loud; handing over the princesses prescribed fenugreek seed, mint and ground sage tea.

"Because my lady, you have been under nothing but a sheet, due to your swelling. It would be viewed as most inappropriate for a visit." The small brunette explained. Callana blushed, than nodded.

"Of course, it would have been extremely inappropriate, of course," with that, she began dressing in the recently laundered brown tunic she had worn for her first and last ride in this kingdom. Miala was smiling devilishly. Callana laughed.

"What are you so happy about mischievous elf?" Miala produced a new pair of green leggings and matching tunic from a large pocket on her apron front. Callana gleefully tore the garments out of the young girl's tiny hands, tittering with delight.

"Where did you get these?" Callana raised her eyebrows.

"Compliments of the queen! She knew you would try riding today," Miala winked. Callana was delighted!

"There is a stipulation...you must have an escort," Miala chastised the princess, arms crossed.

"What? Some *bored* guard bothering me around all morning?" Callana was shoving her legs angrily into her new leggings, wincing against the soreness in her left hip and didn't notice him coming in.

"Well, I see my reputation precedes me," Jiden was standing, hands on hips, frowning in the open doorway. Callana glimpsed Miala's cheesy grin, having been in on this little surprise. Callana finished pulling up leggings and belting her tunic, fidgeting with nervous hands, hoping she did not look as stupid as she felt at that moment.

"Forgive me, my lord, I was not aware of the identity of my escort." She bowed her head politely, suddenly realizing her hair was in complete disarray!

"I would be most appreciative of your company today". She added.

Jiden smiled bashfully, glancing around at the young servant. Miala bowed and excused herself, leaving the betrothed a moment's privacy. Jiden came to Callana at once, bending, eagerly to kiss her lips. Callana closed her eyes and allowed herself a moment's fantasy as he pulled her close with his body hard against her; tenderly slipping his arms around her trim waist, careful to avoid her hip.

"I missed you immeasurably my love," He whispered between kisses. Callana brought her arms up around his neck, her fingers lost in his curls.

"And I you sire," Jiden moved his kisses over her cheek and to her throat.

"Please do not call me sire at a time like this." Callana pushed him away suddenly. Jiden was shocked and attempted to tug her back to him but she held him at arms length and looked up at him, eyes pleading.

"Please, sire, I cannot give in to anything that might spoil your feelings for me!" Callana stepped away and bent to pull on her riding boots. Jiden tried to compose himself, frowning with her refusal.

"How could *enjoying* each other ruin anything Callana?"

"Because you assume you will *enjoy* me, and when I disappoint you what then?" Callana was standing now, with her back to him, unwilling to endure his burning eyes while baring her insecurities. How ironic, Jiden thought to himself. He had the very same fears only days before, but had somehow, learned to disregard them whenever she was near. He turned her to him and kissed her forehead.

"For give me, Callana. I should not rush such a thing," He knelt down to finish lacing her forgotten boot. She was confused.

"We are to be virtuous on our wedding day, are we not my lord?" Jiden stood slowly, a wicked smile playing upon his lips.

"I promise not to tell your husband if you won't tell my wife!" Callana slapped his arm with that.

"So how about a ride?" Jiden grinned, raising one menacing eyebrow. Callana's mouth fell open. Jiden snickered boisterously.

"I meant *horseback* my love!" he smiled wide.

"Of course your majesty." The two locked arms and marched out together to find a very eager George and a not so willing Leviathon already saddled and waiting in the court yard. Nicholas held both pairs of reins, smiling generously upon sight of the riders.

"Thank you cousin!" Jiden shouted down the steps to the handsome young man. Callana reached the bottom stair and returned his bow graciously.

"Princess Callana, pleasure is all mine to be sure," Nicholas took her hand, leading her to the left side of her mount and positioned himself behind her to assist, seeing as she had to use her tender left leg to mount. Nicholas took a quick glance at the tightly clad rump, shooting his cousin a sinful smile and a nod of approval. Jiden rolled his eyes, shaking his head in exasperation.

"Thank you, *Nicholas*, I think she can handle it from here," Jiden clenched his teeth with the last.

"Right my lord, have a good romp then!" Callana turned a bright red with the knight's deliberate postulation. Jiden, reddening with both embarrassment and anger, snapped his head towards the grinning fool.

"That will be all, *Squire!*" he snarled. Nicholas feigning shame, bowed low for lord and lady, and turned sharply on his heels to stroll away through the court yard. Jiden smiled sheepishly at the princess, than mounted his white stallion.

"Where are we heading sire?" Callana asked, desperate to change the subject. Jiden pointed towards the eastern wall of the court.

"To the Green Mountain falls, my lady, I trusted you wouldn't mind, we won't be back for a few days." Jiden noticing the stern look from Callana quickly added,

"I am supervising the changing of the guard. The new detachment left this morning before dawn, to set camp. We shall meet them there. Sir Nicholas is covering my morning patrol." Callana smiled and turned her great purple horse towards the gates of the court yard.

"I will be on my best behavior, Princess, but I cannot promise the same for my men!" Jiden held his hand to his heart in oath. Callana giggled and the two set out on for a much needed ride on a luminous sunny day.

．．．

"Why can't I remember you in my life?" Rogala had her second bout of evening morning sickness and was resting in her nuptial bed. Nia had refused to leave her side until she had regained her full strength. Rogala was trying desperately to get a grip on this new distortion of her life. Nia shook her head sadly,
"I was just another maid, as was the agreement, my angel. I was to *have* you not *rear* you. Your mother and father wanted you to have a rightful claim to Rogadon."
"But when they were murdered? I was only four, and I *needed* someone …I was so terribly sad! Where were you then?" Rogala cried. Nia's troubled eyes welled up with tears and she trembled with every breath.
"My child, I begged to stay with you, I did! Know that I did! But Bromell, he was so fearful I would tell you the truth and he would lose his *precious* kingdom! He detested Kiera for not producing an heir. His contempt for her was so that king Granlund banished him for the first few years of their marriage! Bromell was granted his return under sworn oath to revere her as his queen and harbor no ill will, but I knew he still did," Nia's frail body wracked with her seething rage. Rogala was bewildered by this. She had never known her uncle to be kind but certainly never so cruel as to be banished by his own brother! Her head was spinning, and she felt weak all over, and overwhelmed.
"I was banished the very day we received word of your parent's horrible murders! I grieved so much that day, and every day since! Your mother was my best friend, the only friend I had on this earth, and you were my very own and he wouldn't even permit me to say good bye!" Nia sobbed. Rogala's heart was breaking for this woman. She had obviously suffered a horrendous amount, more than Rogala ever wanted to know. She sat at once to hold the shaking woman through her crying.
"I am with you now, and we will never be apart again, my mother," Rogala squeezed her mother with all the tremendous love she contained and had lost the chance to bestow on her own loving parents. She would give it all to Nia; she swore it to her unborn child. He would know he was loved, infinitely.
"I love you Rogala. I have always, always loved you my beautiful girl," Nia rocked back and forth, holding her child as her own for the first time in her life.

Renk was cooking a rabbit stew, minus vegetables never purchased, outside over their fire pit. He had a good feeling about this woman being part of their lives. His child would have a grandmother! He could tell she cared for Rogala. It must have hurt her deeply to lose her child. His child was not even born yet and he already felt an agonizing love for him. Rogala had been raised by a calloused, cold man, only interested in her basic needs but had never shown her how to love, or be loved. When Renk had first seen her, she was only thirteen, and he was already on the edge of sixteen. It was his first night watch in the tower's of Rogadon and she was crossing the dark court to get to the library. She loved books! Renk would discover that Rogala invented herself through the stories she read, since she had no idea of who she was supposed to be. She had no outlet, no friends, no siblings and worst of all, no one who loved her. Her uncle had no intention of wasting any teachings on a girl, caring only for who he could marry her to, securing his hold on Rogadon through matrimony. Even though, it appears, he knew he had no such claim. Renk felt shame for the battles he had waged for that traitorous man. How many taxes he had collected for a king who would just as soon let his city starve while he himself scrapped half of every meal! Renk learned much about his rotten king during his secret courtship of the young princess. So much he had regretted knowing, for it would be three years before he could try to persuade the princess into a grown up relationship and leave. Renk allowed a small smile to turn up his lips, remembering how fast their relationship had turned physical. She was an unrelenting source of heat and lust and he could not resist. His naughty remembering was interrupted by an eruption of laughter from the cottage. Renk collected the boiling stew and climbed the wooden steps to find out what was so funny to the two women he had left weeping only a short time ago. Rogala and Nia were cackling hysterically when he entered. Renk had to ask,
"What has gotten into the two of you? You sound insane!"
Rogala pointed at her mother and Nia spoke, wiping tears from her eyes,
"I asked to listen to the baby's heart beat and pressed my ear into her tummy and said hello there I am your grand mum, and nearly peed myself when I got a snarling growl in response!" Rogala erupted again and had to hold her stretched stomach muscles that burned with exertion.
"I am hungry, I couldn't help it! It was too funny my love! It was so loud and scary!" Rogala wiped a tear out of her eye. Renk sniggered, enjoying the bond they had formed so fast.
"Well *hungry*, supper is served!" When Rogala nearly leaped out of her bed and plunged face first into her wooden bowl, Renk glanced to Nia and raised his eyebrows.
"Now that's loud and scary!" He whispered. The three started up again, Rogala nearly choking on her stew. Nia came to the table to eat with her new family, glowing with pride over her ravenous daughter.

....

Riding east, over the verdant rising and falling landscape, Callana couldn't help but feel she belonged here. She felt meant to be in this moment, in this place. It made her wonder what Jiden was thinking. While he rode gracefully enough, he had his mind set on formations and reports. She felt an incredible reverence for the amount of stress he seemed to take in stride. She herself may have had chores, but she was not in charge of how or who accomplished all the things necessary to run a household let alone the entire Inn! Jiden was so young, only sixteen, and had a kingdom on *his* shoulders. His father, a good man in all rights, had settled down to the bureaucratic side of ruling. He held congresses and balls, even committee's on findings, or lack there of, from morning patrols. Jiden had taken on the army's training, feeding, sequestering of armor, and rotation of the guards, and he was doing all of this keeping his boyish charm in tact. She had a deep warmth spreading through her as she loped along beside this gloriously adorable man! The courtship, splendid as it was, was a formality. She already knew she would be marrying the man she had dreamed of all her life! A gorgeous prince, who adored her, was going to take her hand in matrimony, have children with her, and grow old with her and her alone! How blessed could one girl be?

"What are you grinning about over there you she devil?" Jiden's curls bounced around his ears while he beamed widely at her. Callana blushed slightly, having been caught in her real life fantasy, than said,

"I was actually thinking of how depressed that magnificent stallion of yours will be when we best you in a race!"

"Just tell me where the finish is love, old George can get a good look at the rear end of this *magnificent* stallion". Jiden winked. Callana guffawed at that. She glanced ahead, over a small rise about a thousand paces away there was a wooden fence around a goat pasture. She pointed it out.

"There sire, to the last post in that fence line," Callana looked to Jiden for a confirmation. He snorted and gave her a look of skepticism.

"*George* will make it another *thousand paces*? You want to put a wager on that love?" He raised his brows, still loping along with his spirited curls. Callana shot him a fiery glare through squinted dark eyes.

"Such as, sire?" Jiden grinned suggestively and Callana shook her head. He feigned pouting; than brightened.

"If Leviathon wins, you will serve me breakfast in bed for a week, and if *George* wins, I shall serve you," The couple veered close to each other to shake. Callana pulled back her hand,

"Wait, we already get breakfast in bed every day anyway," She argued.
"Yes, but *mine* is delivered by Nicholas, need I say more? Now, deal?" Jiden deepened his voice. This time they shook hands. Jiden leaned forward and glanced eagerly at Callana before shouting,
 "Go!" Leviathon leaped into the lead, switching his lead leg as he did. Poor startled George had jolted sideways. Callana prodded him in his belly with hard wooden stirrups and George sprang forward, arching his neck and lifting his tail. They were trailing the white steed, but not by much. Jiden was laughing, cockily, having every confidence there was nothing an old gelding could do better than his young stallion! Callana was slightly irked at the thought of someone counting her George out before it was over. She stood in her stirrups, bending into a crouched position and leaned closer to George's bobbing ear and whispered.
 "Get up George!" She had been using this phrase to ignite the great purple horse since she was a little girl when she had misunderstood her father's command of 'giddy up'. Callana only used that phrase when she wanted real speed from her trustworthy mount, and it worked like a charm. George yanked his head forward, taking the reins, and pounced into a long stretching stride. He passed Leviathon, and his astonished rider, and within moments, they were lengths ahead. Callana's hip burned with the effort from her injured muscles straining to balance her with every huge bound. Despite his slight disappointment, Jiden had to admire the pair. They were a single unit, moving as one, gracefully soaring over the uneven plains. Purple and red banners of long mane streaming out behind as they whooshed passed the fence posts, almost to the finish. Jiden respected the old boy for his spirit, much like his rider's; relentless. Callana slowed, sitting back down in the saddle and threw her arms up in the air.
 "The winner! Yeeeees! George is the greatest horse in the world!" As George slowed to an easy walk, Callana preceded to bow left and right as the champion to an imaginary crowd. Jiden clapped wildly and hooted his approval.
 "All right, I admit it, that's a glorious horse." He leaned forward to Leviathan's listening ear and whispered.
 "We had to let them win boy, girls are terrible losers, cry babies and all!" He winked at Callana. She smiled back and patted the wet neck of her champ.
 "How did you get him to pick up like that? Leviathon is no slouch, and you passed us like posts." Jiden was genuinely impressed, causing Callana to well with pride for her remarkable horse and the remarkable man who had trained him.
 "Well, my father taught me to ride when I was young, and I thought he was saying get up," She giggled, than frowned when she saw Jiden's confused expression.
 "Your *father* taught you to ride?" He seemed doubtful. She grimaced for a moment, holding her hip that had only just stopped burning and blinked;

searching her mind for what she could have said wrong. Rogala had a *father*, right?

"He did... why so surprised?" she finally asked.

"It's just that he died when you were just four, or have I been given false information about you? Chamberlain Illiam is usually quite proficient." Jiden was still frowning.

"No, no that's correct sire, I just, ah, remember him so well because we were... so close." Callana tried to smile brightly, hoping to sound credible.

"Of course," Jiden agreed, allowing himself a small smile. He was startled by the immediate panic he experienced at a single moment of doubt in his beloved princess. He shook his head and decided his previous aversion to marriage was trying to get the better of him.

"So sire, how often do you change your mountain top guard?" Callana tried desperately to start a new subject, disappointed their relationship was to be stained by a betrayal she needed to keep secret. She must be more diligent, staying in character at all times. She did not want this to be ruined for Rogala; or herself, for that matter. She was very much falling for Jiden. Jiden hadn't fully believed her just now, and she felt a cold fear in the back of her mind. She didn't want to lose him. Jiden cleared his throat before speaking.

"On the last day of every month, I bring new knights and supplies and take the new guard to replace the old, who in turn, come down to the lake at the bottom of the falls where they give over their information to me and me only, and we have a splendid swim and supper and head out first thing the next morning for home. There is no need to go through the day's trip down the cavern's trails and than half a day home, so I always insist they have a night's rest in between. Besides, there are two men stuck for a month together in a wooden hut eating only dried pork and figs; it's a matter of health that they have a good meal and a bath before returning home and back to regular duties." Callana mused while the prince spoke, thinking of how dreary those mountain top huts would be in the winter while the peeks were covered in snow.

They rode on, this time in comfortable silence. The quiet ease between them gave them a chance to actually hear the world around them. Callana watched Jiden, unconsciously smiling; observing small orange breasted wrens flitter about from one leafy branched oak to another; in the tree line to the south, a red fox came darting out of her den than back in upon seeing the riders; the slight breeze lifted the leaves and tickled the tall grass. She was happy to see him enjoying his kingdom. She was new to this valley, so she couldn't help but be overwhelmed by the landscape, but Jiden seemed just as amazed by his surroundings as well. Callana guessed he had probably never really *viewed* this beautiful place, never listened to the birds or the wind or taken a day to just explore for fun instead of perimeter checks. How could he not take such things for granted as pleasure? His daily life was demanding from start to finish. Even today's ride, disguised as a lovely jaunt through a majestic valley, was yet another duty to attend to. She could feel her pride in him intensify inside her and swirling around with it was a tingling sensation she had never felt before. She respected him deeply, she was definitely attracted to him, but something else was there. Callana had turned her wistful attention back to the shimmering limestone falls, only about an hour away now. Jiden had followed his musing gaze to the southern plains spilling out around the red, dusty base of Mount Andoria, and the western face of the Shadows forest along and behind them on the far side of the iridescent sapphire Lake Ceruleana. He was surrounded by intense beauty everyday and couldn't remember the last time he had stopped to take it all in. He sighed to himself. Today was wonderful; no other words would do it justice! She was wonderful! He could just *be* with her and he felt.... *happy.* He could spend weeks on end with his knights and every day with Nicholas and, for the most part, he was content in their presence. But he had never experienced any moment with a woman that wasn't horribly awkward and suppressive. He felt suffocated around other princesses at the kingdom's yearly ball. They seemed to seek him out just for being *available* and smother him with their petty comments and shameful flirting! Callana was so different, so brilliant! She was here for the ride, not just his company. She was enjoying herself, not contemplating ridiculous things to say to try to sound important or socially prominent. He doubted she even cared about idle gossip or prattling conversations to fill the silence. He adored her soft appearance, intelligent eyes, and open heart. She had proven herself to be brave, saving Sir Galland's son, and she had proven herself to be chaste, unfortunately for him. He knew something was happening between them, felt it building. Layers upon layers; he had lusted after her immediately, than he had experienced the incredible fear when he heard she had been injured. He was so distraught he might lose her he couldn't be calmed until he had seen her face, seen she was all right. This new gradation of feelings for her was tearing at him more than he wanted to admit. Jiden had loving, devoted parents who adored each other as well as him. Still, since he could remember, he had carried the fear of giving yourself whole to another person the way his they had. His parents made love look so easy, but in truth, how easy is it to worry about another's life more than your own? To care about someone else so much that you cease to exist in your own life? You become a *couple* instead of an *individual.* Jiden had never wanted to lose himself in love, yet no matter how hard he tried to contest himself, he knew loving Callana was inevitable. With every beat of his heart he wanted to love her, and feared it as well; His insecurities would have him cordially calling off the wedding, sending her back to Rogadon forever to *loath* him. Jiden had to defeat one personality or the other, but the stronger he felt for Callana, the more he knew he could no longer wear both faces.

Jiden was starting to make out figures over the tops of the undulating ground. There was the mule driven wagon loaded with fresh mutton, porridge and rice, apples, figs, and pickled eggs; there would also be iron cooking pots, steel weaponry and apothecary herbs; such as vervain, valerian, oregano, mint, horehound, thyme, rosemary, sage, myrrh, comfey, aloe, and wine and honey for mixing herbs and making teas. These would be the responsibility of Lustene's talented assistant Silvio. The wagon's driver, Fredrick, would double as the cook. Jiden also saw about a half a dozen bodies lazing about in this hot summer sun and he shook his head, laughing to himself. Yes, those were his honored knights all right! He halted his mount, gesturing for Callana to do the same. She snapped out of her day dream and followed his gaze.

"Great, we are almost there!" She sighed with relief. Her hip was all but threatening to tear itself apart from her body and burst into flames. Jiden noticed her wincing and grew concerned.

"This was a long trip in your condition, are you all right?" His eyebrows furrowed as he looked her over. Callana nodded and quickly shrugged off the pain.

"It is nothing sire." She suddenly decided it would be inappropriate for her to show up with her hair billowing loosely all around her and hurriedly made a thick braid, pulling all of her hair over to her right side and tying it with a yellow ribbon she had kept around her wrist.

"You ready love?" He smiled warmly. She nodded, grinning brightly.

"Ready sire," Jiden frowned slightly with that, they were all alone any way and she had never stopped addressing him formally. It was a matter for a different time. He stiffened, transforming himself from casual Jiden to the 'Prince' in a quick re-adjustment of attitude; they headed out towards the camp. Callana giggled watching motionless bodies become suddenly alert; jumping into action setting up cows skin canopies and digging a fire pit. Callana could hear the crashing of the tremendous falls into the clear pool below, spilling into a rushing stream leading south through the valley, trickling towards the castle into the south eastern tip of the lake. It was a welcome sight in this summer heat; as welcome as the softy mist she felt billowing around her as she neared. The men must have been looking out for the prince because she was sure no one could have *heard* him over the plunging water. When they had reached the knights, a familiar figure hopped out of the back of the supply wagon to take the horses

"Edward! How nice to see you," cried Callana, dismounting and pulling the skinny young man into a hug. Edward was blushing bright red as he bowed politely to her.

"Is most pleasing to see you again Princess, to be sure. May I take your horses for you Sire, my lady?" The couple nodded their permission and the great purple horse and his gleaming white companion were led to a make shift post about ten yards from camp to be unsaddled, curried and fed a bucket of barely and carrots. Callana turned to join Jiden in greeting her camp mates.

"This is our young cook, Fredrick, our training surgeon, Silvio, and six rather lazy knights. Gentlemen, Princess Callana," Jiden held her hand and she curtsied low for them. Each bowed heads politely and almost in unison said, "My lady". Jiden recognized a familiar face. It was young Jerrik, a rather 'hands on' dancer from the ball. He caught the boy's glance, causing him to drop his head and stare intently at the ground in front of him.

"No worries, Sir Jerrik," the Prince grinned, "There will be no dancing tonight to get you into trouble!" Jerrik gave a simpering smile and straightened his shoulders for inspection.

Each man must bring a spear, dagger, sword, shield, a weeks worth of socks, extra boots, chainmail, fur lined blankets for nights, and a change of tunic. Barrels of water, dried salted pork, vinegar, cereals, fava beans, torches and oil, ale and bread were carried by mule to each of the four watch huts. Most of the food was sent from Felonia, Maulen, and Tasdalad, as a token of appreciation for the knights' service. The Adalonia watch towers were strategically built to view both the Adalonia valley itself and their neighboring kingdoms' valleys as well; a post the neighboring kingdoms were not equipped to cover themselves. The rest of the food was provided by Prince Jiden himself. The actual huts had beds and a broom to keep them clean. They were occupied at all times, so had to be kept in good repair, most of which was done in the summer. Tree sap was used to fill all small openings in the walls and the skin roof tops were replaced yearly. Jiden was closely eyeing each knight and the corresponding display at their feet. Jiden also wrote each name and which post down so there would be accountability other than his memory for each man.

Sir Lance, Mount Rising

Sir Donovin, Mount Rising

Sir Reynolds, Green Mountain

Sir Jerrik, Green Mountain

Sir Lashend, Mount Andoria

Sir Laden, Mount Andoria

Satisfied each man was ready; he dismissed them to pack their gear for the long hike through the cave behind the falls. Promptly upon finishing his inspection of Sir Laden's gear, the young man bent and covered it with vomit. Jiden was concerned. He waited for Laden to right himself again.

"Go see Silvio, he might have a tonic. Can you still ride?" Laden was pale, and covered in sweat. He nodded his head but his terrible expression betrayed him. Jiden knew he needed to stay put, till he could ride. To make the rendezvous time of dusk tomorrow, the knights had to make haste. Jiden knew he would have to fill in as replacement. Sir Ren, a man over forty, who had accompanied Silvio as guard; although a most courageous knight and highest caliber swordsman could not be expected to make the trip through the mountain. Callana was steadying Laden, and helping him to sit in the shade of the wagon. She saw the look of Jiden's profile and knew what he was must do. He turned forlornly towards his princess then, his plans of four days in paradise with her ruined. He took her hand and kissed it.

"My lady, I will be leaving you here. Sir Ren will be at your beckon call," with that, a medium built, red haired, mature knight stepped forward and bowed graciously.

"On my honor, you will be safe my lady," he swore.

"Than I am most safe! Thank you sir Ren," She bowed graciously and turned to Jiden.

"Your turn for watch sire? Which mountain top shall I say good night to every evening then?" Callana was hoping if she smiled enough her aching heart would not be so evident to her audience. Jiden bashfully fidgeted his hands in front of him and pointed to the rounded red peak to the south east.

"Mount Andoria, my lady. I promise to blow you a kiss every morning!" Jiden was suddenly morose. He was earnestly going to miss her, but this was his duty as the prince and duty came first. He suddenly remembered he needed to change his list.

Sir Lance, Mount Rising
Sir Donovin, Mount Rising
Sir Reynolds, Green Mountain
Sir Jerrik, Green Mountain
Sir Lashend, Mount Andoria
Sir Laden, Mount Andoria—relived for illness
Prince Jiden, Mount Andoria

He turned to ready his replacement mount, a small brown mare hitched to the back of the wagon. Out of the four mules left to graze on short ropes near the crystal water's edge, three were collected by Edward; to be loaded with the three barrels assigned each watch hut, strapped to each side and on top of its sturdy back. He informed young Fredrick that he should expect the six returning guards no earlier than two mornings from now. That would give him and the replacements ample time to traverse the cave trail, winding up the rocky interior path to come out on the far side of the top of Green mountain, where Reynolds and Jerrik would relieve their counterparts, and the four other men would branch off; Sir Lance and Donovin heading west taking the deep crevices on the far face of Mount Rising and Lashend and

Jiden south east, following the red clay trails spiraling to the top of Mount Andoria, to relieve the other guards. The relieved six were to meet up and go back down as a unit; all around it was a day up and a day back down.

Silvio had given Laden a tonic, mostly mint leaf, and moved him into the now nearly empty wagon to rest. When Jiden was ready, as well as his five knights, they mounted and set off. Callana smiled empathetically and waved to her prince. He turned around, coming towards her with a solemn face. He stopped beside her and reached down as if to kiss her cheek. He held her shoulder and whispered in her ear.

"There is a dagger in Leviathan's saddle." Callana balked, but Jiden's eyes were severe.

"Callana, trust *no* man." She nodded her promise, though it did little to settle the anxiety now bubbling in her empty stomach. He turned back to join the waiting crew, throwing one last glaring look over his shoulder. He was watching to see if she was going to obey. She walked to the saddle, which straddled a two posted rail and pulled the dagger out of a leather pouch on the saddle; quickly sticking it through her belt. Jiden watched, and then finally nodded his nervous farewell once she was armed. She looked after the band of brave men and mounts as they splashed through the shallow pool, and around the reach of the falls. He was gone; Callana felt a current of sadness flood her entire self, so intense she felt as if it might well up and rush from her eyes. She continued staring after him, until she had regained control of her emotions, and turned to busy herself with what ever she could. Silvio was busily taking careful documentation of his patient's symptoms, treatment, and current condition. Lustene would expect as much. Laden was pasty to the touch, but sleeping, so Callana left him alone. She fanned herself with her hand at the intense heat of the evening.

"Fancy a swim my lady?" Edward who had stripped to only his pants hopped out from behind the wagon, and was gesturing towards the welcoming water.

"Yes, I would!" She replied, un-belting her tunic to join her friend in the water. Sir Ren had taken his chainmail and boots off and was sitting on the edge, soaking his feet in the cool water. Callana noticed and swam towards him, careful not to stand and expose her clinging tunic.

"Why not swim Sir Ren?" She tilted her head inquisitively. He shook his head.

"I am not much for swimming young lady, as much as sinking!" He chuckled with his own jest.

"Well, hows about a lesson? Come, I swear you will be swimming by supper!" Though he tried to protest, Callana and Edward each took a huge hand and pulled Ren to a standing position in the churning water. Callana began by showing Ren how to stroke each arm through the water and kick his feet. He tried over and over, sinking slowly each time and flailing his way back to the surface; Callana had to keep reminding him the water was shallow and he could stand. However, hours later after Edward had tired himself thoroughly and climbed out to join Fredrick and Silvio in audience, Ren was swimming, albeit splashing sporadically; he was on *top* of the water. His small crowd cheered!

....

By torch light Jiden led the way through the cramped dripping cave, slowly climbing higher and higher. They would walk about a thousand paces tonight, leading their horses due the caves lowered ceiling height. They would rest for a few hours at dawn, assuming they reach the opening by then. It was a grueling climb, so Jiden took care to have fresh, young mules and horses for the journey. Leviathon absolutely hated water and would never have made it past the falls. The thought made Jiden smile. He adored his young stallion. He had made Jiden's eleventh birthday extraordinary! Jiden detested the formal ball, although seeing his uncle Leonard and aunt Camela from Mualen, aunt Lunette and uncle Rasden heralding from Tasdalad, and his favorite uncle Felonin and aunt Melanie from Felonia; beyond Mount Andoria, were all very good reasons to have a ball! His Uncle Felonin and Aunt Melanie had been the ones to bring him the white stallion as a gift, bred and raised to Odin's standards in secret far away in Felonia. He frowned, realizing he would not see his aunts and uncles again until the wedding. *The wedding*! He had just absently thought about it without causing himself to panic! He missed Callana already, and he hoped desperately she missed him too. Jiden found himself stepping a little lighter with the thought of her; humming to himself and causing the exhausted tail end of his cavalcade to groan in protest over the quickening pace.

....

Silvio, a rather studious and quiet young man, with stern features, had been kind enough to lend Callana a dry tunic in soft white linen, so she could climb out and dry without giving her new company an embarrassing outline of her figure. She hung her green wear over the saddle rack post. It was a glorious day, and after her swim she felt alive, alert even. Sir Ren was in full chainmail again, riding Leviathon in a quick perimeter check around their small camp. Callana realized she had not eaten since breakfast and her stomach sounded off; catching the attention of the young cook. Fredrick jumped to his feet, and hurried to start a fire. She mouthed a silent thank you and decided she had to do something to take her mind off food. She took George off his long rope and bridled him. She would take him bare back and collect some more fire wood for the coming dark.

"Where are you making off to my lady?" Asked Edward, causing Silvio to peer up from his writing as a concerned frowned contorted his young face. She shrugged and pointed towards the Green mountain side where there were some fallen trees and dry brush in a cluster of old oaks.

"I was just going to gather wood for the evening's fire," she announced nonchalantly.

"No, don't think so, Sir Ren told us to stay here," Silvio contested her matter of factly. Callana waved him off and laughed.

"But you can see me every step of the way, its right there!" Edward glanced at Silvio who in turn slowly nodded to Callana.

"All right Princess, but if you get into trouble, scream like a girl!" Edward snorted, seemingly finding humor in his own statement. Callana nodded and coaxed her old gelding to a trot. Only a short hundred paces or so away she found a promising tangle of dried up, small branches and dismounted to start a bundle. Callana was breaking and smashing longer tree limbs to make them easier to carry when she heard a crackling sound she did not make. George had fallen asleep, she noticed, when she slowly turned to find out what was there. It was quiet again, but Callana noticed it was *oddly* quiet. No birds, no rustling, nothing at all. Something felt wrong; she felt a cold chill race up her spine. She pulled the ribbon from her hair to start lashing the wood together saying a silent prayer of thanks that she had re belted Silvio's tunic and was therefore, armed.

Callana was suddenly aware of eyes on her as if an icy invisible finger was tracing its way down her very soul. She flinched, afraid to actually see something when she turned around this time. She reluctantly twisted around, meeting the fierce stare of her stalker. The creature's eyes were rimmed in red, and crusted in the corners. His long grey hair had fallen out in spots exposing a protruding, heaving rig cage. This wolf was big, not that she can say she had ever *seen* a wolf to compare him to, but he seemed gigantic. He was crouched on a fallen oak, only a horse's length away, literally. Her gelding shifted in his slumber and the wolf flattened his ears to his head in response. Callana slowly bent to lie down her stick collection, and upon standing, carefully unsheathed Jiden's dagger. It glinted in the orange setting sun and the beam flashed across the hostile eyes causing them to squint. His breathing was only now audible to her as he crept ever slowly towards her. He was snarling now, so ravenous, he was not even considering her sizeable horse as any kind of a deterrent. Callana couldn't tell if she was still breathing; she was trembling with a fear she had never known. Her stomach was on fire with anxious bile, gurgling and churning, threatening to come up. She fought to keep control of her shaking muscles as she held the dagger out in front of her. The stand off had begun and would only end when he made a move. There was a nauseating moment of clarity, every sense coming aware of everything around her. How dry the air was; the deep fiery orange of the sunset behind her mingling with the brilliant clear blue sky of the coming night behind her adversary; she could feel the blood pushing through her veins, the slowing of her heart as she fought to control her fear. There was a smell in her nostrils, a wretched, sickening smell, most likely her own stomach ingredients. He was still, frozen in place, watching her, listening to every heart beat; calculating the means to take down his prey. Callana crouched slightly, trying to keep her muscles ready. The world quieted; the thundering of her rushing blood filled her ears, drowned out all distractions. She felt a sharpening of her senses; her eyes were seeing clearly minor details she had not noticed before. The wolf was tired, obviously malnourished, and graying around his eyes with age. There was a change in the air, barely noticeable; it was thicker, heavier, weighing her down; pinning her in this spot. She fought against it, pushing her concentration to its limits; willing her arms to harden in her solid, defensive stance. An eternity would pass before, with a terrible growl that surged through gritted teeth, he leapt! Callana closed her eyes at the same moment, jabbing the dagger forward. She was thrust backwards and onto her left side, gasping for air, landing face to face with the grey wolf. She blinked; shocked by what she believed she had done, as she watched the once, fiery eyes of the desperate animal, flicker and than hold. He was dead and she wasn't! She pulled the bloody dagger out of the bony chest, just as Sir Ren came crashing through the crackling brush to land by her side. Callana realized the blood pushing through her ears had drowned out Leviathan's hoof beats. Finally awake, George was prancing around the now dead predator.

"My lady! I could see him but was too far away," He explained through his panting breaths, turning her to him; wiping her tears away, tears she didn't even know she had cried. He lifted her and, thoroughly inspected her to asses none of the blood was hers.

"I...I killed him." Callana trembled and stumbled into Ren's arms.

"Brilliantly too I might add! Your first battle kill? He was hunting a human, which means he would again. Look around you at the farmers and families. You did what needed to be done my lady." His voice was calming and stilled her quivering body. She remembered the farms she had passed on the way to the falls, letting their safety strengthen her and she pulled herself away and tried to smile up at the warm man.

"Thank you for being so kind to me good knight; a princess has no right out here alone for sure!"

"Princess my foot! You are now a qualified knight, through and through!" Callana smiled and allowed herself to be enveloped in another one of Ren's marvelous hugs.

On the third morning, just as dawn peeked above the Falls of Green Mountain, the exhausted guard emerged from the dark of the hidden cave. Callana had helped an extremely nervous Fredrik ready a thick morning gruel, composed mostly of slow cooked fig and porridge, for the famished lot. As the knights emerged, Callana saw a few proverbial faces. She recognized the enormous figure of Sir Galland and the thick and sturdy Sir David from Prince Jiden's royal guard. They both smiled upon seeing Callana and she laughed, rushing to greet them. Each dismounted and wearily bowed to the princess, who immediately insisted on hugs. The rest of the mountain top guard bowed respectfully and introduced themselves to the princess, one day to be their ruler. There were two brothers, James and Jeremiah, both short but stout with adorable turned up noses and big toothy grins. The brothers had occupied Mount Rising. Then the pair from the farthest point, Mount Andoria, was Nevens, a beefy young man about average in height, and his companion Ellis, solid and strong and very dark skinned. Then from the Green Mountain there was the bullish David and massive Galland.

"I am told I owe you a huge debt of gratitude," Sir Galland knelt as he spoke, taking Callana's hand. He looked up at her, his golden eyes wide with reverence.
"Gant is my boy, he is my life. God bless you princess. I am forever at your service." He bowed his head with this. Callana was speechless, scrambling through words in her mind but coming up short of anything of worth to say in return.
"Please, Sir Galland, you think too highly of my actions..." she tried.
"What story is *this* now?" interrupted Sir Ren. Galland rose and gathered with the rest around the morning fire to devour their long awaited breakfast, regaling the others with the tale passed to him at the changing of the guard at the top of Green Mountain. Sir Ren then told his over embellished rendition of Callana killing a giant man-eating wolf. After tending to the mules and horses, Fredrik and Edward sat slack jawed in amazement as one tale turned into a string of accounts of different misadventures the knights encountered on their respective mountain tops. Galland told of a giant cat, long and sleek, watching him from atop a boulder only a few paces away! David had tripped with a hot iron pan, hurling the searing projectile inadvertently directly at the predator, and sending it yowling away in terror! The circle erupted in laughter, and congratulated the accidental hero. The brothers James and Jeremiah had seen a small fox chasing a long eared hare, only to have the hare turn the tables upon realizing his larger size. The brothers then ran for their saddles and produced two soft pelts, one of bushy red and white and one of the silkiest brown. Everyone applauded the twins.

Callana thoroughly enjoyed the warmth of these gallant men. She was almost sad when it was time to turn in.

 Guarding over the cluster of bed rolls, Sir Ren took first watch, to be relieved by Sir Galland and than home in the morning. Although this party left her feeling a sudden pang of home sickness, Callana fell asleep lost in blissful dreams of her prince, happiness and her legion of new friends.

....

Rogala eagerly awaited the messenger today. Every month on the last week, she was to send a letter to Callana for her uncle back home with Dakin, the carrier from Adalonia, who should be bringing much awaited correspondence from Callana. Rogala was to then forward a letter for Callana's family on to Windt with her own carrier, Stephen. Dakin was a prompt messenger, always mid day, sometimes right after dinner. Today she should be receiving a response back from her uncle also, having had weeks to answer. Nia waited with her daughter. They had rarely been apart since they met nearly three weeks ago. Renk was walking the market, buying fresh fish, lamb, salt, vinegar, pickled eggs, fresh and dried pork and beans. He had already paid for all of Nia's green apples, seeing as how she hadn't made it to market to sell them herself.

He glanced over at them and grinned. It was remarkable how much Rogala mimicked her mother in personality traits, even being estranged from her for so long. The blonde heads bobbed in excited chatter about plans and names for the baby, both absently twirling their curls while talking, intently staring at the dirt road as if *willing* Dakin to appear.

Once he did show the news he had to tell was good. He had heard in the Green Mule tavern about Callana's rescuing of young Gant and a knight over hearing the story had added how brave Callana vanquished an enormous wolf. Rogala was proud of her friend, happily dismissing Dakin with her own letter, bread and cheese for the trip home and a generous purse of gold for his urgency and discretion.

Meanwhile, Renk had found a way to make money fishing from small boats with nets on the ocean, enough for their modest lifestyle anyways. He was perfect here; useful, loved and happy. Castle life held no more attraction for him as it had when he was young and envious of the rich and powerful royal elites. He felt an overwhelming contentment, welling in him and spreading out around him. It was consuming Rogala too. When they had begun life on the run, she was miserable in their lack of comforts. But now, she seemed to flourish in their miniature, modest home.

Later, by candle light, enjoying a delicious lamb and apple dish, Rogala read aloud between juicy bites about how enchanted the prince and Callana were with each other and how she was friends with many knights and a wonderful serving girl. Callana adored the noble king and admirable queen and was terrified to lose them over her betrayal, hoping they could forgive her if she was discovered. Rogala wrote back immediately.

Dearest Sister C,

Please take heart, for I can honestly say that no one who has met you could ever harbor ill feelings for you! You are a beautiful soul and from what I hear, you are something of a hero there in Adalonia! I have some news, I have found my mother! My father, for lack of a better phrase, made me with my mother's servant, due to my mother's inability to carry a child. I have absolutely no royal ties and my uncle knows it! Give me time dear friend and I will find a way to turn this to our advantage delicately, as to preserve your relationship with your new love and country. Please do not despair, for you have just as much claim as I do and if your prince really loves you, it won't matter from where you came.
With all the love in our hearts here in Sea fair,
Sisters R and N and brother R

Rogala would send it with next month's visit from Dakin. She and Nia were determined to find a way to keep Callana in good standing with her new family, but impersonating royalty was a crime. Renk was resolute to see King Bromell pay for serving his own niece up as offering just to secure his kingdom. What difference did it make who married the prince? It wouldn't change the ownership of Rogadon. When Bromell was dead, Rogadon would be absorbed by the kingdom fastest to claim it, unless all sides involved could keep up the façade with Callana as acting princess. If she was *believed* to be a blood princess and heir to Rogadon, no other kingdom would have reason to challenge her. But how to make Jiden, Odin, Lena and Bromell go along with such a thing, without outing Callana and Rogala's treachery to all of Adalonia? This would have to be handled, carefully and soon.

....

One more week until Jiden would return. Although she missed him severely, Callana and Miala had found brilliant ways to spend their time! Summer would be ending soon, the days were shorter already and the greens of the oaks and maples were lightening to muted ambers and browns. The girls were spending most afternoons roaming the village, and buying imported pears from the trade boats that met Adalonia's smaller oar boats at the mouth of the lake, off the larger tributary coming directly from the sea. After snacking, they spent a great deal of time in the water or basking on shore. Miala's father was a stream fisherman, mostly working in the shadow's forest, permitted by law by Rogadon, who retained ownership of the forest; Miala had learned a great deal from her father about spear fishing. It took great patience, standing waist deep in the lake, motionless for long periods of time, but the reward was well worth it and the pair had taken to bringing their catch back to the castle kitchen to be served as evening supper. Gillian was grateful, for she could plan and supervise the preparation of the evening meal without taking time to walk the market for fresh meat. The magnificent trout and striped bass were usually served with apples or fig over rice. Odin and Lena were most impressed; although Lena had decided it was time to start spending more time with her new daughter in law to be. For it was all well and good she had made such fast friends with Miala, and it was a blessing the princess was showing such extreme humbleness spending all her time filthy with a servant; but a princess, someday to be a queen had routines to learn and duties to perform and oversee where Callana seemed content *not* to be implicated in the castle's operations *at all*. Lena hoped a fitting for her royal wedding dress would inspire the princess to show at least a *slight* interest in her new role and kingdom.

....

"Good morning!" cheered Miala. She was ready to leap from her own skin to begin today's planned adventure. She had even woken up a bit earlier than usual and finished all of her duties except Callana's bed chamber, which they always did together. Fall sunset hour was shortening play time as it was. Miala couldn't remember the last time she had been so happy to see anyone as much as she was to see Callana. They were best of friends, sisters almost, and nothing would ruin that bond.

Callana was up and already dressed in her green on green wear, just as keen to go as Miala.

"Good morning! So, to market for a quick bite and ..." Callana started.

"*And off for some more muddy mucking about and just about anything that you two can conspire to do that has nothing to do with being a princess, aye?*" Both the young girls flailed around to see the queen, looking spotless as usual; standing in the open doorway and covered in pink silks.

"Queen Lena," Both girls bowed in unison with bright red cheeks. Callana rose and slowly met the queen's judicious gaze.

"Your majesty, forgive me, I let my curiosity lead us both a stray! Please, do not punish Miala for this I ..."

"*Punish?* My dear child, I am not *that* kind of a queen! I assure you, it has not escaped me that you are young and need amusement. I was young once too, and although I was never permitted to gallivant about with *my* servant, I can appreciate your want to do so. However," she clasped her hands together and began slowly pacing as she spoke; circling Callana.

"As Jiden has taken responsibilities on with his engagement and coming of age, so should you. Did you not have such demands in Rogadon? I shall write that uncle of yours immediately!" Lena warned, coming face to face with Callana.

"No!" Callana quickly recovered. "I mean, it is my own lack of discipline not lack of responsibility my lady. Please, can we not involve my uncle in such matters? I...ah...have had no such role models as you and that is not my uncle's fault. I will give myself over to you to be molded into the princess I *should* be as of this moment!" Callana stood pertly, clasping her hands in front of her with her back straight and tall, mirroring her queen.

"Well, I suppose he has enough on his table right now," The queen was obviously referring to king Bromell's recent health issues keeping him on constant bed confinement. Callana had read as much in his recent letter to Rogala.

"I presume that you are sincere in your interest in Adalonia?" Lena asked, raising both delicate eyebrows. Callana nodded vigorously.

"Then you and I have a very important trip to make. And, of course," the queen curved her elegant neck to take Miala into view, "you will need an attendant." Both girls squealed and embraced the objecting queen who in turn, awkwardly patted them both on the top of their heads. When she left, the girls scrambled through Callana's clothes for the finest and then fled to Miala's families' cottage to collect her attire, stopping twice to purchase a few new fine linens for the young maid. Racing back to Callana's bed chamber to heat the hearth to warm water for a shared bath; afterwards the girls took turns carefully pinning each other's hair on top of their heads. Stunningly dressed and fresh as spring, the girls carried their shared luggage down the hallway and steps to load in the awaiting carriage. When the queen joined them, she informed Miala that she herself had never kept a servant;

therefore Miala would have to attend to both women, but would be paid accordingly. Miala was too excited about the trip to give a moment's care to *any* stipulations and anxiously nodded her agreement.

King Odin was standing on the limestone steps, solemnly watching Lena's carriage circle the courtyard. She carefully raised her hand and blew him a kiss, blushing slightly when her two companions took notice. Odin jumped slightly, his right arm grabbing in the air to catch her kiss and hold it to his heart. Lena took a deep breath and blew it out slowly. Callana could see how hard it was for them to part and it was endearing. Watching their behavior around the castle, always proper, always appropriate of course; but little movements gave them away; a quick surveying glance, a wink, and a tender smile across the table. They were truly in love and even after nearly twenty years of marriage, they were still very much infatuated with each other. Callana's heart was heavy with strong emotions all bottled and befuddled inside. There was the warm, tingling sweetness that swallowed her up whenever she thought of Jiden, always accompanied by a twinge of sadness for the false pretenses under which she had begun their. The constant trepidation lurked behind every kind sentiment, terrified for the day she could be discovered and lose him forever. Her stomach churned, she wanted to see his face, hear his voice, right now! Maybe if *he* felt this way for *her*, he could forgive her? She hadn't wanted anything except to help a friend and change her own destiny. He could understand that, who couldn't? A prince, that's who; a prince who had been born of a praiseworthy family, in a castle, surrounded by knights who would die for him and servants to see to his every need. Jiden would have difficulty understanding what it's like to be born into a situation like Callana's. She had never known this feeling, this, *love*. The worst part was the not knowing if Jiden felt it too.

As they passed through the courtyard, followed by Lena's six mounted royal guards, Callana suddenly remembered someone very important.

"Wait!" Their carriage driver barely had time to slow the two horses down when Callana leapt from the carriage and fled to the royal barn.

"Edward!" The light hazel eyes darted up and down the exquisite golden gown that flourished into the barn.

"Edward, it's me, Callana!" At once Edward was blushing, turning his shoulder and avoiding eye contact with her. She turned him to face her.

"It's still just *me*; your friend. I need you to do something for me, please?" She begged. He bowed his shaggy head.

"Anything for you Princess. And might I add, you must be the most beautiful wolf killing princess I's yet to see!" Callana kissed him with that.

"Please," She pleaded with her dark eyes, "Take George on just a *little* ride, every morning? *Just a little one?*" She grimaced. Edward furrowed bushy eyebrows and glanced over at the side stepping gelding, who was expecting Callana to take him for his scheduled romp and sighed.

"Of course my lady, I would be honored to take care of such a horse."

"Thank you sooooo much dear friend! I will owe you for this. I will see you in a few days!" Off she went, leaving an agitated purple horse to stomp and snort his frustration until his replacement rider had finished his mucking. Callana ran back to the carriage and jumped in. The queen was giving her a puzzled look so Callana quickly explained the importance of George's scheduled rides. Apparently satisfied, the queen turned her gaze back towards the carriage window.

....

Sir Lashend was sleeping soundly, having been relieved of his two hour watch by his bunk mate. Mount Andoria, known as the red peak, was a hard packed dusty clay mountain with very little vegetation; therefore it was the only one of the watch locations that offered little in the way of hunting opportunities. August had arrived, cooling the evenings earlier then only a few weeks ago.

Jiden sighed as he watched the sun slowly sink into the farthest most western edge of great open valley of kingdom Felonia; igniting the fiery red eastern face of mount Andoria; at the same time darkening the edges of far-reaching farmlands of Adalonia to the west. Having few trees to block the view was good for sun sets in the least. Jiden and Lashend had to monitor their rations closely, closer than the other two mountain posts due to the lack of wildlife that occupied them and his stomach growled in protest as he ruefully remembered that in their last week watch they had already devoured the end of the cereal and salted pork, leaving fava beans, vinegar and bread. Jiden had eaten his dinner portion but ached to taste roasted beef, or soup, or fish, or anything but *fava* beans! But, if there was anything Jiden had acquired growing up as a prince, it was self restraint. He shook his head with that thought. He couldn't generate self *restraint* around Callana if his life depended on it! He missed her more than he missed any food or comfort of home. He couldn't believe how much he *needed* her in his life. He had one day of watch left before he and his five guards would meet with their replacements, than make their way down the slick sloping cave trail to the falls. After a day of rest, he would be on his way to her. It felt like an eternity until he would see her again. Her eyes were burning into his memory and setting flame to his heart. Eyes like deep, lipid brown pools, so intensely dark as to rival the murky, sunless depths of the sea itself. Jiden felt all other cares fade away as he sank into a day dream of Callana. Holding Callana, feeling her pressed to him; reveling in the softness surrounding the hard core of her. He wanted to be with her, around her, inside her. He snapped his mind into attention. Self restraint! Ha! Jiden walked out of the open doors into the cool of the early evening to make the long jaunt down to the only tree line near enough to use for fire wood. He gathered several long branches and began using his training sword to carve them into smaller sections. He glanced around himself often, but thanks to the openness of mount Andoria's burgundy façade, he could've seen someone coming long away. Jiden came back to the shelter to build a fire and settle down to watch the sun rise flood the flourishing lush green valley of Felonia; as the red mountain cast its enormous shadow over the goat farmers of Adalonia, he allowed himself another of many, enjoyable fantasies of his dark eyed princess.

....

"How beautiful it is here!" cried Miala, pasted to the carriage window as they approached the busy city of Dellandore. Traveling south west through the gloomy Shadow's forest for an entire day and night had temporarily dulled the explorers' senses; emerging into the bright blue sunny morning quickly re-kindled the trio's excitement for the trip. The queen was smiling out her window, sitting pertly up right, hands folded in her lap. Callana was suddenly aware of her own horrible posture. Lena happened to glance over at Callana, who was straightening her spine and trying desperately to emulate the queen's royal demeanor. Callana, looking over to review the queen again, met the tiny woman's gaze and flushed; Lena grinned and pointed her small finger at Callana.
"Caught you," she whispered. Callana giggled.
"Oh princess! Look at all the shop signs! I have already seen *three* dress shops and *two* for shoes! Oooo! Chocolates!" Miala clapped her hands in excitement. Lena laughed out loud, startling Callana and Miala who gawked in utter astonishment. Lena covered her mouth with both hands after such an outburst and her face was a bright red. Callana and Miala grinned.
 "Excuse me," Lena apologized. The girls stifled giggles. All three turned back to their respective windows, anxious not to miss a single sight! The roads here were clear of vendors or carts. No animals to be seen. Just shimmering satin clad women and velvet covered noble men. Callana sank back against the cushioned bench of the carriage. She can't fit in here! She will be discovered for sure; her lack of poise, her over exuberance for all the finery, and her limited vocabulary. The queen will be humiliated and immediately call off the wedding and who could blame her? Callana was no *Lena*! Adalonia *deserved* a Lena!
The delicate queen was examining her again. She had watched the young girl's excitement turn cold in an instant. What could make a princess so

insecure? Lena wondered. From birth princesses are honored, groomed, and educated to sit side by side in rule; kept on pedestals of high regard. She must have been told constantly that she was beautiful, she is beautiful! Lena was overwhelmed with compassion for Callana. Bromell was not known for anything honorable and his destitute kingdom was a stain on the valley as far as Lena could surmise, but, would never say aloud, not even to her husband. Apparently, Bromell even lacked the basic knowledge of expressing affection? Dolt! Losing her parents must have been painful enough, but to have tolerated a life in that *cold* castle with that *frigid* man! Lena burned with hatred for him suddenly and had to breathe deeply and tell herself to calm down. *She* had Callana now, and *she* would stop at nothing to raise this girl to her rightful place in *this* kingdom. With that, Lena rapped on the coach roof, slowing the driver to a stop. A rather small man with a booming voice jumped down.

"Simon, we will walk from here. You are free to roam the city yourself. Give us till dusk and then we shall meet up at the Purple Dragon. Here," she handed him a pouch of gold coins. Simon's eyes popped open and he gaped at her as if she had sprouted wings!

"Your majesty, I was paid in full prior to departure by your King." He protested adamantly, but she waved him off.

"And you have *seven* children...I am sure one is having a birthday or something!" Simon bowed low.

"You are entirely too kind!" He sincerely praised her. The queen smiled courteously and put out her hand for help from the carriage. When the dashing threesome had cleared the coach, Lena leaned in to whisper in his ear.

"There are many shops full of fine things for a certain young woman looking to attract suitors and will need an appropriate gown for the wedding ball," and with this, she pressed another gold coin into his hand. Simon grabbed her and brought her to him in a huge squeezing embrace! Lena gasped, causing two of the guard to draw their swords and dismount.

"I am all right!" She quickly assured them. Simon's color drained as he quickly bowed again and scrambled back to his sitting perch on the carriage.

"Sir Graven would you have two of your men see to it that Simon is safe? I would like four guards with us, if you don't mind," Sir Graven nodded his slightly graying brown haired head.

"Of course, my honored queen." He turned and made his assignments and the group parted into two, Sir Graven, as customary, staying with the queen.

"Now," the queen turned to the nearly prancing young girls.

"We shop!"

· ·

Uncle Bromell,

You might notice I am no longer addressing you as king, as you are no more a king than I a princess. I have met an old acquaintance of yours, you will remember her as Nia, but I will from now and forever call her mother! I do not wish to marry Prince Jiden, however, I am not without honor, and although I have not one drop of royal blood, I know the reasoning behind this arrangement. I have an agreeable replacement, more than willing to marry in my stead. If you acquiesce with this proposal, and sign the treaty at the ceremony as planned, than I swear to not make public what I have learned. You may send correspondence to the city of Windt addressed to the Stone's throw Inn. I will send someone monthly to collect it. Thank you for any attention you decide to give this matter,

Rogala

Rogala had woken early, searching out the Sea Fair messenger's home. Stephen was only nineteen years of age, but already had two children and a very young wife. He had tried to object because of the early hour but could not turn down the rather large leather pouch of coins the pretty blonde was offering. He was mounted and on the road to Rogadon before sun's light had peeked over the far evergreen trees. Nia had made her way reluctantly back to her own cottage days ago now, insisting the couple needed privacy but promising to visit every day until the baby was born, when they would travel to Windt. Rogala had turned her daily visits with her mother into all day events.

Renk was waiting for his sneaking wife, arms crossed heatedly, in their door way when she returned from town. Rogala tried her best innocent face, cuddling close to the large irritated man.

"And where were you my villainous wife?" Renk held her shoulders, forcing her to look him in the eye. Rogala's blue eyes were wide with blamelessness.

"What? I just needed a morning walk my love, there is no crime in that is there?" She batted her eyes and released him to walk inside. She chopped an onion and scooped it into a wooden bowl of vinegar. She then salted strips of pork. Gathering their breakfast ingredients and cast iron pan, she waddled down the stairs and to the pit where her husband had built a fire. She hummed softly to her stomach, rubbing her rounded protrusion absently while sautéing; a cooking method she had read about in her youth. Renk was still skeptical about her whereabouts. Rogala had finally gotten over her morning, evening, nightly sickness, no longer requiring her anise plant and mint leaf tea, but relished sleeping late when Renk was home on his one day off. He watched her, taking her in; her glowing skin, radiant blonde waves, and her soft lips, pursed in concentration and came to kneel beside her.

"Let me cook for you love," he tried to take the handle out of her hand, but she nudged him away.

"Let me cook for my beautiful husband on his morning off," She insisted. Renk hopped to his feet.

"*Aha*! That gives it! You *despise* cooking! What have you done?" realizing the flaw in her performance, Rogala slowly stood.

"I, I just went to send a letter, to to..." she stammered, searching for a name. He knew she could only send Callana letters with Dakin to make them appear to come from the carrier's scheduled trips to Rogadon. Renk was quick to see through his terrible little liar.

"You didn't! You didn't write your uncle. Did you? Did you!" He was demanding now, his voice rising with his frustration.

"I," Rogala stammered, desperate to forego an argument.

"Oh for the love of God Rogala! You told him didn't you? We were to come up with a plan! You gave Callana up?" Renk was blazing with fury now. Rogala recoiled; she had never seen him so angry.

"I didn't! I didn't give a name, I just said if he allows *someone* to marry in my place I would not let it be know I am not royal, that s all!" She tried. Renk turned to pace back and forth, not sure what to do with his hands, now clenched in fists.

"He is no man to be threatened, you very well know that!" Renk was circling her now, lost in his aggravation. "We no longer have the element of surprise on our side, you understand? We haven't had time to plan! To...to..." He stopped short upon sight of his wife's heaving. Rogala was crying now, breakfast forgotten, she turned to climb the steps to their house. She was so furious with her uncle for betraying her and forcing this marriage to secure his kingdom that she wanted him to *know* she had found him out! She never wanted to hurt Callana. In fact she wanted to coerce her uncle into letting Callana *be* the princess she really could be, and marry Jiden. Renk turned, calming himself at once upon seeing her upset. He grabbed her and pulled her back to him.

"Don't cry love, we can mend this still, you did not ruin anything. I promise. Come, you need to eat." He used the long sleeve of his red tunic to cover his hand so he could grab the now blistering hot pan handle and bring it and it's crispy contents, into the house. He served her, sitting beside her with his arm around her making sure she ate every bite. He did not just hate to see her cry he *loathed* to see her cry. It burned him up from the inside out. She was his world and it was his God given destiny to make up for the cold, abrasive manner by which she had been raised. She finished eating and turned to look up into Renk's immense brown eyes. He looked down into her face; reddened with crying, slightly swollen lids, but so open and young and kissed her gently.

"I love you wife," his voice was deep and soft. Rogala was filled with passion for him immediately and smashed her lips to his. When she pulled away, her eyes smoldered with her intense desire for him. Renk was quick to reciprocate, scooping her up to carry her to their bed, his mouth never leaving hers.

....

A petite brunette seamstress was measuring Callana's generous bosom. "She will be a difficult fit, my lady, very...curvy," she said sliding the cord down to the small waist and than back out again to encompass the wide hips.

"But not impossible?" Lena confirmed. The older woman shook her head.

"Not impossible, your majesty." With that she left the room to fetch samples of fabrics for the queen's approval. It was customary for the mother of the bride to make the decisions on fabric, cut, and style. But color was essentially up to the bride. Lena turned to Miala.

"Miala, could you go for some more mint tea my dear?" Miala nodded and half skipped in delight out of the room, happy to be of service. Lena leaned in to speak candidly to Callana.

"To avoid an embarrassing situation, may I inquire, what color would you like your gown dear?" Lena smiled kindly, feeling awkward about asking. Callana blushed brightly. Wearing blue to symbolize purity was tradition, but not a rule. If Callana were to choose another color, however, it might make a certain mother of the groom suspicious. Having already decided on a different color, Callana felt it necessary to explain herself.

"I would *like* yellow, your majesty, but I *could* wear blue, if you like, I mean, I am *able* to wear blue," Callana answered, rolling her eyes at her floundering attempt. Lena released a breath she had been inadvertently holding.

"Oh splendid!" She clapped. With that, Miala bounced back into the room with a giant smile and steaming black pot of tea. Their seamstress also returned, with an array of fabrics, in unassuming white, careful not to offend. Lena stood, taking each piece of satin, linen, knit, and velvet up against the creamy white of Callana's neck. She tilted her head, examining how each played off Callana's skin and eyes and hair. This was the most important day in a woman's life, and she absolutely must be the only thing worth looking at in the room.

"I am set on velvet; it's simply scrumptious against her skin Talera." Lena stated pointedly. Callana was ecstatic; she loved velvet! Lena winked at her before turning to face the pleasant little wrinkled woman.

"And the color my lady?" Talera asked, although she was more often than not indignantly informed that the color was obviously blue!

"Yellow, if you please," Callana smiled, tickled by the startled look on the woman's leathery face.

"Exactly what kind of yellow, my dear? Saffron dye is a tricky thing; I will need an example to match." Talera put her hands on her hips. Lena glanced around the room for something yellow. Miala spotted daisies through the window at the back of the room and dashed out of the door returning quickly with a beautiful yellow daisy with white petals.

"That's it!" clapped Callana. "That's the perfect yellow!" Talera plucked the flower out of Miala's hand, turning it around and around, cocking her head from side to side to catch the different depths of this particular yellow.

"Give me a month," assured the little leathery woman. Lena clasped her hands together and turned to see the glowing Callana whose eyes welled with tears.

"Oh my goodness! I have never imagined anything as lovely as a yellow velvet dress! Thank you thank you my queen!" Callana captured Lena in an appreciative hug, constricting her with delight! Lena returned the gesture, if not a little less aggressively. Miala squealing with joy joined in the affectionate embrace.

"You really want to show appreciation? You'd better be wearing a blue ribbon in your hair on your wedding day!" Callana gasped and the three burst into laughter.

....

Walking through the crowded streets of Dellandore, Lena was consumed with a giddy excited spirit! She was having more fun than she could remember ever having, outside of time spent with Odin. Callana was a delightful girl with an exceedingly contagious spontaneity to her. Lena was well groomed in the ways of a queen; Calm, collected, and always appropriate. Callana was none of those things, yet she somehow seemed more of a princess for all she lacked! Lena could not help but love this young lady. She was the perfect woman to marry Lena's dutiful son. Although she would never complain about Jiden's obedience to duty, and strict moral code; she did feel a bit ashamed he had never learned how to do something for the mere *enjoyment* of it. Odin had taken him hunting hundreds of times, but Jiden could take no pleasure in killing animals and would only kill what he was to eat. Odin was a very playful soul, but resigned himself from falling out of his kingly character in front of his son; save for his abominable flirting! Jiden was everything a kingdom needed and Callana was everything Jiden needed. Lena's soul soared high with the serenity that comes from knowing your child's future was secure; more than that he would have love; real, true love!

Blissfully walking side by side with her cohort, Callana was snapped out of another fantasy of Jiden, when she thought she glimpsed a familiar face. A tall, thin man was leaning against a shop front, assessing ladies walking the main way. Callana was staring at him; trying to recall why he was so memorable. She couldn't quit place him until he smiled; a sinister sneer curling his mouth and causing her palms to sweat; stirring some recollection. Something was wrong, something was definitely recognizable about him but it must not be good. As the three approached, followed closely by the four royal guards, the dark haired man bowed slightly, never breaking eye contact with Callana.

 "Eh girl," he spoke, hardly louder than a whisper. Callana's heart stopped beating. She halted briefly, shaking her head, pretending he had mistaken her...

"Good sir, surely you have manners enough to know you do not address a lady as *girl*," Lena indignantly swirled to face him, as a guard quickly put himself between the queen and the stranger.

"Hold your tongue. These respectable ladies don't have time for the likes of you," Sir Graven was unnerved by a dirty stranger addressing Adalonia's new princess in such a way. The man laughed loudly with a deep resonating voice that shook the very depths of Callana's soul. How would she explain him away?

 "Sorry, must of mistaken you for another red headed girl I met once in Windt, but she was no lady, she was a whore." He gave a low bow.

"Sorry for the misunderstanding... I was just anxious to show off my clean, shiny boots." He stuck one leg out and twisted his boot to glint in the sunlight; the queen returned his bow tartly and turned along with Sir Graven and Sir Reinhold and Miala, the other two guards staying behind the stunned Callana. She turned her terrified brown eyes to the wicked man; the same eyes he had looked into in her bed chamber in Windt, right before she threw up all over those same boots! She was trembling, she knew she needed to walk away as if he was a stranger, but she couldn't move. Her eyes pleaded with his; cold and gray. His smile faded; he had no idea which she was *pretending* to be, the prostitute or the princess, but he felt sure she wanted to keep their meeting a secret. The queen turned to see Callana staring, seemingly upset by this man's rudeness.

"Princess Callana, pay him no mind; he said he was mistaken," Lena reminded her. The man's cloudy eyes sparked with that.

 "Princess Ey? Oh, well than you couldn't be the girl I know, could you?" A tear rolled down Callana's cheek as she turned to follow Lena and Miala down the road way. She peered back over her shoulder at him with a mournful look in her eyes. His face turned solemn and he couldn't help but feel a bit sorry for her. Something about her beseeching eyes made him abstain from any further comments.

....

Although the Purple Dragon Inn was gorgeous, shining, polished and warm, Callana went to bed that night with a sadness clinging to her heart. Thank God the queen was in her own room, so Callana only had to fib to Miala about not feeling well to miss supper with no arguments. Callana's mind was spiraling. She was who she was, and Jiden had the right to marry her because he loved *her*, the *real* Callana. Most days in this real life performance she was living had been moderately easy. She had no personality to emulate because she was a princess no one in Adalonia had ever really known. No one *anywhere* knew Rogala, therefore no one had any reason to believe that Rogala didn't ride horses every morning or wear men's leggings and play with servants in the mud, or kill wolves! Even when her actions surprised the people around her here, they still had no basis of comparison to hold her to. She was the real *her* in Adalonia, with Jiden. But if he was to find out about Windt, he would have no choice but to assume she had been playing a part, and would not be able to trust his love for someone he didn't think he knew. Ahhhh! Callana screamed internally, burying her head under her pillow to smother her confusing thoughts. After hours of self wallowing, she made a decision confess to Jiden. She would admit everything to him the next time she saw him. He would most likely call off the wedding, but Callana would warn Rogala. Maybe Bromell could be persuaded to sign the treaty anyways? Having reached this momentous revelation, she quickly collapsed with exhaustion.

....

"Oooo Callana, look! How dreadful!" Callana glanced in the direction her young friend was frowning. From the window of the Inn's dining hall, Callana could see that the chilled breeze they had felt during their morning meandering through town had brought with it a blanket of thick, gray clouds, sagging with rain. Callana sighed; it was as if the sky was mimicking her very feelings. Miala watched her friend closely, finally leaning in to investigate.
"Beg your pardon my lady but what is *the matter* with you? You are in a beautiful Inn in a dazzling city with the knowledge that as we speak someone

is designing *your* gorgeous gown for *your* fantastic wedding!" The tiny maiden chastised, startling Callana with her uncharacteristically harsh tone and furrowed brow. Miala raised her eyebrows as if this act alone would force a response. Callana frowned and stretched across the table to whisper to her friend.

"If I told you something, could I trust you to never repeat it? On your soul, could you keep it?" Callana was so serious; Miala was taken aback by the stern stare. The young girl's hazel eyes darted around the room to find the queen, safely too far away to hear as she settled the bill.

"Of course, I am first and foremost your friend Callana." Miala took her friend's hand. Callana relaxed slightly, and smiled at her dimpled ally. "When we pack in our room I will tell you. The queen must not know anything is wrong so remain composed." At that moment Lena rejoined the girls.

"Morning ladies, we-"

"Baa...!" Miala nearly barked in surprise. Lena gave her a sideways glance as if expecting the girl's reaction to be some hideous and obvious warning signs of a bizarre illness.

"Forgive me your majesty! My mind was wondering, ha ha..." Miala quickly stood and bowed to the queen. Lena returned the bow, confused as to why it was offered, than turned to Callana.

"I trust you are feeling better my dear? You still look a little pale. Maybe it's this wea...-"

"Ready to pack princess?" Miala interrupted the queen with a high pitched squeal than quickly turned and strode away to their shared room, leaving a red faced Callana and an appalled Lena staring after her. Callana excused herself politely, after shrugging off the servant's wacky behavior. Safely in the room, Callana threw her hands up in the air.

"Thank you very much for looking completely insane!"

"I am sorry princess, I got so nervous! I promise you can still trust me not to tell, please?" Miala had both her olive skinned hands clasped in front of her face. Callana sighed and sat down on their shared feather bed and patted the space next to her.

"You should probably sit down for this."

....

An hour later, a skittish Miala had become a confused, frantic Miala. When it was time to start the full day and night's long ride to Adalonia, Callana was sure she had made a mistake telling the fidgety maiden. However, it was a fairly smooth ride after the initial rough start, when Miala started to take Callana's small trunk to load it for her, than suddenly dropped it, unsure if she was still to treat her as a princess in front of the queen. Miala, exhausted from the exertion of keeping her new found knowledge to herself, quickly slumped against the plush backed seat to fall asleep. Over the snoring, Lena and Callana talked for almost the entire first day of the trip. Lena told stories of Jiden's youth and how he had been her shadow for the first young years of his life, due to Odin's constant absence during the land skirmish between Felonia and Rogadon. King Felonin was by marriage to Queen Melanie, cousin to Odin, and had called for aid. The then, young and newly appointed King Bromell, had been very stubborn about his borders, although he was proven to be stretching them. The conflict lasted years, fortunately not claiming many lives. Bromell had finally relented the few hundred acres beyond the Shadow's forest where he had tried to exaggerate his boundaries.

Of course, Callana was expected to know the history of her own kingdom, therefore after every, 'go on' she had to add an 'I just adore the way you tell the story'. Lena asked about Callana's childhood, although she dreaded hearing about it and was pleasantly surprised when Callana regaled her with tales of her first rides with George and the daily treks she made into the countryside to find just the right location to watch a sunrise, or sunset for that matter. Callana told the truth, being sure to leave out any anecdotes or descriptions that involved her real family or village. Lena opened up about her strict childhood of daily rituals and severe schedules; routinely subjected to voice instruction, dancing lessons, balls, fittings, fasting, studies and constant primping, lest she be caught with a hair out of place. Fun was unknown to Lena until she met Odin. Lena secretly hoped Callana would do the same for Jiden.
Callana and Lena talked on for hours, delving into each other's deepest fears and wildest fantasies! Callana felt so understood, so cared for. It made her miss her mother and sisters, but, for the helped her to feel accepted by the mother of the man she wanted desperately to receive her most of all. Lena's naked honesty about herself made Callana ache to admit her deception. However, when they both had apologized profusely to the other for involuntarily closing tired eyes, Callana let fear and exhaustion rule out any courageous notions of outing herself. The last hours through the dark forest, they slept, and in that sleep Callana dreamed of her handsome prince, like she had every night for these past few amazing months.

....

Dearest family,
This secretive writing is hard for me, I never know what I can and can't say!
I want to tell you there is not a day or night that passes without a thought
to each of you. My heart breaks to see you, while it soars to be here. Is that
nonsense? I love him, I love him I love him! However I fear it may not be
enough, when he hears the truth. I wish to tell him, do you think it wise? Oh
please help me to decide! Whatever your thoughts, I will gratefully receive
your council on this matter. My love to all, you are in my daily prayers.
Please expect me when Ro is due to give birth. I would not miss it for all the
treasure in the kingdom!   *With so much love,*   *Sister C*

Hellena read her daughters letter over, this time out loud than sighed and turned to her red headed band. Crystalline paced the floor, searching the wooden planks for an answer.

"She should tell him, that is that." She stated simply.

"He loves her, why would it change anything if she is not a *real* princess?" Cylan added; ever the optimistic.

"She should just tell him Rogala is not a princess either, right?" Crystalline posed.

"Marrying Rogala or Callana is the same thing, neither is a real princess, so obviously he would chose to marry the one he loves... Callana." Cylan continued her earlier thought.

"Just write her back and tell her to tell him the truth, go on! It's the right thing to do anyways and he will appreciate her honesty." Cella bossed, retrieving a parchment and ink well for her mother with her command.

"Wait! She can't just tell the truth now, he will feel betrayed! She should wait to be married, so he can't leave her and break her heart." offered Caran, concerned as usual, with the emotional strain on everyone involved.

"It *has* been a betrayal from the beginning, and no matter how long she waits to tell him, it will still hurt his *majesty*! She tells him now or never!" Cella ordered, crossing her arms, having firmly decided.

"How can you suggest such a thing? Marry him under false pretenses? If he found out he would never forgive her!" Crystalline chastised her younger sister.

"Think about who are at risk in this sister," Caran softly reminded. Cella shook her head.

"Caran is right, this is not just about our dear baby sister keeping her love, or a noble prince's broken heart. We've all read the letters. King Bromell was such a king that his own *niece* abandoned his city! But how many were left behind to suffer? This wedding means so much more to those people than *we* could know. Callana taking on this responsibility is nothing less than noble, but until she can convince Jiden, he can *only* feel betrayed." Cella looked around the room at her beloved family. Hellena was smiling, a wet sheen over her orange eyes.

"I am so proud of my daughters, every day." She had sat quietly, letting her brood talk out the issue, knowing that between the differences in personality, there would be unassailability in the ensuing logical conclusion. Hellena wrote back immediately. Anna would be leaving for her northern deliveries at dawn and Hellena would send it directly to Adalonia, for she had no intention of keeping Callana in suspense.

Dearest bird,

The council has come to a swift conclusion. For the sake of all involved, we feel that your secret should remain just that. Too many people are counting on this union, and need it desperately. The noble thing is to follow through. You are beautiful in every way and your endeavors are honorable indeed, so do not lose heart, my angel. You have us on your side and we will keep searching for a solution. Until it surfaces, be the best princess you can be and remember, you are loved my little bird!
Love from all,   Windt

....

Today was Callana's first day in training, and she was bursting with raw nerves. Miala was morose at the loss of time with her friend, yet was feeling, admittedly, rather shamefaced; having come to terms with her own complete aversion to duty as of late. She had to attend to Callana in all she did around the castle, so she would still *see* her friend. Callana had bathed, made her hair exquisitely affixed to the top of her head, her neat bun encircled with burgundy hellebore blooms; a hardy flower, blooming in many colors from as early as November through April; freshly picked by Miala herself to set off the shimmering white silk of Callana's chosen gown. The princess was also wearing a green jasper stone necklace, promoting her faith in her kingdom, boasting the same color in its standards. Miala gasped when they had finally finished readying Callana for the queen's inspection. She was glowing, not just with freshly scrubbed gleaming skin, but with the expectations she secretly held for the day.

Morning report would be first, and it was the absolute pinnacle of Callana's morning. Having been a few days over a month since she had seen her prince, she was eager to fill her eyes with him, lest she forget any infinitesimal detail! Callana turned to see herself in the small mirror above her lemon oil rubbed chest of drawers and hardly recognized herself, and doubted if anyone of her sisters would not burst green with envy upon seeing her as she was now.

Miala was ecstatic. She too would benefit from the princess's acceptance and regality. Miala couldn't wait to be at every event or regal appointments Callana found herself obligated to attend. Miala could think of no one more deserving of honor than her dear friend. Callana was brave, giving, kind, all the traits that earned the prince *his* praise and adulation. Callana lacked only royal blood, and how silly a thing to hold so high was that! Blood! Only visible when drawn in battle and completely unrecognizable was the difference between royals and commoners; only scribed family links can make legitimate the claims to royal lineage! Ha! Jiden would be a fool to see her as anything less than admirable and her love for him was pure. Surely the only reason to keep this secret was the subsequent retaliation from the horrible King Bromell. Miala sighed, for she had no solution to offer for that problem. Lena's soft tap on the door brought both girls back to reality. Miala rushed to answer, bowing for the stunning lavender dressed queen.

"Oh, princess, you are simply divine! Miala, you have done something of a miraculous job with all that hair for sure." Lena grasped one of Miala and one of Callana's hands, smiling brightly.

"You two are ready then? No swimming, no mud, no wandering today. Just duty, understood?" Both girls nodded, anxious to prove their worth.

"Follow me please," Lena's voice took on an authoritative tone as she turned quickly and led them out of the tepid bed chamber and into the cool hallway. Twisting their way through the castle to the enormous formal hall, Callana's heart flitted with anticipation. She could hardly stand the building excitement, rushing through her very blood just thinking about her prince! Was he just as eager to see her? She felt a slight disgrace for the erotic fantasies she had let run wildly through her mind last night. Maybe it was her exhaustion from the long ride home from Dellandore, or maybe she was just absolutely depraved. Jiden had been naked, well, as naked as she could only imagine a man, from the waist up. They were in her bed, he was kissing her hungrily, desperate for her touch. Callana blushed slightly, irrationally fearing, that somehow, someone would know what was on her mind right now!

The large doors were open; allowing the three to walk straight in to begin the preparations Lena arrived an hour early to accomplish every morning, save for Sundays. First, Lena led the girls through the adjoining kitchen, where the squat, pleasant Gillian introduced herself. They were shown the storage cellar where, among many things, there were small bundles of wood. Odin had several wood cutting families he employed for keeping the castle supplied with oak fire wood and fast starting seasoned fir kindling. The trio headed back to build a roaring fire, for this particularly chilled August morning; slowly but surely warming up the large room for the morning council. Next, there were four marble vases, spaced evenly along the length of the cedar table. These were to be filled with fresh water and freshly picked flowers. Whatever was in bloom would do, save for snow drops which were much too tiny a blossom and tended to wilt immediately. Today, Lena wanted hellebore; coming in a variation of yellows, purples, and gleaming white. The flowers were large enough to be appreciated and they were abundant around the castle walls. The three went together, first to the rain barrels, positioned on each corner of the limestone castle, filling the smooth, mottled white vases then stuffing them with the simple, yet elegant varied blooms. The cold of the morning sent the women to racing back up the slippery steps to the warmth of the hall. Lena than took the girls back to the kitchen, where they were shown the large dish washing barrels. A high water table from the mountain made for a fairly shallow well, only a few paces from the back kitchen entrance. Emptied daily then re-filled with fresh well water for rinse in one while the second was filled with a mixture of well water, olive oil, and lemon juice. Lena plunged her hand in, retrieving a sopping cloth she than wrung out and cleaned the table with; the lemon in the water gave the wood a glossy finish, and also added a fresh scent to the now comfortably warm room. "Now," Lena said, "Gillian's servants will bring out the silver trays with meats, cheeses and sliced pears." The queen nodded to the capable little woman, who sent six simply but smartly dressed girls rushing into the room; placing trays of food evenly down the table, along with goblets full of fresh water. The room was clean, elegant, comfortable and ready. Lena sighed, taking her place at the head of the table, in the superb green velvet covered throne next to her husband's. She quickly informed Callana she would sit to Lena's left, as Jiden would sit to Odin's right, to face each other. Miala was to stand behind Callana, available for anything the princess might see fit to send her for. Both girls took their positions. When Odin came into the room, all were to stand and bow. He kissed his queen's golden skinned hand and acknowledged Miala with a wink. He than turned his fiery sapphire eyes on Callana. She blushed slightly, unsure of his mood. He smiled, and turned to his queen.

"She finally joins us? But who will catch dinner?" He teased, feigning worry. Callana grinned with that and Odin bowed slightly.

"Good to have you with us, my dear. Your presence is just as important as mine. I hope you see fit to share any knowledge you have on any topic we discuss." Odin spoke warmly, but Callana heard the serious tone in his normally jovial voice and understood she was to be fully engrossed in the coming meeting. She nodded and spoke softly but firmly.

"Even if I do not speak sire, I assure you I will be listening, eager to learn by example, my king, my queen," She bowed respectfully to both, then with their responding bows, she sat. Callana vowed internally to sit straight and tall and diligently cling to every word everyone attending had to say, no matter how trivial. She had just thoroughly prepared herself for absolute devotion to service when Jiden appeared in the doorway. He was dressed in a green tunic over chainmail, flushed slightly, having hurried in from his morning patrol to see his princess. He seemed to search the room for her, his fervent green eyes locking on hers. Callana's very name eluded her then, let alone any trace of her self restraint. Jiden came to her as she rose to meet him, and without a word in greeting to anyone in the room, he smashed his mouth to hers! Callana though surprised, couldn't have agreed more with the notion. She kissed him back, briefly, and then they both stopped, flustered, turning simultaneously to face an open mouthed queen and a glaring king. Jiden hurried to his mother's side, bowing graciously and kissing her hand.

"Forgive me mother and father," he turned to look at Callana, "But I have been dreaming of doing that for a month!"

The October chill quickly dropped to an icy November frost as Callana was fast becoming very adept at her daily responsibilities. She still squeezed in an hour's ride with George before dawn before morning council, followed by market trips with the queen, castle before dinner for cleaning, than bed chamber inspections, dinner, kitchen inventory, involving a list for the next morning's market trip, and last but certainly not least, Callana was to accept all if any citizen's reports, complaints, or requests. This was Callana's favorite time of day. For one, it meant she was almost done and on her own for the remaining few hours of fading sunlight, and for another, it gave her a sense of closeness to a people she would one day serve. In her first weeks on her own, Callana had already mediated between two incensed goat farmers fighting over field rotations; found space for a cordwainer and his son seeking a shop in the cramped upper village; and granted a wonderful middle aged, barren widow, named Tressa, guardianship over a recently orphaned girl she had found stealing food from her cart at market.

Today, Callana was seated in the elegant formal hall, where the dark skinned; rather dashing Sir Ellis was ushering in one villager at a time.

"Good morning, princess Callana," the small woman bowed her blonde head in respect. Callana nodded an acknowledgement.

"Rise, good woman, and tell me what I can help you with," Callana perkily offered. The emaciated woman's eyes were red rimmed and Callana immediately sent Miala for wine and bread. The woman burst into tears as Callana rushed to her side, to take her hand.

"*Please*, do not cry. What saddens you?" Callana pleaded.

"I am sorry, I had no where else to go." Callana didn't understand.

"What do you mean? You are not from Adalonia?" Callana stepped back. The woman shook her head vigorously.

"No my lady, I am from Rogadon." She glanced into Callana's eyes momentarily, afraid to speak ill of the young girl's home kingdom.

"What has happened that you flea your home?" Callana asked after collecting herself.

"Your uncle, king Bromell, he has become," She broke her sentence off, obviously wary of offending the princess.

"Go on, please? You have no enemies here. I insist you speak freely." Callana encouraged.

"He has gone mad as of late, tripling our taxes. His knights collect first of the month and those who cannot pay are jailed! I fled my lady! I have four children, I, I….can not go to jail! Please, so many of us in Rogadon are so very poor, why does he do this?"

"I… I will write him at once, I …" the woman lurched forward, grasping Callana by her shoulders, causing Sir Ellis to step closer.

"No! Please, he must not know one of his own citizens gave up his cruelty!" Callana furrowed her brow, waving the cautious guard away.

"Why ever not?" She demanded, with her hands on her hips.

"My lady, King Bromell has issued a death penalty for deserters! We are trapped there, to suffer his wrath!" She collapsed into tears with this. Callana fumed. She must find a way to talk to Rogala and soon!

"Where are you staying now my dear?" Callana asked the woman.

"With my cousin, Sir Jerrik, my lady," Callana nodded. She remembered the *frisky* knight from her reception ball. Miala, having returned with a goblet of wine and square of bread for the woman, was immediately sent to Callana's chambers for gold coins. When she had retrieved the monies, Callana poured the satchel out into the woman's trembling hands.

"Until I can right this, please, accept this as a means to feed your children. Inform Sir Jerrik that if he has *any* needs of support, that he should see me *personally*. This is no matter to trouble the prince with at this time. You understand?" The gracious woman nodded and rose to leave but turned towards Callana again, bowing as she spoke.

"Adalonia is truly great indeed, and you my lady, are a savior!" She fled from the castle in search of a vendor's home, so she might purchase foods for supper. Callana sighed.

"Is there any one more today good knight?" She asked Sir Ellis, rubbing her forehead in worry.

"No, your majesty." He answered, slightly bowing. "My lady?" He asked.

"Yes sir?" She answered. The knight flashed a gleaming white smile.

"Well done," he left her with that. Callana turned to her friend, absently frowning at the worries in her mind.

"I need to see Rogala. She will be staying in Windt for the month of November in anticipation of her birth; how can I slip away for a few days?" Miala shook her head, than brightened.

"Say you are visiting your uncle!" Miala bounced, clapping her hands together. Callana grinned wickedly.

"You young lady, are brilliant! Fancy a trip?" Miala clapped wildly in response.

"Now, to ask the queen," Callana turned and strode purposefully into the dinning hall. Moments later, Callana and Miala were set to ride out in three weeks time. Meanwhile, with a quick change of attire, Callana was off to the north shore; where she and Jiden had found a splendid new way to spend their afternoons.

....

"Hold, now exhale, and release!" commanded Sir Galland. With a whistling and a thwack, Callana's arrow hit her target, dead center.

"That is incredible, princess! And in only a few weeks' time!" The large knight commended her. She blushed coyly at the compliment, secretly relishing the astonished praise. She had taken to archery most commendably, seemingly born with a knack for it. Jiden had only invited her to practice so he could have a viable excuse for seeing her every day, but had noticed quickly how innately she had grasped the technique. Sir Galland was an amazing instructor for sure, and with Callana being such an adapt student, the pair had molded the young princess into an archer whose talents rivaled those of the prince himself, to his slight dismay. He had been training under Sir Galland since he was a child, to hone his abilities, while his beguiling princess seemed to call upon some kind of *dormant* astute faculty! He smiled to himself, rather impressed with her. After all, she was an attribute to *him* and *his* kingdom; therefore, her exemplary performance was an accolade for him. This realization did little to lesson his sore male ego, but it did give him a swell of pride in his wife to be.

"She is amazing to watch, my lord. And not a bad archer either," grinned Nicholas. He was elbowing Jiden in the side, trying desperately to get a reaction. Jiden pointed into the distance, causing Nicholas to turn; while distracted, he thumped Nicholas smartly in the shoulder. Nicholas held his shoulder and pouted but when Jiden stepped forward to take his turn, Nicholas tripped Jiden; sending him flailing awkwardly and nearly toppling to the ground. Sir Galland turned his head, as to hide his devilish grin. Sir David stifled a chuckle while Sir Laden guffawed loudly; seemingly unaware laughing at your prince was viewed as rude. Jiden flashed a steely gaze his way, silencing the young, ever happy knight. Sir Lashend, the newly promoted youth, Sir Franklin and Sir Senren had innocently gone back to their shooting practice; although Sir Senren shook slightly with some left over muted laughter.

"Here, here, weak ankles are no laughing matter!" Nicholas chastised the men. Jiden tried to muster a retort but failed, laughing loudly in spite of the jab and the entire group erupted into snorting chuckles around him. Jiden turned to his cousin, now grinning from ear to ear, and pointed to the shooting lane to his right.

"A round at the Green Mule says I can split your next arrow!" Now the men were ooooing loudly, goading the two princes on. Nicholas tried his best shrewd look, scratching his chin in feigned contemplation.

"I see your round and raise you a ...*kiss* from the princess?" Callana giggled at Nicholas's wiggling eyebrows. Jiden smiled, inwardly flashing with hot jealousy at the image of Callana kissing anyone else.

"You're on!" Jiden chided. An hour later he was placing a large leather satchel of gold on the bar, covetously watching Nicholas claim his reward.

Hours passed as the men sat drinking with their prince. Some, like Sir Galland and Sir Senren, were old enough to have seen the prince grow into the solid, admirable man he was today, while the other knights had grown up *with* Jiden. The prince sat, laughing, joking, and trading stories with the men as a part of them, as he had always been. Nicholas himself, although always a prankster, had become an exceptional second in command, leading the patrol for the entire month of Jiden's absence. Callana sat sandwiched between the two look a likes, blissfully warmed by their closeness and the ale; giggling along, blushing when the tales involved herself. Jiden had his arm around her for most of the night, holding her close, however Nicholas kept a running joke, saying aloud, "Now, for my prize!" and kissing Callana every half hour or so until finally earning a punch in the arm from his cousin. The table fell into laughter when Nicholas toppled off the wooden bench with the force of his cousin's clout.

Sir Senren arm wrestled Sir David, then Sir Galland for drinks, goading them into his game with the same boast; "Ah, come on! Your *sister* put up twice the fight!" or the even less popular, "Your *mother* put up twice the fight!" Callana had never laughed so hard! Sir Laden and Sir Lashend were giddy all night, having never been drunk before. Sir Franklin leapt onto the table, performing a disturbing strip dance, on a dare from Nicholas. Eventually, closing time found them all stumbling out. Nicholas ordered the inebriated although still dependable Sir Galland to escort Callana home to thwart any drunken passions. Slightly miffed, Jiden pretended to choke his cousin, before accompanying him back towards the castle. After a few minutes of ambling crookedly up hill, Jiden cleared his throat to speak.

"I ah, was thinking," Jiden stopped abruptly.

"What do you want? Out with it jackass!" Nicholas sighed. Jiden laughed.

"I was wondering where you stood on the whole 'virginity' issue?" Nicholas snorted.

"What *issue*? You are not *children*. If you have no such demands of yourself or your princess, than who is to stop you? You *are* marrying her after all. Odin and Lena are the ones you have to answer to, if you are caught." Jiden nodded solemnly with this. His stomach fluttered slightly with his cousin's echo of Jiden's own sentiments, confirming, no, *promoting* the prince's wanton desires towards the princess.

"Therefore, to avoid having to answer to them, they simply just cannot find out, thus, we need a reason to disappear, together, alone and no one to know about...us, alone?" Jiden asked, slightly confusing himself.

"Yes, *like an archery tournament in Dellandore, far far away*," Nicholas agreed sarcastically. Jiden jumped in response, suddenly excited.

"She *is* a brilliant archer! Once my father sees her in action he will agree and she will accompany my team and me!"

"Team and *I*," Nicholas corrected.

"Well you too cousin, of course," Jiden offered.

Nicholas shook his head, brows furrowed.

"Can you do me a small favor to show your gratitude dear cousin?"

"Name it!" Jiden nodded profusely.

"Invite her friend!"

....

Hellena was frantically readying for the princess's arrival. Rogala was due the first week of December, three weeks from now. Their room would be the largest, Hellena's own bed chamber, with its own fire place to warm the newborn through the coming freezing nights. Crystalline had cleared their 'schedules' so to speak, leaving all free to cook and wait on the couple, as Hellena had no intentions of having the two do *anything* but parent. Crystalline was far too excited, being the oldest of the brood, and still single, she relished a chance to test her motherhood skills. She had often wondered what it would be like to be a mother and what a splendid mother she would be, she promised herself. Hellena was a ferociously loving, wonderful, gracious mother, the best example Crystalline could have to follow! But who would marry an old prostitute? She sighed, and dejectedly accepted her lonely life style and set about to live vicariously through other's happiness. Hellena was no fool; although she herself felt loneliness, she was sure she only felt the cold emptiness of single life so strongly because she had once experienced the bliss of true love. Hellena felt for her daughters, all of them. She shook her head against the depressing thought of *four* single daughters, and fantasized instead of four princes searching out her beautiful girls! Well, at least *one* of her angels was in love. Cella barking out orders pulled Hellena's attention back to matters at hand.

"She will be here today! Have you got supper cooking yet? She'll need lean meats for protein for endurance..."

"*And carrots for strength*!" Cella was interrupted by three voices, mocking in unison. The demanding red head frowned, putting her tiny hands on her wide hips.

"Well I only repeat myself because it's important!"

"We know, dear sister. We are ready." Caran patted her sister's shoulder. Cylan, always looking for a reason to hug, embraced both girls, *squeezing* her excitement into them. Hellena sighed, brushing a loose strand of silky red hair out of her eyes, then huffed, turning towards her bed chamber, calling out, "Forgot to turn down the bed!" Returning to her well warmed room, Hellena hurried towards the bed, stumbling over herself in the darkened room and thumping into the wall. Something heavy thudded to the floor with a cracking sound. Caran rushed in with an oil lantern .

"Mother! Are you all right?" Soon her entire clan was standing in the door, lighting up the room.

"Why didn't I have the candle lit in here, fool, I broke the mirror your father gave me on our wedding day! Oh dear, hurry, we need to get the broom. Cant have shattered glass all over," Cylan rushed for the broom and pan, while Caran helped her mother to stand. Crystalline took the mirror's frame out of the room, leaning it in a corner near the fire place, surprised by its heaviness. Christopher bent as he let himself through the front door. He bowed, always gracious, grinning sheepishly at Crystalline as he spoke.

"Mum, the princess is here," His announcement enlivened the already ecstatic red heads. Caran and Cylan rushed to bring in and unpack luggage for the couple, Crystalline begin setting bowls of steaming stew on the table, while Hellena finished stowing the last of the broken bits of glass out of the back door, tossing the tiny shards under the house. Christopher bowed to the weary couple as they entered, rushing out past them to tend to their frothy horse. Rogala was sweating with nausea from her bouncy trip and Hellena fled to the well to fill a bucket with fresh water to mix a special tea for the mother to be. Cylan and Caran had come back, moving quickly to the awaiting bed chamber to unpack, leaving the couple little to do but rest. Rogala was wrapped around Cella, who had helped her in. Renk and Rogala made it to the table through a gauntlet of hugs and kisses from five awaiting red heads. Christopher returned as the couple fell into eating; Hellena returned and instantly filled a small cauldron and placed it on the iron wrung above the fire to boil. The house was bustling about, some talking, some eating, and some serving. Christopher, unnoticed, cleared his throat to speak.

"I'll be off than, miss Hellena. Send for me if you need me, good ni..."

"Stay for supper," Cella commanded, fully aware of the young man's affections for her older sister. Crystalline reddened slightly, but nodded towards the waiting suitor. He smiled a stretching smile, spreading up in creases to meet with and light up his dark, grey blue eyes.

"Well if you insist,"

"She does," Helena assured him, earning her a wink from Cella. Renk, having noticed the young man's earnest infatuation with one of his new sisters, insisted Christopher sit next to him. Christopher was much taller than Renk, but Renk was an intimidating man in his own rights, and the stable boy was well aware of the fondness the dark man had for the beautiful red haired family. He swallowed hard, sitting warily next to the mighty knight, who eyed him closely before slapping him hard on the back.

"Good to see you Christopher, is it?"

"Yyyyes, sir, Sir Renk," the tall man stuttered.

"She's beautiful, as beautiful as any princess, and she should be treated as such, you agree?" Christopher nodded, his now glowing eyes never leaving Crystalline's smoldering orbs.

"Yes sir, I, I will, would! If she were m..mine," Renk winked at Crystalline, causing her to blush hot red. She rather enjoyed the innocent affections of a man interested in *her* and *not* her body. Well, not solely her body!

Rogala smiled brightly around the room at her adopted family, so warm and caring. She loved being here, even having found her mother, she only felt the completeness of family here in Windt. The only thing missing was Callana. But Rogala held no hopes of her young friend leaving undetected by her new kingdom.

"Where is your mother Rogala?" Hellena asked. Rogala shook her head between delicious bites.

"Running behind us a day or two… settling our financial affairs on our property and selling off the rest of her wares in Sea Fair. She'll be here," Renk loved to see the loving glow Rogala's face emitted while talking of her mother. Nia was something of a God sent these past few months, always helpful, yet respectful of the couple's intimacy needs. She was going to be a wonderful grandmother. Though he would never voice as much, Renk worried about his ability to raise a child. His father had died when he had been a young boy, and he had few memories of him. Renk knew he loved this baby, and hoped that would be enough to guide his actions.

Rogala finished her third bowl, patting her enormous rounded belly. She was so very tired, but anxious to re-connect with the girls. Renk was talking to Caran and Cella about his role during birth, half telling, and half asking what he would do. Hellena was talking to Rogala's tummy, pretending to fall backwards at the force of the baby's kicking. Crystalline said her good bye's to Christopher, kissing his cheek before closing the door and bursting into giggles! It was good to see her so happy about a man. Hellena honestly never thought Crystalline would see a man for anything more than a *job*. Even when Christopher had started showing obvious signs of his adoration, Crystalline had blown him off, seemingly unaffected. Weeks earlier, he was all but completely certain she had no feelings for him and confessed his love to Cella in confidence, begging for her advice. Cella in turn told Crystalline, who had all along thought Christopher was simply a shy customer not a suitor; she was thrilled to learn he cared for her and from then on had allowed him to court her. Two down, Hellena thought, three to go!

Rogala's eyes wandered around the large home, to take it all in. The wafting aroma of her fennel, mint and sage tea; successfully untwisting her stomach and alleviating her nausea, mixing with the smell of burning pine pitch from the fire. Fennel was also used to promote good breast milk production, Hellena informed Rogala, who had recently grown at least a hand's full bigger in her breasts, readying for the onslaught of milk. Renk, upon hearing this, had widened his eyes, staring at his wife's breasts, as if they would grow before him. Rogala laughed, slapping his arm. He smiled at her. Their love had grown such with the expectation of the baby that he found himself completely overcome with the need to be next to her. It was a feeling she was reciprocating fervently as the days ticked by.

Cella moved the mirror frame to the farthest corner near the front door; sure someone stoking the fire in the night would stub a toe. Rogala was closely examining the intricate details of the frame and gasped out loud with the realization that she had seen that design before.

"Well well, Hellena, I know you still think regally of me but to have the royal seal present for my arrival…" She pointed to the polished wooden frame. Hellena gave her a puzzled look.

"*Royal* seal?" Hellena asked. Renk turned and nodded as Rogala rose to trace a finger on each identifying feature.

"See the lion on this side, and the horse opposite? That's representing the red lion of Rogadon and the blue horse of Felonia. Then on the bottom, here, the image of a sun, cut into a crescent by this whole moon, that's the eclipse, the symbol of Tasdalad, then on top, this is the crescent moon representing Adalonia, and Maulen is represented by the eagle flying over the lion's paw. This is the royal seal of the original Della Verde Kingdom before Triden divided it into five smaller kingdoms, keeping Adalonia as his own. Where ever did you get it?" Rogala casually sipped tea, while Hellena sat slack jawed.

"My husband gave that to me on our wedding day," Hellena's voice was barely a whisper. Cylan's head snapped towards her mother.

"*Father* gave that to you as a wedding gift?" She asked, incredulously.

"Who gave it to *him*?" Cella asked, suddenly ignoring her second bowl of stew. Hellena faltered, momentarily going blank.

"He, ah, he said it was a family heirloom, passed down from his mother," Helena finally croaked.

"What?" Rogala spit some tea over her shoulder. "Your husband had a royal *seal* as a family heirloom? Hellena, you cannot *pay* for a royal seal. You *inherit* one, and that's only possible if you are-…"

"Royal," Renk finished, staring down Hellena, absently wiping his wife's tea off his forearm. The room was silent as imaginations ran wild, trying to come up with a clue as to how a soldier in this remote village could come to be royal and how to investigate such a claim. Rogala was turning the heavy ornamental wood from side to side, examining it from every angle when Hellena glanced something yellowed, stuck to the back of the wooden square. She rose and reached to carefully remove it. Rogala, spotting the target, twirled the frame's back to face Hellena. With shaking hands, Hellena delicately unfolded what appeared to be a letter. She could only just make out the words and began reading aloud.

Dearest Cale,

My love, it seems ages have passed since we last kissed. I cannot find the words to express how deeply I miss you and my Cassen. How is he fairing? Does he cry at my absence? What a terrible woman you must think me to be. If my kingdom was to know about our affair, I fear my family would die from the shame! You are so much more than your status proclaims, why can't you be seen by all as you are by me! Please forgive me for sending you both away, for I do it for my people. They would never allow him the throne and I could not bear to see him ridiculed. My broken heart is a fitting punishment for the vulgarity of my actions. When I fell in love with you, it was true, but my Nathan, God rest him, had been dead less than a year. How could I be so terrible? Loneliness is so cruel, even more so having held my child, only to let him go. I ache to feel him in my arms again! I will never forgive myself, please, never tell him of my treacherous nature! I think of you every moment. With every piece of my shattered, unworthy heart, I love you both.

Love,   Camden

Hellena turned confused eyes up to her audience.

"Why would my husband have someone's love letter?" she frowned. Rogala's own eyes were wide, her mouth gaping open. Hellena noticed the pretty blonde's husband mimicked his wife's astonishment. Hellena shrugged, "What?"

Rogala looked to her husband for she had lost her ability to speak. Renk rose to hold Hellena's hand. He found his words, although not sure he should speak them.

"Hellena, I fear I must be mistaken," he turned briefly to glance back at his wife, who nodded.

"But, the original Della Verde valley was ruled by Triden who then split it into five kingdoms ruled by Triden of Adalonia, his brother Ryden of Felonia, brother Boden of Maulen, his brother Nyden of Tasladad, and his only sister.....*Camden* the original ruler of Rogadon."

Hellena shook her head, furrowing her brow, a numbness spreading throughout her chest and arms as her neck flushed with blood.

"That's not possible; it can't be the same woman, how, how...*why* would Cai keep this from me?"

"Maybe he didn't know mother," Cylan offered, only half convinced herself.

"Perhaps the letters were sealed in the mirror without father's knowledge?" Caran presented. Rogala rose to speak to her friends, eager to make her point clear.

"If your husband was a product of *royalty*, and we can trace his lineage, you understand Callana, and *all* of your girls, would be direct descendants of one of the *original* rulers of the Della Verde! Callana *would* be a rightful queen of the kingdom Rogadon and may have actually been betrothed from birth to marry Jiden!" and with that, Hellena collapsed.

....

King Bromell,

I have heard of your recent failing health and wish you the speediest recovery and offer any assistance I can. I may however, have news that should raise your spirits. Your princess has shown model skill as an archer, and I was hoping to take her to the tournament in Dellandore, second week of December, where she would compete under the red lion of Rogadon. I eagerly await your consent.

Sincerely,

Prince Jiden of Adalonia

"Last week of practice men! The king will be inspecting this afternoon and although I determine my archery team, the king has overall decision over who represents Adalonia." Jiden was walking the line, making sure to watch each candidate closely, for accuracy under pressure, as the prince's presence seemed to disturb some of the men. It would be even worse during a tournament; the judging circuit, made up of princes, kings, and sometimes queens who have mastered the art, would have free reign to leisurely stroll amongst competitors and even speak to them. Jiden had written a letter to King Bromell for permission to submit the princess to represent Rogadon. It was doubtful, however, that the elderly king would even respond, seeing as how he had not sponsored a contender to any tournament in nearly ten years. Jiden was desperate to take Callana, even without her uncle's permission. She was good, too good to never in the least, *experience* a tournament and Jiden had a hunch she could take this tournament rise. She was just as good as he, maybe even a slight bit *more* determined. Jiden himself had had the privilege to claim the winning purse in the name of Adalonia last year, alleviating the pressure to prove he could do so. Callana was so intense, even without any knowledge she would be competing. Jiden planned on surprising her upon final inspection from his king. Under cover of a green hooded Adalonia cape and green men's leggings, Odin would notice her exemplary skill, not her sex and Jiden was confident she would be chosen by the insightful man and once he selected her, he wouldn't dare put his own judgment into question by changing his mind. It was a little back handed on Jiden's part, but she deserved to go. Not to mention Jiden had *intentions* of his own he was having an exceedingly difficult time pushing to the back of his mind.

Callana was in top form today. The extra practice over these last weeks had done wonders for her arm strength, and she had mastered incredible focus and breathing control. He found it hard not to admire her a little more every day for her grit, although he could only watch her for a few moments without indiscreet images flashing into his mind, breaking free of his questionable self restraint.

He moved quickly to watch some of his choices for team Adalonia.

One young man who showed an adept aptitude was Sir Lashend, the prince's newest royal knight. He was a thinner version of his enormous father and uncle duo from Odin's royal guard, but possessed remarkable strength of upper body and had yet to miss red today. Farther down the line of runners up, Jiden had also zeroed in on two of the oldest knights in the kingdom. The mighty red headed Sir Ren or 'Red Ren', and the large and gray Sir Galland, had all but flabbergasted the prince the first day of target practice this season. An unspoken competition between the two had ended with the nick named 'Galland the gray' splitting the Red Ren's arrow dead center. The pair could not seem to miss, and Jiden was all too happy to have them along. Not only did he trust Sir Galland with his life but he had always felt a fondness for the widower. The kind and large man's adorable wife had left him and Gant to travel to the southern city of Esildad to care for her ailing parents. She contracted their plague, and upon her parents death bed could only write loving letters to her husband and son until her own terrible death weeks later. Galland had all but died along with his beloved, Gant becoming his only reason to live on. Jiden had more than respect for the big knight, he loved him. Red Ren had also captured the prince's admiration by coming to Callana's rescue, albeit a little late.

Jiden was sure of Sir Laden's abilities as well. Although ceaselessly smiling, the youth was a true master of his sport. Jiden himself had tried and nearly failed to beat the wiry lad. A team was comprised of seven, so beside himself and the obvious Nicholas, Jiden had to decide between two men of equal ability. One was his own Sir Senren, and the other was Sir Kern, from his father's royal guard. Sir Senren, although with his incessant jabbering was quite annoying, his archery skills were commendable. Sir Kern, a large, graying knight was steady and accurate. This was a tough choice for Jiden to make. However, as the afternoon wore on, rapidly approaching evening and Odin's inspection, Jiden finally decided to let his father break the tie.

Jiden called the company to attention, pivoting to face his king, saluting him before pivoting again to face his regiment of candidates.

"Archers, at the ready!" Jiden barked; on his forceful command, all archers in unison answered, "Aye Aye," before pivoting to take aim. Form was as important as the shot itself, so they were to hold their stance, bows loaded, bent, creaking for release until Odin gave the command to fire after an agonizingly slow and critical observation of each and every archer. Odin approached Callana, a tale tale red braid betraying her femininity. He glared at his son, although, admittedly, was impressed with her stance. He turned to Jiden again who mouthed, "*For Rogadon?*" Odin gave him a serious look, but Jiden leaned in and whispered.

"Just watch." Odin nodded, and then continued his inspection. Once satisfied each archer was holding their stance firmly, Odin bellowed the long awaited command.

"Take your aim ..." Breaths were sucked in and held.

"Fire!" Thirty final round aspirants released, sinking pointed steal into stretched canvas and straw with a resounding thwack; resonating off the limestone castle walls a couple hundred paces behind the shooters. Now, Odin's booming voice called for the final command, signaling the beginning of the accuracy portion of the inspection.

"Fire when ready!" Now the archers were to load, aim, and fire, over and over at their own pace. This practice was not only for speed and accuracy, but an exercise of endurance and consistency in the force behind each arrow. Overall, Odin's keen eyes would be searching out the flawless archers to represent not only the power of his kingdom, but its potency. It was an arduous examination but in the end, Jiden knew that his fathers few scrutinizing hours were just as reliable a basis for selection as Jiden's many weeks of watching.

The King was an expert, after nearly twenty years of tournament teams chosen by his self, and six years before following his father, Goden through his grueling inspections. Jiden had already benefited from the generations of knowledge his father had to offer, and Odin was acutely aware of his son's competence. He filled with pride, glancing over at the handsome blonde who was patiently awaiting his father's approval on his selection. Odin turned to the plump little nervous man following him, taking notes on each archer. Chamberlain Illiam was a painfully strict man when it came to annotations. He noted his own observation of each subject as well as Odin's to be sure there was a clear description to go with every name for later when the Chamberlain would be drawing up entrance forms for the team. Illiam's hand writing would be compared and verified a week before the tournament began, as it had for twenty years. When a kingdom changes its chamberlain, the king must personally accompany the replacement to every event to witness and verify the standard to be compared to all writings to come.

Odin bowed in return to the small man's head nodded acknowledgement and he read aloud the final list.

"Will these archers please step forward; Representing Adalonia, Prince Jiden, Prince Nicholas, Sir Lashend, Sir Laden, Sir Galland, Sir Ren and Sir Kern," as the chosen stepped closer, receiving deserved pats to the back on the way, Illiam continued.

"Representing Rogadon, princess Callana, please step forward." Callana gasped, dropping her bow to clasp both hands to her mouth. The men around gave grunts and nods of approval, having seen her undeniable skill. Callana hurriedly collected herself, plucking her bow off the ground as she rushed to the welcoming circle of comrades. She bowed low to King Odin, who nodded to her before clearing his throat to speak.

"You are the team to represent your respective kingdoms, the prince and I having agreed you are the finest we have to offer. Remember what you stand for in every thing you do while in the host city of Dellandore. You will be judged not on your archery skills alone, but on your conduct as knights, and" Odin turned to Callana, "a princess." Callana smiled, her excitement slightly dulled by the reminder that she was already failing her future king.

Jiden was beaming. Nicholas had to smile to himself, knowing his cousin's anticipation was for more than heated competition. He couldn't help but notice Callana did not seem as eager. Of course, Nicholas doubted Jiden had pre-warned her of his *real* intentions. Nicholas found himself frowning, wondering if Jiden had really considered the possibility that Callana might not *allow* pre-marital relations. Nicholas was more concerned that *Miala* might not allow pre-marital relations either! He hardly knew *her;* he was not even courting her! He had tried his best to flirt, winking at her during morning reports; her behind Callana, him behind Jiden. He had tried to tell her once in passing, in the castle hall that she was beautiful, but it had come out as "*Aye, ah Miala, it's beautiful in the room you are in, now.*" She only blushed with his advances. He didn't even know if he had feelings for her other than his undying appreciation of her perky breasts, olive skin and enormous hazel eyes. He shook her out of his thoughts long enough to be dismissed from the archer's circle. With a heavy mind and mixed heart, he plodded through the hundred paces or so to the Green Mule to drink until he was too befuddled to be confused.

....

Rogala,

You ungrateful, belligerent, completely horrible girl, your back stabbing request is granted, I will uphold your choice. If she is found to be false, however, that is on your head. May you and your mother rot slowly in Hell. Do not write me again, our dealings are forever done.

The <u>King</u>

....

Dearest Prince Jiden,

Thank you for your concern for my well being, it is most appreciated. I am sure to pull through and although I appreciate the offer, I can think of no assistance you can provide beyond protecting my darling niece. I can think of nothing that brings me more joy than to hear she is acclimating well and has acquired a fine skill. I am most pleased to accept your proposal and plan to make the arduous trip in December to witness her skill first hand at the tournament. Send her my love, but I beg you, one small favor. Do not alert her to my coming. I wish to see her face upon seeing me there.

Most sincerely,

King Bromell

Callana squirmed with restless impatience. Today was creeping by painfully slow; sluggishly getting from one chore to the next. She and her friend were to travel to Windt tonight, under cover of darkness; this was the only way Callana had surmised she could evade the morning guard ordered to escort her on her fraudulent trip to Rogadon. She would simply explain that she was anxious and withstand a lecture and stern look from the queen when she came home half a month from now from the tournament. Edward had agreed to saddle George and Miala had agreed to ride double, even though Callana could sense the large purple horse was the tiny girl's living nightmare! Callana had already explained to a somewhat agitated prince, that she was positive she would not forget to meet him in Dellandore in a week's time! He had submitted her form of entry, paid her competitor's fee, and reserved her stay for the duration of the four day event in the Purple Dragon Inn. Callana almost laughed at his dauntless determination to see her compete. Finally, Jiden had accepted her word and left her to pack, and secretly pray that Rogala's baby was on schedule. Miala had gone home to gather her own things.

Callana, having received Rogala's promise to come up with a solution and her mother and sister's conference that she keeps her secret, had decided to follow their advice. She knew they had her best interests in mind, as well as the kingdom's. Her lie had grown from a recurring panging through her heart to a constant suffocating grip! What was worse was the enormous trust her king and queen had bestowed upon her. She had all but replaced Lena in the castle chores, save for the morning reports, which Lena still attended. Odin had even let Callana lead his royal guard inspection when he had a particularly important 'father son' talk to attend. She knew she loved Odin and Lena and Jiden, but would it be enough once she was discovered? Why did she feel the need to tell them *now*? Would it really make the deception any better on them *before* the tournament? Callana could not see this tournament as anything less than a way to prove her merit, hopefully lessening their doubt of her worth when they learn she is not a blood princess.

The strange thing was, she had read Bromell's letter, expressing his pure hatred for Rogala but his willingness to go along with the treaty, upholding Callana at the wedding. So why did she feel like *he* would be the one to betray her? He had nothing to gain from canceling the wedding, no one to bestow his crown. In fact, if Bromell were to reveal Callana, he would find himself bombarded by greater kingdoms' attacks! An all out war even, to secure Rogadon immediately, long before he was ready to relinquish his ill gotten crown. Dellandore itself was Rogadon's western and closest neighbor, and King Ulei would all but burst at the chance to expand his somewhat narrow albeit, gorgeous kingdom.

Callana sighed. She had no commoners to see today, so she was released early from her duties but declined Jiden's eager offer to join her for one last practice, complaining of a headache. She needed some time to herself on what could prove to be her last day in this kingdom. She rushed to change into her green on green riding gear, along with a thick rabbit fur cape to ward off the chill of the day and fled to the stables.

George was more than excited to get two rides in one day. Edward, long excused for the evening, had left the stables immaculate, as usual, so Callana was careful not to make a mess pulling George's gear out to ready him for a short ride to find the sunset.

Today, Callana prodded George into a loping canter to the North. Sunset would be most visible between the sharp slope of Mount Rising and the still bristly evergreens of the Shadows forest's edge. There was a small swell that would lift her up to cast her own long shadow at its crest. It would take a day to reach the mountain itself, but the subtle rise would only take her an hour to reach, and she would have another hour or so to wait for the moment when burning red sun melted to an intense golden horizon. Having lied to Jiden, *again*, she thought to herself, that she was ill, she knew he would excuse her from evening supper with his parents, so she had been sure to bring along a cloth with cheese, dark bread, and an apple. She had also smuggled a bottle of wine from behind Gillian's generous back this morning before her ride and had hidden it in George's saddle pouch.

After an hour of easy riding, Callana pulled George to a stop, dismounting and dropping his reins. He was instantly grazing, eagerly sniffing out and pilfering Callana's apple as desert. She laughed at the magnificent gelding, probably the closest friend she had ever had, save for her sisters, and now Miala. He always knew when she just needed to think, and wandered just far enough away as to not bother her or cause her to search. Callana wrapped her cape around her, bending to sit on her knees while she ate.

The sun was most beautiful today. The hot yellow of the center was swirling with a dark ginger, spreading to a fiery red-orange halo, encircling it as it sank; igniting the land it touched, little more than an outline of the flat of the far Adalonia plain's end.

Callana was lost in thoughts about the *ordinary* people out there, living in the sunset valley beyond; so far from their king, yet protected by his ever watchful patrols. What was it like to be them; raising your family by your own standards, living your life by your own wits? To have no one challenging your authority in your own house; with only plentiful soil and marvelous sunsets to fill your waking thoughts. It must be glorious to be yourself, expected to be nothing more or less than what you were. Callana had no delusions about her own reality. She had *chosen* to make chaotic a once peaceful existence. No one forced her to leave home and all she had known, nor did anyone or anything force her to take Rogala's responsibility as her own. Perhaps, somewhere deep inside, she had expected Jiden to turn her away, for he had already made known his aversions to this marriage. Than she would have saved the dignity of her friend and gone on to live a normal life; like the sunset valley villagers. Expected to do little but survive, never being seen as anything but durable. No celebration dinners, no fancy clothes, no adoring prince. Callana cried softly into her elbow. How stupid could she have been to believe she could conjure up a better life? She had everything she wanted now; acquired, not earned. When she inevitably lost him, lost them all, how the emptiness would consume her. The more she gained, the more she stood to lose. There was no winning and she wept for her selfish nature, her lost innocence, and her soon to be lost love.

....

Jiden was doing his own contemplating this evening. He had not seen Callana leave for her sunset ride, but felt just as dejected by her absence tonight from supper for a headache he was sure she did not have. She had been acting oddly about the archery trip from the beginning; all but passing out when Jiden had happily announced her uncle had accepted her admission to the contest to represent Rogadon. Jiden couldn't bring himself to ruin Bromell's surprise and tell her to expect her uncle there. Jiden had thought she would be at least a little excited about a trip together. He had mentioned the four nights in the Inn, next door to each other, with no parental supervision and Callana had paled, noticeably, and nodded her understanding with complete absence of anticipation. Could he have read her wrong? Was it just losing her virginity that made her suddenly fear his advances? Or was there something more? There was no mystery if they would end up together, being betrothed, but it was still unclear to Jiden if this was to be a happily ever after kind of marriage, or a miserable life time commitment. He knew she cared for him, maybe even loved him. It was there in her smile, in her touch, and burning behind her eyes. Was that not enough for her to make love to him? Maybe she did *not* love him. How would he know? She wanted to be with him just as much as he wanted to be with her, it was evident in her actions and excitement in even the slightest invitation; *usually*.

He grunted, rubbing his head as he flopped onto his bed; straining to find answers in his green velvet canopy. As the orange sunset filtered through his painted glass to flood his room, he rose to stoke the fire and undress. When he climbed back into his large bed, he closed his eyes and filled his thoughts with her, finally deciding that if she allowed him to take her, than she must love him. Having come to a conclusion, he allowed himself to imagine, step by step, how he would seduce and have his princess. He thoroughly enjoyed his fantasies of her, for in them, he was not insecure, fumbling and fidgeting. He was a supreme example of the male species, and she was very much impressed and satisfied. Jiden fell asleep with a grin stretching his face, long before the full blue moon rose to illuminate it.

....

Hellena woke with a start, having no idea of how long she had been out. Her girls were all around and Renk and Rogala were each rubbing one of her hands. Renk noticed her eyes open first.
"Thank God! You are awake," Renk leaned in to help her stand. Rogala followed her to the bench to sit by her; the young blonde's pretty face was frowning in worry.
"I am afraid to ask, but do you remember what we were...talking about when you collapsed love?" Rogala swallowed, half sorry she mentioned it. Hellena blinked than nodded.
"Yes, so sorry love, you should not be troubled in your state, please," Hellena tried to rise but was forced back down by Cella's gripping hands.
"Sit!" She commanded. Hellena sat, knowing she was in no shape to battle with *that* one. Crystalline had a goblet of wine for her mother, who quickly finished it off. Caran spoke softly, seemingly sure that the lower her tone, the lower the chances of shocking her mother.
"Rogala was telling us that there is a royal library in Adalonia where we could search out a family line," Caran calmly explained. Rogala nodded.
"The Rogadon library is vast but our chamberlain has long since been relieved and I fear the records will be sloppy, if any." She added. Cylan was frowning now.
"How can we show up and ask to look through the library?" She asked.
"You can't," Said Renk, "You all look like Callana. It would be too difficult to explain it as coincidence."
"We need an insider," declared Cella.
"Yes, someone who roams freely in the castle," Crystalline added.
"Callana herself would be too closely watched and the chamberlain would be far too curious as to why she wanted to research family lines" She added. Hellena was feeling better, and very much intent on solving her daughter's predicament and thrusting her girls, upwards in standings, if they are rightly deserving of it. Rogala was scratching her head, searching her mind for an ally. With tired bodies and weary minds, the clan finally decided to sleep on it; each with the overwhelming objective of dreaming up the answer. One thing was certain; an announcement this big needed some substantial proof, and only royalty had entrance into the royal library. Hellena knew they

would think of something. For right now, she just hoped no one discovered Callana before she could be proven to be of royal blood. Hellena thought nothing could ease the cold fear for her daughter's safety that clutched her heart. Early the next morning, however, some solace came.

....

"Callana!" Hellena screamed with delight, leading the herd of sleepy companions thundering down the hallway. Callana was captured in hugs and kisses, joyously returning as many as she could. Renk grabbed her, lifting her up and spinning her around. Rogala waddled over to catch the landing red head in a huge embrace. Callana cried with the excruciating elation that flooded her heart. She could barely stand it; she was desperate to hug each and every person at least a hundred times! In her excitement, she had forgotten to introduce her haggard companion.

"Oh, sorry love; everyone, this is Miala! The girl I told you about," before Miala could speak a hello, four Callana duplicates surrounded her, examining her and murmuring to her and each other.

"Of course! You are Callana's best friend! I am Cella,"

"I am Crystalline, the oldest,"

"I am Caran, this is Cylan," Miala struggled to remember the names; although the faces were all so similar, she feared she would never distinguish them from Callana's. Hellena rushed in, shushing the girls away.

"Dear, come come, eat and rest. We can talk later," Miala was most grateful for the rest, and her mouth watered at the thought of food. Crystalline had already been sent for fresh well water for tea, and boiling water for eggs as well. Boiled eggs, sliced apples and mint, fennel, sage tea, were the planned breakfast here at Stone's throw, in honor of the princess and her growing inhabitant.

Miala spent the next few hours basking in the love that filled the little Inn to bursting. Rogala and Renk were everything Callana had said they were; fun, lovable, loving, caring, and crazy about Callana and her family. Miala found it hard sitting here, listening to the buzzing of all the varied conversations, to imagine how Callana had given all *this* up to come to the loneliness of a castle? She knew that these women were all prostitutes, but it didn't seem to define them. They were wonderful, amazingly brilliant, funny and kind. What they did for a living did not change any of those qualities and Miala adored all of them.

....

"What do you mean *she had already gone?*" Jiden was snarling with rage. Sir Jeremiah cringed slightly. He was the senior knight leading the four guards who would accompany Callana and her maid however, when he had gone to the stables to collect them, he had noticed the purple stallion already gone.

"Sire, when I went to the stables..." Jeremiah began again, assuming the prince to be confused. Jiden jumped forward, interrupting him.

"I know what you mean; I mean *why* did she leave without her guard?"

"Sire, I assure you, I cannot speak for the princess. It seems she left you a note, however. It was on the stable door when Edward..." Jiden snatched the note out of the knight's hand.

Dearest prince Jiden,

The fault is all mine, please do not take it out on your guard. Miala and I left last night. I felt an urge to see my ailing uncle immediately and did not want to wake the guard. I assure you I will be quite all right, and will meet you in Dellandore in a week's time. Please do not worry. Send my love to the King and Queen.   *With love, your Princess*

                                                  Callana

Jiden inhaled deeply, blowing out slowly; desperately trying to free the angst from his lungs. She had left *alone!* With her only protection being a scrawny *maid!* She would hear about this, but his parents would not. He looked up to meet the guard's gaze.

"So help me God she will be the end of me..." Jiden mumbled to himself, causing the twin knights to exchange smirks.

"Take two days off, and make sure to remain un-seen by the king and queen. At least *they* will believe she is safe." Sir Jeremiah bowed, taking care to not show too much happiness at being released for two days. He and Sir Jerrik, Sir Ellis, and his twin, Sir James, rushed out to the Shadow's forest, for an unexpected but much appreciated hunting trip. Jiden met his cousin and his seven royal guards, to assemble the rest of the candidates for a much needed run in full armor.

A puffing column of smoke trailing them, the small detachment ran for two hours, before Jiden and his royal guard dismissed the others to mount up for morning patrol.

Jiden did not like the way his day had started. Callana was proving to be a might trickier than he had given her credit, and it was eating away at him. There must be a reason she did not want the guard to accompany her. Jiden tried to dismiss his mistrustful feelings, knowing he was prone to them due to his ever present fears of commitment, but they kept resurfacing. *Who* would voluntarily ride through the shadow's forest alone? Two *women* no less! Jiden tried to reason with himself. She was quite *different* than any other princess he had met; brave, and intelligent. Maybe he just wasn't giving her enough trust and she was setting out to prove herself capable on her own? Yes! He would believe that for now, wanting nothing to ruin this trip for them. Jiden was going to find out if she loved him once and for all. He would never denounce his marriage as nothing more than a duty, but he still wised, even *needed* to know if she loved him. He had a week left of training before the tournament, and let his quest ignite him, burn through him; practicing and planning until collapsing every night with exhaustion.

....

Over the next few days, Hellena's house was alive with activity. Having decided to keep secret their new found suspicions until they were proven facts, Callana's extended family resolved to come up with a plan after the girls had left for the tournament. No need to get any hopes up, in the chance that this could turn out to be merely some coincidence. Rogala had taken Callana's news of her uncle's abuse of his constituents into deep consideration with the pledge to think something up to help them all.

It was marvelous to have Callana home again, and Miala was fitting in splendidly. Caran had found a kindred spirit in the young maiden, and the two spent a great deal of time together discussing the landscape and gardening; which was apparently a hot topic for both, unbeknownst to Callana. Crystalline had managed to have Christopher over every evening for supper, and Callana could hardly contain her exhilaration for their fast developing romance. Nothing could make her happier than to see all of her sisters in love, including Miala! Caran, although possibly the sweetest creature on all the earth, had yet to set her sights on anyone and Cella had no interest in *breaking* anyone as of yet. Cylan was so high spirited, so full of optimism, it seemed that true love would seek *her* out as the perfect vessel in which to inhabit! There were hundreds of single knights, more than a handful Callana knew personally, who would adore women such as these. She sighed, suddenly heavy hearted. Jiden only vied for *her* affections because the two were, to his knowledge, *betrothed*; a maid and three prostitutes was a harder sell indeed.

Callana had to smile to herself, being here again though, surrounded by such love! She had a slight suspicion that her situation was linked to her sisters' own prosperities. Perhaps, once she was officially married and a lawful princess, if not blood, she could move them all to Adalonia? Her family would be well taken care of in honor of Callana at any rate, and they could stop trading their bodies for food and shelter. Yes, Callana decided, they would live as she did, and the verdict stirred her desire to take this tournament and prove herself worthy to her prince.

"Today, we head for Dellandore, father. Chamberlain Illiam has readied the knights' papers of lineage, as well as a copy of each individual's entrance form, lest there be any confusion once there." Jiden was extremely tense this morning, and Lena was not the only one who noticed.

"Thank you son. Is there anything else you wanted to discuss before morning council arrives?" Odin was prying, but Jiden only grimaced in confusion.

"No, sire, I will give morning report than finish some packing. We will leave after mid day dinner," He announced as if this would clarify his stand off attitude. Odin shook his head.

"Bring me the toys," The king rubbed his forehead in feigned annoyance. Lena, although fighting it, could not contain herself, and a small giggle escaped. Jiden fumed.

"Do not mention the *toys* in front of the council!" He was nearly growling trough gritted teeth. Nicholas was bent in quiet shakes of silent laughter and Odin grinned wickedly at Jiden, who very well remembered the last time he had seen 'the toys'.

Once when Jiden had been a little boy, a teenage maid had winked at him in passing in the hall. He had instantly assumed they were in love, and ran to tell his father. Odin had played along, encouraging Jiden to talk about what he believed a husband and wife do. Odin had a collection of hand carved wooden shapes, some boats, some horses, and a few likenesses of the queen and himself and other family members long passed. They adorned the stone mantel of the large formal hall dinning room; lemon oil polished and beautiful, Jiden had been drawn to a few figures and Odin had taken them down for Jiden to play with. Lena had walked in the room just in time to see Odin place a wooden likeness of Triden on top of a little wooden carving of Queen Nella, Lena's grandmother. Lena was appalled by the tiny characters engaging in such a crude act, corrupting her young son and was further enraged at the howling laughter of her husband. However, when Jiden had innocently failed to notice the vulgarity of the wooden lovers' pose, Lena finally gave in to giggling. From then on, it had become the family joke to lighten heavy moods and this morning it was working for everyone except the frazzled Jiden, who boiled blood red. Morning council filed slowly into the long room; mercifully saving Jiden from further humiliation.

"Sir Galland led a small detachment north and west and had nothing to report. Sir Nicholas and I and two Knights rode south and east and also saw nothing out of the ordinary, sire."

"Good to hear prince Jiden, and as Sir Kern of my own royal guard is accompanying you for the tournament, do you have my replacement?" Odin asked, back to his Kingly state of mind.

"Yes sire, a noble knight named Sir Keiton. Keiton of Biddingwell, son of Breiton, descendent of King Fayton of Frellis. He has accompanied the queen before on market trips and is most interested in promoting and eager for a chance to prove his worth."

"Good line indeed. He will have his chance." Odin nodded.

"Sire, the morning patrols have been without incident, but I have been advised that farmers to the north have experienced a few animal attacks on live stock. Sir Keiton has lived there most his life and has asked if he could interest you in a wild dog hunt while I am away?" It was Jiden's turn to smile now. Sir Keiton was eager indeed, so Jiden had all but placed the royal guard position in his lap, teasing Odin with his favorite sport. The big king's blue eyes lit up with excitement.

"Give this Sir Keiton my word, first thing after morning report tomorrow, we hunt and if he draws first blood, he's a royal guard!" Odin was all but glowing with enthusiasm now. Jiden was pleased. He had been watching Sir Keiton for a while, as he had many knights, and had seen a quiet integrity to the big yellow haired man and was satisfied he had done his best to give the good knight the best chance he had. Now it was entirely up to Keiton. Jiden bowed, excusing himself to pack, with Nicholas close behind to do the same. The anxious prince seemed to fly to his door way. Nicholas laughed.

"Well, cousin, if I didn't know you better, I'd say you're excited to go!" Nicholas grinned. Jiden flashed him a devilish smirk.

"So, she has agreed to your devious rendezvous?" Nicholas crossed his arms, halting in front of Jiden's door.

"Well, she would if I would have *asked* her, so that's the same as a yes. Now go away. I will see you in the stables in one hour." Jiden frowned. Nicholas saluted crookedly and pivoted towards his adjacent room.

....

"Oh Rogala! I leave tomorrow and not even one cramp? I mean honestly!" Callana was beside the pudgy little blonde, rubbing the bulging tummy with the protruded belly button. Rogala sighed, and kissed her friend's cheek.

"It seems this baby is already as defiant and stubborn as his father," She grinned at her husband, who sat clutching his hand to his heart; pretending to be hurt by her comment. Callana stood to stretch, groaning with the effort and the soreness in her back. She had been taking Rogala on morning and evening walks, making her drink plenty of mint and sage teas in the day and a hot bowl of chamomile and rosemary tea to help her sleep all night, and had forced at least two apples a day down her throat. Hellena only had one more trick to try and that was motherwort, but stimulating contractions was only necessary if the baby was very late. Rogala was sleeping most of the day, her body preparing for the ultimate test of stamina a woman could possibly endure, so the signs of birth were there.

Hellena and Nia were hitting it off most beautifully. They seemed to agree on every tea recipe, every baby name; every thing! It was funny to Callana, but everyone seemed to pair up for most of the day. Renk and Rogala were closer than ever, Hellena and Nia, Crystalline and Christopher, Caran and Miala, and the inseparable Cella and Cylan. The only one on her own was Callana. She felt very selfish for thinking it, but it was almost as if the home she had known had gone on without her, staying the same while she had changed; she was a stranger here, where her friends were now more at home than *she* was. How odd, Callana marveled, how fast growing up seems to happen. She had left this tiny village with pity in her heart for her broken little family, only to return as a *pretend* princess, to find them thriving in her absence, while she herself, who was to marry into greatness, felt humbled in their presence. Could Jiden ever see *her* family as great? If only in character? Her engagement to him held little consolation when she compared it to the happiness her family embodied. The love here was simple and real. There were no false pretenses or layering of lies to unfold. Callana suddenly felt shame, sitting by the fire in this wholesome home. She felt alone in a full, buzzing room; a fake among the genuine, no longer able to assert her incorruptibility.

Hellena had been watching her daughter. In all her girls, she saw her Cai showing through in Callana the most; shy but courageous; honest but cunning; caring but hard. Callana was a living puzzle, not yet sure of how to piece herself together. Nothing would delight Hellena's selfish side more than keeping Callana all to herself, stuck out here in Windt. But, Hellena wasn't looking at the same naïve girl that left only half a year ago. The beautiful woman before her had grown far too grand to fit back into this miniscule place. Callana knew about the real world she had once only dreamed of, while gazing out of her window. She *was* the princess from fairytales who finds out that love, though righteous, does *not* rule the world as she had been led to believe; and that knowledge had hardened Callana; roughened the softness of her, sharpened her very thoughts. Hellena's baby was gone.

"What's in that pretty head of yours, love?" Hellena squeezed next to Callana on the fur rug in front of the fire. Callana leaned to put her head on her mother's shoulder.

"Mother, how terrible of a disappointment am I to you?" Hellena shushed her, rocking side to side, holding Callana's shoulders.

"You will never disappoint me, my bird." Callana sighed as a tear rolled down her cheek.

"I know I *planned* on lying to him, but I never *wanted* to lie to him. You understand?" Callana was so tired; her head throbbed with the exhaustion of keeping all she felt to herself. Hellena hugged her close.

"You are not the princess he was supposed to meet, but is it the mere station of princess who he fell in love with? No, he fell in love with *you*; your face, and your heart, all of the things that make up *you*. Do you really think he would have fallen in love with *anyone* who rode up to meet him that day? Of course not! He was meant to love *you*." Hellena kissed Callana's forehead and Callana held her mother close for a long moment.

"You are right as usual mother," Hellena smiled brightly.

"I know dear, it is a curse!"

After a few more hours of cuddling, and talking, Callana and Miala excused themselves for bed. They needed to ride out before dawn to make Dellandore by the morning after next when they were expected. With the sunrise, the two set out with plenty of cheese and apples, rabbit fur lined capes, tunics and boots, about a thousand hugs, and a tearful promise from Rogala that she would cross her legs until the two could return to Windt in route home to Adalonia.

Miala sat behind Callana, clutched against her warm friend, and shivered with the icy wind. Callana's feverous purpose drove her on through the cold. She needed Jiden to love her strongly enough, that that love would transcend her deception; as powerfully as she felt for him. She deeply believed he could, and if Jiden was on the verge of falling for her, she was determined to do whatever it took to lure him over the edge.

Dellandore was alive with colors this morning; from welcome banners to winter crocus flowers hung as decorations and even the clothing. Brilliantly colored competitors were showing up in formations, boasting their kingdom's crests for all to see. The massive arena, bordering the green expanse of the archery field, backed up to the staggering Mount Lisia, whose rocky, sloping base supported the tremendous south facing spectator's stands. The first bright streaks of sunshine to break through the clouds all morning were starting to warm the early dawn crowd. Blue sky was peeking through in numerous cloud breaks, promising a clear day for celebrating. Fire pits built before dawn still blazed, warming the partially covered stadium seats to combat the frigid day.

This entire city was incredible. Even having just seen it a year ago, Jiden, Nicholas and Sir Galland had forgotten the vivaciousness of Dellandore and its constituents. The people here were completely different from people in Adalonia. Though the Della Verde valley held many balls and celebration dinners, opening the main hall to guests was a mere gesture compared to the *welcoming* nature of King Ulei, who had commissioned an entire structure, separate from his castle, to non stop entertaining! Callana would love it here, Jiden mused; Hundreds of dancing partners and new friends she would no doubt make. He smiled to himself; she *was* easy to like.

The first to arrive had been the majestic, plum caped knights from Dellandore itself; the winged gold horse embroidered across every purple cape and standard. The eager crowd had filled the wooden structure early, most excited to watch each kingdom's champions arrive. The fans roared for their very own representatives, throwing crocus and hellebore blooms out to the gallant purple knights. Next to show was Lena's sister Lunette and Odin's cousin Rasden's kingdom of Tasdalad. The squadron of knights wore the sky blue velvet capes adorned by the large golden sun with orange flames being eclipsed by a full black moon. The crowd erupted in a new wave of cheers for the vividly colored formation, already choosing their favorites to root for during the games. Maulen, Lena's brother Leonard's kingdom, was next to arrive; vibrant yellow capes and standards illuminated by a noble shimmering white eagle in flight.

The next kingdom represented by a gray velvet cape festooned with a large black wolf, was Esildad, coming from far south; enthusiasts howled their appreciation for the gallant kingdom. Next, Odin's cousin Felonin's kingdom of Felonia, showing off their dazzling sapphire rearing horse, fiercely contrasted against gleaming white capes and standards. Jiden, his royal guard, and his team were next; presenting vibrant jade capes billowing with the shining silver crescent moon of Adalonia. The veneration of their welcome upon entry was overwhelming enough to silence even Sir Senren, who stopped short of finishing a tall tale a now taken Sir David hadn't been listening to. This was Sir Franklin, Sir Laden, Sir Lashend and Sir David's first time in Dellandore, and their awed expressions revealed as much. The crowd stomped and cheered for the returning champion of archery and in turn, Jiden gave his best smile and waved to the audience. Behind Adalonia was the kingdom of Frellis. Being a sea side kingdom, their crest illustrated a giant russet sail boat with a large white sail, tossing about on a sparkling blue ocean.

Jiden waited impatiently, fidgeting with Leviathan's reins as they stood in formation with all the opposing teams. He quickly took notice of his competition; He gave a quick smile to his dear friend, King Elei of Esildad. They had been friends for nearly Jiden's entire lifetime; meeting yearly at balls and competitions; Jiden was sure Elei was one of the few royals worthy of their rank.

Jiden went back to worrying angrily again. Callana was late. He was irritated with his lack of judgment, not collecting her himself from Rogadon. Dellandore's King Ulei's appearance and dismissal would signal the start of the few hours of entertainment while each team filed in to the receiving canopy to turn in lineage papers and check competitors' names against Dellandore's own lists. Mid day dinner would be served and then the Kingdom of Dellandore would open its famed dancing hall to all for the opening day ceremonial dance. There would be no competition today, just reception; giving all who had traveled far, one night of merriment and rest before the early start dawn tomorrow.

Jiden noticed the crowd had quieted and he followed their gaze towards the wide open city gates. He was instantly taken aback by her, motionless, and framed by the enormous wooden doors with sun pouring down on her. It was his beautiful Callana. She was atop her giant purple horse, looking around, most likely seeking Jiden. The innocence on her alabaster face was endearing, framed by her silky straight lengths of fiery red hair, emblazoned by the sun's rays. Her large brown eyes were wide when they met with Jiden's. He sat stunned, almost unable to move. Callana had hushed the entire crowd with her beauty, and with her midnight cape ornamented with the blood red lion of Rogadon. Not only was she representing a kingdom that had failed to appear for years, but she was the *only* representative! Callana's eyebrows rose towards Jiden, as if signaling that she was unsure of what to do. Nicholas elbowed the prince, who finally snapped himself aware and prodded his white stallion to move out to meet her. Once he encircled Callana, coming to her side with a huge smile, he took her hand and raised it to the multitude, finally inspiring a roaring welcome. Callana slightly blushed, as she followed her prince to line up.

"I was about to send a search party for you my love," Jiden chided, his eyes reflecting his serious concern. Callana looked up at him, so happy to be near him, so warmed by his presence. She grinned and tried her best to look innocent.

"Whatever do you mean, great prince? I was exactly on time to make a fashionably late entrance!" Jiden's brows softened and he winked.

"I missed you Callana. I have come to the conclusion that you can never leave me again." Jiden was smiling, but it did not touch his eyes; blue and green, alive with his amorous affections for her. Callana felt a flutter undulate through her chest. That look was easy enough to read, she had seen *lust* before. Only this time, she actually *enjoyed* the way it made her feel. A raging ocean of intense stimulation rose and fell inside Callana. Her lips were parted and she was breathing heavily, eyes locked on Jiden's. He leaned to kiss her, but was interrupted when Nicholas cleared his throat, causing the couple to face forward; both turning a bright red. Jiden was pleased by Callana's reaction to him this morning. She was, uninhibited and responsive and Jiden felt his body throb with the exhilaration of the possibility of Callana accepting his indelicate proposition. A week of worrying after her ebbed away, leaving only his sincere relief to see her and his intense need to be near her.

The tall and handsome King Ulei stepped out in front of his citizens and visitors, causing an enormous response from the multitude behind the formations. It was no secret that Ulei was a well loved king, not for the same reasons as Odin, but revered none the less. He had a mighty army, prospering people, but he wasn't known for these, but more for his, devilish side. Dellandore had its quiet, stately shops, yes, but it had an intense night life as well. This was the only kingdom Jiden had ever known where a person could be employed as a *permanent* entertainer, working nights and sleeping days. Not that you could call entertaining *working*. Most of Dellandore's income was from its many shops, employing villagers to make or grow products, but it made a considerable amount of money hosting large parties for most months of the year. This was the place where you escaped the worries of your life; where the celebration never really ended and no one seemed to sleep. This was the perfect place for the prince's indecent intentions.

King Ulei raised both hands for silence, although once he spoke, it was evident he probably could've been heard over an avalanche.

"Friends! Welcome all to Dellandore! I am honored to receive our many guests in our humble city," He bowed deeply to the throng and was answered by an eruption of cheering. The king's golden brown eyes were caught by a lone black cape billowing in the slight morning breeze. He was drawn to the beautiful red head on the tall roan horse, as well as intrigued by the single Rogadon delegate, or *any* Rogadon delegate for that matter. Ulei spoke again to his fans without breaking his eye contact with Callana. She bowed her head respectfully to the king, self-conscious under his penetrating stare. Jiden felt a flash of jealousy tear through his self esteem; his jaw tightened and he clenched his fists.

"Knights, and my lady," He bowed to Callana separately, "and friends, please, in the tradition of enjoyment, let the show begin!" He waved a hand, signaling for the music to start. As young boys fled into the stadium to lead the knights horses to the kings vast stable, the men dismounted and some started filing in to the reception tent to sign in with Dellandore's many scribes, while others stayed to watch the acrobats flipping and leaping out in the grassy square between the stadium and the king's raised platform, where he would watch from his monumental purple throne.

Jiden turned to walk with Callana to check in when Nicholas leapt out in front of the two.

"Aye, where is your...ah...maid?" He asked, slightly anxious.

"Oh, Miala? She checked in to the Purple Dragon first. She...does not travel well," Callana winced with the memory of Miala vomiting off George on the way into town this morning. The timid girl had over come her *fear* of horses, leaving only her great *disdain* for them! Nicholas nodded slowly, seeming to understand but disappointed; his dampened spirits signaling to Callana he had feelings for the little brunette.

"But, Sir Nicholas, she *will* be joining us for dancing later," Callana smiled at Nicholas, causing him to grin from ear to ear.

"Oh, well, that's good to hear, isn't it? So, I will see you all for dinner?" Nicholas arched an eyebrow towards his cousin. Callana was slightly taken aback, having thought *everyone* was to have dinner together. Jiden tensed visibly.

"Yes cousin, we *will* be at dinner. Why don't you go check in the men?" Jiden insisted as Nicholas bowed his exit to Callana. She felt she was missing something from that conversation, but decided to dismiss it.

"Well my lady, it seems we need to sign in and have dinner," Jiden was suddenly edgy and almost yanked Callana towards the canopy.

....

A well rested and bathed Miala awaited Callana when she finally pried herself away from Jiden long enough to get in the carriage ushering visitors to the Purple Dragon Inn. She was exhausted and there were only a few hours before the dancing would start. Miala looked amazing, fitting perfectly into Rogala's royal clothes as Callana had long since given the tiny girl her entire Rogadon attire that had been tailored for a tiny princess. Callana had purchased linen, velvet, and silks in various colors and had paid an ever eager Miala to make her new wardrobe of clothes to fit her more robust figure in exchange. Today, as Miala was Callana's maiden, therefore also representing her lady's kingdom, the enchanting brunette was wearing a brilliant red velvet lace up tunic lined with soft white rabbit fur. She was stunning to say the least! Her hair was down, curly and shimmering, framing her olive skin and hazel eyes. Callana gasped and held her hands to her mouth. Miala was glowing with excitement for the coming evening, especially after hearing Sir Nicholas had asked after her! The girls danced in a circle, squealing with anticipation of the promising night ahead. Finally, Miala rushed from the room to have the house maiden bring in the hot water she had requested for her friend. Callana mixed olive oil and dried rose petals in the water to soften her skin and give it a clean, fresh fragrance. Miala had also brought in some blooming white winter crocus and drops to make a crown for her false princess. While bathing, Callana helped braid gleaming white snow drop blooms and white crocus, together with a thick thread, than Miala took the length and wrapped it tightly around a slim, stripped branch, lashed together at two ends to form a circle. Callana had quickly dunked her hair under water, running her fingers through it to unleash all the tangles, than sat up so Miala could towel dry it while Callana scrubbed her filthy hands and face. Bathing in the wooden tub directly in front of the fire place helped dry her hair faster, and after an hour, she had dried and dressed in soft rabbit fur linen under tunic. Miala and Callana were looking for the royal gown that had been in the Rogadon wardrobe along with the kingdom's black cape when someone knocked on the door. Miala leaned against it and asked,

"Who is it?"

"Sienna, the house maid, my lady, with a delivery from King Ulei for the Princess of Rogadon." A girl answered. Miala opened the door and gratefully took the wrapped item. Callana was confused; she didn't know the king, why would he send a gift? Miala tore it open, unable to wait to find out what the king felt necessary to send. The petite girl's mouth dropped open as she unfurled a sleek, black velvet gown. It had a spotted deer fur lining that was incredibly soft to the touch. Callana gaped in shock! She had never seen anything so beautiful in all her life! Miala helped her to put it on, lacing it up tightly in the back. Once on, Callana's sleek body resembled a glossy black cat; silky and slinky, her movements catching candle light from every angle, the deep black contrasting against her milky skin, with her cascade of long red hair flowing down her back. She was breathtaking, and Callana could *feel* an appeal radiating from her, its equal she had never known. Miala was speechless; especially considering the alluring gown was a gift from an available man such as King Ulei. Miala had heard about little else from the maiden's of the Inn. How handsome, strong, and charming he was and how he could get *any* woman he wanted. Miala had a suspicion he *wanted* Callana, but she new her friend's heart was taken with her prince husband to be.

Dressed to turn heads, the two boarded the bouncing carriage to the great dancing hall where they were to meet their counterparts for the evening. Both girls trembled with the revelation that two handsome princes were out there *waiting* to see them! How could anything be as marvelous as this night? She would be meeting up with her prince, soon to be her husband. Callana could hardly contain her flittering heart! Jiden loved her; she was almost completely convinced and was absolutely certain of her love for him. She was still tingling from the hungry way his eyes seemed to devour her, bringing out feelings in her she had never experienced. She *wanted* him, and was feeling less ashamed of that desire, because she saw it reflected in Jiden's own eyes. He wasn't testing her resolve; he was trying to test her heart! She needed to tell him how she felt about him, and she would, tonight.

....

Jiden and Nicholas, alone, having dismissed their boisterous guards for the less daunting tavern, were awaiting the girls on the front stone steps of the great dancing hall. Jiden held his hand out to help Callana step out of the carriage, as Nicholas did for Miala. Jiden was impressed by the moonlit silhouette of his princess, although it did not prepare him for the vision of her under the glowering light of the hundreds of candles lining the halls and chandeliers. Jiden turned her slowly to see her at every angle. The glossy, soft black velvet, outlining her tremendous curves and small waist, with the silken red tresses falling down to touch the round of her lower back was a jaw dropping sight. Her creamy skin and soft pink lips gleamed against the dark gown that dipped down just enough to expose ample cleavage, and her deep, dark eyes danced with the reflection of hundreds of tiny flames. Jiden had no words; his awestruck expression however, said enough for Callana. He wasn't the only man appreciating her either. Heads turned as Jiden took her arm and arm into the large inner hall. Jiden was walking forward but his eyes were on Callana, causing her to blush. Miala and Nicholas slowly passed, concentrated on one another as well. Callana, noticing Nicholas's dress attire, pulled Jiden's arm, forcing him to stop so she could turn him to her.

"Is it *my* turn to *evaluate* my prince?" She asked, cocking her head to one side, sending a wave of red hair splashing out from behind her back. Jiden was blushing now. He hadn't even spoken to her yet in his stupor, not even to say '*good evening*' or '*so happy to see you*'. He smiled bashfully and bowed his head slightly.

"Of course, my wife to be," how he answered her with that low tone in his voice, or maybe it was his use of the word 'wife' caused Callana to become acutely aware of her intense attraction for him. She felt a shiver run down her spin then race back up, rippling her skin in goose bumps. She forced her eyes away from his to look him up and down. He had worn his Adalonia formal wear that had been impeccably tailored, and Callana was appreciating the fit immensely as he turned for her. Jiden was wearing a thin, silver crown, adorned with emeralds to represent his kingdom's hope, and it twinkled in the candle light from its bed of sleek blonde curls. His tunic was made of brilliant green, supple velvet, with its spotless white rabbit fur lining. It was belted at his trim waist by a wide leather belt, accentuating his hard, flat stomach and wide shoulders. His trousers were rich black velvet that clung to him, *everywhere*, making Callana very aware of Jiden's form, making her neck pulse with a jolt of exhilaration. When Jiden turned to face her, he smiled, a series of dimples creasing his cheeks; his twinkling, mischievous eyes mirroring his jeweled crown.

"Will I do, my love?" Jiden flexed his eyebrows and held his arms out to his sides, waiting for her verbal approval of him. Callana nodded, but did not smile. She was looking in his eyes with a smoldering expression in her own. An intense want shivered through his stomach, exhilarating him in a deep, instinctive way, he had never known. He felt as if she was granting permission to his unspoken desires, however, they *must* make an appearance, so he took her by the arm and led her towards their fellow attendees to await the King's commencement. He turned to her while waiting for King Ulei to make his way to the front of the room.

"Callana?" He asked in a subtle voice. Callana turned to him.

"Yes Sire?"

"Tonight, call me Jiden?" Callana bowed her head, blushing red cheeks with embarrassment. She had a feeling he was not just talking about during the dance, and her own insinuation sent her pulse racing again.

The large room was bustling with music, conversation and laughter. Minstrels played instruments and sang; the melodious sound reverberating off the polished stone walls and filling the room. Couples held hands; single men boasted loudly of hunting conquests and scars to grab the attention of single ladies. Kings and Queens, princes and princesses gathered in large groups telling stories and jokes with commoners and royals alike. Generous circles of partakers had started flirtatious games, and Callana stopped to watch. A beautiful, mature woman with long black ringlets of hair had been blind folded, and was spinning herself around slowly. When the circle called for her to stop, she held a pointer finger out, unknowingly selecting one of the clustered. Once selected, the rather timid young princess had to come forward and kiss the blind folded woman! The watching men could hardly contain themselves as the two women shared a tender kiss before the player was allowed to remove her blindfold to see her partner. The older woman blushed, as the younger girl reached for her again, and the circle erupted into gregarious cheers in response to another female to female kiss. Callana and Jiden clapped and laughed as they made their way to the inner hall.

The immense stone room was surprisingly warm despite the cold chill outside; for each corner had a great, roaring fire place. The impressive room itself was vibrantly decorated. Dozens of giant elm log rafters crossed over head draped in bright banners in brilliant blues, deep reds, bright yellows, lustrous gold, shimmering silver, rich greens, plum purples and crisp whites; falling down to dangle just out of reach of the vociferous, gyrating crowd. The chandeliers were rubbed pewter rings of ascending sizes, held by delicate lengths of chains and ablaze with candles. The impressive eastern stone walls had been polished smooth and featured copious floor to ceiling art works; commissioned, and hand painted by visiting and local artists alike. One was a rather spot on likeness of a younger, attractive King Ulei atop a giant black horse with colossal hooves. Jiden explained it was called a shire horse, bred for its strength for the fields as well as carrying heavily armored knights. The next colorful painting depicted Dellandore's majestic countryside, the castle with the dance hall, and even the arena where the sword competition would be held in two days time. The last was of an exquisite woman, wearing a tattered tunic in the lush purple of Dellandore, bracing as she gripped a red-wooded bow and pulled back a jagged silver tipped arrow to fire upon an open mouthed golden dragon.

"Her name was Anna," Jiden explained when he noticed Callana studying the beautiful woman.

"She is breathtaking," Callana was caught by the intense look on the pure white face, the eyes a rainbow of colors.

"She is that, for sure. Anna was believed to have lived a hundred years ago, in the days of dragons. Legend tells she was the hunter to take down Sunfire, the last known dragon." Jiden was very much an admirer of such women; strong and fearless, not the trembling damsels his cousin seem to chase. He tossed a glance over his shoulder at Nicholas, just in time to see Miala blushing and giggling at an apparently forward comment. Jiden smiled, Miala *was* beautiful, in a miniature kind of way, and she may not have been Jiden's type of girl, but she was captivating to Nicholas and that made Jiden quite happy. Nicholas was usually the jester and tried his best to appear nonchalant about women, but Jiden knew his cousin was dying to have someone to romance and protect. It made the young prince smile to think his cousin may have found her. Jiden turned back towards the attractive dragon hunter, ever poised to strike, looming high above him.

"The dragon is much smaller than I thought dragons were said to be," Callana mused. It was true; the dragons of myth were thundering, gigantic beasts, big as castles! This one was only slightly bigger than a large horse.

"Good eye, my love. Sunfire was said to be a female, therefore she would be depicted quite smaller than a male because females are the weaker..." He stopped short as Callana raised an eyebrow, curious to see how he finished this particular insult.

"It's only true with animals, actually, yes...ah... women are much stronger, when you compare a woman's size to a man's...see...a man,"

"Oh shut up!"

"Yes love," Jiden eagerly changed the subject.

"Seems your maid has fallen for my cousin," Jiden considered as he watched the couple. Callana nodded merrily.

"I know. I am very happy for them. I think they are a complimentary pair." Jiden nodded his agreement.

King Ulei finally mingled his way towards the front of the room, but stopped when he spotted Callana. Jiden felt suspicion knot his stomach. He may not be a sexually *experienced* man but he knew what this man thought about when he ogled Callana and Jiden did not appreciate it. King Ulei approached Callana and she bowed respectfully. The king nodded in response. He was quite a bit taller than Jiden, glancing down at the young prince, blatantly sizing the younger man up. Despite his urge to club the arrogant prig in the face, Jiden bowed his head to the king. King Ulei nodded a response, with a flicker of amusement dancing in his eyes for his apparent affect on the attractive young prince, before turning smoldering golden eyes on Callana, who blushed.

"Lovely princess," He pulled her hand to his mouth and kissed it than held it to his heart.

"The dream comes to life before my very eyes. You are truly a vision; shimmering white moon reflected on the dark ocean at midnight." The king's finger traced her neckline as he spoke.

"I knew you would do this dress justice my lady." He smiled. Callana's cheeks burned red as Jiden's stomach boiled.

"Thank you, your majesty, you flatter me with your much appreciated gift," Callana graciously bowed again.

"Yes, it *is* greatly appreciated, sire," Jiden added, grinning wickedly up at Ulei, grabbing the man's outstretched hand in an un-welcomed hand shake. Ulei glared down at him.

"I was just contemplating if I am to address you as Prince Jiden of Adalonia or luckiest man alive," Ulei grinned maliciously, baiting Jiden to deduce that the king believed he did not rate such a woman.

"Either works for me, your majesty, or should I address you as most eligible bachelor?" Jiden was enjoying this now. It was public knowledge that Ulei had been married six times, and all six he had kept less than a year than sent away. He was more than infamous for the multiples of children he had created and subsequently ignored with wives, maids, prostitutes and visiting royals alike. The very same behavior that gave him his virile reputation among his own constituents only made him appear tawdry to most of his fellow kings. Jiden hoped to make known the virtuous Callana had been told of his roaming lusts, and would be turned cold by the knowledge. Ulei glanced awkwardly at Callana, who stared uncomfortably down at her feet.

She could not be sure, but she had a feeling that the two were trying to insult each other but she did not know why.

"You will have to save me a dance, Princess Callana of Rogadon," King Ulei bowed to her, than turned on his heel to make his way to the front of the room. Jiden smiled down at Callana.

"You will have to explain that to me later," She said, hooking her arm into his.

"Not much to tell, we were just having a pissing contest, and I won," Jiden winked. Callana frowned slightly.

"And what may I ask was the intended prize?"

"It's an arrogant man thing, love. The winner keeps his pride, that's all." Jiden squirmed uncomfortably. He was treating her like an object right in front of her and it did not flatter either one of them. She was innocent but not stupid and Jiden warned himself not to forget that fact again. He decided not to bring up her wearing the impious man's gift, obviously intended to charm her.

In the front of the large room, King Ulei raised both hands to silence the swarming guests and musicians.

"Ladies and gentlemen. We are gathered here to celebrate! In the spirit of sportsmanship and friendship, tonight, we honor our competitors and spectators alike! Royalty, do not be surprised to find yourselves dancing with blacksmiths and farmers, princes with cooks or shopkeepers, and princesses, with *me*!" The room erupted in cheers at this. Jiden rolled his eyes and decided to ignore the egotistical king, instead turning to look for Nicholas, who seemed to have wandered off.

"Cheers!" The king raised his glass to the room. The room responded, "Cheers!" The king drank some of his red wine before starting the dance.

"Well what are you waiting for?" He gestured. The minstrels commenced; strings, flutes, pipes, castanets and drums rang out melodically, enticing people into movement. Jiden, having decided his cousin must have ran out of resolve and made his move early, spun Callana around to begin their dance. She was fluid, beautiful and inviting, rhythmically swaying her supple hips to the tempo. Callana was impressed with Jiden's sure footed movements and firm hands as well. He was an excellent dancer! She found herself losing her feeble hold on her inhibitions.

Jiden encouraged her to share his wine, and Callana found the taste sweeter than she had remembered from her celebration dance in Adalonia six months earlier. She reeled with the thought; six months, half a year, she had known Jiden. She had been instantly attracted to him physically, but something else had taken hold now. She knew she loved him, knew it as she knew her own name, but this was more. She *wanted* him, every part of him, and she would no longer put off his advances. Jiden loved her; she felt it when he touched her, the lightning spark that jolted her body when he kissed her. When he looked at her, she saw his great love for her, burning behind those green eyes;

the same incredible eyes filled with lust tonight. His body was visibly responding to her and she was desperately yearning for him to tempt her, like he had before, and this time she would relent. Could he see how much she wanted him? She knew what to do to make her feelings known. He spun her again and when she reeled around to face him, she stilled, looking into his eyes, holding herself close to him. His eyes softened as he stared down at her. He was drowning in his *need* to have her and would not have the strength to resist her much longer, but he knew his pride could not bear for her to turn him away again. She was leaning into him, brown eyes yearning up to him. Was he imagining her desire? Did she *want* him? She was so beautiful, so open right now, causing him to feel as if they were standing on the edge of something only he could plunge them into. His hands traveled up her back, pulling her tightly to him. Jiden yearned for her to know he wanted all of her, heart, soul and body. He *needed* her to know she was more than important, but necessary to him. He leaned down to kiss her whispering into her mouth.

"I love you Callana," and with that, he kissed her. She fell against him, her hands against his chest, pressing her mouth into his. When he pulled his lips away, he looked down on her with an intense expression on his face. Callana had all but melted against him, lips parted, eyes lipid pools. Jiden's voice was austere.

"Callana, I want you tonight," he commanded. A flame danced across her dark eyes as she answered.

"I want you too," She breathed. Jiden moved his hands to cup either side of her jaw as his eyes burned into hers.

"Say I want you, *Jiden*," he growled through his teeth.

"I want you Jiden," Callana responded compliantly, her voice full and soft. Jiden's breath caught in his throat. He kissed her again, than looked towards the large, now closed wooden doors. Without another word, he pulled her through the room towards the awaiting carriages.

King Ulei watched the amorous couple's rising moment with amusement. The king had been around long enough to know virgins when he saw them. He laughed to himself as he imagined the prince's blundering first attempt to pleasure his princess. King Ulei had his own group of fervent admirers tonight, so he dismissed the curvy red head for now, but he had a strange, lingering feeling about her. He shook his head and downed another goblet of wine which was quickly re-filled by one of his zealous temptresses.

....

Jiden led Callana to his room at the Inn, first checking for any sign of Nicholas. He ushered her in, lighting a single candle by his immense feather bed, adorned with soft green linens. The house staff had a fire burning for returning guests and the room was aglow, burnt orange with its warmth. Jiden moved Callana to the foot of his bed than turned and bolted out of the room. Callana was trembling with the excitement of this moment, and nearly jumped when Jiden burst back into the room with strawberry wine and two goblets. He poured a drink for each of them, than sat next to her on the foot of the bed; shaking slightly when he raised the wine to his lips. Callana's own tension melted away to see his endearing nervousness. He was staring at the fire, as if silently waiting for the wine to instruct him how to begin his seduction. He cleared his throat to speak, turning to face her with concern in his eyes.

"I have no idea what to do, I mean, I have an *idea* what to do, just never done...It," Jiden was rambling, his eyes darting around the room then back to meet Callana's. She smiled up at him, her eyes shinning in the candle light, leaning forward to silence him with a kiss. When she pulled away, his eyes were dark, and full, all reservations dismissed. He stood and took her wine away; placing it next to his on a bed table, garlanded with purple crocus in a bed of fern leaves. He reached for her, taking both of her hands in his own, pulling her to a standing position. Face to face, Jiden turned her around to unlace the back of her velvet gown, softly brushing her hair aside to reveal her shimmering soft skin; her spine creating shallow creases darkened by the fire's glow. Callana submissively dipped her shoulders one at a time, allowing the black dress to pool at her feet. Jiden filled his eyes with her. She was firm and shapely; so perfect, he was afraid to touch her, for fear his calloused hands would damage the delicate, creamy skin. She slowly turned to face him, and his jaw clenched as his hungry eyes devoured her again; thin, firm legs, the sweeping curve of her hips, the soft, trim middle, swaying upward and curling around the great fullness of her breasts. Jiden's eyes traveled slowly past her clavicle and over her throat until he met her beautiful face, her brows scrunched with apprehension. Jiden came close to her, lifting her chin to look in her apprehensive eyes.

"What is it, my love?" His voice was throaty and low as he spoke. She glanced at the floor than back up to meet his burning gaze.

"Am I disappointing to you?" Callana had confused his intense look as he appraised her as a hard look of displeasure. Jiden stared into her eyes, his hands moving to hold her face as he kissed her. A warm sensation spread from his lips to hers, than throughout her entire body, leaving her wanting when he stopped to speak.

"I am only disappointed that you have no idea how beautiful you are," Jiden's face was so earnest, so sincerely in awe, Callana felt her insecurities start to fade. He pulled his eyes from hers to let them roam her naked form once more before stepping back to undress. He took off his crown, removing his belt and began pulling his tunic off over his head, slightly mussing his riotous curls. Callana's attention was immediately drawn to the rich tan color of his skin, tinted orange by the fire. He was exquisitely defined, muscles rippling his bronze stomach and chest; hard biceps flexed on strong forearms with the effort to take off his pants. Callana forced her eyes to meet his, although her curiosity to watch his body as he undressed was bubbling over inside her. He was still looking at her, his eyes full of his lack of confidence. He bent and pulled his boots off, than his pants. When he stood, Callana was acutely aware of his physical attraction to her. She blushed slightly but did not take her eyes off his naked manhood. She was fascinated, and frightened all at the same time. She wanted to touch him, all of him, but was intimidated by his flawlessness. Jiden came to her, suddenly filled with determination. He knew what he wanted and she was willing; He kissed her eagerly, his contagious passion consuming her as well. Callana slowly trailed her hands up his chest and around his neck while Jiden gripped her waist and held her to him. Her warm skin, and full, soft breasts pressed against him, igniting a heated, intense rising need in him; a primal call to answer. He bent to lift her onto the bed, his mouth covering hers. He was over her now, breathing deeply, his eyes dark with his desire, hers wide with unspoken acceptance. Callana was filled with an intense arousal she had never known; fearing it and craving it all in the same lasting moment as she waited for him. Jiden moved forward slowly as he entered her, shuddering with the tremendous feeling of her. Callana gasped slightly, the initial pain forcing her body to tense against him, her legs gripping around him. Jiden was moving slowly, pushing further into her every time. He kissed her softly at first, holding her to him. A deep sensation was building inside him, pulsing through him with every movement. Callana felt every thing inside her body tense in overwhelming anticipation. Her kisses grew fervent as she moved against Jiden; desperate for him. Jiden could feel her powerful need and it broke his hold over his release. Callana watched the slowly building storm raging through his eyes as an intense climax racked through his body, coiling his stomach muscles. Her pain had subsided; a climbing, hot pleasure replacing it, curling her body up to meet him as a powerful orgasm throbbed through her.

They collapsed together, his sweating body covering hers while he breathed into her neck. Callana's legs were still around his waist, her arms holding tight around his neck. Jiden lifted himself up to his elbows to look down at her and kissed her; searching her face for any trace of regret. When she spoke, her voice was sincere.

"I love you," Callana pulled Jiden to her, forcing him into a ferocious kiss, thoroughly eradicating any doubts from his pounding heart.

....

"Christopher, hurry, get some water boiling. Crystalline, we need some clean cloths and sterilized blade; Caran fetch her water to sip; Cella and Cylan, I need my ground valerian for pain and ready the yarrow to help stop the bleeding after birth! This is it!" Hellena knelt between Rogala's tiny knees, bracing the girl for another painful contraction. Renk was holding his wife's head on his thighs, pulling sweat soaked hair out of her face as she squeezed his hand and puffed through her anguish. Her contractions were so intense but nothing seemed to be happening. She had been dying to push, but Hellena had inspected and decided she was not dilated enough for that yet. Something was wrong and Hellena was terrified to admit it. Renk knew, Nia suspected, she could see it in his twisted face! He was mortified with the thought of Rogala in pain for this long as it was but if Hellena was to confirm his suspicions he would go over the edge. Rogala's mind reeled with torment, lost in her tremendous pain; she clung to the image of her husband's face leaning over her. She could not speak, could not think, she was a crashing ocean wave, smashing and rolling over a jagged, rocky shore of sharp pain. Hellena's mind scrambled. Rogala had been in pain for too long, she would not be able to withstand it much longer. She was pale, so pale, her eyes were blood shot and she was collapsing between contractions. Hellena snapped to attention with an idea; a painful process, but effective. When Hellena would not dilate with Crystalline, the surgeon used his fingers to force her cervix open. She would have to try and get Rogala to push soon or she might lose the strength.

"Renk, hold her tight, she will fight me. I am going to dilate her so she can push!" Renk nodded, and wrapped his arms around his shivering wife. Hellena nodded, and then reached inside. Rogala screamed out, a horrible sound, causing the returning girls to cry, running to the tiny blonde's side. Nia held tight to Rogala's hand and sobbed, praying to take her daughter's pain on herself.

"All right Rogala, angel? Can you hear me? I need you to push, push this baby out love. You can do this! Push through the next contraction, got it?" Rogala was openly sobbing, exhaustion and pain racking her depleted body. She wearily looked up at her husband and nodded. Renk looked at Hellena with tears welling in his tortured eyes.

"She understands," He said, his voice cracked as he spoke. Nia and Renk exchanged a long look, both hurting for their beloved Rogala, not knowing how to help. Hellena turned to her girls.

"We are going to help her. She is weakened by her hours of labor. I need you all to push down on the top of her muscles, here," Hellena placed a hand on the rise between the dip under her breasts and the full roundness of her belly.

"When she starts pushing through her contraction, ready?" Hellena was sure to get a confirmation from each teary eyed helper. Christopher was waiting to bring whatever they needed, leaving them all free to stay by Rogala's side. The young woman sat slightly, her head supported by her husband; she clutched her mother's hand, and squeezed with all her might. Hellena bent, watching for the head. Crystalline, Cylan, Caran, and Cella pushed down on Cella's command.

"One, two...*push*!" Rogala cried out as the force moved the baby down into her canal to crown. Hellena nearly squealed with relief.

"He's coming! Keep pushing!" Hellena signaled for Christopher to hand her a towel she had hung by the fire to warm. She placed the towel across her lap, readying to receive the new life. The head moved out, than sucked back in, and Hellena's breath caught as she realized Rogala's knees had fallen slack. She watched as Renk grabbed his wife's tiny shoulders and tried to shake her awake, but she had slipped into unconsciousness, her poor body unable to deal with the torture any longer. Nia sobbed and turned to Hellena with red eyes.

"What do we do?! *Please*?!" she begged. Renk was crying now, lost in his worry for Rogala and their baby. Hellena pulled herself together, nearly barking her orders to the room.

"On my count, push for her girls, hear me? I will pull. We need him out now! One! Two! Push!" The girls heaved on the flaccid form, forcing the baby's head out completely. He cried out, his wrinkled, bloody face agitated by the ordeal. Hellena called out again.

"One, two, push!" This time, shoulders came out, and Hellena was able to grasp his slippery body enough to pull him free of his mother's unconscious form. Nia was torn between her urge to hold her grandson and her worry for her own little girl. Hellena held him out to her, calling for Christopher to put the blade directly into the fire and then bring it for Renk to cut the umbilical cord, than she pushed Cylan aside to feel for Rogala's pulse.

"She is weak, so weak, but," She added quickly to the horrified faces of Renk and Nia, "She will be all right."

"Nia," Renk turned to his mother in law, but she preempted his request.

"I will take care of your boy, now take care of my girl," Nia was crying, desperately wishing she could do both. She bent to show the now quiet, puffy eyed infant to his puffy eyed father. Renk smiled, beaming through his tears with pride for his creation. Nia kissed his forehead, than Rogala's sticky cheek, before reluctantly rising to bath the precious baby. Christopher and Crystalline attended the baby with Nia, while Hellena and Renk, Cylan, Cella and Caran set a recovery plan in motion for their helpless Rogala.

"Yarrow to stop the bleeding, but how will we get her to take it?" asked Cella. Hellena paused, than decided.

"We will put it straight on her tongue, to absorb. The taste will not matter with her in this state, quickly, run and get it dear," Hellena turned to Cylan, "I need you to make the lemon balm paste we used when you were girls. Do you remember?" Cylan nodded and sprinted to the cupboard. Hellena directed Caran to fill the wooden tub with two boiling hot pots of water and two cold of well water, to get warm soaking water that Hellena would add fenugreek to submerge Rogala in and bring down her vaginal swelling, in turn easing some of the pain. They could add coltsfoot to water for her to drink once she woke up to also combat her swelling and pain. Across the room, Nia cooed gently to her new grandson as she used a piece of cloth to scrub him clean with olive oil soap. Renk pried his eyes away from his wife's face long enough to look to Hellena.

"What can I do?" Hellena tried to smile to reassure him, but failed. She shook her head and grabbed his arm.

"The rest is up to her love," With that, Renk leaned down to whisper in his wife's unhearing ear.

"Come back to me, please? Come back for him."

....

Callana opened her eyes to see her handsome prince lying on his side, facing her, his head resting on his hand. She smiled sleepily up at him.

"Good morning love," he grimaced down at her.

"I have already ordered breakfast, and it should be here before long, and I have ordered a bath to share while we watch the sunrise," He was prattling on nervously, and it occurred to Callana he was self conscious about his performance, as was she.

"You were amazing," She interrupted. He halted, then smiled bashfully.

"*You* were amazing," He finally grinned, relief lighting up his green eyes. Callana hugged him close, kissing his neck as he curled around her. Jiden rolled her onto her back, his arousal pressing against her leg. She pulled him to her eagerly but was interrupted by a knock on the door. Jiden leapt off the bed, pulling the blanket with him and wrapping it around his waist, leaving Callana exposed. She gasped and shot him a scornful look, getting only an apologetic shrug in response.

"Just a moment," He told the door. Callana quickly donned Jiden's discarded tunic and tried her best to look natural, leaning against the bed post.

"Come in," she said primly. A bright red Sienna pushed the door open to bring in their breakfast meat, cheese and fruits. She was followed by three house boys carrying cauldrons of water to fill the wooden tub in front of the fire Jiden had built earlier that morning. All four tried desperately not to make eye contact with the couple, knowing what had most likely conspired here. When they were alone again, the couple grinned sheepishly to each other. Callana giggled, pulling his tunic off over her head and jumping into the warm wooden tub. Jiden dropped the blanket and joined her, carrying the tray of food. The amorous pair ate and laughed while they watched the coming of dawn from their shared bath; as the sun rose majestically, shinning on their glorious new beginning.

"Ey, where have you been?" Jiden slugged his cousin in the shoulder as they awaited the king's commencement of the archery portion of the tournament. Nicholas glared at him through squinted red eyes. Jiden flinched back. "Who pissed in your boots?" Jiden crossed his arms as he interrogated his angry cousin.

"You did, you horny little prig!" Nicholas snapped. Jiden glanced around to see a few knights of Esildad had caught his cousin's snide comment, and found it hilarious. Jiden turned to face Nicholas with a stern face.

"Ey, watch it! We are about to be in competition with these men. Show some respect for Adalonia," Jiden chided. Nicholas nearly jumped in response.

"*Me? Show some respect?* You locked me out of my own room! I had to sleep in Sir Galland's room, like a fool." Nicholas was nearly steaming now. Jiden relaxed his shoulders.

"Forgive me cousin; I had assumed you had, ah, made other sleeping arrangements." Jiden apologized. Nicholas looked confused for a moment, than realization struck and he laughed out loud.

"Ignorant donkey, she agreed to let me court her, not *ride* her!" Nicholas laughed again, igniting Jiden's own chortling. Nicholas sobered suddenly, leaning in close to his cousin.

"So, how was she?" Jiden's laughter stopped abruptly, his face turning serious.

"None of your concern *pervert!*"

"Oh, I guess I should have asked how were *you?*" Nicholas grinned widely, obviously enjoying his cousin's annoyance. Jiden glared at Nicholas, than, suddenly grinned devilishly.

"*I* was amazing," He bragged. Nicholas shook his head.

"Says you maybe,"

"Said *she*, good sir!" Jiden grinned from ear to ear.

Nicholas snorted putting his hands on his hips.

"Really? *She* said that?" he snorted in disbelief.

"Aye and she said she loves me!" Jiden grinned with pride. Nicholas rolled large blue eyes.

"Only *you* would get turned on by a woman saying she *loves* you in the sack," He snorted again. Jiden was curious now, asking earnestly.

"Why? What would a woman say to turn you on in *bed?*" Nicholas pondered that for a moment, finally shrugging.

"*Anything* a woman says to me in bed would turn me on!"

"You are daft, you know that?" Jiden laughed out loud and shook his head. Nicholas bowed, feigning reverence to the young prince. Jiden sighed, shaking his head in a show of disgust.

"I hate you," he mumbled.

"*I hate you too you big stud,*" Nicholas whispered in his most feminine voice. Jiden punched him hard in the side, sending him stumbling.

Ulei's appearance finally sobered the two as they turned to bow respectfully to his royal arrogance. Jiden crooked to see Callana, down near the far western end of the row of archers. She saw him and waved discreetly. Jiden smiled, and nodded before turning his attention back to the king. The tall man raised both hands to silent the anxious crowd.

"On this first day of competition, we will hold our archery contest. Today, forty nine, oh, pardon me," he bowed to Callana who blushed slightly.

"*Fifty* of the finest archers will have three chances to compete for a place in the top five. Those five will be determined by our panel of judges, free to roam the field during competition. The five chosen will go on to battle for champion archer of the Dellandore tournament. Good luck to all. You will empty your quiver as rapidly and accurately as you can until time is up. The first round begins…now!" Only a moment of silence hung in the air before it was shattered by fifty thwacks. The crowd begun to cheer on their favorites; Callana being referred to as the *'black widow',* for her all black tunic, pants and cape; her red Rogadon lion billowed out behind her as she fired upon the small red circle. Jiden, Nicholas, Lashend, Laden, Galland, Ren, and Kern were pulling back and firing in unison, as they had practiced for months before. Sir Galland was an incredible leader, rhythmically sucking in breath as he pulled back on his bow string, exhaling then releasing his bow, setting the pace for his crew. The team representing Felonia and Esildad had a similar strategy, only their release commands were verbal. The target was set at fifteen paces to begin. Once all had successfully emptied their quiver of twenty arrows, the targets would be moved back. A representative for each team stood patiently on the northern sideline, awaiting the command to spring out and replace and move the targets. Edward was the Adalonia appointee, dressed head to toe in green and silver, standing near Miala who was dressed in the sleek black of Rogadon. Judges and their scribes walked behind each team, pausing for as long as they needed to observe the skill and focus of each competitor, dictating to their scribes as they watched.

Callana was elated with her presentation thus far. Sir Galland had taught her to forbid herself to lose time trying to glimpse other targets or shooters. She forced her eyes front, her mind completely engrossed in her breathing and release. Her red target was all but a blur of dyed black feathers. Two more to get off, she breathed out, relaxed her ribs, released and pulled the last arrow out, breathing, releasing and landing her shot, before finally sighing with relief. She may not be the most amazing archer out here, but now that she allowed herself to look down the line, she could see she was not the worst.

"Time!" King Ulei bellowed from his platform. The silence pounded in Callana's ears, now ringing from the residual thudding of a thousand arrows.

She only now noticed the group of judges had congregated behind her. Her ears burned with their attention and she blushed against the cool morning air. Cheers erupted from the exuberant crowd behind her. She was curious as to what happened to cause such a stir when the king's voice rang out in answer to her questioning thoughts.

"Targets to twenty paces!" On cue, eight colorful attendees flew onto the field to grab their appointed targets, removing the numbered wooden face full of arrows and pulling them off the field, returning with a brand new target to place on the wooden stand. They each in turn lifted their targets. On the command of the field captain, they each took a long step, one at a time, until they had gone five, standing their targets up to be checked and in some cases, adjusted by the field captain. When he was happy with the line, he turned and bowed to the king then hurried off the field. The king dismissed the attendees and turned to face the archers.

"This is the second part of the competition. Your assistants will be bringing you another quiver to empty." On cue, Miala popped up behind Callana, winking to her friend and filling her quiver deftly than exiting swiftly.

"On my command you may begin. Ready..." The king spoke again, and the line raised their bows, pulling tautly back against the string. This was the part of the competition Sir Galland had warned her about. The king had the power to make you hold for as long as he felt necessary to test your nerve. Moments seemed to pass slowly. Jiden was more than ready for such a test. His weekly armored jaunts with his knights, sword training, and daily archery had strengthened his upper body and hardened his reserve. He was all but grinning with the audible groans and grunts of protest coming from the line. His team was solidly holding their pose and it was well noticed by the judges.

"Fire!" Fifty arrows whistled through the air. Some had unfortunately lost their necessary force and sailed too low either striking the bottom or missing the canvas entirely. It was a test for sure, but Callana was confident in her aim. The king bellowed again.

"Fire at will!" Now the timed portion of the second round began. Freeing as many as you could for time, hoping to empty what appeared to be fifty arrows. Callana set her rhythm as Sir Galland had instructed, fast enough to correctly unleash as many accurate arrows as she could. As long as you did not sacrifice your technique, you are not going too fast, she heard his words echo through her busied mind.

Jiden was in top form, his team's rhythm faultless, landing accurate arrows into his red circle. Sir Ren and Sir Kern were doing a marvelous job, feeling their experience surging through every release. Sir Galland was flawless, poetic, and even majestic to watch, not that Jiden could take the time. Sir Laden was doing well, having missed bull's eye only a few times. Sir Lashend was doing just as well but was tiring. Sir Ren fired away perfectly, matching his friendly foe Sir Galland's performance. They fired as a team, but as the arrows emptied one by one, the tiredness wore Lashend down, throwing him off pace. Sir Laden and Sir Kern missed red a twice; the tall blonde mature man swore out loud at his disappointing performance. This was the toughest part of the competition for Jiden. To watch your team fall apart, like all teams were sure to do, knowing your friends would be eliminated before the next challenge, beating them selves up internally for failing their prince. Jiden had to keep focused. Judges were still walking the line, peaking over shoulders, almost purposefully trying to ruin competitor's concentration. The purpose was to ready you to concentrate during the distractions of battle, which is what your archery, was meant for. Minutes wore on, as archers reached for their last arrows. As Callana released her last arrow, King Ulei's voice rang out.

"Time! Judges, make your eliminations!" The Judges started at the far west of the line of targets. If they tapped your shoulder, you were to respectfully bow to the king and exit the field. Having reviewed the first targets pulled to the sidelines, the judges would now one by one review the second, and if your combined red hits were of sixty or greater, you would move on to the third round. The first target was calculated and passed. The crowd erupted in a cheer for the first competitor, who turned to remove his plum colored hooded cape to wave to his new found fans. Callana gulped down her stomach bile as she quickly recognized the tall dark haired man from Windt. Of course! She verbally reprimanded herself for not figuring it out before, when she had seen him here while fitting her wedding gown. He is a knight of Dellandore! She was staring absently at him, her thoughts reeling, when she noticed he was staring back at her. A sly smile played on his lips, as he bowed to her. She felt sick, and forced herself to look away as if she didn't know him. She glanced down to see Jiden and was horrified to see he had noticed the knight's display of respect and had obviously taken it to be a flirtatious action, for he was glaring at the knight now. Callana tried to slow her breathing down to appear unaffected. She hadn't even noticed that her target was being evaluated right then. She snapped her attention back to her quest, to win; and vanquish any disputes of her worth as a royal representative to her prince. She nervously watched the judges tally scores than nod and walk on to the next target. The crowd was screaming her nick name.

"Black widow!" they cheered for her. She composed herself and removed her black hood to turn and wave to the horde. She was more than grateful for their support, and found it difficult to contain her emotional response to such acceptance from mere strangers! She felt over whelmed by gracious thanks as she bowed low to them, setting off another round of cheers. She waved again and turned to see that only three competitors remained between her and the dreaded purple knight to her left.

Callana turned to Jiden who had calmed himself, slightly, enough to smile and blow her a kiss, obviously proud of her performance. She smiled back, renewed by her love for him, and strengthened by his love for her. More were eliminated, the respectful crowd clapping and cheering, *"Good show!"* to keep dampened spirits from sinking too low. It was a wonderful kingdom, Callana thought to herself; almost as wonderful as Adalonia.

Jiden, Nicholas, Ren and Galland were left to compete in the third round. At the end of the eliminations, there were four blue and gold knights left for Tasdalad, three grey and black for Esildad, including King Elei and two of his royal guard, Sir Falen and Sir Don; three purple knights of Dellandore, four green and silver knights of Adalonia, two yellow and two ocean blue knights of Maulen and Frellis and one lone black representative of Rogadon. Sixteen archers would compete for five spots; five to compete for one.

The sun was brilliant against a cold, light blue sky, warming the morning slowly, although the archers' breaths were still visible puffs. The final event of the day would end around dinner at mid day. Callana was relieved to put this much of the competition behind her, but her arms were starting to burn. Seeing the dark haired man had shaken her nerve to say the least. She fought to fortify her resolve. On cue, the targets of the dismissed archers were removed, and the remaining competitors were moved to take up their spaces, leaving only the three Esildad archers between Callana and the sneering knight. He winked as he walked to his new, nearer position.

"Hey girly," He laughed in his deep voice, sending a shiver of fear down Callana's spine. She kept her eyes forward now, deciding to ignore him. There was no one here to prove her other than a Rogadon princess so what was she afraid of?

"Third round will begin. This time, you will have to fire on my command and my command only. Move the targets to thirty paces!" The king called out new instructions for the third round. Callana gasped. *Thirty paces?* With her arms burning through his hold commands? She would have to call upon strength she did not know if she possessed. She glanced to Sir Galland who was watching her. His eyes opened wide as he inhaled and exhaled, gesturing for her to do the same. She did. He smiled and mouthed the words, *'you are doing great!'* But she didn't feel great. Her stomach was turning slightly with her nerves over this round and that purple knight. She inhaled deeply, exhaling slowly as she watched her tiny friend remove her target and replace it, than move it ten more paces on the line captain's command. She looked at Jiden who stood focused, eyes on target, awaiting his order to strike. She nodded to herself, and followed his example. She knew she could do this, she *knew* it, felt it in her soul! She steeled her arms, mentally renewing their fortitude. The king bellowed again.

"Ready!" Callana inhaled slowly, knowing full well she would not be able to hold her exhale for his long wait time, choosing to breathe normally until told to fire. In this sequence, he would be calling for aim as well, giving her three commands to hold through. Her bow creaked against the bend, her fingers turning red than purple as she stretched her string back. Moments passed like decades, archers at the ready holding still, as a mural on one of the king's grandiose dance hall walls. Callana's eye held her red target, keeping the little black arrow perfectly aligned. There would only be five arrows this round, but they would last an eternity.

"Aim!" The king finally called out. Callana inhaled, exhaling slowly, waiting for the command to fire. She would inhale and exhale three more times before finally hearing it.

"Fire!" Thwack! The sound reverberated through the stands behind them, bouncing off the now quieted crowd. Out of respect for competitors' concentration, they were not to cheer until the end. The next three arrows were similarly commanded, archers' arms burning from exhaustion and yearning for release. Callana was satisfied with her first four, all in red. She forced her self not to look at anyone else's target, although she was dying to see how her friends were doing. The king was all too excited about the last arrow, making Jiden suspicious. He had something wily up his sleeve, and Jiden turned a sideways glance to his team, nodding a silent warning towards the king. They all nodded in understanding to be vigilant.

"Ready!" The smiling king called out. Inhale, pull back, hold...

"Fire!" Callana was startled, she held her arrow, unsure if the king mistakenly called fire out of sequence or if she was supposed to adapt. Three arrows had released one from Tasdalad, one from Frellis, and one from Felonia, taking the kingdom's last representative out of the competition. The king smacked his forehead, pretending to be suddenly aware of his blunder.

"My mistake, aim!" Judges moved to the premature archers and dismissed them. The crowd booed and hissed at the king's trickery, although, he was *allowed* to do anything he wanted to distract the line so the archers had to bow respectfully and leave. Callana was still holding, her arms shaking slightly with her severe exertion.

"Friar!" He yelled, laughing at his own play on sound. Three more arrows were released, followed by one very livid King Elei, cursing and throwing his bow into the booing crowd. Frellis and Maulen were now out of the competition and their cheering section was especially disappointed in King Ulei's cruel humor. Callana was thanking God she had sharpened her ears for any more tricks from the irritating King. She was visibly shuddering now, her arms still holding her in the aim position. Jiden was steady, along with Sir Galland, but Nicholas and Sir Ren were starting to shake.

"Fire!" Callana exhaled and released surprising herself with a dead center hit. Jiden had done the same along with Sir Galland and the purple knight. Esildad had only one of two knights hit center, Tasdalad had three red hits, but no dead centers. Sir Ren and Nicholas had hit the edge of red. The crowd waited anxiously for the judges to make their decisions. One knight of Esildad was left, sending the crowd into a furry of roaring congratulations. Sir Galland, and Jiden remained, Sir Ren and Sir Nicholas's fans erupting in cheers for their valiant efforts as the two bowed and exited. The purple knight remained also, to Callana's dismay. He seemed to have quite a following cheering him on, which was un-nerving to her as well. She was counting in her head when the judges quickly examined her perfect hit and nodded to the king that she would be one of the five finalists! She gasped, clasping her hands to her face before turning to her riotous admirers and waving. She looked to Sir Galland, beaming proudly at her and blew the big Knight a kiss and he jumped to catch it. She was so ready to end this, so ready to be happy with top five and call it a day. But she knew she had to finish her self assigned mission. If she lost to Jiden, that would not be so bad, but she refused to lose to that purple knight. The King rose, swaggering slightly, having been drinking throughout the entire morning.

"Final five, your last test will be one arrow, one chance to win. You will fire one at a time on the same target at thirty five paces!" With that all the attendants rushed out, removing all the targets while the line captain set up the single target.

"You must move across the line, firing on the run….from horse back!" Callana turned, and as the king commanded, an apathetic Miala was reluctantly leading Callana's prancing roan up to his bewildered rider. She mounted, lining up behind the purple rider on his great grey horse. Leviathon was first in line, Jiden atop him, seemingly un-shaken by this change of venue. Even Sir Galland astride his enormous Palomino mare appeared completely at ease. Callana had never fired from horse back in practice, not since she was a child and only for fun. She frowned with worry but forced her mind to focus. Jiden rode on King Ulei's command.

"Ride!" Jiden knotted Leviathan's reigns, freeing both hands to pull his bow off his shoulder and remove one arrow, pulling back and firing, hitting a little off center, but still red. The crowd was jumping with excitement. Sir Galland was next, easily riding out to strike just right of center. He returned to the side line to receive a slap on his large back by his proud prince. The knight of Tasdalad rode out; standing in his stirrups to help his aim, but his arrow sailed wide left, striking the outer ring of the red circle. The crowd was still on its feet for the impressive archers. The purple hooded knight turned to grin maliciously at her before riding out. His arrow was a perfect dead center hit. Jiden and Galland exchanged hand shakes with the knight for his brilliant display. This was the moment Callana had been waiting for. The crowd had already settled on Dellandore's victorious champion and was only counting Callana's attempt as a formality. She was furious! She knew what she had to do to win. A little trick her father had taught her as a girl. She turned to face the king, awaiting his command.

"Ride!" He waved nonchalantly, already dismissing her. Callana leaned in to whisper to George.

"Get up!" The purple ears straightened as he leapt into a full gallop, much faster than her predecessors' easy lope. She tied the reins, and carefully, yet gracefully stood, one foot on the saddle, one balanced on the big horse's back. She pulled her bow off her shoulder and an arrow from her quiver, inhaling and blowing out, releasing a speeding arrow. Her black feathered arrow fired towards dead center, splitting the purple arrow straight down its middle. There was a stunned silence, before the crowd erupted wildly, screaming for their new heroin.

"Beware the black widow!" They chanted, yelling and stomping for her. She dropped back into her saddle and pulled up to stop in front of her prince. She was beaming with pride, hoping to see the same in her lover's eyes. Jiden and Sir Galland were slack jawed and wide eyed. Finally, Jiden shook away his shock and jumped down off Leviathan's back to pull Callana down to him in a huge embrace. He spun her around and around before kissing her lips. Sir Galland's big arms encircled the couple as he squeezed them tight, kissing Callana's forehead, his eyes shinning with pride for his pupil. Miala was squealing, jumping up and down holding hands with Edward on the sidelines, both ecstatic for their friend.

As the judges, her friends, the King and fellow archers surrounded Callana; she felt her heart surge; a tear slid down her cheek from the exhaustion of her accomplishment and the somewhat bitter sweet bubbling of self esteem. This was her highest moment! Her good friends adored her, her fellow archers respected her, and her prince loved her! She could want for nothing else in her life! Callana had forgotten all about her now vanished purple foe as she was carried away to a celebratory dinner in her honor, her heart swimming with happiness and hope.

"Congratulations, most beautiful, Callana of Rogadon, for you are truly deserving of the golden medallion for archery!" Everyone in the large dinning hall raised their wine goblets in response to King Ulei's presentation of the archery medal. Sir David stood, turning to the filled room, to toast his princess.

"Cheers for Callana!" He bellowed the young, blonde knight, tipped his goblet into the air, splashing some red wine into Sir Senren's fiery red mop; who in turn flailed about, tossing his wine into the quick tempered Sir Franklin's lap. Contagious laughter spread through out the room, mingling with riotous applause.

"Cheers for Callana! Cheers for the Black widow!" The room called out, causing Callana to blush a radiant red. She stood to receive her prize, lowering her head for the King to place the medallion around her neck, on the black and red twisted ribbons used to signify it belonged to Rogadon. She bowed graciously to the King and then to the room, which was still applauding.

"Your majesty," King Ulei turned, gesturing for a haggard, unshaven old man to stand. The man was wearing a black cape with the red lion of Rogadon, and a crown. Callana's heart seemed to halt in mid beat. She felt the blood drain from the top of her scalp, slowly emptying her body and filling her feet, making her wobbly. Her breath froze in her lungs as the awareness struck.

"Thank you, great King Ulei. In honor of my kingdom of Rogadon, I accept the purse, won by my very own niece," The gruffly voice boomed through the room, as he turned a contemptuous face to Callana.

"Or so I have been led to believe." The room quieted, many unsure of what the king had said, while a few assumed he must be senile and unsure himself of what he had said. King Ulei grimaced, turning a furrowed brow to his fellow king.

"She is the clear winner, voted by a panel of *astute* judges, King Bromell, I assure you. Callana *is* the champion." King Ulei waved a hand towards Callana, who had begun to pale visibly, clutching her heaving chest as she awaited the inevitable. She turned her head, trying desperately to avoid Jiden's confused stare, as she searched for her solitary confidant. Miala was there, hands clasped over her mouth, eyes wet with pity for her friend.

"I do not question her archery skill, good King, but her *identity!*" The crowd sucked in a deep breath at once. Callana swallowed hard, willing her body to keep standing, though her knees threatened to give. Jiden's glare was burning into her now, forcing her to turn and face him. The young prince's stomach was swirling, sickened by his confusion. A flickering panic burst through his heart. He shook his head, his voice coming out in a forced whisper.

"What is he talking about Callana?" His teeth were gritted together as he spoke. She couldn't respond; she closed her eyes, tears spilling down over her cheeks. The surrounding people started murmuring, informing the rest of the room she was weeping.

"Yes, tell your prince, young *impostor*, who you really are; *whore* from Windt!" Bromell pointed. Callana was panting out loud as the crowd began to shout out now, some in protest of her, some in her defense. All of Adalonia's Knights were on their feet, irately objecting. An uncharacteristically riled Sir Galland stood, his fists clenched. Sir Ren was irate!

"What is the meaning of this? How dare you speak of the princess this way?" He boomed, filling Callana with a shame so intense, she shook with its resonating pounding that crashed through her very *soul*. They were fighting for her and she was a fraud! How could she have not seen how this would affect her friends? She had made a fool of each and every one. She turned to Jiden again, trying to say something in her defense.

"Jiden, I…"

"You *what*? Tell me this isn't true! Can you? *Can you*?" He growled. She shook her head, shoulders slumping in defeat. Jiden was on fire, nearly vibrating with rage. *She had betrayed him*? It wasn't possible, was it? Jiden faltered, unsure of which to pursue; his sickening curiosity or his crumbling sense of dignity. Callana shook, glaring through watery eyes at the sneering King, and immediately spotted his informant. The dark haired man with the cutting grey eyes stood up, grinning widely, taking his place next to King Bromell, who in turn placed the large leather satchel of gold coins in his hands.

"Good Sir Erik, Knight of Dellandore, seeing as how you are *rightful* winner, had it not been for this *pretender*, I offer the winner's purse as payment for exposing her deception." Sir Erik bowed respectfully to the King, turning a wicked smile on the crying Callana and her fuming prince. Of course! Callana realized, he was the *only* person here, save for Miala, who *knew* who she was, and now, he was seeking revenge for her besting him today! Jiden stood and nearly leaped across the room, clearly aiming to clobber the traitor. He was stopped by Dellandore guards, and forced out of the hall, his own royal guard mobbing after him. Callana sobbed openly, the room calling out loudly for her immediate arrest; booing her, only moments after she had been their hero.

"Guards, take this imitation princess away immediately!" King Ulei pointed to Callana, who collapsed into tears as she was surrounded and brutally dragged from the room. Miala jumped up to follow and was pushed backwards, nearly falling to the stone floor, by one of the guards. Nicholas caught her in his arms, lifting her to her feet and promptly rushing to intercept the retreating King Ulei.

"Wait! Sire, how can you *believe* these accusations?" The King halted, turning to face the young prince, eyes flaring with anger.

"Young prince, I will ignore your impudence because you are rightfully *disturbed* by this turn of events, but I warn you, you are accusing a *King* of dishonesty and that is not taken lightly in Dellandore!" The arrogant king turned quickly, leaving the young man glowering after him. Nicholas ran a frustrated hand through his hair, nearly growling with aggravation. He turned to Miala who was openly crying, and pulled her from the room, racing back to the Inn. They rode in tense silence, both minds tumultuous, trying to sort what they knew and what they *used* to know. Once in his room, he pushed her inside and closed the heavy door.

"We need to get them out of this, I don't know what's going on, but we need to *prove* her innocence, then they will have to release them both..."

"She is not *innocent*, Nicholas! It's true, all of it is true!" Miala interrupted her soft voice uncharacteristically sharp. Nicholas stopped pacing, turning to face her, his eyes squinted with derision.

"You *knew*? You, you knew a *whore* was setting herself up as eventual *queen* of Adalonia?"

"She was never a *whore* so do not call her that! She is my *friend*, your *friend*, the archery champion who saved Galland's son and killed a man eating wolf! Who just so happened to be born poor, destined to be a prostitute, when she deserved to be a princess, you arrogant, all mighty prig!" Miala raged at Nicholas, causing him to flinch back as she forced him up against the wooden wall of the Inn. He had his hands held up in surrender as she closed in on him, nearly snarling as she screeched in his face. When she had finished her rampage, the infuriated crinkle in her brow immediately relented as she slapped her hands over her face, flabbergasted by her own outburst. Nicholas slowly lowered his hands, tentatively placing them on her tiny shoulders.

"I have never raised my voice like that in all my life. Forgive me sire, it's just that,·"

"No, no I am so sorry, Miala, I did not mean to speak of your friend in such a way, I was wrong. I should not have been so quick to judge her. Forgive me? " Miala relaxed her shoulders, her hands falling to her sides as tears streamed down her delicate oval face. Nicholas pulled her close, trying to control her shaking, and ease her pain. He was astounded by the loyalty of this maiden for her friend, although, he had to admit, he was having a hard time seeing Callana in such an unfavorable way, but *he* had only reacted on *his* own undying loyalty for his cousin. He shook his head; how alike he was with this exquisite little creature he was still getting to know. He pushed her back to look in her face.

"Aye, give me the night, to think about this. I promise I will meet you in the morning with a plan...trust me?" She slowly nodded, than allowed herself a small smile.

"Of course, sire," she bowed respectfully, although her addressing him as sire was somewhat irritating, he nodded his acknowledgement. He bent to kiss her hand, and then released her. He couldn't help but notice she seemed in quite a hurry to see him go, but he had other things to worry about now. He quickly rushed to the stables to his chestnut stallion, hastily saddling him and riding out across the valley between the Inn and the Dellandore dungeons.

....

Renk was awakened by a slight movement, he had mistaken for Rogala, painfully disappointed when he realized it was only Nia checking on her slack daughter. Renk was acting as permanent cushion for his wife, leaving her rarely, only to relieve himself, for days now. She was soundly sleeping, sunk against her husband, holding him in Hellena's enormous feather bed, her pulse still weak, but steady. The lemon balm leaves had effectively stopped Rogala's vaginal bleeding, helped slightly by the tongue full of yarrow Hellena administered daily. The placenta had come out not long after the baby, and Hellena had informed Renk that the umbilical cord was unnaturally short, maybe causing a slight premature detachment, which would explain the excessive bleeding. Renk was in a state of constant exhaustion, despite his lack of activity. Worry for his wife was eating him alive, while he longed to be the father he should be. He had held his son often, cradling him next to his mother, hoping it would rouse her to wake and meet her amazing creation. Renk was so grateful for Hellena's courage and knowledge, undoubtedly saving his son and wife's lives. Knowing he had no way to ever show her enough gratitude for what she had done, but he resolving to desperately try.

Nia was also proving to be remarkable, stuck to the beautiful dark skinned boy almost constantly, and successfully holding him to Rogala to nurse. Renk winked at the petite woman bending over him, worry creasing her eyes as she stroked her daughter's matted waves, silently willing her to rise. Nia smiled at Renk, briefly, turning back to attend to her beloved daughter. The two had their morning routine down now. Christopher was there every dawn to help Crystalline fill and boil water for Rogala's soak in a rosemary, vervain, and olive oil bath, followed by a fresh poultice of lemon balm on fern leaves to her healing body. The baths were helping tremendously with her swelling, the hope being that her pain was consequently subsiding. Her clothes were changed daily, the clean tunic hung first over the fire to warm, before it was tugged down over her head. Nia used a long woolen sock to hold her poultice in place, and two long wool socks were kept on her delicate feet and legs for warmth against this chilly, albeit subtle winter. Usually in December, snow fell daily in Windt, but this year it had yet to fall. Christopher had been chopping the wood, tending the horse, stoking the fire, anything he could do to help. He was an admirable young man, Renk mused, who was very happy to see Crystalline with someone so responsible and caring. Crystalline would probably be married by now if Rogala was well, having no time limits on engagements as commoners. Only royals were required to wait a year.

Renk lifted his beautiful wife, pulling her tunic over her head, and gently placing her in the warm water. Christopher respectfully busied himself outside while the other man's wife was nude, and Renk made sure to thank him every day for braving the elements on behalf of Rogala's dignity. As she soaked, Renk supported Rogala's neck in the crook of his elbow, while his free hand gently rubbed her skin. Nia felt the stimulation would incite Rogala to wake, or at least feel loved, lost in her sleeping world, only memories of terrible pain to haunt her. Nia worked her fingers gently through Rogala's submerged hair, massaging her scalp and gently untangling the knots.

Caran, Cylan, Cella and Hellena busied themselves with the housework, cooking, laundry, market trips and of course, baby care. When ever Nia required a break, even a short one, there was always someone there to hold the darling little blue eyed boy. The girls spent long parts of their days near Renk and Rogala, Cylan soothingly talking to Rogala about her son, describing in detail how incredible he was and what he had learned that day; Caran would braid and unbraid, comb and play with the little blonde's hair, desperate to rouse the sleeping girl. Cella had taken to Renk maintenance; washing his hair with a pot and olive oil and mint, bringing him food and water, rubbing his aching shoulders and generally attending to his every whim, so he could remain there with his still wife. Hellena had a generous savings, so she had called off all gentlemen callers for December, and thankfully had received no visitors, due to travelers avoiding the cold.

This morning, something happened that reinforced the hope that pulsated through the walls of the Stone's throw Inn. Rogala, usually limp, had stiffened during her soak, pushing slightly against Renk's arm, and her eyes had flickered open. Renk exhaled, tears springing into his eyes as he looked down at her face. Nia rushed around to the side of the tub to see her baby, calling out to the house.

"She is awake!"

Hellena had been anxiously awaiting this moment. She quickly filled a goblet of warm broth she had slow cooking for dinner, and mixed in fenugreek for inflammation, garlic for infection, and fennel for milk production, and rushed it to Nia. Nia nodded eagerly, and Renk raised his wife's head to drink. Rogala's brow creased; she was confused at her surroundings, but drank, hungrily finishing the entire goblet. Hellena rushed to get more of the same and Crystalline ran to the well to get a pot of fresh well water, for the undoubtedly parched little woman. Rogala drank again, still too weak to sit up on her own, but trying. Renk held her firmly upright, delighted to see her getting nourishment. Rogala looked around her, still slightly fuzzy cognitively, but seemingly recognizing the tearful faces around her. She drank three goblets of the medicated broth, than five full of water, before she closed heavy lids, and slumped back against her husband. Nia whimpered slightly, calling her name.

"Rogala, my angel? Rogala? Oh, I didn't show her the baby! Oh how could I have forgotten? My poor girl!" Hellena grabbed her friend, embracing her and shushing her softly.

"There now love, that's enough of that!" She forced Nia to look her in the eye. "Listen to me, love, she's eaten, she drank; we've received our sign that she has the strength to recover, she just needs time and rest. Look at her, she looks better all ready!" It was true, Nia had to admit, Rogala was still paler than usual, but not as ashen as before. She was so frail looking, floating in that wooden tub, but it was good to see her eat something, for that meant she could keep feeding her baby, even if she was unaware she was. Nia nodded up at her friend, than turned to Renk who was openly crying and pulled him close, squeezing his neck tight.

"She will make it, I know it. I know it!" Renk nodded against her, still cradling his thin wife. Hellena and her brood encircled the trio, hugging them close, comforting their friends in this bitter sweet victory.

....

"I am here to see the prisoner, Prince Jiden; I am his cousin and squire, Prince Nicholas." Nicholas informed the two guards, their huge frames filling the entrance of the Dellandore stone prison. The two dirty faced giants exchanged glances before parting to allow the smaller man in.

"Make it quick," One sneered. Nicholas ignored him and hurried to the last cell. Jiden was pacing, angrily shaking his head, puffing out hot breaths in the putrid stone structure, when Nicholas rounded the slimy corner.

"Can you believe this? Is it not poetic? I didn't *want* to marry the princess in the first place and the instant I want nothing *less*, she turns out to be a prostitute?" Jiden was furious, crossing back and forth over the filthy, dirt floor of his cell.

"I know you are angry, cousin, but..."

"*But? But?* You have a bright side to this story Nicholas? What is it?"

"Please, Jiden, I am only trying to explain..."

"Oh perfect, brilliant! You are on her side?"

"I am on *your* side cousin, but..."

"She was ideal, perfect for me! Innocent, brave, wonderful, beautiful, like my very own fantasy come to life. How did she do that? How..."

"How *indeed?* Do you hear yourself?"

"What?" Jiden snarled.

"Out of your own mouth, she was *perfect* for you! Do you really believe she faked all of the things you love about her?" Nicholas scolded.

"*Loved*, about her, but not any more," Jiden snipped, crossing his arms in defiance of his own feelings. Nicholas sighed, stepping close to the bars to speak sternly to his closest friend.

"Jiden, if you can say you no longer love her than you really never did, right?"

Jiden stilled, staring down at his feet. When he met his cousin's stare, he had calmed his temper.

"How could I be this stupid?"

"It's a gift," Nicholas shrugged. Jiden shook his head and kicked dirt at his cousin's boots.

The creaking of the outer doors caught the two's attention. Callana was led in, black velvet archery suit and cape torn and tattered, covered in rotten food, head down, shamefully hiding behind matted red hair. Following the two guards with Callana was King Ulei, smirking towards Jiden, openly pleased that the young prince's life had taken such a traumatic down turn. Jiden's skin bristled when he saw Callana, remorse and disgrace simultaneously flooding his heart, turning his neck a heated red. The King's smirk was noted, although Jiden could hardly feel anything less than humiliation in front of him now. The tall blonde came to stand next to Nicholas, who bowed dutifully; Ulei glared down at Jiden, absently nodding a response.

"Although your violence in my dinning hall was considerably rude, and unbecoming of a prince, I am after all, a man, and understand the rage you must have felt over the whore's betrayal," Ulei nodded to his left towards Callana's cell as he spoke. Jiden felt a shiver run up his spine. How he wanted to climb through these bars and throttle the royal tyrant for addressing Callana that way. He forced himself to calm, breathing slowly, biding his time before the king would release them, so Jiden could deal with her himself.

"Therefore, you are free to go, to leave Dellandore; your men have been disqualified from the remaining events of the tournament, you understand."

"Your majesty?" Nicholas asked.

"Well, frankly, dear squire, I can only assume that Adalonia was conspiring against Rogadon, using a prostitute to replace the princess, aiming to secure the crumbling kingdom for its own."

"*What?*" Jiden jumped towards the king, iron bars keeping him from his intended target.

"Temper temper, young prince," Ulei tisked.

"Sire, you have no evidence that Adalonia is nothing more than a victim of the girl's betrayal, just as King Bromell was," Nicholas tried, but was cut off by a wave of the King's hand.

"I have no evidence to the *contrary*, therefore, King Bromell has ordered you released to return home and gather your *evidence* to support your claim that you are above suspicion,"

"And Callana? What happens to her? Sire," Jiden sneered. His stomach was twisting with the realization that her fate was up to this condescending pig. Jiden had not counted on this; He had assumed Callana would be held to the judgment and punishment determined by Adalonia, and himself.

"She will be publicly executed, King Bromell will settle for no less in the face of her wide spread deception." Ulei answered nonchalantly.

"No! King Ulei, show mercy, she is a mere girl!"

"Prince Jiden..."

"She has harmed no one; I will call off the marriage!" Jiden promised.

"Prince Jiden..."King Ulei tried again.

"I will banish her from the Della Verde valley, King Bromell can keep his God forsaken kingdom, Adalonia does not want anything but peace!"

"Prince Jiden, you are protesting my judgment?"

"This is not justice, my lord!" Jiden was gripping the bars now, his eyes pleading. King Ulei relished his position of power, openly reveling in the prince's torment but Jiden didn't care; his pride was no longer an issue. He would beg if that's what it took.

"Prince Jiden, this is *my* kingdom, and *my* ruling is final. Be sure to tell your father, the *mighty* King Odin that if you are found guilty of conspiring against Rogadon, you will share your lover's fate," He grinned maliciously before walking away, waving off Callana's cell as he strolled past. The guards waited until the King had long gone before they opened Jiden's cell, pushing him and Nicholas out of the prison.

"Can I at least speak to her? Stop!" Jiden's protests were ignored, most assuredly on King Ulei's orders, and Jiden and Nicholas were shoved through the dank stone hall and the outer doors. Jiden caught only a glimpse of Callana's trembling form, crumpled and crying on the cold floor as he was shoved by, calling her name.

....

Outside, Jiden was frantically running around the stone building, still calling Callana's name hoarsely, as if his sheer will would pull her through the wall. Nicholas felt numb; he had no soothing words for his hysterical cousin. He had not seen this end coming for Callana. He searched his mind, tearing through ideas to find the saving grace, the plan to end all plans. As he pondered, he vaguely noticed a dark form, leaning against a tree near the prison's entrance.

"Who goes there?" He called. Jiden skid to a stop in his ranting, turning to see who his cousin was talking to.

"Show yourself!" Jiden demanded his self control hanging by a thread. Sir Erik stepped from the murky shadows of the trees and into the dim orange of dusk. Jiden snapped, his hold lost, fury boiling over. He lunged at the taller man, smashing him to the ground; pummeling him in the face. Erik took both fists and balled them together, bringing them slamming down on the prince's diaphragm, knocking his breath out of him. Jiden rolled off, the veins in his neck rising to the surface from his lack of oxygen. Nicholas started towards the knight, but the bleeding man put both hands up in surrender.

"I do not wish to fight *either* of you," Erik's gruff voice stopped Nicholas, who flailed, turning his attention on his fallen cousin. Jiden wheezed with a sudden intake of air rushing into his burning lungs. Nicholas pulled him to a standing position while he sucked air in loudly.

"Why? Why did you turn her in? What did she do to deserve *death*?" Jiden demanded in his strained voice.

"I did not mean for her to *die*. It was sour grapes is all, I lost to a woman, and I was humiliated!" Jiden heard the sincerity in the older man's voice. He stood, still spinning inside with the sickening knowledge that Callana was to die. Nicholas was grim, staring out towards the large field and immense wooden stands where only hours before, Callana had been a champion in this city. How quickly they had turned on her, how easily her fame had come and gone. Was it possible she had planned even this? Taking a tournament for a sport few women even entered, let alone excelled in! He shook his head, clearing out any thing that was not strategy, when he noticed a familiar large, plum gelding thundering out of the Purple Dragon's stables, only a few hundred paces from the prison's position on the southern base of the daunting Mount Lisia. He frowned, trying to place the horse and why it was significant, when as it pounded slightly closer, he realized there was a delicate maiden, puffing out heated breath into the cold air, clinging to its back. He jolted as his mind made the connection of horse to unlikely rider.

"*What* is she doing?" he muttered, mostly to himself.

"Who?" Jiden asked, turning abruptly, following his cousin's stare.

"Miala, she is riding Callana's horse. She *hates* horses!" Miala was riding past, now only about sixty paces from them, but she did not see them. Nicholas sprang away, untying his long legged chestnut from the post, and mounting him quickly.

"She knows all about Callana, she told me as much. I need to find out what she's up to! I will meet you in Adalonia!" Jiden had no time to protest as Nicholas spurred his mighty horse into a roaring gallop, soaring away, on the heels of his un-knowing prey. A slightly confused Jiden turned back to Erik, who was using his glove and sleeve to wipe his bloody nose. Jiden was panicking, he didn't know what to do, who could help? If he could just, talk to her, find out her motives, perhaps someone would vouch for her character and the King would relent? Oh who was he kidding? King Ulei was all too happy with himself for his authority over the couple. Jiden could not begin to think of what kind of *evidence* he could conjure to prove he had no knowledge of Callana's true identity. If only he could get her out....

"That's it!" He concluded out loud. Erik looked into his now bloody glove, mystified over its apparent relevance.

"I just need to ...." Jiden stopped himself, unsure of his company. Erik shook his head.

"Yes?" The dark knight encouraged. Jiden glared at him, his eyes burning into the stranger's as he tried to determine the man's intentions.

"Never mind, *traitor*, I was just thinking out loud," Jiden scowled at him, briskly turning to sprint back to the Inn, his plan formulating as he ran, his long strides easily devouring the distance of rolling plains between the low lying prison and rising perch of the Inn. Erik started.

"Wait!" He sprinted to catch up with the agile youth, huffing and puffing as he paced next to him.

"Prince Jiden, wait, I want to help..." Erik panted. Jiden turned a glaring eye on his adversary.

"Really? How helpful you have been already, having my love *jailed and sentenced to death*!" He barked the last out angrily, slightly increasing his speed. Erik huffed out each breath. It seemed Dellandore's standard of training may be lacking compared to Adalonia's.

"Jiden, er, ah *Prince*, Jiden, I made a mistake, please, let me help to amend it!"

"Toss off!" Jiden twisted to belt Erik in his jaw, snapping the taller man's head sideways, sending him smearing face first across the hard, flat ground. Satisfied he had rid himself of his nuisance, Jiden loped on to the Inn, determined to free his pretend princess.

....

Prince Jiden, along with his archers, royal guard and Edward rode out of Dellandore at dawn; their departure supervised by King Bromell, King Ulei and their respective royal guards.

"And where is your young squire and his maiden?" King Ulei asked, apparently confirming no Adalonia visitor was left behind to stain his city of sin.

"*Prince* Nicholas and his companion are gone, *King*, since last evening. We are all that's left of Adalonia here," Jiden snapped his retort, gesturing widely with his hand towards his loyal band. King Ulei turned to his old time friend, King Bromell and nodded to the lesser King. King Bromell cleared his throat to speak.

"In three days time, if the *real* Princess is not found, I will have no choice but to condemn your imposter to death, and any man found to be guilty of aiding her in any way, young *prince*." Jiden flinched at the almost merry tone in the scraggly man's voice. He *wanted* her dead. Jiden was Callana's only chance.

"How noble of you; May the legend of your vanquishing a mere *girl* spread far and wide, *mighty* King Bromell," Jiden responded with a patronizing tone to his voice. Sir Galland and Sir Ren exchanged glances of disgust for the rotten king, before the bevy departed, leaving behind a now somewhat lackluster Kingdom of Dellandore. Once the Dellandore escorts had finally turned back towards home, beyond the inner city's colossal gates, Jiden pulled his squad to a halt.

"Sir Galland, make camp, wait for me here undercover," Jiden turned Leviathon towards the back side of Mount Lisia, as Sir Galland protested.

"Sire, you should not go alone, it is our duty to..." Jiden cut him short.

"One man can go undetected, not a squad, good Knight. Besides, this is *my* mistake to put right, you will do as we discussed!" With that he was gone, a white billowing tail trailing out behind his giant stallion. Sir Galland was having a time trying to console his twisting stomach. Both his charges were gone, out of his sight, and he was left to worry after them, and his Callana. Still, he was an obedient knight, true to his place and he had a direct order to follow. He turned crossly to the remainder of his party.

"Well, you heard the prince! Find a secure location far off the road to make camp."

....

Deep into the middle of the following chilly day, Jiden still climbed, having had to leave his trusted mount when the earthen mountain had turned to sheer rock. Once close to the top, he started his sideways scaling, tearing his arms and back as he pushed through snagging thorn bushes growing between the sleek rocks along his way to the southern end of the great mountain. The sun was blazing down on him, burning into his exposed head, while the rest of him remained chilled by the flurry of the cold winter air. In a few hours, the guard would change over, the oncoming returning with Callana, he had surmised as much at least, the evening before when he had been let in and out by two separate sets of guards. The second had brought in Callana, who, from the looks of her the day before, was being submitted to daily humiliation in the stocks; He needed to be in place for that moment and that meant he had to push on, though his muscles and stomach protested angrily. Jiden's trained body moved him forward as his mind spun; shooting off on different tangents of thought, trying desperately to focus. He had all but convinced himself that having her back again would right all the wrongs. His heart was tearing between his love for her and the sting of her betrayal as he scrambled slightly westward towards the dingy prison, all the while trying to force the images of her crying face out of his burdened mind.

....

"Miala!" Hellena pulled the shivering form into the heat of the Stone's throw's large hearth. Miala had been crying, her nose and eyes red and sore, and her lips had split from her wind blown ride. Christopher immediately rushed to secure an anxious George in the small stable while Crystalline wrapped the tiny girl in a woolen blanket. Hellena sat her on the bench to fill her with hot soup.

"Something terrible has happened!" Miala chattered, her teeth clinking the words out to the puzzled red headed woman.

"You mean Rogala? How did you know love?" It was Miala's turn to look quizzically now, creasing her brow as she spoke.

"No, *Rogala*? I was talking about...what? What happened to *Rogala*?" Hellena nodded to Caran, who turned to retrieve Nia from the back bedroom, aglow with its fires light. Nia emerged, carrying a delicately swathed form. Miala's breath caught in her throat as tears began welling in her eyes. Nia gently placed the dark skinned baby in the young girl's waiting arms. Miala nuzzled him, his tiny hand reaching up to grip her cold nose.

"Oh, he is perfect! He has his mother's eyes!" Miala suddenly remembered what Hellena had said.

"What has happened?" She asked the circle of sunset eyes peering wearily down at her. Cella sighed, looking to her mother for permission to speak.

"Miala, Rogala is, unconscious, the pain of the birth was too much for her. She has been asleep for days now." Miala looked back down at the cooing little boy, blissfully unaware of his mother's anguish to bring him into this world. Tears spilled, splashing on his blanket as she rocked him gently, hoping soothing him would ease her own breaking heart.

"Miala, darling, what were you saying? Has something happened with Callana? Why did she not return with you?" Hellena was pressing, terrified for her own baby now. Miala shook her head before forcing herself to look around the room, making eye contact with every pair of reddened, tearing eyes as she filled them in on their beloved false princess's terrible fate.

Out side, only moments behind his quarry, Nicholas pulled his sweating chestnut to a stop, watching from the forest beyond the crossroads as a tall, young man, was leading a now rider less George into a stable.

"Stone's throw Inn? She rushed off to seek *shelter*?" Nicholas asked his mount. The horse only snorted a cloud of exhausted breath in response.

....

"Tavern, tavern, that's all you talk about; well, cottar, we gots no money for no tavern so put a cork in it!" A dirty, large guard sat at a rickety wooden table, talking to another guard Jiden couldn't quite see from his hiding place in the thick, dark of the trees and brush only paces from the prison doors. He was cursing himself internally; sure he must have missed the exchange, when from the exposed edge of the outer rock side of the structure, limped Callana with her two sizeable escorts. She was covered in rotting food; clothing in even worse condition than the day before, her hair was a red clot stuck to her ruined cape. Jiden felt a pang of guilt upon seeing her, but forced it out of his mind. He needed to concentrate if this was to work. He was no match for four, and although two were only slightly less daunting, it was the best odds he was going to see; he had to wait for the first watch to be long out of earshot.

"Here, you lock her up, she stinks to high heaven!" The new shift pushed Callana forward, her weakened legs stumbling, as she collided, hands bound behind her, into the barrel chest of another complaining guard.

"Ugh, my stomach! I think I am going to be sick, take her take her!" The un- seen guard grabbed the discarded prisoner, pulling her hair back out of her face and using his large body to force her into the far wall. A fiery anger sprang up in Jiden upon seeing her swollen eye and split lip. The guard pressing into her leaned forward, licking her cheek.

"I like my women *dirty*," he breathed into her face, his hands traveling down her body. He forced a hand between her legs. Jiden stirred, anxiously snorting from his helpless location. His mind was screaming! Just as he felt his control breaking, Callana jerked, her knee meeting genitals, buckling the hefty guard instantly. He groaned out as the three others spewed a roaring round of laughter. Once recovered, the humiliated man stood and back handed Callana across her face, the sound bouncing off the walls around her, infuriating her watching prince.

"Whore!" He grabbed her arm and jammed her into her cell, clanging the door shut. The chortling crew exchanged keys, and the relieved pair left, apparently heading for a drink. Jiden sighed; glad to see her torture over for now, a new flaring determination filling him, pouring strength into his depleted muscles and staying his throbbing stomach.

"Tough to watch, isn't it prince?" Jiden jumped at the sound; spinning in search of his invisible audience.

"What are you doing here?" Jiden growled, recognizing the shadowed face of Sir Erik. The beaten man came forward, the dim beams allowed to penetrate the evergreen pines shone on the bruised jaw and swollen nose, compliments of Jiden himself. Erik was grim faced, almost sorrowful.

"I have been watching for a while, they have not been kind to your lover."

"I told you I didn't need *your* help!"

"I am doing this for *her*, not you, ass. She is to be hung at dawn, King Bromell insisted, for fear you would return with your army and force her release."

"You *know* this?" Jiden asked. The snide tone had all but vanished from his voice as fear crept back into his heart. Erik nodded.

"Heard the two talking this morning, when they came down to..." Erik stopped. Jiden grimaced angrily.

"What? They came down to what?" He pressed.

Erik sighed.

"They have not been... *civilized* to her, is all..." Erik resigned to keep quiet about Callana's graphic rape, as the young prince was teetering on the edge of madness as it was.

"This ends now, we must rescue her." Jiden turned, clinging to his tree like a giant cat, leaning to watch the one visible guard, playing cards with his unseen partner. Erik nodded, coming to Jiden's side.

"Right! So? What's the plan?" He whispered.

"I am going to distract the guards, drawing one outside, incapacitating him, his absence drawing the other out, and than we just have to grab those keys and release her!" Jiden pointed excitedly to the keys hanging off the discarded belt near the guard's feet. Erik nodded again, looking to Jiden.

"Sounds good. How are you going to distract them?"

"I am going to throw rocks!" Jiden was hyper now, having put entirely too much blind faith into his ill formulated plan. Erik shook his head.

"Ah...prince...." But it was too late. Jiden tossed a rock, hitting the side of the prison's outer wall. The guard nearest the door turned slightly, eventually shrugging off the noise. Jiden moved to the cover of another sticky pine, tossing a larger rock, this time hitting the door.

"That got him!" Jiden grinned hysterically. Erik was worried now, fully aware of the guard's superior size and his new comrade's delusional state. The massive man moved to the door, followed closely by his bulky companion. Erik moved to stop Jiden from throwing another rock, but the excited prince released it as he reached for his arm. The rock pinged off the guard's head this time; his snarling face turning in the direction of his invisible attacker. Daylight broke through close to Jiden's moving arm as he reached for another rock. Erik flinched, realizing the guard's eyes caught Jiden's movement, and now the giant man was charging towards the tree. Jiden jumped to meet the big man, ducking at the last minute to avoid his grabbing arms. He spun the large man around, punching him square in the jaw, frowning when the monstrous man only grinned in response. Jiden turned to move out of his reach, running smack into the chest of the other guard. Jiden dipped, dropping to the ground as the two both swung, their powerful fists striking each other in unison. Jiden crouched between as the two large men wavered and fell like a mighty tree splitting down the middle, each half slamming to the ground. Jiden stood, dashing for the small stone building. Once inside, he found the cell was empty and turned back in time to see Erik signaling from the forest with Callana in tow. With no time for tearful reunions, Jiden joined Callana and her once accuser and the three tore through the brush, ripping tunics and slicing skin as they plunged deeper into the woods to begin the arduous climb to tenuous salvation.

Hellena went to answer the knock at the door, muttering to herself.
"Who could that be at this hour?" She opened the door to a handsome young blonde.
"Good evening love, what can I do for you?" She was trying her best at hospitality, though her mind was in shock over her Callana.
"Good evening, good lady," Nicholas begun, bowing, somewhat in amazement over this woman's resemblance to Callana.
"I...ah...I am prince Nicholas of Adalonia," Hellena's wide eyes squeezed into a squint.
"Ha! *Prince*! *You* and your cousin, *Jiden*, leaving my daughter to die! And for what!?" Nicholas was agape, not sure of what to say to this obviously irate mother. Hellena yanked him inside, slamming the door behind him; the sound drawing out four other Callana look a likes, a tiny older blonde and a disheveled Miala.
"Nicholas! You followed me?" Miala crossed her arms angrily over her chest.
"I... wait! I thought you....you..." Nicholas was confused.
"You what? You tell your mighty King Odin to have my daughter released on princess Rogala's orders!" Hellena commanded furiously, backing Nicholas into the closed door. What was it with small, angry women lately?
"Wait! Don't kill him!" Cella roared. The horde of women turned to her; visibly disappointed their apparent execution was halted.
"Kkkkill...Kill me?" Nicholas squirmed. Cella brought the wooden frame forward and held it in front of him.
"Recognize this?" She demanded more than asked. Nicholas nodded warily.
"Of course, it is the royal seal of the original Della Verde Valley...where...where did you get it?" Nicholas asked tentatively. Cella nodded to her mother, and the group of dogged woman surrounded the intimidated prince, forcing him to the dinning table, where they proceeded to feed him, fill him with drink and finally, impart the mirror's possible history and how *he* was going to verify it to free Callana at once.

Callana's mind was numb. She was only vaguely aware that her brain was sending signals to her legs and arms to lift, grab, lower, release, but she could not *feel* her body responding. Her hands and forearms were shredded raw from the prickly brush reaching out between the rocks, as she climbed her way east, to an unknown destination. Jiden was leading her, turning a concerned face to check on her progress incessantly; while Erik was behind her, using reassuring words to motivate her upwards and onwards. Her heart was aching inside her chest, sorrow surging out of it to infect her very soul. Jiden had rescued her, yes, but he would never love her again, and how could she expect him to? She tricked him into an engagement, no matter the fact that she fully intended to serve proudly her attained rank and new city, he could only suspect her of attempting to usurp; had the marriage gone through, she could claim Adalonia and Rogadon for herself and the promotion of her own line. To tell him she only meant to become *someone*, to better her station, would be useless, for she would have to give up her dear friends' to prove as much. She was dizzy from her lack of food, rest and relentless worrying. The only thing she was sure of was her undying love for a man who now despised and mistrusted her. Callana felt herself shutting down, her unfeeling limbs grasping at ledges her painfully frozen fingers were too weak to grab. Callana's swollen eye was throbbing mercilessly, the thudding nauseating her, churning the bubbling acid in her empty stomach. She felt a cold sweat break out on the back of her neck, her head spun as the feeling swirled to the crown of her head. Jiden was anxious to keep moving, having no idea how long it would be before the guards would awaken and sound the alarm, but Callana's appearance had him very distressed. She had visibly paled, even more so than when they had first rescued her, and her breathing was labored and ragged.

Jiden glanced ahead. There was a break in the rocks, only a deep split in an enormous boulder, but it would do. Jiden signaled to the closely following Erik, and the three slowly edged in, huddling into the crevice, mercifully escaping the frosty wind.

"She does not look well," Jiden tried his best to sound as if he was making a mere observation, but a crack in his voice gave away his exhausting concern. Erik took a sideways glance at the collapsed red head, heaving against the deepest wall of their rocky shelter, her eyes closed, mouth open, hands and arms covered in blood. She was strong to endure the punishment of this climb, as well as the torture during her short but violent stay in that vile prison, but she was exhausted, in every aspect of the word. So much more than her *physical* fortitude had been tried as of late. Erik felt a fresh surge of guilt wash over him as he sank back out of the wind, grateful for the rest for Callana *and* himself. He was having a hard time keeping up with the lithe young prince, and his lungs were protesting the bitter cold air. He coughed loudly, rousing his new comrade out of a deep trance of thought. Jiden was grimacing, hungry and tired, but desperate to push on to the safety of camp and then home. He glanced over his shoulder at Callana, curled in a fetal position, snoring into her shivering arm. She needed rest, *real* rest, warm, bathed, fed, and safe; would she ever know such things again as safety and comfort? How long could he keep her in Adalonia before her sentencers would follow and find her? He ached to hold her, than cursed himself for his weakness. She had *deceived* him, although, he as of yet did not know her motives, she had herself admitted to her crimes. How much of herself did she pretend and which aspects were her own? Was he a fool to still love her? Still care for her? His mind was reeling through memories of shared time with her; the ride to Green Mountain falls, archery practices filled with laughter and friendly competition; the warm, fire lit room in the Inn. Her beautiful naked body, porcelain, glowing skin, the inviting look on her face, and her eyes; they had been so deep, so dark, and so full of desire. He grunted, shaking his head as if he could loosen the memory and empty it out of his frozen ears. They had made love, yes, but was it nothing more than a strategic act to further *delude* him? Securing his heart by quenching his lust? She was a prostitute, after all, and would know that men could easily be led by their urges, especially a virgin. How had she imitated the innocence of that night? She had appeared so vulnerable, almost surprised even, by her own orgasm. Could such a thing be *practiced*?

"She needs to eat and..." Erik started, but Jiden's anger had flared with his thoughts.

"What do *you* care? Because of *you*, she has been sentenced to death! It's your fault we are on the run in the first place!" Jiden snapped, snarling the words through gritted teeth. Erik recoiled, but recovered quickly.

"What do *I* care? What about you, your *majesty*! You were awfully quick to turn on your *lover* weren't you?"

"Says her first customer!"

"Is that what bothers you? Disappointed you weren't her first, *virgin*?" Erik was grinning now, playing off Jiden's possessiveness for Callana. Jiden felt a jolt of rage he was unable to control, causing him to lunge from his crouched position, smashing into Erik and pressing him to the rock wall behind him. A loud, forced groan escaped the older man.

"Come now, oh mighty prince, is that all you've got?" Erik jeered Jiden on, antagonizing him, smiling although he was clearly in pain. Jiden pushed off of him, heaving as though his heart might pound through his chest. He put his hands up, ashamed of his own lack of restraint.

"Forgive me, knight, I let my anger get the best of me," Jiden earnestly regretted his outburst. He was supposed to be a leader, an example of good and honor, not some jealous *child* throwing a tantrum! His shame was all over him; his head hung down, his shoulders slumped, he was humiliated by his own actions. Erik scoffed, shaking his head.

"You surprise me prince," He laughed. Jiden was confused by the knight's reaction.

"You are a *knight*, why does it surprise you that I should apologize for behavior unbecoming of a future king?" Jiden crossed his arms, furrowing his brow as he looked down at the now kneeling knight.

"You apologize to the man who has inadvertently condemned your own *wife?*" Erik shrugged. Jiden glared at him now.

"She is not my *wife.* I can not possibly marry her now, now that she has...such a... *past!*" He pointed an aggravated finger towards Callana as he spoke. It was Erik's turn to puzzle now.

"*You can not marry her now?*" Erik mocked sarcastically. Callana stirred, her snoring quieted. Erik noticed, but in his angst, Jiden did not.

"Of course I can not marry her! Dolt! Marry a prostitute? *Me?* The direct descendent of Triden? The original ruler of the Della Verde? Are you mad?" Erik's smile faded as he straightened to speak.

"So you do not love her anymore, ey?" He sighed.

"*Love* does not matter, you well know that! Our marriage, *my* marriage to the princess of Rogadon was arranged to join our two kingdoms, nothing more. Love has *nothing* to do with marriage when you are a prince." Jiden's voice had softened as he spoke, looking out over the darkening landscape below.

"You did not answer my question," Erik's grey eyes gleamed with his mischievous goading. Jiden sighed, turning to look back at the crumpled form of his sleeping Callana.

"It matters not, Sir Erik." Jiden's face was defeated. Erik turned to gaze out into the deep blue of the early evening sky.

"Aye, suppose not."

The two men sat in silence as black night devoured all of the pink dusk from the sky. A low cloud cover was blowing in from the south on the blustering wind that had plagued the entirety of their climb; its puffy outline reflecting the bright light of the new moon.

"My men wait, not more than a few hours away now. We should cross the road under cover of dark," Jiden suggested from his sitting position opposite Erik's. The un-shaven knight nodded.

"We could give her an hour to sleep than push on?" Erik offered. Jiden nodded his acceptance. They would be moving down the back side of Lisia; he recognized their position and remembered it to be less than a hundred paces till the sleek rock turned to hardened earth, hopefully making the descent a bit easier. Sir Galland would have a lookout, invisible to the road's travelers and patrols; Jiden would be spotted and led to camp where Callana would be warm and safe. He, Sir Franklin and Sir Laden, all tremendous hunters, could do some short distance hunting for fresh meat, for the men's dried pork, fig and bread supplies would no doubt be dwindling by now. Once under the protection of his guard, Jiden could concentrate on getting home and stalling Callana's sentence long enough to find a way to rescind it.

Both men sat in silent contemplation, minutes turning to an hour, until Jiden cleared his throat to announce the moment for departure had come. He turned to crawl in to gently rub her frigid arm to wake Callana.

"Callana? We must move on. You awake lo...you awake?" Jiden hoped his slip of the tongue had gone un-noticed but it had not. Callana had been awake for most of the two men's conversation anyways, and was fully aware that Jiden would no longer entertain any feelings of love for her; only pity and disdain. She sat slowly, moonlight illuminating the hair stuck to the side of her face, and welling red eyes as she nodded to Jiden. Behind him she could see the eerie blue light, glowing off the crouched profile of Erik, and she winced under his piteous gaze. Callana flinched when Jiden reached to help her. Jiden pulled the offending hand back, unsure of what he had done to frighten her.

"Not far now, we should reach the camp before long," Jiden assured her, his voice soothing and low, as if comforting a crying child. A thoroughly irritated Callana pushed passed him to follow Erik out to begin their slow descent. Jiden reached for her arm but she pulled away.

"What's the matter? Are you injured?" He asked anxiously, his voice only slightly louder than a whisper.

"Immensely! But a royal *prince* such as you should not worry his *noble* head about a *whore* like me!" Jiden balked back from her scathing retort. He had no experience with relationships, and a purely theoretical understanding of women's emotions, therefore Callana's apparent offense was a complete mystery to the baffled young man. Callana had turned back to her descent, leaving Jiden to slink into his place behind her, frowning in his desperate attempt to decipher her behavior.

"You are cross with *me*? I...I do not understand," Jiden stammered, following the mass of red hair, clumped with mud and food.

"Evidently," Erik laughed out hoarsely, entertained by the couple's spat.

"Callana, what did,·" Callana cut Jiden short, turning to face him, resentment flashing in her dark, moonlit eyes.

"My feelings are no concern of yours, *Jiden*, nor is my past, which you know nothing about!" She barked. His worried brow turning up as his confusion changed to exasperation.

"The blame falls to *me*?" Callana turned, ignoring Jiden's question. The rocky wall had given way to steep, soft ground now. Erik had disappeared into the black cover of a grove of trees, slanted towards the road ahead. Jiden reached for Callana's swinging hand, turning her around to face him.

"Let off!" Callana tried to wriggle her raw wrist free but Jiden's thick fingers clamped down, nearly buckling her.

"You are hurting me!"

"Than stop fighting me!" Jiden demanded. Callana stilled, tears spilling out when she lifted her face to him. Jiden's heart throbbed, aching to be the one to bring her comfort, instead of grief.

"I..." Jiden tried to sound forceful, but his voice faltered. Callana's jaw tightened as she spoke.

"Why did you rescue me?" She demanded. Jiden grimaced; appalled by the question he thought had a clear answer.

"I..." Callana cut him off, yanking her arm free.

"You *pitied* me, is that right?" Her arms were crossed now, her stance obstinate. Jiden shook his head.

"I did not think you deserved to die," he tried but Callana cut him off again.

"What do I *deserve*, mighty, all knowing *prince* Jiden?" Callana's tone was antagonistic. Jiden was furiously confused now.

"To live...wait, how did *rescuing* you make me your enemy?"

"Precisely the same way *loving* you has made me yours!" She sniped.

"You *lied* to me! Did you not?" Jiden had reached his boiling point and he gave in to his rage.

"You lied! You offered yourself to me as a false princess! Nothing about you was real was it?" He accused.

"*Everything* I said and *everything* I did was *real*," Callana protested but Jiden stepped closer to look down in her face, his fierce green eyes cutting her answer short.

"You *played* your role, and made me your *fool*! You had me believing you were my *own, virtuous, princess wife to be,* but you are none of those!" Jiden's hand sliced the air, putting fervent emphasis on his words. Callana burned with humiliation over his supposition.

"I was never a princess, no, but I was... *virtuous*....before you," her voice had quieted, her eyes darting around to make sure no one was near to hear her talk of their intimacy. Jiden threw his head back and laughed.

"Ha! Lied the self admitted prostitute in the company of her very first patron!" Jiden's arm flailed out, gesturing in the direction of the shadowed woods Erik had evaporated into only moments before. Callana turned, following his pointed finger, realization dawning on her of Jiden's misconstrued conclusion.

"Jiden," She took a tentative step towards him, but anger had taken over, and he stepped back.

"Do *not* address me common!" He snarled. Callana flinched at his bitter tone.

"Forgive me, *prince* Jiden, I only wanted to assure you my... virginity...-"

"Is not my concern, as you most astutely pointed out. Now if you are done wasting my time with your make-believe, I suggest we move on!" Without waiting for her response, Jiden stalked passed her, into the dark woods, leaving Callana demoralized and severely frustrated. She took a moment, not quite sure if being hung could possibly be any worse than enduring that excruciating look of contempt on Jiden's face. However, she finally turned to follow, her aching heart still clinging to the hope that Jiden would one day hear her reasons and forgive her, even if never to *love* her again. Erik was waiting in the dark when she crossed into the cluster of evergreens.

"This way," he called. She numbly followed his deep voice, only slightly interested in finding Jiden's knights, once her dear friends, who now undoubtedly harbored ill will towards her for her treachery, just as their prince did. Erik reached to take her hand, leading her in between the trees and around the squat thickets. He knew she was crying, and he knew why, having over heard as he sat in wait for them in the shadows. Jiden had mumbled something about going ahead to signal his guard, but Erik knew better.

"It will be well again, soon as we get you to Adalonia, love. Odin is a fair king; he will not allow Bromell to hurt you anymore," Erik's voice was soothing. Callana knew he was trying to make her feel better, but all she could do was sniffle in response. Her tears were burning hot, uncontrollably pouring down her wind stung, chilled cheeks. He stopped just short of the clearing for the main road, the hard packed red earth glowing eerily in the moon's unearthly bluish beams.

"Callana," Erik turned to her, cupping one cheek in his hand.

"He is *young* and prideful; do not take his words to heart. It will take time for him to heal. You must be patient, right?" Callana nodded, awkwardly, unsure of how to respond to her once accuser's moment of compassion.

"*Hate to interrupt*," Jiden blurted out, startling both Erik and Callana, who immediately separated.

"Do not be *jealous*, my lord, I was merely comforting the down hearted young woman, nothing more." Erik grinned, enormously happy with his affect on the young prince. Jiden crossed his arms over his chest widening the stance of his legs.

"I have nothing to be *jealous* over, knight. I merely wanted to inform you both that I have been signaled. We need to move," with that, Jiden shot Callana a scathing look, before turning back to the road. Callana's heart sagged with shame. Not only did he think she had been a *practicing* prostitute, but he assumed she had actually *slept* with Erik, and now he would not even hear her explanation! She slumped after the two, crossing into the glow of the illuminated road.

Jiden was moving with such determination, Callana started to wonder how he knew which way to go. His direction changed, than again. She strained to see, but could not determine any visual signals. She noticed, however that his hands felt up and down each fur tree he passed. She watched him, than mocked his movements, placing her hand in the exact spots where he had had his. That's when she felt it! One miniscule line had been cut into the fur's smooth bark, slanting slightly upwards and forward, leaving an almost invisible trail to the unknowing eye, but a trail you could *feel* nonetheless. Callana gasped at her discovery. It was a most ingenious marker!

"We must leave, I ...ah...am terribly sorry..." Nicholas stammered through his apology. Hellena grabbed him, pulling him close to her in a warm embrace, smashing him into her generous bosom. Nia, Caran, Cylan and Crystalline did the same, but Cella had her arms crossed. She was surveying him, scrutinizing him from across the room, and apparently coming up disappointed in what she saw. Nicholas frowned, unsure of himself under her penetrating glare.

"Now Cella, he has agreed to help your sister. We must trust in him love," Hellena soothingly stroked the stubborn girl's shoulder as she spoke, carefully removing the wooden frame and wrapped letters so she could hand them to Miala.

"Miala, you will see him through this, you swear?" Cella was trying her best to appear aloof towards Nicholas, but he could see the fear behind her lovely light orange eyes. Miala nodded, tearing up, already missing her new family.

"Please, Cella, everyone, I have every intention of helping Callana. She has become a dear friend to me, and I know Jiden will stop at nothing to save her life." Nicholas was addressing the room, but his eyes never left Cella's. He was determined to see her comforted before he walked out holding their family's entire legacy in his hands. Cella wavered, than nodded, shaking his hand firmly, as a knight would.

"I believe you, young prince. But, please hurry. She does not deserve to sit in prison," Cella urged the two out of the door. Miala ran to the back bedroom, kissing the sleeping Renk, Rogala and their still un-named baby boy. She could not bear to leave them, but she could never live with herself if she did not personally see to it that every effort to save Callana had been tried. Christopher had fed, watered, curried and saddled the two nervously prancing horses. Their instincts told them there was trouble, and the absence of George's loyal rider made him edgy. Miala dreaded riding the giant purple monster, but she knew that riding double on Nicholas's chestnut would slow them down, and time was of the essence. The pair mounted, turning to wave once more. Tears streamed down Miala's delicate face as she pulled her scrounged, rabbit fur lined green cape tight around her against the frost of the evening and set off after Nicholas and his long legged chestnut. The pair thundered down the road at top speed, to reach Adalonia by mid day next day, God willing. Nia turned to her baby responsibilities; she had a few blessed moments of reassurance these the last few days, as Rogala had woken and fed, always during her bath, and then fell to sleep just as suddenly. It was a small victory, but it was enough to keep the worried mother in hopeful spirits.

The rest of the girls returned to their knitting and mending, what ever they could do to take their minds off their sorrow for their captive sister. Christopher went about tending the fires, the way he did every evening before kissing Crystalline and heading home. Hellena began her nightly busy work as well; sorting herbs, preparing a broth for the event of Rogala's next awakening, clean up, heating bath water for the house hold, and praying vehemently for her missing angel.

"Lord, please watch over my bird, keep her safe and bring her back to me, amen..."

....

"You *idiots*!" King Bromell was boiling with his contempt for the two completely inept guards who had lost their small charge. The pair shuffled their feet impatiently, unsettled by this minor king's assumed authority over them. King Ulei shook his head, only slightly discouraged, squeezing the top of his large, noble nose to stop his headache; for he had lost any interest to see her dead, alive or at all, nor to hear Bromell's whining about it. It was a formality that he had even jailed her. *He* was king of Dellandore, not Bromell, and if he had said so, she could have received lashings in the town square, or immediate banishment, but he did not see her crime as punishable by *death*. Ulei was fully aware of the apparently powerless man's incentive for desiring the young girl's demise; Rogala had fled from him, from her own city, to avoid this marriage that Bromell so badly needed to secure his failing kingdom. With no heir of his own, no doubt due to his unfortunately, and recently demonstrated impotency, his kingdom was assuredly to be over run and confiscated by the first aspiring king to learn of these fateful truths. King Ulei grinned maliciously as Bromell turned angrily to face him.
"You stand there smiling? While the whore runs free? Undoubtedly to the safe harbor of Adalonia and her taken King Odin?" Bromell was leaning hard on his walking cane, his rage shivering through his frail body.
"I stand here smiling, because her escape, disappointing as it may be," He shot a harsh look at the two enormous men and their matching blackened eyes as he spoke.
"Is *your* problem, not mine, *king* Bromell." King Ulei spat out the title, making known his distaste for the weaker king. Bromell swallowed hard, suddenly aware that enlisting this powerful man as aid in his personal war against Rogala, and her puppet, Callana, also made known to the mighty king, all of Rogadon's defenselessness. Bromell's army had all but evaporated with his noble brother King Granlund's murder and the city's following collapse had left it half as potent as before. King Ulei had ample coin to buy Bromell's subjects, army, castle and lands, and Bromell welled with the fear of his realization.

"We had a deal! The girl was to die for her treachery and later be connected to Rogala's death! You will receive full credit for her capture and execution! Adalonia would have no choice but to grant me a division of their army to protect Rogadon from any other kingdom's attack!" King Bromell was nearly blubbering now, horror distorting his face as his ex-confidant drew a crooked dagger from his belt.

"With your blood, I shall forge a *new* deal with Adalonia. See you in Hell, *king* Bromell!" Ulei pushed his blade through Bromell's heart, deftly, ending his abysmal life while mercilessly smiling down at the dying man, winking as the last flicker of life filled than drained from widened, fearful eyes.

....

Hours of following fleeting glimpses of her former betrothed and her dark haired once adversary, breaking through low hanging limbs, tangling in spiky thorn bushes, and tripping over fallen oaks, proved to be too much for Callana, as her body begged to collapse. She was determined to prove herself laudable, however impossible it seemed and willed her legs to keep moving. If Jiden wanted to see the *real* her, he was going to see her for all she was worth! She would not let anything break her again, not like that terribly wicked king Ulei had done. Oh how she boiled with hatred for that man! How he had taken her, repeatedly, his own royal guard holding her down! She had cried out, even screamed! But no one came for her, and her protest and struggling had only excited the perverted *dog*. The disgusting king Bromell had only watched on in sickening wait, but had failed to rise for his turn. Apparently he was incapable, his humiliation witnessed by all, he had returned his fury on Callana; beating her and cursing her until he had drained all the anger from his system. She hated them both. Hated them furiously! Fuming as she absently followed Erik through the forest, she had not noticed the warm glow not far ahead.

Callana's ears alerted her long before her eyes recognized the band of knights around the welcoming fire. Oh! She wanted to dance with elation over the end of this very arduous escape. Her happiness faded however as she neared the ring of men, who quieted upon sight of her. Sir Galland, Sir Gracien, Sir Franklin, Sir Laden, Sir Lashend, Sir Kern, Sir Senren, Sir Ren Sir David and Edward; they were all there, Jiden now among them, staring at her, as if she had fallen out of the sky! She lowered her tear stained dirty face, shame welling up in her, threatening to spill out of her heavy lidded eyes. They did not want her with them; she was below them, as a wretch. A low, crawling creature they only loathed now.

Erik stood next to her, unsure of his welcome in the midst of these men as well. Callana knew how she must appear; covered in blood, rotting food, and dirt. Clothes torn and filthy, hair matted and frazzled; face swollen and split, she could feel them examining her. After a few crawling moments of awkward silence, Sir Galland finally spoke.

"Callana," he boomed, forcing her to lift her eyes to him, terrified to see hatred burning in his. She was surprised to see something else.

"Do not fear, love, you are *still* among friends," as the big man came towards her, the circle of knights called out.

"Aye!"

Sir Galland lifted her, embracing her tightly, her feet dangling a foot off the ground. Callana squeezed his neck with her frail arms, fully aware of how fortunate she was to have retained her friends, if not her love.

"Oh Sir Galland! I was afraid you would detest me as well!" She cried into his neck. He pulled back, gently placing her on the ground, flashing a concerned frown on her.

"*As well?* Who here *hates* you, love?" Callana shot a quick look passed Sir Galland's left shoulder at the now glaring Jiden, than looked back down at her feet. Sir Galland followed her look, than turned back to her. Jiden had turned his back to them, shaking hands with Sir David and doing his best to appear nonchalant.

"I only meant...thought, perhaps you *all* did," Callana's voice was quiet, and delicate, striking to the core of the big, gentle knight. He pulled her close, kneeling to look up to her.

"He is wounded..." The expressive golden eyes flashed towards Jiden, then back to Callana. His voice was hushed.

"And a bit spoiled, if truth be told." He smiled and winked as he spoke, consoling Callana, as only her father used to be able to do.

"I know you are *good*, my little archer, and he will see in time. Chin up, ey?" She smiled down at him, and then knelt to kiss his prickly cheek.

"I love you Sir Galland! You are a most noble friend," She said. The giant man stood and grinned down at her.

"You smell a bit like Senren, love," He whispered, pinching his nose in protest. She grinned sheepishly down at her feet.

"What was that?" Senren asked, hearing his name.

"Seems there was an awful lot of rotten food to throw in Dellandore," she shrugged. Sir Galland laughed.

"First things first," he grinned.

....

An hour later, Callana had stuffed her gut with bread, cheese and almost a cauldron full of water from the nearby creek that wound its way towards Lake Ceruleana, and Sir Galland had graciously boiled a large cauldron of water and added mint leaves for her to wash with. Sir Laden and Sir Ren had obediently stood, backs to Callana, holding their capes out to shield her from view, so she could thoroughly scrub her whole self, including dunking her hair and running her fingers through, donning the gracious Sir Lashend's extra rabbit fur-lined tunic and pair of leggings. She felt full, clean and rejuvenated; thoroughly scrubbing away her horrific prison experience, shoving it to the back of her weary mind. She now felt warm and welcomed, by all, save for one. Thankfully, Jiden had convinced the rest to trust Erik based on his assistance in her rescue, and the now nourished knight was sitting on a fallen oak, regaling his friendly audience of his numerous female conquests. Callana smiled at the sight; her Adalonia family, and her new found friend, sharing a fire. She casually glanced around to find Jiden, glowering over the fire at her, obviously assuming she was admiring Sir Erik. She could not contemplate how he could be so envious of her affections for anyone else when he did not want her for his own! She had never been involved, never seen a man in *love* before Jiden, and it was proving difficult to determine if what he *said* was what he *meant*. She pulled her eyes away from his, turning back towards the group and Erik's tales.

Jiden sighed, exhausted to his core with this entire affair. He had loved her, he was sure of it! It was so strong, beyond anything he had known before, and it did not fade the morning after their consummation. His father had explained to him once that lust faded with sex, because you obtain all that you had desired, but love remained, even grew, making it all the more appealing to indulge again and again....Jiden turned suddenly, raging into the nearby woods, furious with his ridiculous hormones. Even in the aftermath of her deception he still *wanted* her! Nicholas had been right, albeit, uncharacteristically; Jiden was not a child, and should have known better than to pursue sex with Callana. Everything was so complicated now; but he missed so much more than her tantalizing physical form. He missed talking to her, the honest interest she had in everything he said, and the calming affect her presence *used* to have on him. Jiden slumped to lean on the far side of a thick fur, out of view of his knights, who would most likely just assume he was relieving himself.

Jiden absently tore at the shredded remains of his tunic sleeve as his mind worked. He had no explanation for the un-controllable rage that boiled in him now when he looked at her. He felt jilted and unfairly forced out of his happiness, by her deception. If they had already been married, the problem would have been theirs and theirs alone to deal with. Now, because she had been revealed by the arrogant King Ulei, in view of Dellandore constituents as well as Jiden's own knights, too many people were involved, with deafening voices and opinions for Jiden to heed, when all he wanted was to hear her out, absolve her of her crimes, forgive her and move on with their lives, together. Perhaps it was true; he had felt sorry for her in prison, obviously, for she did not deserve such a fate. Did that make him a terrible man? Was it so demeaning to her that he pitied her, the victim of abuses he had never known?

Jiden shook his head; of course it was belittling! He would not want anyone to assume he was any less of a man just because he was ill-treated or wounded. His stubborn nature was holding him back from apologizing to her and his pride would not let him lower himself to do so. He was, a prince after all, and she was of a low station, even lower than a peasant. Prostitutes were forbidden in Adalonia; although Jiden was sure they were not only practicing in outlying villages but thriving. Look at him, he was a *prince*, heir to a great kingdom, and his physical desires were still threatening to over power *him*! What chance did a common man, a man with out the benefit of years of training and teachings have against such temptations? Worse still, Jiden grimaced as he contemplated, in all of his angst to push her away, all of his prideful condemnation of her, he *still* wanted her, needed her even. And he *still* loved her.

"How long till she is forgiven, your majesty?" The gravely voice of Sir Galland's answer to Jiden's internal conflicts roused him back to awareness. He tried his best smile, though it did not touch his eyes.

"Who? Callana? Oh, well, I ah…see….it's not possible…" Jiden was using his best nonchalant tone, though his stammering was giving his uncertainty away. Sir Galland chuckled, slapping the young man on the back.

"Do you not remember who it is you are speaking with? I was thirteen years old at your *birthing* celebration!"

"I know Sir," Jiden tried but Galland was not done.

"Sixteen when I became a royal knight under your father, and twenty three when Odin assigned me to *your* royal guard; you were only ten! I have seen you and your obnoxious cousin, through every horrendous stage of your adolescent lives, including *this* one!" Galland was slurring slightly, having helped himself to the ale, as did Erik and Senren. Jiden had to laugh; he had the truest of respects for the large, noble knight, and had never been very good at deceiving him. God knows, he and Nicholas had tried and failed numerous times to convince the old knight they were innocent of offenses the big man *knew* all too well, they were guilty of.

"You are one of my very, very, very, very *old* friends," Jiden taunted the big knight. Galland guffawed loudly, stumbling forward to wrap his huge arm around Jiden's shoulders, turning him slowly back to stumble towards the fire.

"I may be drunker than you, so catch up, *than* we can have an *intelligent* conversation!" Galland challenged. The knights laughed loudly, Sir David gladly handing the young prince a jug of ale as Sir Galland forced him onto a stump near the fire. Callana was smiling, carefully avoiding Jiden's eyes, as not to provoke any more aggravated glares. Sir Lashend was standing first watch somewhere close in the darkened, cold woods, and the camp was over two thousand paces from the road, therefore, Jiden could relax and succumb to the affable knight's demands. He took a long swig, his head tilting back, eyes closed, thoroughly enjoying the warmth, spreading down his throat and into his gut, comforting him almost immediately. Enough so that he even found himself laughing along with the others at Erik's anecdotes, filled with obvious but hilarious embellishments. Callana was sandwiched between Sir Ren and Sir Laden, warm and welcome, giggling at the slurring in Sir Galland's speech and Sir Erik's legendary tales. In the orange glow of the fire, she felt herself un-controllably watching Jiden. She was sitting to his left, with Sir Galland and Sir Ren between them, at an angle that allowed her to watch undetected, as Jiden was looking to Erik, who was across from the now visibly affected prince. Jiden glanced sideways, pretending to look for his jug, his eyes stopping on hers. She had been watching him intently, caught in a secret memory. His smile had faded, and he quickly broke eye contact, easily returning to his jovial self, joking and chortling with his men. Callana felt a jealousy eating away at her; a fierce, raw gnawing, something she had yet to experience in her young life. How could he sit there, relaxed, laughing, eyes glowing and warm, so quick to recover, even forget he had once looked to her with the same joyful content? She sighed, excusing herself, and rising to walk into the dark trees. Jiden's eye caught the movement, and he stared after her, causing Sir Erik to turn his fervent attention from the story Sir Ren had begun, to watch her swaying exit. Jiden cleared his throat, bobbing his head towards Callana's backside.

"Wh, Where are you going, Callana?" concern noticeably strained his voice. Callana tossed her hair over her shoulder to turn and answer sarcastically.

"Forgive me, sire, I forgot to get your *royal* permission to urinate, how disobedient of me," She curtsied briefly with mocked reverence, rising and turning quickly, swinging into the shadows, thoroughly antagonizing Jiden into anger, and the knights into drunken laughter. Jiden's jaw clenched, the large vein in his neck rising to the surface of his skin. Erik elbowed Sir Gracien to his right as he goaded the vexed young prince.

"I think she just challenged you mate... Aim high my lord!" The circle erupted again as Jiden stood, wavering, and stumbling out of the fire's light. Sir Galland started a story about catching Nicholas and Jiden peeping on a young castle cook, taking turns standing on each other's backs to gape through her cottage curtains. Jiden frowned, staggering back towards the fire to forbid the tale, but spun too quickly and fell down in the dark.

"Callana? I need to talk to you, you...woman!" Jiden's hand reached out for a tree to help him stand but grasped onto a firm thigh instead. He looked up from his sprawled position on the cold ground, his stupor blurring his vision as he forced his eyes to focus on the small form looking down on him, moon light shimmering off a cascade of silky hair. Jiden smiled; too inebriated to remember momentarily, that he was cross with her.

"So? Talk." She sniped at him, hands on her generously rounded hips. Jiden swallowed, straining to regain his composure, his restraint all but forgotten.

"I...you, you ruined everything, you know that?" He started, gripping her thigh with both hands as he used it to stand. He leaned forward, his hand bracing against the pine behind Callana, holding him in a slanted position to look down at her.

"*You* are drunk," she declared, as if anything he said would be dismissed as rambling. Jiden pointed a finger in her face.

"I am! But it does not mean that I am not meaning what I mean to say, got that?"

"What?" Callana was only half sure of what he was attempting to say and completely sure he was not.

"I said, what I am saying is what I *mean* to say," Jiden furrowed his brow with the obvious effort of concentrating. She sighed.

"You have not said anything, prince," she informed him smugly. Jiden put his hand on her waist, taking her completely by surprise. There was a tingling, rushing out from the point of contact, that spread through her body.

"I still...." Jiden's face was fully illuminated by the moon as he gazed down, dazed, as if only just realizing he was touching her. He moved his hand, slowly, tracing the hollow of her waist, the soft protrusion of her ribs, and the roundness of her breast, and finally to her neck, where he firmly grasped her hair; forcing her head back so he could look directly down into her eyes. She was breathing roughly, taken aback by her own immense arousal, when only moments before she had been livid.

"You still *what?*" She asked, her voice straining against the tension of his tugging hand. Jiden's eyes were fierce, almost animal with his primal need.

"I still..." Jiden blinked his eyes, frowning suddenly. He glanced down at her, pressed up against the tree by the force of his pulling and angrily yanked his hand out of her hair, pushing himself away.

"Nothing, I was just..." Jiden stopped, bereft of explanation for his body's shameless loss of control, staring in horror at his own hand.

"You were just drunk, that's all, right?" Callana finished for him. Jiden's head snapped up towards her, infuriated with her assessment.

"Yes, drunk, that excuses my actions, right? Is that your evaluation of our night at the Inn? We were just drunk?" Jiden sneered. Callana gasped at him.

"I was *not* drunk!" Callana was adamant. Jiden tilted his head to one side, shifting his stance and crossing his arms over his chest.

"About that, you are the expert, how was I, in your professional opinion?" Jiden's antagonistic tone cut Callana as a sharp sword.

"I have no basis for comparison, Jiden, I already told..." Jiden barked over her.

"*Prince!* Prince Jiden! Is it so hard to remember? *My rank* is real, charlatan, I have *earned* it!"

"You did nothing more to earn your precious rank than be born to it!"

"And what did *you* do, Callana, to earn *your* rank? How many did you have before me or was Erik the first?" he scoffed. Callana sprang forward, slapping him across the face. Jiden easily absorbed the force of her slap, a malicious grin spreading across his face.

"*You* were the first! Ignorant prince!" she demanded. Jiden shook his head, his voice seething now.

"I do not believe a word that falls out of your lying mouth," Jiden turned to leave but Callana reached out and grabbed his hand.

"Stop! I am telling you the truth!"

"What is that worth? The truth as told by a lying whore?" Callana was crying now. She shook her head and released his hand.

"I am *no* whore," her voice had quieted, her anger replaced with a throbbing hurt. Jiden watched her surrender, exhaustion wrinkling the corners of her crying eyes. He sighed, the desire to argue extinguished in the face of her defeated tears.

"It pains me to call you such a thing, and I give you my word that I will never call you that again," Jiden's voice was gentle and earnest. Callana, who had now turned her back to him, nodded her acknowledgement, afraid if she spoke she would incite another outburst. Jiden felt suddenly sober, and spent, but he did not want to leave her like this, alone, crying in the dark.

"Callana come back to the fire, you should rest for..." Callana spun and cut him off.

"Yes, I *should* rest. As you wish, of course, my lord," She bowed her head, quickly walking away before he could say anything else. Jiden slammed his fist into the tree. He had come so close to telling her he still loved he. Even now his pride thwarted him.

Jiden waited in the chill of the dark forest, for a few stretching moments of staring into the moon, in desperate search of some answer, some help, to relieve this tremendous pain in his heart. He finally returned to the fire's warmth. He walked back into the middle of Sir Ren's story of Callana killing a giant, man hungry wolf. Although he was sure Erik was the only one *new* to this tale, all eyes were on Ren, bodies leaning in, anxiously hanging on every word. Jiden rolled his eyes. Callana was cuddled in a sleeping roll between the fire and Sir Galland's large, snoring form. She had her back to the knights on the opposite side of the fire with her beautiful red hair splayed out behind her.

"Than, as the wolf sprang to devour her..." Jiden finished for Ren, breaking the circle's concentration.

"Callana wielded *my* mighty dagger, slashing him deftly through his heart as the force of his lunge brought them both crashing to the ground! Hooray Callana! Now turn in, *I* will relieve Lashend," Sir Ren gaped at the prince's snide rendition of his famous story, as did the once avid audience. Jiden stormed off to the look out position, a few hundred paces from camp, to take his two hour watch.

"Aye sire," The knights answered, almost in unison. Erik obediently lay down, happy to be offered a spare sleeping roll next to the blessed warmth of a roaring fire, amongst noble knights such as these. He had never been welcomed wholly by his own knights of Dellandore, due to his reputation for consistently vanishing. It was actually quite nice to be accepted as you were, and, Erik feared, he would miss this when he moved on, eventually. After all, all good things had to come to an end. He closed his weary eyes, stomach full, mind busy, and muscles depleted, he quickly gave in to his exhaustion and fell into a deep, dreamless sleep.

....

Renk was roused out of an unusually restful sleep by the dawn's golden beams. Nia had been dutiful in opening the curtains for this daily occurrence, as it had always been Rogala's preferred way to be awakened. His young son had yet to budge, his pudgy little arms clasped tightly to Rogala's thin, limp hand. Renk kissed the blonde mop sagging against his chest, sighing with his restlessness. Hellena had been so kind, selflessly giving up her extremely comfortable bed for Renk and his tiny family, while she herself was sharing a rather small bed with Cylan. How the guilt was eating away at him, as he lay here, day in and day out, afraid to miss one moment of Rogala's chance awakenings. Today, however, he was aching to move his tingling muscles and patiently waited for his beloved mother in law to make her morning rounds. Nia had already been in once, apparently; the roaring fire evidence of as much. She was a marvelous little woman, Renk mused. How on earth magnificent women such as Nia and Hellena remained unattached was baffling to Renk and proving to be a source of great ache for him as well. He would give anything to see them blessed as he was, albeit undeservedly so. Oh, Rogala, please wake up! *Please* meet our son; Renk closed his eyes with his daily prayer. Right on schedule, as the dawn itself, Nia came in, humming softly.

"Oooo, good morning handsome, and how are you this bright day?" She was always over compensating for their situation with her slightly forced, blissful disposition. Renk smiled at the busy little woman.

"Oh, me? Well, I am doing well, however....I need to move my legs a bit," He gestured for Nia to help, and she compliantly lifted the flaccid form, so Renk could slide out without disturbing her or his son.

"Thank you, mother," He groaned as he reached down to grab his dark brown toes, his joints popping and clicking with the effort. Nia smiled softly down at her new son in law, admiring his dedication to her suffering daughter. When he stood, she reached up to pull his forehead down to her lips. Renk smiled bashfully, kissing her hand as he turned to make his way to his shoes in the main room. Just as he reached them, an excited Christopher burst through the door, the heavy wooden planks swinging inward, slamming into Renk's side, the force knocking him to the floor.

"Ey!" Renk growled. Christopher rushed to help him up, all the while stuttering.

"Dellandore, marching...outside...hundreds!" Crystalline, who had been chopping carrots for stew, threw her suitor a confused glare.

"You did not even knock! What if Rogala had been bathing?" She scolded him, but he was too busy gasping for breath. He pointed to the west side of the room. Renk shook his head, but walked over to part the draperies, suddenly stilling with the sight. Crystalline huffed, stomping over to stand next to both men.

"What's gotten in to the two of..." She stopped short, eyes wide, mouth dropping open at the sight of what looked like a thousand purple caped soldiers, marching towards the Inn from the west, abruptly turning north and east, their pivoting feet twisting in unison, not a hundred feet from the Stone's throw. Hellena emerged from Cylan's bed chamber, slowly walking over to join the stiff frightened trio.

"Oh, Heaven help us!" She caught her breath, her hands covering her mouth in horror. Nia came jogging in now, along with Cylan, Caran and a sleepy Cella.

"What is it mother?" Cella grouched, annoyed at the commotion so early in her day. Cylan, Caran and Cella all joined the onlookers and gasped at the staggering spectacle.

"Who do you suppose they are marching on? This is a declaration of war, right?" Nia asked out loud, although not sure if any one could answer. Renk shook his head, never breaking his gaze from the horrific moving mass.

"They would not dare march on Adalonia's far superior army....do they march on Rogadon?" Cylan deduced.

"It makes sense!" Renk suddenly turned to face Cylan as he spoke.

"If Rogala is missing, and Callana has been found to be false by the knight of Dellandore, than King *Ulei* has discerned that Rogadon has no *heir* and he means to seize the kingdom! He marches on his own *neighbor*! The villain!" Renk was fuming now, having long despised his *own* king, his hatred of his king's weakness came second only to his intense loathing of the womanizing snake, king Ulei. Playing to people's sinful natures to ensnare them, duping them into believing he has their interests in mind, when he only knows selfish and lustful plotting.

"Does Rogadon have a guard? A look out to warn them?" Nia asked. Renk gritted his teeth.

"We *had* many things, but Bromell, the fool, has long lost influence over his knights. I can not be sure if *anything* is as it was when I, *we*, left," Renk glanced towards Hellena's room and his sleeping Rogala. Hellena suddenly swung around to face the dark knight.

"Would Adalonia help? I mean, in light of Callana's, deception…would they *still* come to the aid of Rogadon?"

"Of course, Odin is a great king, a fair king. He will see this as the back stabbing offense it really is and send his army to crush Dellandore! And if I can somehow…."

"Say you are friends of Callana's! Then Adalonia will see King Ulei for the demon he is! Odin would never allow such a king to hang a *hero*! Who had stood in for Rogala to save Rogadon from eminent war!" Hellena finished Renk's thought, growing more and more excited as she spoke. Renk grinned, and then frowned.

"What? No good?" Hellena's brow sagged.

"It's brilliant love! I just…I …" Renk's giant brown eyes glanced in the direction of his wife and son.

"You have my word; we will protect them with our lives!" Nia came to her friend's side to reassure her son in law. Renk nodded, his eyes welling with his fears.

"Aye!" Crystalline barked.

"Aye!" Cella agreed.

"With our lives," added Caran.

"Because we are family," finished Cylan, locking arms with Nia, who in turn locked her arm with Hellena, Hellena with Caran, Caran with Cella, Cella with Crystalline, and Crystalline with Christopher, encircling Renk. The dark man nodded again, turning purposefully to Christopher.

"Ready my horse?" Christopher nodded eagerly and fled the room. Cella turned, placing herself at the front of the group, clapping her hands together.

"Now, Crystalline, pack the knight's foods," Crystalline nodded and hurried away.

"Caran, gather his winter wear," Caran was gone in a moment.

"Mother, you and Nia will attend to Rogala's bath," The two women bowed obediently to the dominating little red head, than rushed to grab cauldrons to fill.

"And you, Cylan," Cella pointed to her remaining subordinate.

"You and I shall go into market to replenish the herbs for Rogala's broth," with that, Cella linked arms with her sister as they collected their fur lined capes and coins, kissing Renk on either cheek as they passed on their way out. Renk was left to dress and quickly devour a small wooden bowl full of porridge. An hour later, he was on the road to Adalonia, and Callana's salvation.

∙∙

Morning's amber rays gently woke the aching prince. Jiden groaned as he rolled onto his tender knees to slowly stand. Climbing the mighty Lisia twice in one day had taken its toll on his joints, and his head was swimming with his slight hang over.

"Here you go," a grinning Laden appeared and handed the prince a steaming bowl of what appeared to be broth. Jiden grimaced at the pain in his elbows as they un-bent to receive the much needed sustenance. Jiden swallowed the hot liquid, reveling in its warmth filling his chest and middle.

"That was perfect! Thank you, good knight," Jiden slammed his head back to dump the remainder of his breakfast down his throat.

"Oh, it weren't me who made it sire, but Callana. She said it has things for makin us all feel good," Laden continued to grin widely, completely unaware of the tension between the two lovers that was so awkwardly obvious to everyone else. Jiden stiffened slightly as Callana appeared from behind a pine tree.

"What kind of *things* are in here, Callana?" Jiden's tone was antagonistic and accusing. Callana glared at him through puffy lidded eyes.

"Do you actually *want* to know or are you just hoping I will say something you can hold against me, *sire?*" Her sarcastic question had the groggy circle of knights looking from one to the other, hanging on every word of the couple's ridiculous spat.

"I am asking, so answer," Jiden growled, scrunching his turned up nose to scowl at Callana, who couldn't help but notice how adorably young he looked when he made that face. She shook her head; determined to retain her stance against him.

"Coltsfoot for the inflammation in your muscles, Chamomile to strengthen your liver and mint for your digestion. Any other questions, *prince?*" She crossed her arms over her chest as she spoke, taking on a tone of irritation.

"Yes, one, how do you know all of those herbs?"

"My mother taught me her knowledge of apothecary, your majesty,"

"So *medicines* are common knowledge among *prostitutes?*" Jiden spat out the last, desperate to get in a scathing remark to set his tone towards her for the day. Callana's eyes watered, stung by his indisputable insult. She dropped her arms and bowed to him.

"Yes, your majesty, thank you for reminding me of my place, I had almost forgotten," She straightened and turned quickly as her red tresses swung out behind in her rush back to the cover of the trees. Jiden shook his head, angry with his childish behavior. He turned to meet eight pairs of mortified eyes.

"Oh she can *nip* at me but *I* am the criminal?" Jiden pointed in the direction Callana had left as he chided; furious his *own* knights shamed him.

"No sire, you are no criminal," Sir Galland retorted, rising from his log and striding out into the woods, quickly followed by Kern, Senren, Lashend,

Laden, Gracien, Erik and Franklin. Sir David was on watch or Jiden was sure he would have stormed off as well. Jiden kicked dirt, splaying a nearby tree with earthen clumps. This was ludicrous! She was *his* to torment, was she not? She had lied to *him*! She had hurt *him*! Why was it that even in her admitted guilt she could make *him* look like the ass? Jiden was furious with his knights, furious with his childish angst, and furious with his heart's loyalty to Callana! But above all, he was furious with the fact that her own accuser, Sir Erik, was able to maintain her *friendship*, while Jiden was detested, as an enemy, and for what? *Rescuing* her? Feeling *sorry* for her? These were the qualities of an *enemy*? Jiden was the victim here, why did they not stand by *him* in his time of need? He was their prince, yet, his own attacker, the very girl who had crushed his heart and threw it in his face, was their charge now? He was frustrated, mentally, physically, and newest and most regrettably, sexually. It was not fair he should be made to carry the blame. Jiden crashed into the forest, determined to put this issue to rest, once and for all. He found her a few hundred paces from camp, alone, splashing cold creek water in her face as she knelt by the water's edge. Jiden cleared his throat, drawing her attention.

She rose slowly, unwilling to be in a disadvantageous crouch while he undoubtedly, degraded her. As she used her borrowed tunic sleeve to dry her face, she was surprised to see the torture in his green eyes as he absently pulled a weed apart while he spoke.

"Callana, please...I gave you my word that I would never call you...*that* again, and I did. I beg you, forgive me?" Callana tilted her head, eyeing him suspiciously. She could not begin to understand his severe change of moods, and it made her dubious of his motives. She nodded slightly, her creamy forehead wrinkled with her confusion.

"*You* are asking *me* to forgive *you*?" She used her delicate finger to point from him to her, as if clarifying to Jiden who he was referring to. Jiden nodded, his eyes still squinted in obvious angst.

"I do not, wait, I mean, I have no... channel ...for the anger and frustration over all that has happened...between us," He explained. Callana relaxed slightly, seeing his earnest effort to put his words in order.

"Ey, go on," she nodded to him. He looked down at his hands for a moment, before turning nervous eyes back to meet hers.

"How would *you* have me...*feel*?" Jiden was reaching out, hoping Callana could release the knotted emotions choking his heart.

"I can not tell you how to feel, sire, I..." Jiden cut her off, stepping closer as he gritted his teeth.

"No, I am not saying *tell* me how to feel, I am saying, how would you...do this?" Callana shook her head.

"*Do* this?" She was thoroughly confused now.

"*Be*, how would you be if I had lied to *you*?" he explained. Callana looked down to the ground shamefully.

"I can not *hurt* you anymore," Jiden started but Callana stopped him abruptly.

"Prince," She began. Jiden shook his head.

"Jiden," he corrected.

"Prince," she continued.

"I think I understand what you are trying to say," Jiden breathed a huge sigh of relief. He was so anxious to have things the way they once were.

"And I want you to know I do not blame you for not loving me anymore," Callana looked up into Jiden's eyes, tears spilling out over her pale cheeks. Jiden frowned again.

"*What?* I was not sayi..." Callana interrupted him, fully sobbing now.

"I was born what I am and you were born what you are and I thought I could raise myself to your level and I was wrong, and I will never forgive myself for hurting you!" Jiden's head reeled. He grabbed her shoulders and shook her.

"I am not asking you to say you are *sorry!*" He said through gritted teeth.

"But I *am* sorry!"

"Damn it Callana! I came here to tell you..."

"Prince Jiden!" Sir Gracien's call interrupted Jiden's explanation. He turned an annoyed glare on his knight. Sir Gracien made a face.

"What is it?" Jiden snapped, reluctantly releasing Callana.

"Forgive me sire, but Sir David has returned from watch with disturbing news. You must come at once!" Jiden nodded, glancing back at Callana. She had turned her back on him, ashamed of her tears.

"Callana, listen..." Callana turned to face him, reddened eyes, swollen from crying, one lid still slightly blue due to previous injury.

"Jiden, if you need me to forgive you, I do. I can not go on like this....fighting with you breaks my heart...." She choked. Jiden reached to put his arms around her shaking form, desperate to make her understand. She shook her head and backed away.

"Please, just go, please Jiden," Callana cried into her hands. Jiden reached for her again, this time interrupted by Sir David.

"Sire, forgive me, but you *need* to see something!" Jiden angrily turned, rushing to follow his knight, his chest tightening with his failed attempt at reconcile with his love. Should have just said *I love you Callana*, he chastised himself while he ran. Simple, self explanatory; *I love you, love me again*, stupid, prideful fool! Jiden rebuked himself until he reached camp where he gaped in shock.

"Where did you find that?" Jiden clenched his teeth as he questioned the stout knight. David pointed to the far off road.

"In the road, sire, when I left my post to check for patrols," Jiden glared down at the muddy green cape, its silver sliver of a moon stained red with blood.

"A knight of Adalonia? Who would be fool enough to travel these woods alone?" Sir Senren asked out loud. Jiden shook his head.

"Nicholas would," he sighed.

"But I fear he was not alone," Jiden finished turning a concerned face to Callana. Realization crossed her face as a shudder of fear rippled her porcelain skin.

....

"You will need to hold still, my dear, or my stitching will be crooked," Lustene had almost choked Miala with a rag soaked in ale, as he heated his needle in preparation of closing her wound.

"This is entirely my fault; I should have had you ride with me! Forgive me Miala?" Nicholas was nervously pacing, his hands going from clenching his sides to pulling his curls as he crossed the room over and over again.

"Sir Nicholas," Miala began, her hazel eyes pleading.

"Nicholas, please," the young prince corrected.

"Nicholas, I will be fine, you heard Lustene," as if in answer, Lustene glanced away from her sliced arm and cheek to shush the agitate man.

"Sire, I need you to quiet yourself, your pacing is breaking my concentration. Would helping calm you down?" Nicholas nodded fervently to his trusted old friend. Lustene pointed to the large boiling cauldron hanging over the fire.

"Please make a goblet of broth for the maiden, just as I say. Are you listening?"

Nicholas had stopped pacing, but was wringing his hands together with all his might. Lustene sighed.

"Sire?"

"Yes, Lustene, as you say, tell me what to do," Nicholas was talking fast, staring into the older man's stern blue eyes, awaiting his command.

"First, throw a few burdock leaves to steep into the water," Nicholas followed the older man's finger, grabbing a handful of the crispy leaves and hurriedly tossing them in the water.

"Wait, what are they for?" Nicholas worried.

"To bring down her slight fever and prevent infection, now, add the ground fenugreek," Lustene began.

"For the *inflammation* of her skin, young prince," he explained when Nicholas turned a concerned expression on him. The young man did as told. Lustene had begun to stitch Miala's cheek now, and she was squeezing her eyes shut against the pain, biting down hard and sucking on her ale cloth. Nicholas was fidgeting again and Lustene continued to instruct him without looking away from his charge.

"Now, the garlic, for taste and also infection," Nicholas found the bottle, and poured generously.

"Finally, for pain, valerian and yarrow," Nicholas sought each label, deftly adding each ingredient and stirring.

"Done," Lustene announced.

"Now what can I do?" Nicholas pleaded. Lustene shook his head.

"Nothing sire, she is all done," The surgeon smiled at the immediate relief that washed over the handsome young prince. Miala sat up, tears stifled, wounds closed and lifted her right arm to take note of the good surgeons' handiwork.

"Marvelous Lustene! The scar will be so tiny, no one will notice!" Miala was happy with the miniscule line zig zagging up from her elbow to her shoulder blade. She had feared she would heal as a scarred, hideous monster. Nicholas kissed her unaffected cheek.

"Say the word and I will have every tree of that forest cut down in your honor!" Miala laughed at Nicholas's reaching offer.

"Why don't we just ride in the day time from now on? And if anyone asks, this was a stray lion, not a tree branch that I warded off mightily in your defense!" Miala flexed her good arm, doing her best to imitate a noble knight's stance. Nicholas and Lustene laughed out loud.

"Of course, tiny maiden, of course!" Lustene chortled, busying himself with cleaning his messy preparation area, thanks to Nicholas's clumsy assistance.

"Lustene," Nicholas's tone was sobered, and serious; causing Lustene to turn around.

"Yes sire?"

"We must get into the royal library, but...."

"But you do not wish to alert your aunt and uncle to Jiden's disappearance and Callana's deception, so I need to keep your visit a secret, is that right?" Lustene finished for Nicholas, causing the young man to blush bashfully. They had already come clean when a severely startled Lustene had come home for an afternoon nap to find the two laying in wait for him. He had been adamant that they rescue the false princess at any cost, and had graciously nourished the famished pair.

"Sorry, good surgeon, I did not mean to assume you were a fool,"

"I know, young Nicholas," Lustene assured.

"Now," Nicholas glanced to his small cohort as he spoke.

"To the matter of getting inside the castle, without being seen..." Nicholas was scratching his chin in thought. Lustene had begun washing some neglected dishes.

"Well if it were me, I would go in through the servants' entrance through the kitchen early morning before Gillian's arrival and Lena's morning duties," the gentle old man casually answered.

"You are a genius!" Miala giggled at the blatant obviousness of the answer to their problem.

"Yes, I am," Lustene nodded. Nicholas laughed at his wonderful long time friend.

"You've done this before?" He challenged.

"Let's just say, in my younger days, I had a few forbidden rendezvous with a rather tempting young chamber maid and had to find my way *in* and *out* undetected," Lustene grinned devilishly, his crinkled blue eyes lighting up with a secret, delicious memory. Miala giggled, and Nicholas slapped him on the shoulder.

"You devil!" The three enjoyed a much needed relief from their worrying as the couple caught Lustene up on all the events of the tournament, including Callana's amazing victory. Lustene regaled them with stories of his adventures, accompanying the king on his rambunctious hunts these last few days, even killing a deer himself!

Holding her prince in the warm, glowing fire that evening, Miala fantasized about riding into Dellandore, birth papers in hand, to free her beloved friend, so they could *both* , someday, marry the princes of their dreams...

"My lord, the east was clear," The lofty and lanky Sir Reinhold bellowed, accompanied, always, by his hefty counterpart, Sir Graven.

"Yes my lord, all clear!" Sir Graven interrupted, somewhat perturbed. Reinhold gave him a stern stare, forcing the larger man to glare in response. Friends since childhood, the twenty year old pair were inseparable, and insufferable. Odin chuckled to himself over the odd couple. The giant blue eyed monster, Sir Keiton, who had been knighted only yesterday, was returning from his northern route with his fast, albeit shocking, new friend, Sir Paul. Sir Paul was not known to say much, and spent any time off duty completely alone, or in the tavern. He had never attached to anyone, save for the newcomer Sir Keiton. Odin marveled over the motley duo as they rode towards him, engaged in conversation when the king himself was sure he had never heard Paul speak. Sir Keiton cleared his throat as he neared to report.

"Sire, the north was clear, nothing to report," as Keiton spoke, Paul was nodding.

"Good, and the south?" Odin asked as the generously proportioned Dashend and nearly identical cousin Earnest pulled their mounts to a halt next to the big king.

"Nothing to report sire," replied Earnest, the vociferous half of the two. Odin grinned, having found nothing to report to the west himself, he was about to turn for home and morning council when he thought he heard the far off thundering of hooves. Paul heard it to, both golden haired men turning to watch the road through Shadow's forest. From their vantage point, it was just a jiggling, puffing dark figure in the dim light of this very early cold, gray dawn. Sir Keiton, Sir Paul and Sir Dashend took their places in front of their king. Sir Graven, Sir Reinhold and Sir Earnest immediately urged eager horses into a charge to head off a potentially threatening intruder. Odin watched with slight amusement, only vaguely worried that any *one* attacker would be imprudent enough to ride upon Adalonia. As he drew nearer, the dark man held up his hands in peace meeting the three guards, a hushed conversation taking place,. He was led, somewhat urgently to Odin. When the stranger pulled his frothy bay to an abrupt stop in front of Odin's three guards, the king took note of the man's Rogadon cape, although it was tattered, badly, a state most un-fitting a knight's apparel. The exhausted man looked upon the knights with dark, weary eyes, a beseeching look twisting their corners. The man spoke with a harsh, raspy voice.

"I implore you, I need an emergency audience with your king," in keeping with the code of behavior, the knights had not divulged who was the king, leaving the option to do so entirely up to Odin. The large king nodded slowly.

"Speak, for I am King Odin of Adalonia, knight of Rogadon," Odin's voice was deep and powerful, conveying his ownership of this great land he held the highest pride for. The dark man quickly dismounted, bowing low to the king, still atop his giant black stallion.

"Mighty king Odin, I have come to report a terrible happening," the man started, swaying slightly as he rose to stand. Odin frowned.

"Give him some water," The king ordered. Sir Earnest produced a water bladder and passed it to the man.

"When you can speak, tell me of this terrible thing," Odin urged, and the man nodded as he gulped.

"Sire, Dellandore marches on Rogadon! Two mornings past," the knight was obviously in horror from what he had seen. Though the Dellandore army was half the size of Odin's, it was impressive none the less, especially to see it in motion. Odin shook his head.

"You are sure?" The man nodded fervently.

"Why tell me, good knight? Surely you are aware that your king refuses any dealings with me until the treaty is signed,"

"I do not come for my king, I come for my people, my family, trapped in that awful city under siege, your majesty," the man's voice was passionate, his eyes pleading. Odin was enraged over King Ulei's sneaking attack, and only months from the wedding to end all conquests!

"Your name, good knight?" the king implored.

"Renk, sire, I am a dear friend of Callana's," Renk answered, swaying greatly again, using his exhausted bay to lean against. The horse tossed his head in response. Odin dismounted, propping Renk up against himself.

"You have ridden far, you need rest. Come, I will have a room made for you," Odin was trying to help Renk back into his saddle, when Renk stopped him, turning to face him as he spoke.

"Sire, I must not stay long, I have to get back to my wife. She has been unconscious since the birth of my son, a week ago now," Odin could see the earnest angst in the young man's eyes.

"I can sympathize young man; my wife too, had a terrible experience with my son, Jiden. It is a frightening feeling of helplessness to see her suffer while you can do nothing," Odin sympathized. Renk nodded.

"What is your wife's name, so that I may add her to my nightly prayers?" Renk smiled brightly with the mention of his beautiful little blonde.

"Rogala, your majesty," Renk beamed until he noticed the consternation scowling across Odin's forehead. Renk knew what he needed to say; the king would know the truth soon anyways.

"And no sire, it is not coincidence that I am a knight of Rogadon in love with a woman named Rogala. She is the princess, sire," Renk began, a confused circle of knights closing in on him.

"Callana? She asked to be called Callana; this is the woman you speak of?" Odin was confused, and already enraged. Renk swallowed hard and continued.

"No sire, Callana and Rogala met in the Shadow's forest; Rogala and I were fleeing our terrible city, and Callana fleeing her village. Callana took Rogala's duty to marry Jiden, so Rogala and I could be free. I fear if your son is not here it is because he is in hiding with Callana, between here and Dellandore,"

"What? Why would they be in hiding?" Odin's voice was strained with his worry. Renk sighed heavily, knowing the shame of being deceived would be heavy for such a noble king, but to be discovered by a king such as Ulei? Renk kept his voice low, afraid to spark the big man's outrage any farther.

"Callana was discovered at the Dellandore tournament, your majesty, by King Bromell," Renk could see the great man seething with his rage.

"I beg of you, King Odin, do not think ill of us sire! The treachery was done in the name of love and *love* alone!" Renk had dropped to a knee, entreating Odin's forgiveness. Odin glowered down upon the dark man, than relented his anger, sensing the man's honesty.

"See this man to a brief stay in the castle so he can rest and get back home where he is greatly needed," Odin commanded. Renk bowed again, mounted, and followed Graven, Reinhold, Paul, Dashend and Earnest up the winding path through the now bustling village market and to the great white courtyard. Odin stayed a moment, turning to Sir Keiton, his anger dissipating slightly, replaced by an immense concern for his son. The large blonde man shook his head. Odin sighed, and followed his knights. Hours later, they were headed out in search of his deluded son and the underhanded red head.

....

Nicholas and Miala hunched over one of the many leather bound, enormous books of lineage, opened and spread around them about a large, dark walnut wood table. They were in the further most row of the immense library, amidst rows of dusty books and lit chandeliers, covered in spiders' webs.

"The lines are clear, Camden *is* Triden's sister's name, but she registered no children!" Miala howled, sorrow filling her hazel eyes, threatening to spill over. She had been so confident in Hellena's discovery, and so happy to exploit it for Callana's sake. Now there was nothing to save her friend, nothing short of a miracle.

"Do not cry love, we will…." Nicholas trailed off. He had no words of reassurance for his beautiful object of affection. The ever present Illiam had allowed them into the library, and lineage records, swearing secrecy of the couple's presence until they had something worth while to report, and of course, only after Jiden was home. The two started turning pages again, determined to find the connection they could not even be sure existed.

"Well, I always knew one day I would catch you sneaking about with a young maiden, I just did not expect to catch you *reading*," Lena's small hands were clasped in front of her petite frame, her intrusion causing Nicholas and Miala to jump and turn. The couple gave the peeking Illiam a scowling look. The nervous little man ducked back behind the great door, rushing away down the hall. Lena shook her immaculate head.
"This is *my* castle, he is under obligation to inform me of all goings on under this roof because I am his *queen*, as I am *yours*, nephew," Lena's tone was stern and scolding, a shameful Nicholas coming to her and holding her hands.
"You *are* my queen, aunt Lena, and I was wrong to sneak, but I have a matter of great importance to research," Lena shook her head.
"First off, are you two an aspiring couple now? And where is my son? How did the tournament go? How did Callana do?" Lena was smiling with her exuberant curiosities and it broke Nicholas's heart to have to bring her the appalling news.
"Callana took the archery tournament, her opponent then turning her in to king Bromell, who denied her as his niece, and who turned her over to King Ulei who imprisoned her for impersonating a princess, and I am willing to bet that Jiden is not home yet because he succeeded in breaking her out of prison and has taken cover in the Shadow's forest," Lena sat slack jawed, as Nicholas rambled on. Miala was in awe of his short work of such a seemingly long story. When he had finished talking, Nicholas nodded to the floor, searching for any where to put his eyes except on Lena's green daggers! She reached out and slapped him, her mouth closing and tightening, it was her angry look, but unfortunately it was too adorable to be taken seriously.
"I am just a messenger, aunt; I was not privy to anything! But we," he gestured between himself and the delicate, curly haired maid.
"We may have found a saving grace for Callana..." Lena jumped to interrupt.
"*Callana*? Why would we save *Callana*? Did you not just tell me she *betrayed* my son? My kingdom? Rogadon?" Lena was furious now and Nicholas backed a few steps away.
"Your majesty, please, let us explain," Miala piped up, flinching after she spoke, for fear she would get slapped as well. Lena turned to her, eyes squinting as she searched the oval face for honesty.
"Well?" Lena growled.
"Oh, well, what happened was Callana was running away from her home and a life of sexual servitude when she ran into a pregnant Rogala who was running away from marrying Jiden because she loved Renk, a knight, and Callana offered to take the princess's place in marriage so Rogala would not be hunted down and punished by her uncle, King Bromell!" It was Nicholas's turn to stand slack jawed now.

"That was amazing!" He said coming to put his arms around her shaking form as she smiled and embraced him.

"Me? You were amazing! It would have taken me years to tell that story correctly," she admired.

"I was thinking about her story and I could not even begin to..." Nicholas was tittering on when Lena cleared her throat to end the chattering session of congratulations. The pair blushed slightly.

"Fine, so she did a *nice* thing, helped a friend, but what of my Jiden? He must be heart broken!"

"We must deal with that later, dear aunt, for we have more pressing matters now," Nicholas grabbed Lena by her delicate shoulders as he spoke.

"We have this letter, Rogala believes it to be proof Callana *is* of royal lineage," He handed Lena the letter and she read it quickly.

"I am sorry to say nephew, but this alone will not serve as viable evidence to support such a claim," Nicholas nodded, reaching to a nearby book case, where he had leaned the exquisite wooden frame.

"This was Callana's father's wedding gift to her mother," he announced. Lena gasped.

"Now *that* is viable," She breathed.

....

"We need to travel the road, though I hate to be in plain sight if Dellandore *dares* to come looking for their prisoner," Jiden was addressing his ring of knights, desperate now to find his possibly injured cousin. Callana had not seen him for the entire day before, which he had used to go hunting for a much needed meat supper last evening. He had not come to lie down until she was fast asleep, and today he had yet to speak to her, and was carefully avoiding any eye contact. Callana could not decide if that was better or worse than his blatant outbursts of hatred. She was cleaning up camp for departure; taking cooking pots and utensils to rinse in the stream and filling up water bladders for all. Erik was helping break camp while the royal guard was in session. He brought some water bladders to Callana at the icy stream's edge.

"Here you go love, this is the end of them," He plopped them down at her feet, buried in a thick, red mud.

"Oh thank you, Sir Erik," Callana bowed her head to him, before turning back to bend to her scrubbing. Erik allowed his eyes to travel over her; red lengths cascading down her back and over her shoulder, a glowing contrast to the grey cold of the day. Her borrowed tunic hung slack at the neck where she had forgotten to tie it and he stood on tip toe to peek at the exposed, copious cleavage.

"Mind your eyes, Sir Erik," Jiden's sneering voice jolted the older knight.

"I bet you do," Erik laughed at his own jest; Callana blushed now in Jiden's presence.

"My God you are irritating," Jiden scoffed. Callana rose; with hands full of water bladders and clean cookware.

"Here I can help with that," Jiden rushed to her side eagerly as Erik turned to her.

"I got it, I got it. This is poor man's work, ey Callana? Much too gritty for a *prince*," Erik grinned, winking at Callana. Jiden fumed with the raunchy man's insinuation he and Callana were two of a kind.

"It's time to move out," Jiden conceded, having no time for arguments while his mind buzzed with worries about Nicholas, and Callana's stalled execution, and the probability that his father will call off their wedding and he will never....never be with her again. Jiden's mind swirled as he followed the two back to camp. It had only just occurred to him they would have no reason to uphold the marriage now that she was not a princess, and his parents would most likely, arrange *another* marriage. But he loved Callana, did he not? He could not *allow* them to be separated. He would not be able to live through watching her leave, knowing he loved her more than anyone else possibly could; aware another man could be holding her, kissing her, loving her every night of her life, when it should be him! Damn her stupid ruse, if only Jiden could carry out the wedding as planned! Than it would not be *him* breaking down his pride, but law that would bind them, and once tied, he would admit he had never stopped loving her. Jiden shook his head. There was so much wrong with his plan he could not even begin to right it. Other matters took precedence now. He crashed through the spiny bush to the clearing and the now broken camp site.

"We need to double up the smaller riders; I will take Callana, seeing as how I am one of the....lighter knights...."He looked about at his men. Galland, Gracien, Ren, Kern, and David *were* large, heavy guards. They would ride alone, and Senren and Franklin were both short but thick as old tree trunks, and heavy. However, Lashend and Laden were tall and thin; Lashend and Laden gave each other a confused look. They were both lighter than the prince, and could have taken Callana.

"That takes care of it! We ride!" he quickly mounted Leviathon, turning when he heard someone clear their throat.

"*And*, what about me?" Erik was standing in the middle of the group, hands out at his sides. There was a stifled snicker from Sir Ren at the prince's obvious distaste for the bristled older man.

"Oh, yes...you, well..." Sir Laden offered up immediately.

"Sir Erik can double with me, if he wishes. I am not nearly as heavy as these piglets," He said, gesturing to Senren and Franklin, who in turn rolled their eyes.

"Brilliant, move out!" Jiden sniped; reaching impatiently down to grab Callana's hand to easily lift her to the big stallion's back. Callana sat awkwardly behind him, trying hard not to read too deeply into his offer to double with her. She could have easily ridden behind Lashed, or Laden, why had he insisted on her being with him? And after he had admitted he did not love her anymore? Didn't he? She could not really *blame* him; she *had* lied, but she could not believe it was so *easy* for him! She could not stop *her* love for him any more than she could stop the falls from rushing over Green Mountain! Perhaps it was so painless for men, making it simpler to *buy* affections from a woman they forgot the instant they were out of her bed? Was it that way for Jiden? Had he forgotten her now? Forgotten how tremendous they had been together? In the quiet, stillness of the night Callana found it hard to think of little else. She found herself waking, only to search out his sleeping face across the fire, the sight comforting her and lulling her back to sleep to dream of him again. What she would not give to know *his* dreams.

Jiden had urged Leviathon into a spirited walk as they made their way through the tangled wood, crunching through fallen, crisp frozen leaves and needles. Even though the pace was brisk, Callana had kept her distance from Jiden; sitting behind the saddle's rim, clasping onto it to keep from toppling off, squeezing the big horse with her knees. Jiden was aggravated at her coyness. They were riding double for Heaven's sake!

"Hold tight, when we reach the road we will be making full speed towards Adalonia," Jiden kept his voice diplomatic.

"Yes, sire," Callana answered just as tactfully, moving her hips forward, pressing into his back and wrapping her arms around his hard middle. Jiden grinned, the excitement of her touch rushing through him. He was caught in the midst of his elation by a wildly grinning Galland. Jiden blushed, and cleared his throat to speak.

"We must be alert for any other signs of Nicholas along the road,"

"Aye!" his knights called out. Jiden strained his neck to put his cheek to the top of Callana's head resting against his shoulder blade.

"Callana?"

"Uh hum?" Callana mumbled into his cape.

"I want you to know...I am....glad, you are with me....us, with us and not in prison," Jiden stammered through another blundered attempt to express himself. Callana smiled.

"That is the first *kind* thing you have said to me for days," she spoke softly into his gratefully warm back, her arms clutching tighter around him. Jiden felt a great guilt wash over him with the realization that since her rescue from prison he had done little else but demean her. He held the reins with one hand, taking his free hand and rubbing Callana's cold hands.

"You are frozen! Hold on," He pulled the horse to a halt, unlashing his bright green cape.

"No! I am already wearing one of Sir Galland's capes!" Callana protested.

"Yes, but this one is lined with rabbit fur," Jiden argued, turning his body sideways in the saddle to throw the cape over Callana.

"What will you have?" She tried to object, but the fur lining warmed by Jiden, was too magnificent to deny. She cuddled into it.

"I will have you," Jiden smiled softly, briefly meeting her brown eyes before turning back to the task of getting home. Callana's injured heart soared! She was completely confused by his swinging disposition but she reveled in this extreme up turn. If he would love her again, she would not ask for anything for the rest of her life!

Once upon reaching the main road, Sir Galland in the lead, with the rest of the knights encircling the prince, they charged for home; careful to mind their speed for the endurance of the horses with twice the burden. Jiden felt a surge of hope rush through him with their encounter. She was still receptive, even after how brutally cold he was to her and with her misconstrued conclusion that he did not love her anymore. He would prove it to her, using his actions instead of his words. Surging towards home, while remaining aware of his surroundings and searching for any sign of his cousin, Jiden could not force the smile off his cold lips.

．．．

Stars are shining big and bright
To shine upon my little one
Soon comes morning's yellow light
To shine upon my little one
And when the day has turned to night
To shine upon my little one
The moon and stars will rise and fight
To shine upon my little one

Nia woke, startled by a soft singing; raspy and so faint, she could vaguely make out the words of a lullaby she would sing to Rogala in the castle Rogadon. The little woman made her way towards Hellena's bed chamber where she had left Rogala and her infant son; hope was bubbling through her chest, threatening to strangle her with excitement. Was her girl really awake? Was Nia really hearing this, or had her hope finally drove her over the edge? She froze in the door way, her eyes drawn to the bed, illuminated by the warm, orange fire's light; her frail angel was breastfeeding her healthy baby boy.

"Oh Rogala!" Nia rushed to her side, wrapping her arms around her delicate daughter and grandson.

"Mother!" Rogala gingerly raised a weak arm to pull her mother into a fragile hug. Nia looked down on the chunky face of her precious grandson.

"He is beautiful; your hair, your eyes, but everything else belongs to his father!" Nia giggled with this. It was true; he had dark skin, huge hands and feet, but blonde, wavy locks and crystal blue eyes. Rogala was crying.

"I have never seen anything so *incredible* in my entire life! He is so *perfect,* so *beautiful;* it hurts my heart to look at him! Does that sound absurd?" Nia shushed her.

"Of course it does! But that's how babies make you feel!" Rogala rested her head on her mother's shoulder as she cradled the now sleeping little man.

"How long have I been out of consciousness?" Rogala asked. Nia shrugged.

"Oh, about seven days, and twelve hours or so, but who is counting?" Rogala met her mother's weary eyes, remorse flooding her own.

"What have I put everyone through? Did my husband finally abandon me?" Rogala was not serious, but admittedly felt very disappointed that he was not here when she woke. Nia frowned.

"Well, I should probably tell you from the beginning, here goes. Callana won the archery part of the tournament," Nia began; Rogala grinned from ear to ear with this news.

"But, the knight she bested turned her into king Bromell, who apparently was in attendance, and king Bromell consequently turned her over to Ulei...to be executed for falsely impersonating a princess," Nia's words were like sharp pains searing through Rogala's heart.

"*What?*" Rogala demanded.

"Wait, there is *good* news. Nicholas, Jiden's cousin, followed Miala here when she came to tell us what happened, and he was under the suspicion that Jiden was working to free her from prison, even break her out...and he is off with Miala investigating Callana's possible ties to royalty," Nia smiled faintly with the last, in hopes of cheering Rogala.

"Words have escaped me...I am horrified! This is all my fault! I should have never let her serve in my stead! Oh mother! We have to save her...we" Nia shushed her again.

"That is precisely why your husband is gone; he left just two mornings ago, to convince Odin that Callana is the one who gave the warning that Dellandore has marched on Rogadon," Nia explained. Rogala gasped.

"What? Are you sure it was not seven *years* and twelve hours I have slept? I feel insane!" Rogala was sweating with the effort of being awake, after surviving purely on liquids for a week. Nia rushed to the cupboards for bread and cheese. She was careful not to wake anyone else. They could catch up with Rogala in the morning. Tonight was Nia's turn. After she had eaten,

Rogala finally let Nia convince her to rest, so the food could nourish her exhausted heart and depleted muscles and tomorrow they would worry about everyone else. Cuddling with her grandson and daughter, Nia felt a pang of guilt for her dear friend in the next room, aching for her *own* daughter. Nia set her mind to figure something out if Renk's mission failed; little did she know Rogala had no intention of waiting for Renk to fail. She was leaving for Adalonia in the morning.

....

Callana was cold, so cold, a freezing, biting cold she had never felt in her entire life. How she had taken for granted the many winters she had spent outside as a child; hunting with her father, riding her horse, or just rushing out for fire wood, but there was always a warm home to return to. These hours of the billowing, blustering, frozen wind whipping her atop this speeding horse with no end in sight was unbearable! She clung to Jiden's warmth, guilt ridden with the knowledge that he was suffering this with only a fur lined tunic! How far had he said Adalonia was? A day? Half a day? She could not remember, and she feared it could be longer.

Callana opened her burning eyes as bouncing landscape rolled passed; she strained to focus on Sir Laden and his riding mate, Sir Erik. They did not look happy about the sudden blasting storm, or miserable. They just rode on, as if this was any other ride and the cold was just a minor detail; a simple fact to accept and ignore. She shivered again, her trembling arms closing in around Jiden's firm middle, pulling her close body even closer, to crush into him. His free hand clasped down on top of her hands and he turned his head sideways to speak into her hair.

"A few more hours still…will you be all right?" His voice was hoarse, causing Callana to turn her face up to see his. When she did, her guilt intensified, for he was pale, terribly pale, with a raw, redness to his turned up nose and his swollen lids. His lips had chapped severely and split down the middle. Callana nodded against him.

"I will be fine, sire," She pulled one hand free so she could yank the hood of one of her capes down tight over her face and burrowed her head into his back. Jiden was feeling the snow, though it had not come yet. He could sense it, down to his very marrow. There was a bite to this storm, different than the regular cold of a rain storm. The grey clouds hung low, almost close enough to touch it seemed, and they were still, solid even, like great marble stones frozen in mid air. There was a wet stickiness that had been clinging to him, his crew, the trees, the ground, even their breath since the night before and it was heavy in his lungs. The wet air was falling now as puffy drops, splatting into his arms and face as he rode; the white onslaught landed on Leviathan's white mane and flung up to smack Jiden in his chest, which was now sopping wet. Jiden forced himself not to shiver. He needed to remain strong, and resilient in the eyes of his men, and Callana. If he broke down now, gave in to his excruciating chill, he would not be able to hold back the persistent tormenting tremors he had been fighting since this relentless cold had taken the forest. Sir Galland was ahead, he and his golden horse charging on like rocks rolling down a steep ravine; no stopping him; no breaking him; no fear nor cold could deter his uncompromising bravado. Jiden steeled himself against the cold, determined to follow in the great knight's example. Mercifully, however, someone heading towards them from a great many paces away slowed them, and Sir Galland moved them off the road.

Jiden's heart beat roared through his burning ears now that they were still. The thundering hoof beats were closing in on them now and Sir Galland had ridden out to meet the group. As they neared, however, Jiden sighed with relief; their green capes signaled he had nothing to fear.

"Father!" Jiden peeled himself away from Callana's rigid grasp long enough to slink to the ground, tingling legs stinging with the effort, as he strided out to meet the large king.

"Son!" The larger, but very similar man leaped off his mighty black beast to embrace his bone chilled son.

"I have been worried about you," Jiden grinned up at his father, sheepishly, than frowned slightly.

"Wait, why would you be worried? With the tournament you would not have expected me for days," Jiden was puzzled. Odin shook his mighty head and frowned down on him.

"I have been *informed*," He stated plainly, giving Callana a fierce scowl. Jiden bowed his head.

"Father, I understand your anger with her but..." Odin pushed him aside as stalked over to the ragged, soaked girl on the back of the big white horse.

"You have shamed my son, me, and my kingdom. What have you to say for yourself, young Callana?" Callana immediately fell off the horse and plopped to her knees in the icy mud at Odin's feet. She looked up at him, tears spilling out over her pink, frozen face.

"Sire, please, forgive me? My intentions were noble; I meant no harm to Prince Jiden or the kingdom!" She begged but Odin's stern stare did not waver.

"When we get to Adalonia, I will decide your punishment, and believe me, if I were less of a king I would leave you here to suffer in the cold before I would let you back into *my* city!" Callana nodded, bowing her head in shame. She could have expected no less from a great man dealing with such a low villain.

"Father, Callana has been punished enough..." Jiden started but Odin turned to face him, a hot temper boiling in his eyes.

"You will do well to keep your *affections* out of this, young prince," Jiden balked.

"You think I am blind to her crimes?" Jiden's own anger deepened his voice. "I will not be questioned by my own son!" Odin's tone was clear; Jiden had crossed the line; used his blood relation to the king to sway his decision. "Yes, sire. We will follow you to Adalonia," Jiden bowed to his father, and Odin nodded, turning to Callana, still in the mud. His eyes had softened at the sight of her shaking in the grimy wet road. He had genuinely adored her just days earlier, but he was the king, and emotions could not rule *his* duty. She had embarrassed him; she had humiliated his son, and she had duped all of Adalonia that had grown to adore her as well. He shook his head, sadness filling his eyes, as he turned his back to her and mounted his horse.

"To Adalonia!" He veered his big hoofed horse around and kicked it into a full canter. Jiden came to Callana, reaching for her hand.

"Callana, forgive him, he is angry..." Callana stood, refusing his assistance.

"I understand, sire," She bowed her head to him. Jiden felt his blood boil against the frigid air. He sighed and mounted, pulling her up behind him. He nodded to the solemn Sir Galland and the now slightly downhearted party moved out at a less than urgent pace. Jiden turned his head to the side to speak to Callana.

"You are holding my father's behavior against me?" His raspy voice was strained with his frustration. When she did not respond Jiden fumed.

"This is it then? You are ignoring me? I am the *rotten prince again*?" Jiden clenched his teeth when he spoke. Callana shrank away from the mad expression in his squinted eyes and furrowed fore head. She was so confused! One instant, he is pulling her to him, the next he is pushing her away? He just stood there and let his own father condemn her; the way Jiden himself had condemned her, but has anyone of yet asked her *why* she had done it? No! Even if she *could* explain her selfless motives, neither man cared. Her actions spoke for themselves and she could not make up for them, not even as a champion archer, a hero, or a lover. She wept into his back, her crumbling heart making her forget all about the frozen world around her.

....

"I am sorry to say but Sir Illiam is correct; if Queen Camden *did* have an illicit affair, less than a year after her husband's death, she would not have allowed her son's birth recorded in the lineage books." Lena was saddened to see the desperate couple, reading and re-reading the dated books, determined to see a connection that just was not there.

"Aunt Lena, where would *you* record such an affair?" Nicholas asked, eyes still combing over the yellowed pages before him. Lena gasped, clutching her hands to her chest.

"I would never *have* such an affair!" Miala giggled as an absurd image of Lena engaged in a lurid affair with her royal stable boy, Edward sprang into her mind. Lena glared at the curly haired girl.

"I just meant, if you were *Camden*, where would you have written down the accounts of your affair?" Lena calmed, sighing.

"I fear she may not have written them down at all," she paced.

"She was Triden's sister to inherit Rogadon, correct?" Lena was basically confirming out loud what she knew to be truth. Nicholas nodded.

"And who did she leave her kingdom to?" Lena asked.

"That part is a little confusing, my lady, it seems she bequeathed Rogadon to Triden's wife's niece, Kiera, who was raised by King Leston, sorry, my grandfather, and grandmother Nella, I mean, your parents." Nicholas's eyes were closed with his concentration.

"Essentially, she did not have children, so needed to leave her kingdom to someone she could trust and in her search she decided on a non blood relative to be arranged for marriage into the Della Verde, which she was not however, for Kiera married Granlund, who was a wealthy man from the village, Kursdalen, beyond the kingdom of Felonia, but Camden would have no way of knowing who Kiera *would* marry." Lena was rambling now and Nicholas turned to shrug at Miala.

"What does all of it mean?" Nicholas asked his glowering aunt.

"Oh, nothing, just that…Camden was Rogadon's only blood heir. We need to get into her home city. She must have left behind personal effects and perhaps, a diary?" Nicholas and Miala joined the queen in her search of Odin to inform him of their new quest.

The trio had finally made their way to the open reception hall in time to hear the trumpeting of horns, announcing her husband's arrival. Although it was not unheard of for the morning patrol to turn up something worth investigating, Lena had been worrying for Odin since his absence at morning council and than dinner. She signaled for Miala to help her stoke the two fires in the large chamber to warm the stone against this chilling cold, and then the two rushed to the kitchen for pitchers of water and breads and cheese. Nicholas stood in the entry way to welcome his king and, most regrettably, inform him of all that has happened. However, when it was Sir Galland who opened the doors for the King, Nicholas knew the bad news had spread.

"Your majesty," Nicholas bowed low for his returning, frozen king. Odin nodded as he rushed by to greet his queen. Lena embraced him, pulling him to her as she eagerly kissed his prickly cold cheek.

"I did not even know why you had gone! I missed you!" She grinned up at the large, curly blonde, his dark blue eyes shinning with his adoration for his marvelous little wife.

"Love, I have found your son, but I fear I have some news," Lena shook her head.

"I already know about Callana my lord, Nicholas and Miala arrived not long after you left out for patrol," She nodded to her grinning nephew and his blushing young counterpart. The large doors opened again, and this time, a filthy, worn Callana and an ice covered Jiden stepped through.

"Mother... cousin!" Jiden grabbed his closest companion in a squeezing hug, chilling his cousin with his touch.

"I thought you had been injured?" Jiden continued. Miala and Callana were hugging now, the younger girl petting her sopping friend.

"Oh, the cape? Yes, well, lets just say, a low hanging tree can be dangerous for a novel rider on her first night ride!" Nicholas explained.

Miala gasped. "You promised!"

Nicholas laughed out loud with her naivety.

"It was *Miala* who was injured?" Jiden came to look over the delicate stitching on the young maiden's face and arm.

"She has seen Lustene," Nicholas assured him. Jiden nodded.

"Seems some of Callana's courage has rubbed off on you, ey?" Jiden winked at Miala, who in turn blushed brightly and bowed her head.

"I can only hope, sire," She giggled. Callana glanced at him. What new game was this? She was so exhausted, and so frightened over her impending punishment and stalled execution! *She was so tired of being exhausted and frightened!* And she was tired of being confused. She glared at Jiden, who nearly jumped back. Lena came to her side.

"My dear, you look frozen! Come, stand next to the fire, get your blood warmed," Lena led the muddied, dripping girl to the limestone fire place to sit on the wooden chair she had pushed close. Jiden was slightly irritated his own mother had ignored *his* frozen state!

Callana huddled near the fire's warmth, determined to regain her composure as quickly as possible. Lena sat next to her, smoothing the long red matted lengths gently, as she spoke softly to Callana.

"I know what you did," Lena soothed. Callana burst into tears with this. Her fragile hold on her emotions broken, she sagged, sobbing quietly into her own hands.

"Now, that's enough of that," Lena quieted her softly.

Callana sucked in her breath, willing herself to stop crying as tears spilled over her cheeks.

"I also know *why* you did it, and I am so proud of you Callana!" Lena was smiling at her now, and Callana felt even more bewildered.

"Wait, you are not cross? I lied to all of you...I faked my way into your city....you do not hate me?" Callana was frowning, dirty wrinkles creasing on her pale forehead.

"My dear, you did all of those and more; you saved Gant, you spared the outlying villagers from losing their herds and possibly children to a rabid wolf! And I hear you were a masterful archer; are these not also true?" Lena beamed down at Callana now.

"Well, yes my queen," Callana nodded.

"Well then, I just can not believe a girl who would do those things could be anything but honorable and therefore, must have honorable intentions for all she does," Lena stated it so matter of fact; Callana had to smile, despite herself.

"Sire, I feel we should discuss this matter in private and the men deserve some time to rest," Jiden glared at his father, impatient to begin a deliberation Odin had already all but declared over. Odin grunted and turned to Jiden's knights, Sir Erik included.

"Good knights, you have served your prince and I well. Take the remainder of this evening with your families. That is all!" The knights nodded as they backed quickly out of the room, all too excited for free time. Odin's guard took their leave to perform a routine check of the entire castle and grounds before retiring themselves. Nicholas turned awkwardly to Miala.

"Ah, Miala, perhaps we should take our leave and..." Lena piped up from across the room.

"*You* shall go to your room Nicholas and *Miala* shall attend to some much neglected house work for the time being!" Lena led Miala and the frazzled young red head to her bed chamber while Odin and Jiden stared one another down.

"Father," Jiden began, but Odin was agitated.

"This wedding is off! I make the announcement at morning council. Jiden, your loyalties are to your kingdom, your country men, and your wife; seeing as how Callana is none of these, your loyalties should be clear!"

"My loyalties to my kingdom are not so *clear* to me! *You* force me to marry when I do not wish it because *you* decide it is good for my kingdom and now that I want to marry *you* tell me I can not because it is *not* good for my kingdom! Do I have that correct sire?" Jiden was maddening with every word, gesturing wildly with his green eyes hard on his father. Odin was beginning to boil now.

"You dare twist these events to make *me* the enemy? I did not arrange for you to marry a *prostitute* from Windt, I arranged a marriage to a *princess* from Rogadon! And furthermore, *I* did not ask for her to join the tournament under Rogadon's colors, you did! In the end, Callana has sentenced *herself* with her deceitful actions and I will not be judged by my own son for *her* crimes!" Odin slammed his fist into a nearby stone wall. Lena returned, now nervous; her son and husband bickered often, but never so enraged. She was not sure how to stop them, without breaking their prides.

"I am not judging you father, or placing any guilt on your shoulders," Jiden sagged with his fatigue. His voice was scratchy, and his throat was painfully swollen. He could not stand to see his father so angry; it did not suite him.

"I am asking you to allow me to right my own wrongs. You expect me to run this kingdom one day, *correct*? But to succeed father, I need to be allowed to *try*." Jiden eyes were weary, but serious. Odin sighed, shaking his bearded head.

"I know, son, I know. But I fear...I fear you will fail," Odin admitted.

"I probably will. Adalonia has had a long line of perfect kings; I will undoubtedly pale by comparison," Jiden admitted. Odin smiled slyly at his son.

"I want nothing less than greatness for Adalonia father. All I am asking for is a chance to show you what kind of king I aim to be." Jiden put his arm out, and Odin grabbed it reluctantly.

"All right, my son, this is *your* problem to sort out now, as it should have been from the start."

"Thank you father. So," Jiden clapped his hands together and rubbed them devilishly.

"*I* get to punish Callana!" He sneered. Odin grinned at Jiden's maniacal posture. Lena jumped.

"You will do no such thing!" She crossed the room swiftly, to stand between king and prince.

"She receives no punishments! Is that understood?" Lena commanded.

"My dear, she *did* lie..."Odin started but Lena snarled.

"She did, but why? Sometimes people lie for *good* reason! Does either of you even know her reasons? Has anyone asked for *her* side of the story? No! Men like Ulei and Bromell decide her fate and you have been content to let her stand accused with no voice of her own! A princess, pregnant with another man's baby, flees a crumbling city and her unwanted duty, only to happen upon a young woman, fleeing her own unwanted duty, who courageously offered to take the princess's place so her new friend could live with her *true* love, exiled in peace. How can either of you argue that she has acted in any other way but nobly?"

Jiden and Odin stood, slightly agape. Jiden's jest unknowingly opened a flood gate of truth that threatened to drown both men. Callana was not a practiced deceiver, trying to secure a kingdom or fame for herself, but an innocent traveler, pitched into another girl's troubles, emerging a wrongfully accused heroic friend? Jiden felt awful for how he had treated her. Odin was feeling the same. In their outrage, they had never asked about Callana's reasons or intent. Both hung their heads low.

"There, now, I have said my bit; let that teach you to *assume*! Good night to both of you!" Lena stormed from the room, leaving the shameful pair sulking in the entry way.

"I have never seen your mother like that Jiden," Odin whispered.

"I was about to say the same thing. She sure came to Callana's rescue, ey?" Jiden whispered back.

"Good sign," Odin nodded. Jiden wrinkled his brow.

"Good sign? Of what?"

"That Callana is good. Your mother is an excellent judge of character. I mean, look who she married! Noble, brave, handsome as the devil..." Odin grinned wickedly, wiggling his eyebrows and trying his best to take on a dashing pose. Jiden scoffed.

"Ha! She was *forced* to marry you!" Odin winked at his son.

"Pity, you were almost forced to marry Callana," Odin teased, urging a reaction out of his son.

"I was..." He nodded his head, his smile fading.

"You know, a great prince once told me that he did not want to marry for duty, *only* for love," Odin's eyes twinkled. Jiden cocked his head sideways.

"I reserve the right to call of your marriage as a duty; the council will demand as much," Odin began.

"If you wish to marry for love, well, that is up to you, young prince," Odin grinned before turning to search of his flustered wife. Jiden exhaled deeply. Finally, he would get a say in this mess! But his love life would have to wait; first, comes war.

....

"Oh, Callana, how dreadful that day was! I am so sorry I could not do anything to stop them from arresting you..." Miala was racked with guilt. Callana sat up in her hot, soapy bath.

"Please! Miala! I did this to myself, the king was right. This is my fault and getting caught, no matter how terrible, was my own fault as well."

"Here, dunk your hair again. I am almost done detangling it," the tiny maiden pushed Callana's shoulder's down to submerge the all too willing filthy girl into the wonderfully warm water. When the red haired beauty popped back up, she was smiling.

"I can not tell you how blessed this feels! I was beyond disgusting," She glanced around to see her muddy, soaking clothing laying about the room. Callana looked up to catch Miala's eyes scanning over the bruises and welts she had received in Dellandore's stocks and prison. Miala blushed.

"Forgive me for staring. I feel terrible for what you have been through. How is Jiden taking it?" Miala gently and deftly combed free the last of Callana's knots, and set about combing it again. The feeling stimulated memories of Callana's sisters and their childhood routines.

"He is ...confusing...but I want to hear about my family. How did they take the bad news?" Callana asked. Miala frowned, her hands dropping to her lap.

"Well....Rogala has been unconscious since the birth of her son, but she and Renk had identified a wooden frame your father gave your mum on their wedding day as the royal seal of the original Della Verde Valley, and Nicholas and I have been trying to use a love letter that may possibly be from a queen to tie your father and you, consequently, to royalty," Miala finished simply, going back to combing Callana's hair. Callana grabbed her tiny hands. "Rogala is going to be all right? Right?"

"Well, actually, I am not entirely sure, but you can ask Renk yourself, he has come to Adalonia. Nicholas heard from Edward today. He stays in the castle, on the prince's wing to rest than head back. He was pleading for help for Rogadon."

"Rogadon? What happened to Rogadon?"

"Dellandore means to claim it, in the absence of an heir," Miala was speaking so calmly, Callana feared she was not hearing her correctly.

"He *used* him! Ulei used Bromell! Don't you see?" Callana asked. Miala smiled brightly, nodding vigorously, before frowning and shaking her head. Callana sighed.

"Bromell is weak, and when Rogala threatened to admit she was not a real princess, Bromell was forced to accept me as replacement for the wedding to bind our kingdoms, and he must have told Ulei everything, hoping to secure the mightier king's assistance in his revenge on Rogala. So Ulei pays Erik to turn me in, Erik knew me from Windt and could care less, so he does, and Bromell orders my execution, tying me to Rogala's disappearance. He wanted to use my deception against Odin, guilting him into lending a part of his mighty army to secure Rogadon for the lesser king!" Callana surmised. Miala suddenly brightened.

"OH! I understand! So, once Rogala admits to Odin she was not really a princess, and we determine you are, you can marry Jiden and bind your two kingdoms, in earnest this time! It's brilliant!" Miala laughed out loud, igniting Callana's long dormant laughter. The two giggled and talked for a while longer, mostly about wonderful, adorable Nicholas; finally, Callana reluctantly climbed out of the now murky wooden tub, and into a silken tunic. Miala blew out the candles nearest the door on her way out, leaving Callana with the warm, orange glow of the fire to light her dearly missed bed chamber. She sighed to herself. Half a year ago, she was introduced to this beautiful room for the first time. Yet the elation of that day could not compare to the immense graciousness she felt laying here tonight, after her experience in Dellandore.

Callana allowed her mind to wander back to that romantic night in the Purple Dragon Inn. She remembered Jiden's eyes, gloriously green, gold flakes sparkling in the fire's glow, as they devoured her before squeezing shut with the ecstasy of their tremendous shared orgasms. She flung herself out of bed, restless legs refusing to still. She could only imagine what her punishment would be. She would undoubtedly be banished, never to see her friends or her love again. Jiden had thoroughly confused her with his ups and downs of feelings. Still, she had to wonder why he wanted the control over her sentence, enough to fight his own father. Was he *that* determined to see her in pain? She sat at the edge of her feather bed, staring at the fire, waiting for its dancing flames to form answers to the many questions in her head when a tap on the door startled her back to reality. She called over her shoulder.

"Come in, you silly girl," She taunted, assuming her friend had come back. The door creaked open, as Callana turned her head, catching her breath.

"Well I am silly but do not let the curls fool you, I am no girl!" Jiden put his hands on his hips as he spoke, trying his best to sound virile, though his hoarse, croaking throat made him sound more like an old man. Callana blushed, and quickly tried to pull her revealing tunic down over her exposed thighs.

"Your majesty, I did not expect you," She bowed to him. He stepped into her room, swinging the heavy door shut behind him.

"For one thing, I have already seen all that you are trying to hide," He grinned as he spoke, his teeth bright in the fire's light.

"And for another, I already told you not to call me that," Jiden closed in on her and Callana stiffened.

"Yes, you did, right before you informed me *your* rank was earned," she mocked him, her voice lowering an octave, her stance obstinate. Jiden's smile faded; his face sobering with her painfully accurate memory of such a hateful night.

"I can not begin to tell you how sorry I am for the way I have been behaving towards you, Callana," He closed in on her, but she backed away, her mind reeling with the emotional hills and valleys his attitudes were putting her through.

"I…understand you are to assign my punishment?" She cleared her throat, having backed helplessly into her bed post.

"I am," Jiden closed his eyes momentarily, stilling his feet.

"*Well?*" She demanded impatiently.

"I have decided that your time spent with me has been punishment enough; you are a free woman," He stated. Callana frowned.

"I am too tired to *play* with you Jiden, just tell me what is to happen to me!" Callana crossed her arms, coincidentally tugging her tunic up high enough for Jiden to tell she was not wearing anything underneath. His physical response did not go unnoticed. Callana steeled herself, forbidding her wounded libido from taking over her thought process. Jiden's eyes traveled down to her feet and back up to her eyes. His pupils had dilated, darkening his eyes to a murky green. Callana had noticed he too had bathed, but had not shaved the stubble growing along his jaw line. It made him appear older, wiser, distinguished, and absolutely irresistible.

"I am not trying to torment you; I find your actions noble and faultless. Well, that, and the fact that a very angry little queen forbade anyone from *actually* punishing you." Jiden smiled slightly, the dimples only creases, leaving his amorous eyes unchanged. Callana shook her head.

"I am so confused by you. *Do not call me prince, call me prince, do not call me prince;* you are mad I betrayed you one moment, the next you applaud my actions? What do you wish of me Jiden? I can not endure these games any longer. You smile at me than snap at me...I hardly know what to say or not say to you.... I just want the truth!" Callana was demanding now. Jiden's smile faded as he closed in on her. Callana flinched back slightly, unsure of his intentions. Jiden reached for her hand and led her to the fire's side of her bed, promptly lifting her by her waist and plopping her down atop it.

"Truth is, tomorrow, everything will be different, for us." Jiden began, but faltered, unsure of how to continue.

"My father wants to call off our wedding..." he started. Callana shook her head.

"But...you told him you still wanted to marry me? Right?" She asked.

"True, I did say that, but, it is not so easy as that," Jiden stood, aware that what he had to say would hurt her.

"What do you mean? You said you found my actions faultless, so you know why I lied, right? *You have forgiven me?*" Callana's eyes were insistent now, her chest rising and falling faster with her increasing panic.

"I do, I mean, I did forgive you. I want you to understand you did not do anything wrong. It will just take time, I mean, I have only tomorrow to ready to meet Dellandore's army in battle and I just need a clear head, you understand?" Jiden's brow was turned up, and his voice had turned apologetic.

"You do not want to marry me anymore?" Callana shook visibly with the subdued insight she had been avoiding since Dellandore. She realized, only now, that she had been sub consciously hanging on to a sliver of hope, and that sliver had finally been cut. Tears rolled down her cheeks.

"What I want is irrelevant right now. I have to plan... I have...I cannot argue away my father's right to call off this marriage of *duty* but, after Rogadon is safe..." Jiden tried. Callana sucked in a breath, willing herself to stop crying.

"You do not have the *time* to decide if you want to marry me? How much time do you need? I mean, I thought you..." Callana shook her head.

"Please do not cry Callana, I only mean that, for now, I need to concentrate...elsewhere..." Callana jumped to her feet.

"Of course, you need to concentrate! Well you can't do it in my bed chamber so be gone!" She pointed a shaking finger at her door, than angrily crossed her arms over her chest, defiantly flicking her eyebrows at Jiden; his blood started to boil.

"I know where the door is! I am trying to talk to you like an adult and tell you I just need you to..." He reached to hold her shoulders but she shrugged him off.

"You *need* me to what? *Wait*? Ha! I wish I would have!" Jiden's brow furrowed in confusion, than comprehension hardened his features.

"Don't! Don't you dare bring *that* into this, Callana!"

"Why? You didn't want to *wait* for our wedding to have *sex* but I am supposed to *wait* for you to decide if there will *be* a wedding now?" Callana was hurt and angry, and desperate to drive him out of her room.

"I did not force sex on you!" Jiden burned with anger, unable to stop the words from flying out of his mouth.

"*You* told me you loved me to get me into bed and *I* am branded false?" Callana turned with that, swinging red hair splaying out around her as she grabbed for the door. Jiden caught her arm and yanked her back to face him.

"*You* dare call *me* a liar?"

"*I* had good reason for lying to *you*, what's your excuse?"

"I never *lied* to you! I truly loved you!"

"If it was *true* love you would love me still!"

"I love a girl who never was! You want the truth, there, that is the truth," Jiden had quieted now, moving to place himself between Callana and the door.

"I loved you, like I have never loved anyone in this world. But *who* did I fall for?" He was glaring down at her now.

"Jiden…" Jiden turned, walking to the door. Callana wanted to plead with him, but she was choking on her words. Jiden's voice was earnest when he spoke.

"I am sorry. I never meant to hurt you." He left with that; spent and unable to bear her tears.

....

"I know he is a grown *man*, but he is still my only *son*!" Lena stalked back and forth in front of their immense, lemon oil rubbed cedar post bed. She was half pouting and half begging her husband.

"Wife, I assured him this was his problem and I intend to let him deal with it; I need you to trust in him, and me." Odin's voice was calm and soothing, as he attempted to lull his wife into a state of obedient patience; he was failing.

"You, you can not be serious! I am willing to allow him to make his own decision to marry or not marry Callana, but I refuse to allow him to go to war!" She stomped her tiny foot and crossed her thin arms, making her statement through stern, tear filled eyes.

"You *refuse* to allow him? Am I to understand that he is man enough to marry but not man enough to fight for his kingdom? The real world will not *allow* him to choose his battles, and neither can we."

"I know you are making sense, I know! But I am telling you my heart will cease to beat if he…if he is lost!" Lena could not bring herself to use the word *die* when she spoke of her beloved son. Odin raised himself from his large wooden chair in front of their roaring fire and came to hold his wife.

"This is merely a show of force. I am sending him with enough troops to squash any resistance Ulei can offer, and our son will be the figure head of the great army to rescue Rogadon. You see? It will not be a blood bath. I will have reports every few days from the lines, we will be completely informed of his situation and if the need arises, I will replace him." Odin was holding his wife's delicate shoulders and peering into her eyes, pleading for her faith.

"I...I will stand behind your decision as my king, and I trust you, husband, to make your decision as a *father*. For my sake?" Lena relinquished the last of her tears as she turned her beautiful face up to petition her husband. Odin leaned down and kissed her lips tenderly.

"Always,"

"I love you, my husband,"

"I love you, my wife," The pair relented to their tired bodies and climbed into bed together, Odin holding Lena as she cried again for her son.

"Rogala, be reasonable! You have only just recovered; you are not fit for such a ride!" Nia pleaded with her strong willed daughter, but to no avail.

"Mother, I will be fine. I can not just sit here and worry about Callana; her favor to me is the very thing that condemns her! I could not call myself her friend if I do nothing!" Rogala hurried about her borrowed room, searching frantically for her and her son's warmest wear, than out into the kitchen, where she found herself face to face with Hellena.

"You are not going to try to stop me too are you?" Rogala asked, annoyed in everyone's insistence that she was fragile, but even more annoyed by the fact that her muscles were already tiring from her efforts. Hellena slowly shook her head as she looked into Rogala's weary blue eyes, so like Nia's; tired, troubled, and guilt stricken. Hellena crossed her arms over her abundant chest.

"I am not arguing, I am telling; all go or none goes." She flicked an eyebrow as she spoke, signifying her readiness to back her threat. Rogala opened her mouth to protest, but was stopped by Cylan clearing her throat, drawing the blonde's attention to the band of red heads she would have to fight to reach the door. Rogala surrendered, crumbling as she reached to grasp Hellena in a huge embrace.

"Oh Hellena, how sorry I am for what I have done to Callana! Will you ever forgive me?" She sobbed into Hellena's silky hair as she squeezed the older woman with all her aching might. Hellena pulled Rogala's wet face back to look her in the eye.

"Rogala! Forgive what? There is *nothing* to forgive, that's the end of that talk, right?" Rogala nodded, hopeless against the fierceness of Hellena's orange glare. Nia sighed behind Rogala, knowing the battle was thankfully lost; Rogala was going to hand herself over to King Odin in trade for Callana, and there was nothing Nia could do about it. Crystalline, Cylan, Caran, Cella, Hellena and Nia circled Rogala.

"Right, first is first; your carriage horse was the only horse here and your husband has taken him. We need to find a good, young horse to pull us all in that carriage." Cella had only just started searching her mind when Crystalline piped up.

"Christopher has a Clydesdale! Magnificent, huge plow horse! He is slow, but he's got triple the strength of any horse I have ever seen!" She was out the door in a flash to procure their transportation. Cella turned to the task of assigning duties again.

"Mothers, prepare our foods; Caran and Cylan, find the warmest garments we have, it is snowing hard out there; I will ask Braden to stay here and watch over the Inn," everyone nodded and set out about their missions. Cella grabbed her cape and set off for Braden's small home. He was a rather small, sweet man who had been labeled the town bachelor because he was half way through his twenties and had never been tied to anyone; but above all, he was remarkably trustworthy. Every one in Windt knew of his severe honest nature and his reliability. He visited the single elders every morning; tending to their breakfasts and fires, and he spent a great deal of time repairing roofs and chopping wood for anyone who asked. Braden fished all summer, off the coast of Frellis, where he made enough money to spend the colder months at home, helping others.

Braden was only a few hundred convenient paces from their house, and Cella had reached his door in time to catch him walking out of it.

"Braden! Did I come at a bad time?" Cella batted her eyes, fully aware of his small crush on her and more than willing to abuse it to illicit his services. Braden blushed.

"Cella, oh, ah a bad time? No! No, just ah…I…ah…what can I do for you?" He was taken off guard by her visit, as the last time he had seen her she harshly warned him to find something new to stare at. He remembered suddenly and stared down at his feet.

"What are you doing?" Cella was running short of patience, as usual, and had no time for his oddities today.

"I am finding something new to stare at, as my lady requested last time," Braden replied, refusing to meet her glaring eyes. Cella huffed, trying her best at niceness although her temper threatened to erupt.

"I was just busy that day, all right? You may, *stare* at me," She waited impatiently for his lime colored eyes to wander up to meet hers, than spoke again.

"I need your help, could you spare a few days at the Stone's throw?" Cella smiled tentatively, causing Braden to falter.

"You… you want me to stay… with you?" He was only slightly hiding his immense excitement at the proposal. Cella's smile turned empathetic.

"No, my dear, *we* will be leaving and I wanted to know if *you* could perhaps, watch over the place?" Braden sagged perceptibly, but nodded.

"Of course, of course. When shall I come? Busy is all, just needed to clarify what you meant, so…ah…when?" He crossed his arms and tried to lean nonchalantly against his door frame but miscalculated and slumped inelegantly against the wall of his entry way, his face now hidden from Cella's view by the door frame.

"Go on," He assured her, his voice echoing into the wood between them. Cella sighed.

"As soon as you can, for we wish to leave promptly," She turned to leave, feeling awkward, but turned back.

"And thank you so much, Braden,"

Braden mumbled inaudibly from his corner, content to hide until she was out of sight. Cella hurried out of the wind and slush in time to meet a frazzled and frozen Dakin just coming out of the forest. She rushed to open the door and bring him in to the warmth of the Inn after such a long, freezing ride. She hurried his painted pony into the shelter of the barn, leaving him saddled and bridled. Once inside, Dakin nearly collapsed in front of the fire while Hellena hurried to bring him some hot stew and water.

"Forgive me ladies," The dark haired, trembling youth breathed.

"Nonsense," Hellena assured him.

"I have a message from Sir Renk for Rogala...he said I would catch you trying to leave..." Dakin glanced around as all six women were in different stages of packing.

"Dam, he's good!" Rogala cursed.

"He told me to tell you the message....as to not have anything written on my person for the Dellandore soldiers to find, and he had me traverse the forest to avoid the main road..." Dakin took a large drink of water before continuing.

"You cannot travel to Adalonia," Dakin finally concluded.

"Says Sir Renk?" Rogala asked.

"Yes my lady,"

"Why ever not?"

"Dellandore soldiers have taken the road. No one gets through, my lady," Dakin said.

"We are supposed to stay *here*? While my bird ...?" started Hellena but Dakin interrupted.

"No, Windt is on the borders of Rogadon. It will be taken soon as well. Sir Renk wants you all to head to Sea Fair, far from harms reach," Dakin nearly choked down his stew. Hellena turned to Nia and Rogala than back to Dakin.

"But my Callana...she needs me!" Hellena argued, but Dakin shook his weary head.

"He told me to tell you he plans to accompany Miala in her search. He said you would know what that means, my lady," He swallowed the rest of his badly needed, hot sustenance.

"I am not scared of this, whelp! Let's just tie him to something and say we never saw him!" Cella offered on her way to fetch rope. Dakin shivered.

"Cella! You scared him!" Cylan scolded. Nia tried a different form of trickery.

"Well, the man of the house has spoken. We make for Sea Fair!" Nia clapped her hands together, intent on Adalonia. Rogala made to protest but Dakin shook his head tiredly.

"Sorry my lady, he has paid me in full to *see* you there," he promised. Rogala huffed.

"Damn! He's good!" Nia echoed her daughter's sentiment.

Crystalline returned with her gentleman and his giant horse in time to find out they were leaving immediately for Frellis. Christopher hitched his large horse to their carriage and kissed Crystalline before turning reluctantly for home.

"Oh no you don't Christopher! You warn the village of Dellandore's coming than get in this carriage!" Hellena commanded. Christopher grinned, before disappearing into the white wall of the oncoming blizzard, returning as the girls had finally finished loading the carriage and securing Dakin's painted horse to the back. Close and cramped, the tangled family started out to their required destination; a bundled Cylan accompanying the thoroughly wrapped Dakin in the driver's seat as they begrudgingly headed east.

....

"Miala, our best strategy is the tunnels, but..." Renk's hushed voice halted. A very impatient Miala stomped a foot.

"But, what?" She gestured for Renk to continue.

"Well, with your prince leaving for Rogadon, and all of Adalonia's guard here on alert, I fear I alone will not be enough if faced with resistance. I have no way of knowing how much of Rogadon will be..." Renk was cut short.

"You will not be alone, *I* will be with you!" Miala pointed a thumb towards herself, obviously assuming this would bring the dark knight comfort. Renk smiled apologetically.

"Of course, brave maiden, but the tunnels are no place for a woman," Renk shrugged helplessly and turned back to his packing. Miala gasped.

"You...arrogant...pig headed...." She was stammering with her unjust now, forcing Renk to shake his head with surrender.

"I only meant that even with your *mighty* help, we are *no* match for soldiers, young Miala." Miala seemed partially satisfied with his reasoning, but sulked with disappointment.

"There must be those that can be spared, for this very important mission, I mean, Callana must be proven..." Renk cut his little friend short.

"Callana's lineage is only important to *us*. Rogadon's safety is the whole of Adalonia's mission for now," Renk scowled again, searching his mental list of ally's for one he could find to assist him, although if going it alone was his only option, he was *still* going. Miala absently set about stoking Renk's guest chamber fire while her mind searched for a name.

"What about Erik? He is not with the Adalonia army, not officially anyways. Can we not ask him for help?" Miala's tiny face was bright with her hope.

"He did voluntarily assist in her rescue from prison..." Renk scratched his chin in concentration.

"It will not hurt to ask!" Miala flung about, hurrying from the room before Renk had time to answer. Renk sighed. His wife and son, and extended family should have received Dakin and his message by this morning; that is if Dakin made it safely through the cover of the forest last night. He knew Hellena and the girls would be devastated that they could not come to Callana's aid, but he would see to his promise to help in their stead. If only he could have more eyes inside the castle Rogadon. Renk finished his pack, stretching his aching arms above his head and pacing in front of his northern facing window. From his vantage point, the dark black of the night had lightened only slightly to a deep grey; the yet to rise sun's reaching light accentuated the undulating cloud cover, darkened further in contrast to the brilliant white snow, blanketed across the land; Renk's eyes climbed up to the engulfed white top of Mount Rising. This would be the worst kind of battle; if fear did not consume the younger knights, the bitter cold could. Renk shivered with his memories of enduring frozen wars long passed, in honor of a once mightier Rogadon. His unwanted flashbacks were mercifully interrupted by a knock on his chamber door.

"Come in," He turned his eyes away from the intimidating mountain in time to see a haggard young man standing in his now open door.

"Morning, I am Prince Jiden. I hear from my cousin you are on a quest; a quest of some importance," Jiden stepped forward and shook the dark man's hand.

"Morning, your majesty," Renk bowed his head, furrowing his eyebrows in confusion.

"You have heard correctly, young prince. Miala is off in search of more help, but I will go with or without aid, I assure you, sire," Renk stood tall, his shoulders squared with his determination. Jiden allowed a grin to turn up one side of his mouth.

"Would you do me the honor of accompanying me on morning patrol? I wish to speak to you of this quest," Jiden's tired eyes sparked momentarily. Renk grinned.

"Absolutely sire," He bowed his head again, eager to be of service of this great kingdom.

"I make for the stables in only moments. I will see you there?" Jiden raised an eyebrow.

"Yes, sire," Renk watched the young blonde turn and leave, surprised by the unshaven, worn-down appearance of someone so young. Renk dressed in full chainmail and fur lined cape before rushing to say a quick good morning to his dear friend.

"Renk!" Callana jumped into the large man's embrace.

"Oh Renk, how much I have missed your face!" She squeezed him tightly, as he kissed her hair.

"I heard of your experience in Dellandore," He started, "I will see you proven royal if I have to draw up the papers myself!" Renk declared. Callana grinned through tear filled eyes. She had dressed in her fur lined tunic and cape and her green leggings with knee high fur lined boots, for her morning ride with George.

"Walk me to the stables?" She asked. Renk smiled and nodded, unaware her inevitable chance meeting with Jiden would not be a merry one. The pair charged down the chilly hall and out into the frozen pre-dawn air. George was stomping wildly when she arrived, eager to make up for their lost time together.

"I missed you too, you great purple stud!" She ran to him, hugging his giant neck while his head tossed up and down with his excitement.

"I have sent Rogala and your family to Sea Fair, safe from Dellandore's reach," Renk began. Callana sighed.

"Oh, thank God! I was terrified for them since I had heard of Dellandore's march but we are not to send mail. How did you get them a message?" Callana was busily saddling George when she noticed Renk was not answering.

"Renk?" She popped her head above George's saddle in time to see her now preoccupied friend shaking hands with Jiden. Her heart froze; stinging with the raw hurt and frustration from the night before. Jiden glanced at her, the easy smile he had mustered for Renk all but evaporating when he met her vicious eyes. Renk's grin also faded upon seeing their unpleasant exchange.

"I...ah...should saddle up, my lord. Excuse me," Renk bowed to Jiden, before he passed Callana to hurry down to the bay at the far end of the enormous stable. Leviathon, across from George, snorted to his rider in protest of the coming cold ride.

"Morning, Callana," Jiden's hoarse voice had gotten worse since last night and the weary look in his reddened eyes indicated he had as terrible a night as she.

"Your majesty," Callana bowed her head, swollen lids and blood shot eyes a painful reminder to Jiden that he had caused her great pain. She turned back to her task, fumbling while quickly bridling George in an effort to get far away from her ex lover. Jiden's eyes turned apologetic.

"Callana?"

"Yes, my lord?" Callana answered but refused to look at him. She could feel her reserve breaking as it was.

"I am truly sorry for things I said last night." Jiden had moved to George's side where Callana was now hiding, staring at the ground, willing Jiden away in her head.

"It is forgotten. Now, if you could excuse me, Prince Jiden, I will be leaving," Callana moved to George's front and started leading the agitated horse towards the nearby door. Jiden sighed, rolling his eyes in exasperation.

"You will not accept my apology than?" Jiden glared after her. Callana turned her face to him, a hardened expression sharpening her soft features.

"I do not have the *time* to forgive you right now, Prince Jiden, but I will let you know," turning to leave after her sarcastic comment, Callana quickly mounted George as soon as she was outside. Jiden's anger flared. He followed her outside, jumping in front of George as Callana attempted to spur him into a hasty retreat.

"You use my own words against me when I said them to *you* in earnest!" Jiden stepped to her side, green eyes burning up to her as he grabbed for George's rein.

"Let me go!" Callana tried to yank the rein free, but Jiden held tight.

"Is that what you want? You want me to let you go?" Jiden was almost pleading with her now, his tentative patience exhausted. Callana looked down at him, her eyes squinting with her failing composure.

"You are so dense!"

"Answer me, Callana! Do I give up on us?" Jiden's croaking voice cracked. Callana glared down at him, her hooded face wet with tears.

"If you have to ask me that then you already have!" Jiden bowed his head despairingly; when he turned his face back up to look at her, his blaring, eyes were wet. He released the rein, throwing his hands up in exasperation as he backed away, allowing Callana to kick George into a gallop as she escaped. Jiden watched her bouncing retreat until she evaporated around the bend before he returned to his now prancing stallion. Renk had inadvertently witnessed their altercation and felt his chest tighten with his angst over his friend's pain and the awkwardness he was sure would render the coming, intended conversation. Jiden was saddling Leviathon, yanking tight on his straps, causing the stallion's ears to lay flat with his gripe. Jiden turned a drawn face on his new acquaintance.

"Sir Renk, I apologize… I know you are friends…" Jiden was so emotionally exhausted he could not form his thoughts fast enough. Renk shook his head.

"Sire, she *is* one of my dearest friends, but I hold no ill will towards you. Your relationship with Callana is yours to sort, not mine." Renk assured him. Jiden tried to smile, nodding his head slightly.

"Thank you. You are almost a stranger to me yet you show me such kindness. I am grateful, sir Renk," Renk bowed his head, waving a hand, dismissing the prince's remarks.

"Let us ride and speak of tactics," Jiden offered, gesturing towards the door.

"Let's," Renk agreed as they both led their perspective horses out to the frozen ground of the upper village path.

"We will find my knights at the rise, just south of the last dwelling," Jiden pointed. The two spurred snorting mounts into a light canter as they pounded along on the sloping, winding dirt towards their patient quarry.

....

Lena searched the castle for her missing maiden; certain Miala was setting out to drive her mad with worry.

"Where has she gotten off to now?" Lena mumbled to herself as she turned to busy her nervous hands in the now warmed council hall. Odin was going to handle morning council, as usual, before joining Jiden in preparing their army for this so called, *show of force*, that Lena was sure would turn into an all out war if Ulei was anything like his prideful reputation suggested him to be. She had finished setting the table and was about to signal Gillian's team to bring out the food when Miala rushed through the large, chamber doors; huffing with her exertion.

"Miala, my goodness, I have been searching for you all morning!" Miala bowed respectfully through gasping breaths. When she rose to speak, she was gesturing wildly towards the door.

"Sorry your majesty...just....Erik...." Miala bent, trying to catch her breath. Lena sighed.

"Well don't stand there gagging, get into the council hall," Lena scolded, shushing the frazzled girl into the fire warmed room.

....

"My lord, may I ask you a question?" Renk bobbed along next to the world-weary prince, heading east towards the falls.

"Of course," Jiden seemed to come out of his fog, his eyes clearing as he turned to the amiable knight.

"Do you plan to attack? Or are you hoping sheer superior numbers will thwart Ulei?" Renk knew Jiden was inexperienced, and wanted to prepare the younger man as best as he could.

"The latter, I pray. I do not wish to lose good men to that supercilious prig," Jiden's stomach was starting to knot as his mind finally pushed Callana to the back, and threw the looming battle to the front.

"Of course. This is a talk reserved for your *father*, if you do not wish to talk to me, that is," Renk offered.

"I do not mind getting free advice. God knows I could use it," Jiden smiled with this, causing Renk to smile back.

"Well, Ulei is a snake, so expect dirty diplomacy; tricks, sneak attacks, anything you fear he may do, he will."

"Good to know," Jiden listened intensely, knowing full well he could easily be out maneuvered in his ignorance.

"If it was me, I would try a few *surprises* of my own," Renk went on.

"Like what?" Jiden chuckled with a sudden laughable idea. "Hide half my army? Ha!"

Renk's teeth gleamed in the grey dawn as a wide grin spread across his face.

"How do I *hide* two thousand men?" Jiden was earnestly asking, no sarcasm or condescension in his tone. Renk *knew* he liked the young prince now.

"On the *inside*," Renk stated. Jiden's brow furrowed.

"How do I get them inside? The castle is most likely surrounded by now," Jiden asked.

"I know of a tunnel system; you would emerge in the court yard, undetected by the outside forces."

"You have *seen* these tunnels?" Jiden's excitement was growing.

"I have *used* them sire, to smuggle ...*something* out of the city," Renk's face was apprehensive now, not sure how the prince would handle this particular part of the story.

"What? What did you smuggle?" Jiden was on the verge of laughing now at the chagrin look on the dark man's face.

"Your fiancée..." Renk grimaced.

"The princess Rogala?" Jiden's face was serious now; Callana flooding his mind again.

"Yes, sire. We fled the city through the tunnels, running south. That is where we met Calla..." Renk stopped himself from saying her name.

"You met Callana as you escaped?" Jiden pried, having never really heard the clear version of this story. He frowned with his sudden awareness that he had never even *asked* Callana.

"On the road, deep in the forest, sire," Renk could tell Jiden was hearing this for the first time and jumped on his chance to verify his friend's intrepidness.

"She actually came to the princess's aid; we had pulled over, well almost, for Rogala's third bout of morning sickness and Callana rushed to help. The two instantly became friends," Renk sighed with the memory of the girls' tremendous bond.

"When...how did it come about that..."Jiden began but Renk finished.

"The switch? Well, when Callana heard of our deep love, and our coming child, she asked why we fled. Once we explained about the arranged marriage, she insisted on carrying out Rogala's mission."

"So, she really did this all for peace and duty?" Jiden asked, reverently.

"No. She did this all for *love*," Renk smiled again, winking, his eyes softening with his thoughts of his beautiful little wife and their magnificent son, liberated due to the bravery of his good friend. Renk ached to be with his Rogala; precisely why he wanted to help bring a quick and painless end to this war.

Jiden sank in his saddle. How ironic; he had protested this marriage of duty, while Callana had accepted the same marriage for love. He felt like a fool; this morning, in the presence of the council, their duty would end, as well as their love. He had wrestled with his feelings throughout the night before; he could not be sure how much of Callana's charm had been part of an act or the real Callana, therefore had to protect himself. If he married her now, could he trust he was marrying the woman he loved? How would he know? The only encounters they had shared since she was found to be pretending had been horrible; sarcastic, spiteful words, angry out bursts, so much said in an attempt to hurt one another. Jiden was heavy hearted with the knowledge that they may have gone to far, said too much, to salvage any chance for *real* love he was not even sure she had ever felt for him.

"I have to stop thinking about her," Jiden accidentally mumbled out loud.

"My lord?" Renk asked.

"Sorry, I misspoke. I was just saying…I need to keep my mind on the task at hand," Jiden corrected, silently hoping Renk had not heard him.

"It is desperately hard to concentrate with a woman around and even harder to concentrate when they are gone!" Renk laughed with this, goading Jiden reluctantly into laughter.

"Right you are good knight, right you are!" Jiden laughed, again heartily this time. When they had both calmed slightly, Jiden scanned the horizon. Up ahead, near the goat fields where he and Callana had raced, he could see his group of knights awaiting him.

"I have made my men wait for me twice now this morning, they are never going to let me live that down, you know?" Jiden spurred Leviathon into a full gallop, Renk following on his large bay.

"Nothing to report North sire," Sir Senren spoke for his team of Lashend, Gracien and Laden and himself when Jiden had halted.

"Clear West, sire," Sir Galland gave the report for his team of Nicholas, David and Franklin. As Jiden nodded to his team, he noticed over Sir Galland's shoulder, that a great purple horse raced back towards the castle, not two hundred paces from them, with a green clad rider, red hair billowing out behind. Nicholas followed the prince's glare then shrugged.

"What about her?" Jiden asked.

"We *saw* her," Nicholas chided, "She is no *threat*," he continued snidely.

"Says you," Jiden mumbled before turning the troop back towards Adalonia's great white castle and this most dreaded morning report.

· ·

Jiden marched into morning council, followed closely by his royal guard, including Erik and Renk for this occasion. His eyes met Callana's, and a confusing mixture of happiness and bitterness swallowed his self assuredness. He was trying to read those dark eyes, but could not decipher what her hard stare suggested. He pulled his attention from her to bow to his father, then his mother. The council filed in as he sat, across from Callana, still in her riding gear. Now that she was not seen as a princess, his mother had released her from any dress code or duties. Jiden could only assume she was here today….to hear his father call off the wedding. Jiden grimaced; his stomach flipping and twisting, painfully coiling with his intense angst. Callana was sitting straight backed, her forehead creased slightly with her own worrying. She and Jiden had turned resentful and hostile towards each other; she could feel nothing more than a sickening, conflicting combination of longing and hatred when she looked at him now, thoroughly confusing her and wearing her down. They sat there, only feet away from each other, each stubbornly waiting for the other to break first, to start their affair over again, this time in earnest. Callana watched Jiden clutch his side; she wondered if he was as upset as she. Odin rose to start the meeting, interrupting her thoughts.

"I begin this council meeting with a heavy heart," Odin began. Jiden and Lena both lowered their heads, fully aware of what was coming.

"We have a saddening matter to discuss. In light of the…recent events…" Odin gestured slightly to Callana, causing her to hang her head in shame.

"I am calling off the wedding; Callana and Jiden's marriage will no longer stay Rogadon's safety, and Ulei is fully aware and taking full advantage," The council nodded, as they had been briefed on the events in Dellandore. Callana sagged slightly, tears threatening to spill as she turned towards Jiden; her eyes pleading with him to speak. Jiden's face showed his anguish. He was truly sorry for all that had transpired as of late.

"The sooner we resolve this campaign for Rogadon, the sooner Callana can return home to Windt, where I am sure she is *dearly* missed." Odin flashed a sympathetic look towards her when he spoke, regretful she would be leaving. "Prince Jiden is leading this…fracas…so I give the floor to him now, Prince?" Odin turned, bowing towards his son and Jiden slowly rose, clearing his scratchy throat to speak.

"I will be leaving this evening for Rogadon and with the king's permission, I need to take this day for preparation and will give a full strategic report after supper in an emergency evening council," Odin nodded his permission and Jiden bowed before sitting again. Odin dismissed the council and set about to begin his own home front defensive maneuvering with the six thousand men he would be keeping back to guard the castle. Callana fled through the doors, avoiding Jiden's eyes in her sprint to her bed chamber. Once inside, she sank slowly to her bed, slumping over and sobbing into her velvety bed spread. After watching her retreat, Jiden came to Nicholas.

"Cousin, I will be in the study....in a few hours I will find you...." Jiden seemed far away; unable to make cognitive connections in his tired mind. Nicholas frowned.

"Of course, my lord...cousin? Do you not think you should rest?" Nicholas clapped a hand on Jiden's shoulder. Jiden mustered something close to a smile and shook his head.

"I have too much to do. No time for rest now. No time for...*anything* anymore. Meet me in the study in an hour and bring Galland, Renk and Erik. Ey? If they are willing, I would greatly appreciate their assistance." Jiden's face was intent now, finally focused, having come to some inner conclusion.

"Ahhhh, so if she is proven royal, you can reinstate your arranged marriage?" Nicholas was grinning like mad, trying to bait Jiden. The tired prince sighed, rubbing his weary eyes in annoyance.

"Be gone, you irritating horse's ass," Nicholas bowed to the disconcerted prince before turning on a heel to head for the knights' quarters on the easternmost wing of the castle. Jiden turned north, avoiding the corridor passed Callana's chamber to take the long way to the study, attached to the royal library; hoping to find a quiet place to fill his aching head with strategy, pushing out all thoughts of his estranged, beloved red head for now. He was to lead an impressive army; such an army deserved his fervent dedication, and that's what he would give them.

· ·

The snow covered carriage set out again after allowing the crammed passengers a brief leg stretch, and urination break in the deep wet chill of the graying evening. Dakin and Cylan came in, frozen from their long day on the perch; Crystalline and Christopher voluntarily taking their place, bundled for their shift. Rogala had already informed them they had another day of travel, so their stop was quick, as everyone was eager to get to Sea Fair and out of this carriage for good. Hellena's heart sank in her chest. This was the first night, first trip away from home, her home, hand built by her beloved Cai since Crystalline was born. She felt a terrible longing for the Stone's throw; having attached all of her affection for her husband long passed into every inch of the wonderful Inn. In the dark, tight quarters of the carriage, next to her sleeping daughters, Hellena silently wept for her love, and the home they had forged and filled together, so many years ago.

· ·

"Here, near the western edge of the Shadow's forest, beyond the farmers' valley. That's the entrance. It opens up in that last mountain's middle. It's a day's ride," Renk was using his thick finger to trace their intended path on a hand drawn map Jiden had painstakingly sketched during his productive hour of solitude.

"I will lead four thousand to the front lines, well basically; I will give you a thousand men for the tunnels. Now, are you sure of your man on the inside? I do not want my men coming out under attack by Rogadon." Jiden's brow was furrowed with his concentration, yearning to get this terrible march started. He had chosen the greater number in hopes Ulei would recognize Jiden's superior force and call off his futile siege.

"I trust Ranik, your majesty. If it eases your mind, I will be sure to emerge first, in my Rogadon wear, to ensure Adalonia is permitted and accepted." Jiden nodded, this proposition indeed easing some of his worries.

"I would be most grateful, Sir Renk." Jiden raised his head to make eye contact with his small committee of Renk, Galland, Nicholas and Erik. "Supper is in two hours; Galland and Nicholas, see that the men eat well and are rested. Erik, you will see to it that Edward and his crew have the horses saddled and watered by then? Renk, seeing as how Miala is *insisting* on going, please see her to the armor for some chainmail and perhaps a training sword?" The four men nodded, bowing before eagerly rushing off to serve their purposes. Jiden set out for his self assigned tasks. First and foremost he needed to see to their supplies and make sure Silvio was ready.

....

"I have equipped my young apprentice well, I assure you young prince. He will be as reliable in the field as I but with more... *agility*," Lustene bowed to Jiden at the conclusion of his report. Jiden nodded.

"Where is your ward now, old friend?" Jiden asked, glancing around the cozy home and office of his life time companion. Lustene cleared his throat and blushed slightly as he spoke, refusing to meet Jiden's stare.

"I ah, he... is.... *visiting* ...a close friend before his departure, sire," Lustene seemed extremely uncomfortable exposing the closest thing he had ever had to a son. He had raised Silvio on his own, since the impressively sharp lad had lost both parents to the plague when he was only nine years of age. His older sister, Siriana, had begun her wedding planning, deciding she had no time or financial capabilities of rearing him herself, and had delivered him from Esildad to the famous castle's steps around the same time Lustene was ending a routine examination of his King. The then only slightly graying younger surgeon had initially taken on the child in the midst of the girl's anxious haste, with no intentions of actually keeping the boy; but after a few days together, Lustene found Silvio to be something of a kindred spirit, and asked him to stay.

Six years later, and Lustene was having a hard time releasing his fatherly command over the young man, who had of late, became intensely interested in a young, chesty brunette whose mother was a seamstress only yards away. Lustene sighed, sorting through his mental images and fleeting memories.

"Ah, I see. Yes, I can understand the need to *visit* before leaving on an undetermined length of absence," Jiden smirked, trying to sound knowledgeable but only convincing himself he wanted to *visit* Callana, now more than ever! Lustene noticed his sudden frown.

"I understand the wedding has been cancelled," he started slowly, careful to note Jiden's sagging reaction.

"I see. You can not marry her because she is not a princess..." Lustene clasped his hands behind his back and nodded. Jiden interrupted the older man.

"No! Not...I mean, my *father* cancelled the marriage of *duty*...I just have not decided...I mean...m...my head has decided *no* because I do not ...know who she or... I mean...who I really loved. My heart is still stuck on *yes*...so I am eeessentially..." Jiden was rambling, making Lustene grin widely.

"In love," He finished for the stuttering prince. Jiden stood, blinking, silenced by the wise man's summation.

"Yes, young prince. I see the symptoms clearly; stammering speech, exhaustion, sudden stupidity," Lustene was thoroughly enjoying this taunt.

"All right, old man, you have had your tease." Jiden tried to joke the conversation to an end; not at all anxious to see where it was going.

"I am laughing but I am dead serious. I know love when I see it, sire," He slowly straightened his smile till it was merely a curl on his lips, his eyes turning solemn. Jiden shook his head.

"Even if I were, *in love*, how would I know if it is her or the *pretend* her I love?" Jiden's torment was starting to unravel his composed guise. Lustene folded his arms across his chest and brought a hand up to scratch his leathery chin.

"Well, let us approach this logically; first, tell me what you loved about her," Jiden sighed.

"Lustene, forgive my impatience but I only have a few hours till I set off for *war* and I do not have time to..."

"Than I must tell the king you are unstable, therefore unfit to lead an army..." Lustene threatened, somewhat nonchalantly. Jiden held up his hands in surrender.

"Fine!" He put his hands on his slim hips as he paced back and forth between Lustene's heavy door and his blazing fire pit.

"I love her face; those dark eyes, the smooth, alabaster skin and those full pink lips…" Jiden had frozen; his mind engulfed with Callana's radiant beauty. Lustene nodded, than held up a finger on his right hand.

"Real," He stated. Jiden turned to him with confusion wrinkling his brow. "Lustene?"

"*Real*; her beautiful face is real. I am keeping score; go on sire," Lustene sternly urged the patient on. Jiden nodded slowly, than resumed his pacing.

"Well, I love her spirit; she is so… exhilarating! And excitable! She seemed to find…fun… in everything she did,"

"Real,"

"God I love her eyes,"

"So you have already said, go on," Lustene pushed.

"Her kindness, caring for villagers…"

"Villagers she knew she had no *real* accountability for, yet helped anyway," Lustene interrupted.

"Of course, in keeping with her princess façade, no doubt," Jiden argued.

"Of course," Lustene half heartedly agreed. "Back to the list," He insisted.

"I love her bravery; she saved Gant, killed a wolf, even in prison, she was fearless," Jiden rambled. Lustene interrupted Jiden's musing.

"She saved Rogadon," the older man stated.

"What do you mean?" Jiden asked.

"With Rogala's escape, Rogadon was without an heir, therefore open to siege. Callana took that burden upon herself, to save a kingdom she did not even know. There could be no braver act," Lustene's bright blue eyes hardened when he caught Jiden's stare. He glanced at his right hand, bending each finger down than back up again as he silently counted.

"I have a full hand of real, and only one fake. So tell me, how much did you *love* her for being a princess?" Lustene was prodding him now, raising his bushy eyebrows and holding both hands out for Jiden to see.

"I understand," Jiden conceded quietly. His eyes had fallen to the ground now, and his feet shuffled back and forth.

"Well?" Lustene asked.

"Well, what?"

"Well, what are you doing *here*? Do you not have *someone* else you need to talk to?" Jiden grinned, than suddenly grabbed Lustene in a crunching embrace.

"Thank you, you are a great friend!" With that, he was out the door, the blasting cold wind and freezing shin deep of snow going unnoticed by the determined prince, ablaze with his purpose.

....

"You do not have to accompany me to the armor; I know how…distressed you have been," Miala smiled apathetically into her friend's swollen lidded, red eyes. Callana slapped her hands to her hips and gasped.

"You think I am going to sit up here and cry through your very first trip to the armor? Ha!" She threw back her head, her green hood flopping back, exposing the bright white rabbit fur lining and her disheveled red hair. Miala had to giggle at her worn friend.

"Very well then, I told Renk I would meet him there. Let us beat him!" The narrow hipped girl bolted through the reception hall for the front doors, tugging one open enough to slither through it as her wider friend attempted and stuck. Callana wriggled, trying to dislodge her hips or open the door, whichever came first. She laughed as she tossed her head up to yell after the tiny maiden when she noticed Jiden dashing up the icy limestone steps.

"Callana? Where are you going?" Jiden pushed on the big door to free the blushing red head; leaning into her as he heaved against the robust wood.

"Sire," She bowed her head.

"I was following Miala…wait… *why?*" She suddenly balked; her forehead crinkling in irritation.

"I was just wondering…you looked like you were having fun," Jiden smiled down at her. Callana rolled her dark eyes, dramatizing her exasperation.

"I am sorry, I could only cry for so long before I ran out of tears. If you give me a few hours I am sure I could come up with more!" Her snapping comment surprised Jiden, and he shrank back away from her.

"I did not mean anything by it," Jiden held his hands up in an admission of defeat. This angry, biting version of Callana was not the one he had come in search of. He suddenly felt tired again.

"I wanted to talk to you," Jiden kept his voice small, hoping to calm her down. Callana only flicked her eyebrow in response.

"Can we get out of the door way? Please?" He asked.

"Oh, you have *time* to talk to me? Why didn't you say so? Let me forget everything *I* am doing for *you!*" Callana crossed her arms as she stepped back to allow Jiden to come in. Jiden stepped just inside; turning to push the door shut against the cold.

"Callana, I do not wish to *fight* with you, only talk." Jiden held his hands out to his sides.

"So? Out with it, your majesty," Callana's tone was serious, and confusing. He was trying to gage the hard look on her face again but decided to just start talking.

"Callana, I have been doing some thinking and I have something to say." Jiden reached for her hand as he spoke, but she pulled back.

"Can you stop being *mad* at me long enough to hear me out?" Jiden's anger spiked.

"I can *hear* you without holding your hand!" Callana fumed at his arrogance; she was supposed to show affection to the man who had only just last evening told her he could not *decide* if he still cared for her?

"Stubborn girl! You make everything so much…harder than it has to be!"

"*I* am making things harder? Forgive me, your royalness! *Please*? Tell me what I can do to make *your* life easier!"

"You could shut your mouth for starters!" Jiden's teeth were gritted with his frustration.

"Should I also stop breathing? I would not want to disturb your air!" Callana was raging now.

"Quit!" Jiden barked, but Callana was completely ignoring him now.

"I could set myself on fire and you could use me to keep warm!" Callana was glaring at him, her brown eyes welling over. Jiden kept trying to talk over her ranting to no avail.

"Stop, Callana! Just stop!" His fury boiled; antagonized by Callana's insistence that he was now her enemy.

"Wait! You haven't heard the best part; I could do you the honor of never speaking to you to spare you from every having to hear my *voice* again!" Jiden grabbed her shoulders and shook her violently.

"Enough!" His growling voice slammed off the stone walls, echoing all around them. Jiden was glowering down at her, his teeth grinding and his nostrils flaring with his rage.

"Jiden!" The snarling prince turned to see his mother, terrified and trembling behind him.

"Mother?" He looked from Lena to Callana, then at his gripping hands. He released Callana immediately, and forced himself to look in her crying eyes.

"I am so sorry," Jiden sank back. Callana could see he was sincere, although it did little to ease her immense remorse. What had she done? She had purposely goaded him into an argument in an attempt to avoid talking to him at all, and she had pushed him over the edge. Jiden was staring at her, his face twisted with guilt over what he had allowed his anger to make him do.

"I need to leave," Callana's voice was shaking and quiet. Lena came to the pair, taking their hands in hers.

"This may be *your* conflict to resolve, but this is *my* castle." She turned hard green eyes on Jiden.

"I will never see this again, is that understood?" Jiden nodded fervently, but would not look at his mother or Callana now. Shame swallowed his voice as he bowed slowly to his mother.

"As for you, Callana, you are forbidden to leave until Rogadon and the road is secure; is *that* understood?" Callana bowed her head, nodding slowly, as tears fell to the hard, grey floor.

"Very well," Lena backed away, giving Jiden a harsh look before quickly leaving to finish her duties before supper. Callana wiped her face with her cape as she turned to wrench open the door. Jiden came up behind her, his arms on either side of her shoulders; his hands on either side of her hands, as he pulled open the door. Callana turned her head and felt Jiden's warm breath on her cheek, as the frigid air swirled around her. Once she could wiggle through, Callana dashed to the armor; Jiden's attempt had failed.

"Good evening, esteemed members of council, mother, father, and knights," Jiden began his presentation.

"I will keep this short. My newly appointed committee and I have come up with a basic strategy, in hopes the council will see fit to accept our plans, with your full support and faith." Jiden gestured widely to the room, being sure to make eye contact with each member of council and his parents. Callana, Miala, Nicholas, Renk, Erik and Jiden's royal guard were in attendance as well as half of Odin's guard; the other half were on high alert on the castle wall posts, as was custom in all emergency situations. Illiam was there to take close and undoubtedly precise notes on the meeting as to answer any questions later and for records of this event.

Callana could not help but marvel over the change of attitude Jiden could so quickly adopt while addressing council. She had noticed it during morning councils. Jiden was commanding, yet humble, and his facial features were hardened by his internal call to action. Jiden caught her surveying stare and faltered. Their exchange did not go unnoticed by the meeting's attendees, and Jiden blushed slightly under their scrutinizing eyes, than cleared his throat to speak.

"As of yesterday, Dellandore has of yet to send scouts our way, as I am sure they are hoping to avoid our interference and I want to use their own secrecy against them; the majority of the designated army will ride south with me, essentially paralleling the road, but using the cover of the forest and splitting into three divisions, a thousand men each; to come at the most assuredly, surrounded Rogadon from all directions. The woods will slow us down but it would be most beneficial to retain the element of surprise." There was a murmuring and bobbing of agreement around the room. Jiden glanced to his right to check his father's response, and was pleased to see his king was also nodding his acceptance thus far. Jiden allowed himself to relax slightly and continued. Callana watched Lena across the room, smiling at the brightness in the delicate queen's eyes as she beamed with pride for her only child. she could tell Jiden had been anxious about the initial reaction his parents would have, and had loosened visibly with their concurrence.

"It will only be four thousand men, but Dellandore needs only a reminder of our superior forces, at least that is my hope. With the other six thousand only a few days away, King Ulei will realize his disadvantage immediately."

"You have thought this out well, my son, I commend your effort. But you do know he will out number you by a thousand once you are face to face," Odin was leaning forward, resting elbows on the sleek cedar table, his hands clasped together. Jiden nodded, having prepared himself for his father's questions.

"Yes father, I have taken that into consideration as well, which brings me to part two of my plan. You are all aware that prince Nicholas has dedicated some time towards researching Callana's family line; as her mother has recently uncovered some evidence linking Callana's father, Cai, to Queen Camden," The room suddenly stilled, the boggling stares slowly turning from Jiden to Callana.

"Actually, son, I had not informed them, as we have no solid substantiation to validate the claim as yet," Lena interjected.

"How does Callana's lineage tie into this war, I mean, obviously, other than the fact that she would be sole, blood heir if proven..." Odin began but was cut short by his eager son.

"Therefore, father, eradicating any false claims Ulei has taken it upon himself to act on. If you will let me explain, you will see its relevance." Jiden maintained a respectful tone, his eyes imploring his father to allow him this opportunity to show he had done his research. Odin bowed his head, and waved his hand.

"Of course, my son; I apologize," Jiden continued with that.

"Thank you, father; our remaining six thousand will also be divided; as is customary, the five thousand will keep our home front. I have no intention of leaving us open in case any kingdoms hearing of Rogadon's plight and our consequential involvement try to assert themselves over our divided forces, and keeping the majority home will almost double our numbers against *any* invading armies with the guidance of our brother in arms, Sir Renk," Jiden gestured towards the dark knight who bowed to the room. "Being a former soldier of Rogadon, has intimate knowledge of a tunnel system I am sending a thousand men through; consequently popping them up directly inside the castle court," Jiden allowed a small grin to curl his lips with the round of awes and approving nods he received for this maneuver.

"I cannot take the credit for this particular tactical maneuver, actually, it was Sir Renk's volunteered advice that made this possible, therefore, I am commissioning him commanding officer of the tunnel brigade," Jiden bowed to a now taken Renk, who bowed after a momentary stunning relented its control over his movements.

"Thank you, sire; I will serve Adalonia as honorably as I can, your majesty," Renk bowed again, than again, unable to wipe a huge smile off his blushing cheeks. Lena stifled a giggle over the man's blatant and adorable surprise. He seemed an honest man, in the least, she thought.

"Sir Renk has comrades on the inside he will signal upon arrival, insuring our army is received peaceably," Jiden added, to quall any doubts the council might have over Renk's newly appointed position of power.

"I am extremely impressed, prince Jiden, and I would like to offer my approval. Is there any among us who will join me?" The eldest member of the council, Corrin, slowly turned his large, intelligent brown eyes on the room. Nona, the eldest woman, was carefully considering all she had heard; her piercing blue eyes staring hard into Corrin's as she pondered. She finally nodded.

"Aye," her singly voice rang out, followed by the rest of the council. Nona was a figure head in Adalonia, having raised seven children on her own after the early death of her husband. Her silky white hair, noble nose, lengthy fingers and incredible carriage, gave her the appearance of a great, elegant crane; and her opinion carried immense sway over her fellow council members. Now Jiden turned to his father and mother. Lena nodded solemnly.

"I am in approval, as much as a mother can be to send her only child to war," Jiden smiled apathetically to his mother.

"Mother, this is a *show* of force, as father has pointed out. I will return, on my honor," Jiden held his hand to his heart as he spoke to her, swearing his oath. Lena nodded, turning sad eyes down to the table's glossy surface.

"I am in agreement, except for one detail," Odin squinted in thought, turning to Renk.

"I am assuming, due to their attendance, that these young ladies intend on going?" Odin looked at Callana and Miala, calculating their worth as a farmer would mentally weigh a sheep. Both girls squirmed slightly under his penetrating gaze.

"*Miala* is father, she has been fitted for chainmail," He nodded towards her, noting the exasperated look on Callana's face. He cringed in response.

"I, ah, was against allowing Callana to go, for fear of what could happen to her if Ulei discovers her." Jiden turned apologetic eyes on the now fuming Callana.

"Than I am in agreement; Callana, although I do not doubt your character, my dear, prince Jiden is right; Ulei would do anything to get a hold of you and I am sure I could never forgive myself if I allowed you to fall into danger. You understand?" Odin had softened his tone but Callana knew he would not entertain any arguments or attempts to tag along. She bowed her head in resignation.

"As you wish, my lord," She raised her head and looked to Jiden, whose face had twisted with his angst over hurting her. She fought back the stinging of what she felt was betrayal, however slight or good the reason, and nodded begrudgingly to Jiden. He sighed and turned back to the council.

"As for Rogadon's fate; as of now, I have only allowed a few moments of thought on the subject but wanted to leave the council with an idea to deliberate; I propose, that is, if Callana is not in line for the throne, that we host a tournament. Winner takes stewardship of Rogadon until a rightful heir can be assigned?" Again his idea ignited a round of excited awes and murmuring as the council voiced their agreement to give the idea some thought.

"Thank you all for your time and if my father has nothing to add," Jiden looked to his father; Odin shook his curly head.

"I adjourn this meeting. Illiam, if I could please have a copy in my chamber before I leave?" Illiam nodded, fervently writing as he hurried from the room. Jiden shook hands with most of the impressed council before turning to catch up to Callana.

"Callana, please, tell me you are not cross? I cannot bear to leave like this," He jogged up to her side but she waved him away. He had no time and begrudgingly watched her escape before turning to rush to his room to dress in his full chainmail. His squire, was close behind while Miala and her champion, Renk, grabbed Callana in a fierce embrace on their way to the stables and a thousand newly appointed comrades. Odin and Lena would watch them all go from the tower, and offered for Callana to join, and reluctantly, she followed; already hurting to see Jiden go.

Only moments later, Odin, Lena and Callana stood solemnly but strong; watching their savior mount his mighty stallion; Leviathan's gleaming coat was blending seamlessly into the snow covered limestone court, with only the lush green of his Adalonia covering to separate the two. Galland, Senren, David and Franklin sat mounted and saluting on Leviathan's right while Nicholas, Gracien, Lashend and Laden saluted from their mounts to his left. Once ready to go, Jiden turned a somber face towards the tower, saluting his king and queen. Callana's heart deliberated; her pulse pushed her chilling blood slowly through her frigid body. She was consumed with a cold sadness as she stood on her shared, lofty perch, amidst such royalty; formally returning his son's salute, Odin grimaced visibly with his own concern. Lena was standing firm, nobly bowing her head in response, as tears rolled slowly down her cheeks. Jiden would never see their agony, but Callana did, and although the prince had calculated and planned, Lena and Odin would still worry, as Callana would. Jiden was waiting for her dismissal, his piercing emerald eyes glowing against the bright of the white snow covered world around him. Callana closed her eyes, and bowed her head; hesitant to allow him to go. She felt panic ripple through her as he turned his battle dressed charger towards the now opened gate of the courtyard, and she had to steel herself against calling him back. Callana was nearly panting, puffing clouds of hot breath out around her as his billowing green caped detachment descended the village path, paralleled with perfectly aligned constituents bowing respectfully as their champions passed.

Callana faltered, looking to the chivalrous couple before she spun quickly, flying down the twisted stairs and leaping through the halls until she reached the main door, struggling to open one just enough to rush through, as she fled through the silent courtyard. The gate guards, heads still bowed, allowed her to pass through as she raced for the rise in the road. Jiden and his royal guard had met with the three thousand by now; Nicholas, Jiden and Galland, each taking the lead over their designated thousand foot soldiers. Callana was sprinting down the hardened ground path; passing blurred villagers and their homes in her pursuit for a better vantage point. Erik,

Renk and Miala met their thousand men and immediately turned them towards the tunnel entrance somewhere beyond the western plains. Callana's heart was pounding now, threatening to tear her chest wide with its desire to see him one last time! She nearly flung herself to the top of the slippery ice covered rocky crop of the rise; huffing her exhaustion out in giant puffs as she longed, for him to turn around; praying to see his face once more. As if in response, as Nicholas, Galland and their two thousand headed east to part ways near Mount Andoria, Jiden called to move out south towards the forest, but stilled in place suddenly. Callana nearly gasped with elation, wanting to jump frantically up and down to have him notice her.

Jiden's head turned, in slow motion it seemed, glancing over his shoulder towards her. Callana felt her spirit sink as he turned back to his men again, apparently having not seen her. She sagged where she stood, miserably aware of the biting cold now that her blood had calmed after her dash to the rise. Callana turned saddened eyes up to watch her prince depart before returning to the castle, when she saw him there, white main and tail flying, as Leviathan's pounding hooves could only now be heard. He was coming back to her! Callana vaulted from her rocky landing and ran to him. When Jiden was near, he swung his right leg over the saddle, stepping out of the stirrup with his left foot as he pulled the reins and stopped his sweating horse only feet from Callana.

Without a word, Jiden came to her, stopping only inches away. They held there for a stretching moment, memorizing one another. Time stood for them, locked in each others' stare; both with so much to say that neither could speak in what could be their last moments together.

"I must go," Jiden apologized, reaching for her hand and kissing it, then quickly turned, mounting Leviathon in one deft movement, and riding off. As the big horse thundered away, Callana watched on, waiting until the entire platoon had disappeared into the forest before allowing herself to make her slow, painfully frozen climb back up towards her bedchamber, and the beginning of her agonizing wait for her prince.

....

"Oh Rogala! It is beautiful!" Hellena nearly fell out of the carriage in her amazement. The salty spray of the rolling sea filled the air around them. Hellena could taste it as she spoke.

"Girls! The ocean! Oh, Cai would be so proud of us!" Crystalline and Christopher stumbled down, joints aching from their long turn in the perch, mouths agape with the sight before them. Cylan knelt to touch this new ground; her silt covered hands trembling with the excitement of her first experience with sand. Cella was, for once, completely speechless; standing with hands over her mouth in awe of the great, swelling waters, stretching endlessly out before her. Caran was crying, clasping her mothers shaking hand, as the two marveled and feared all at once, the glory of the mighty sea. "I feel...insignificant! I am *nothing* of God's creations compared to *this*!" Hellena cried; inundated with the expanse of the sea's blue reach as well as its roaring and crashing white waves. Rogala's charming little raised cottage went all but unnoticed by the overwhelmed inland family. Rogala held her snoring infant as she stood shoulder to shoulder with her mother. The two smiled knowingly at each one another as they remembered *their* first time seeing the ocean. It was an emotional response no one was immune to.

"I have seen the tremendous peaks of Mount Lisia, hidden in clouds, as if the angels themselves could reach down and stir them; but I have never seen the likes of this sea! My eyes are not big enough!" Christopher was captured by the beauty before him. He grasped Crystalline's delicate hand and dropped to a knee. Crystalline's gasp drew her family's torn attention.

"Crystalline, I can think of nothing more magnificent than this sea, and even with all its magic, it fails in comparison to you. I love you; I love you from the depths of my soul. In the presence of your family and this glorious sea, please, say you will marry me?" Hellena could scarcely handle these attacks on her heart. She nearly collapsed into Caran as the entire clan held their breaths in wait for Crystalline's response.

Her graceful face was pale; her shimmering orange eyes releasing their hold on stinging tears she had conjured for the sea as her lips parted and she caught her breath. Crystalline nodded slowly at first, then fervently as her shock relented. She grabbed Christopher's collar and bent down to him.

"What took you so long?" She did not wait for a response, pulling him to her and kissing him hard. Cylan and Caran squealed and danced around the couple as Rogala and Nia rushed to Hellena's traumatized side.

"Love, are you all right?" Nia asked her friend. Hellena nodded and finally shook her head clear.

"Yes, sorry, yes!" she cheered as she came to the kissing couple, clearing her throat. Crystalline finally relinquished her stupor entranced fiancée long enough to allow him to stand, and tower over her again. She embraced her mother.

"Mother! It is all right, isn't it?" Crystalline was so happy, so filled with her love for this lanky young man, and Hellena was all to consumed with her own joy over her daughter's fortunes, that she could not form words to suit the moment. She just nodded and squeezed the two of them as hard as she could before everyone turned back to the task of settling.

Standing, basking in the almost unbearable magnitude of this sea, and surrounded by her family and friends, Hellena marveled at the intense trek life truly was. How youth flashes by so fast, you forget to remember every detail of all of your firsts; the first time you ride a horse, spark a fire, catch a fish; your first true love, and the first time you see passion chase the innocence out of your lover's eyes. There were days Hellena would trade her soul to have one more *first*; in the mature years of life when we have made all the mistakes, and earned all of the praises, what is left? Was she only to *watch* others live now? Is that the fate of true love; to suffer the loss of your only partner? *Alone*? Until your own death? Hellena could not believe that the same God who gave the world this incredible ocean could have intended for widows and widowers to pass unloved through the remainder of their lives. Seeing her children through was her responsibility; once grown, seeing them *in* love was first and foremost, for as far as Hellena was concerned, everyone deserved to know true love and every soul on earth was created to intrinsically bind to another. Hellena allowed a small hope to shiver through her as she beheld the ocean; maybe there would be another match for *her*, after all. And what of Nia? Who had been in love with a married man in secret? Did she not deserve true love? Real love she could shout about from the roof tops and not hide in shame? Hellena made a decision; however long this temporary designation would be, they would make the most of it; as a family, and she would pray for peace, happiness and love for them *all*.

....

"Oh please? I promise I will stay close and cause no trouble...you wont even know I am there!" Callana begged Odin; creased forehead, and large, lipid brown pools implored the big king, cornered against the front doors of the castle. Odin scratched his head, glancing over the red head's shoulder at Lena, who was standing with her arms crossed in the door way of the council chambers. Odin feared he would have an angry female either way he answered, but he understood Callana's need.
"Fine, you may ride on morning patrols," Odin began, catching a scathing look from his tiny wife.
"But," he continued, stilling Callana's dancing celebration.
"You will need chainmail and you go no where alone, understood?" Callana nodded then turned and crushed the queen in a grateful embrace.
"I know you are worried for me my queen, but I will be safe, I promise!" Callana released the suffocated woman long enough to bolt for the armor. Odin came to his wife; a beseeching pout on his lips.
"Please do not be cross, my beautiful, incredible, magnificent..." Lena slapped him across his face.
"I worry for my son every minute and now you will make me insane worrying about *you and Callana*? Why can you not assign your royal guard to conduct patrol without you? This is a time of high alert, is it not? You of all people should not be out in plain view of any assassins!" Lena was shaking with her fury, but Odin could see the genuine fear behind her lovely green eyes.

"I love you; because of many reasons but none as much as for your strength, my ferocious little queen. And you love me for many reasons but none more than for my bravery; you know very well I refuse to hide in fear, relinquishing my duty to my own kingdom. I will have my guard with me, as always, and Callana will be safe; on my honor!" Odin stepped back and raised his right hand, looking quite like his son Lena noted. She sighed, having lost this battle one two many times this week. She looked as if she might storm away, but instead, turned and grabbed Odin in a fierce embrace. She *was* really worried, Odin mused, as she rarely showed any physical signs of affection outside of their bedchamber. Odin had a slight inclination he was standing in for her son, who made it a point to hug his mother every day and was not here to do so. Odin held her tight, kissing her immaculate hair as he whispered in her ear.

"Everything will be fine, you will see, my love. Now," He barked the last, forcing Lena back at arms length.

"Let me go woman! There is man's work to be done!" Odin was trying his best chauvinistic attitude, finally inducing a small smile out of his wife. He kissed her lips and slapped her on the rump before easily pulling open and shut the large wooden doors but not before Lena caught a glance at the cold, icy white world beyond and was reminded of her boy, out in that terrible cold, on his way to war, and she shivered violently.

Callana was all too excited about this mornings ride. She and her great purple mount had not been permitted to ride for the last four days since Jiden had left, and without Miala in the castle, Callana could only do chores and read to keep her mind busy, and it was just not enough. Her body needed to move, not just fidget, and she needed to *feel* the air in her lungs. Once she had donned her heavy chainmail, she flung her luxuriously warm fur lined Adalonia green cape over her quiver and bow and tied it around her neck, before racing for the barn. George nearly flew out of his stall when she entered, and she had barely gotten a foot in the stirrups when he burst down the winding village path. She was well ahead of the king but his royal guard met her with open smiles near the rise in the road. It was more than just the ride or comradery she needed, it was the chance to hear from Jiden, although, it would not actually be Jiden, but a message from him nonetheless.

Jiden had no doubt, reached his predetermined camping spot where he would have to remain, undetected, for another day, allowing Nicholas and Galland, coming from the east through the farthest point of the Adalonia farmlands at the base of Mount Andoria, before splitting, where Nicholas would turn west, after both armies crossed the tributary, now frozen, and push in on Rogadon, and Galland would make even further south, almost to Stones throw, to come north through the forest. Both battalions would be closing in on Rogadon; Nicholas from the east, Galland from the south, and Jiden's force would meet them from the west; leaving Ulei no escape, backed into the castle to fight, where he would find his army attacked from within the very walls of the city itself by Renk and his thousand.

Callana believed in Jiden's plan and Jiden himself, but could not help but fear for him. Silvio was with Jiden's detachment, and once the three companies were joined, he would serve them all, and Callana had confidence in him as well, therefore she could not logically explain her fear. Lustene had insisted it was, irrational, and apparently common in women, to worry needlessly. Callana convinced herself that being among the first to hear from the front lines would ease her tensions, and the messages would more than likely be coming during morning patrol.

"We was thinking of doing some archery after patrol if you is interested?" Sir Kern wiggled his bushy blonde eyebrows at Callana and winked. Callana giggled at her recently forged friend and nodded.

"You are on, sir!" She laughed. Kern grinned and gestured towards Dashend and Earnest.

"Told you she would go for it," he turned back to Callana and pointed at the cousins.

"They thought you would say no on account of the cold, but I told them you'd go," he assured her, turning a defiant sneer on the two. The nearly identical cousins shook their heads.

"It weren't a *woman* thing, Callana, nothin like that!" Dashend promised. Callana laughed out loud at the innocent look on the large man's face; so much like his adorable son, but almost twice his size.

"I will try not to hold it against you!" she warned him. Earnest's chapped lips curled in an evil grin.

"*You can hold it against me*," He flicked his eyebrows at her, causing Graven and Keiton to 'boo' him. The silent sir Paul pinched his nose in protest.

"Boo! In poor taste!" called Reinhold.

"You don't talk to a beautiful woman like that!" Graven announced, than pulled his tall brown mare up next to Callana, turning his massive body in his saddle and doing his best to look debonair, with his disheveled brown hair and large hazel eyes. He grinned at her, enormous white teeth and creased dimples over taking his scraggly face.

"I must be asleep, and I pray I never wake for only in dreams could such a vision as you exist," Callana blushed, bashfully bowing her head. Graven glanced around the circle of knights.

"See, blushing is always a good sign," He winked at Callana who smiled up at him, having finally recovered from his brilliant attempt to flatter her.

Reinhold guffawed and pointed at Callana.

"*Blushing* means she is a lady, twit, nothing more,"

"Jealous?" Graven taunted.

"Of what? The women you usually take home are only *drunk pretty* anyways!" Reinhold answered, igniting a cackling response from the group.

Callana was confused. She turned to Reinhold as Odin rode up behind the tall man.

"What is *drunk pretty?*" she asked. Reinhold made to explain but stopped when he heard the puffing of Odin's large black mount behind him.

"If you answer that I will have you beheaded!" Odin growled.

"Aye, your majesty," Reinhold bowed his head and pulled his mount backwards in retreat to the back of the band. Odin's stern glare stifled a few snickers before he turned his attention on Callana.

"I welcome young Callana on morning patrols on the condition she is treated with utmost respect and you *will* maintain your bearings!" Odin made sure to lock eyes with the, now ashamed, Reinhold as he spoke. The last thing the king needed was a hooting circle of under sexed hyenas losing focus and getting each other killed. The knights straightened in their saddles and answered in unison.

"Aye!" Odin seemed satisfied with his reprimand and his face relaxed, giving him back his jovial appearance.

"Sir Graven, take your *perverted* friend west, and be sure to watch for any signs that any unwanted attention has been drawn to the tunnel's entrance,"

"Aye!" Graven turned, his childhood friend close behind, as they headed down the path before veering to the west and urging their mounts into a gallop. Odin faced Paul and Keiton now.

"Sir Keiton and Sir Paul, make north for Mount Rising," both rather quiet men nodded, immediately spinning back towards the castle to head around its large, limestone outer wall. Odin turned cool blue eyes on Callana and Kern.

"You two will ride with me," Callana felt a pang of foreboding cause her heartbeat to skip. If she were to ride with the king, that meant she would be personally responsible for his safety! She was not ready for this! She glanced around at the departing guard, than frantically at Kern who furrowed his brow.

"What is it?" He asked. Odin was watching her, a smile of amusement curling his lip.

"I...ah...just thought that someone...*better*...should be assigned to your majesty, sire," Callana stammered with her anxiety. Kern huffed.

"Ey, I am just as good a knight as the rest of them!" he defended. Callana shook her head. Odin laughed out loud at Kern's indignant reaction.

"No, I did not mean *you*, Sir Kern, I meant *me*!" she corrected. Kern calmed, satisfied she had not insulted him. Odin was still chortling.

"Callana, my dear, what ever did you think all that archery practice was for? *Winning?* Archery *tournaments* are for trophies, but archery *itself* is for defense. Who *better* to protect me than a champion?" Callana looked to Kern for any sign of distress, but he seemed collected, almost unaffected by his assignment. Callana bowed her head finally, when realization set in that she had, essentially, begged for this *very* obligation just this morning.

"Aye, your majesty; I will do my best," she pulled George to Odin's right, while Kern flanked the king's left, and the trio headed south than east, with a very paranoid Callana jerking towards every snapping twig and plopping of snow.

....

Miala sat frozen to her saddle, atop her borrowed, short backed dappled gray mare. The wind had finally subsided as they skirted the dreary forest, but the glaring white sun light hidden by grey cloud cover, was starting to dim with its slow descent across the darkening sky. The clouds rolled and flashed with lightening as they filled and threatened to release their chilling rain. The young servant girl had never traveled the outlying valleys of Adalonia; the pastureland was under over an ankle deep of snow and all the livestock were shut up in large, wooden barns and seemed to illuminate the true expanse of this kingdom. From her vantage point, along the dark forest's western edge, she could still look over her right shoulder and glance the ominous white limestone pillars of the castle's watch towers; the upper village dwellings only tiny brown dots on a blanket of white from here, with billowing grey smoke puffing out of indiscernible chimneys. Miala shivered against the cold again thinking of those cozy, little warm houses; full of family and friends she had known since birth. She felt her heart thump against her chest, longing to turn back, but to what? If their mission failed, not only would Jiden, Galland, and Nicholas be out numbered, but Rogadon would fall to that wicked man; its constituents to once again be left to suffer under the greed of an unworthy king. Oh! Miala could feel her blood boil when she thought of that man and all he had done to her friend! To see him sit in rule over an already broken city made her absolutely furious! Her gripping white knuckles and grinding teeth went unnoticed by her preoccupied companion.

Renk was keeping a weary eye on his surroundings, riding point with his little friend, eager to push harder, but aware of his foot soldiers limitations. Today would be the hardest march as they needed to clear the valley to submerge themselves into the cover of the tunnels. Erik had agreed to ride the rear, on a spirited buckskin, only weeks out of breaking. The prancing male was enormously irritating to the weathered knight, but the young horse had exceptional endurance; giving Erik the advantage of backtracking often to assure no one was following and riding ahead to converse with Renk numerous times throughout the march without wearing down his mount. The wagon wheels seemed to slice easily enough through the freshly fallen snow as Edward guided the two mighty plow horses in the lead of the thousand marching men. Edward had his own guards, flanking either side of him in his perch and two facing out in the back, as well as his own chainmail and sword, although it had done little to ease his mother's worry when he was enlisted for this skirmish.

The men marched on relentlessly; easily tramping along in the flattened path ahead of them. Renk had ingeniously tied both ends of a log, length wise and slightly askew, from the rear of the wagon, to smash and divert the snow down for the foot soldiers, in hopes of easing their long progression. The snow was falling steadily enough now that their tracks had all but vanished only hours after they had passed ; keeping their mission a secret thus far. Erik caught up to Renk in another, predestined to fail attempt to tire his young horse to end his incessant prancing. He pulled up next to the dark knight and leaned in close.

"So if '*big breasts*' is not proven royal, will you be entering the tournament, good sir?" Erik grinned ear to ear at the now frowning knight as Renk's tiny counterpart flashed him a nasty look.

"Whether *Callana* is proven heir or not, as soon as this battle is over I will be heading *home*, to the coast," Renk smirked at Erik with his declaration. Erik shook his shaggy head, sending fresh snow flakes flying from his unruly hair.

"Too bad, Rogadon could use a great man like you, Renk," He smiled at Renk, winking over the dark man's shoulder at Miala. She huffed.

"Maybe they could use a great *woman*? She raised her eyebrows at Erik.

"Well hell, who couldn't?" He smiled to his dark friend again before blowing Miala a kiss and turning his bouncing horse back towards the rear of the formation. Miala nearly hissed.

"Sometimes I want to...to..." she stammered, searching her mind for an appropriate expression.

"Punch him in the face?" Renk offered. Miala nodded vigorously.

"Aye, he seems to have that affect on most," Renk laughed with that, as he twisted in his saddle to watch the older knight flouncing away, his horse's anxious hooves throwing snow in the faces of agitated foot soldiers.

....

Nicholas heaved a large stone towards the center of the iced tributary, and frowned when it cracked the surface. He cast an disconcerted look towards Sir Galland, who was already cursing under his shivering breath.

"Two thousand men crossing that rickety bridge will take over a day! We will be behind our meeting time, leaving Jiden to assume us to have failed." Nicholas scathed, staring down the flat wooden glorified raft just feet from where he stood.

"You know as well as I do that your fool cousin will attack, with or without us," Galland pointed an angry finger at Nicholas as he spoke. Nicholas nodded.

"Aye, and we have no way of knowing if Renk has made it through yet either," Nicholas was bitter, unwilling to admit defeat, but unable to hasten what had to be done. Galland stopped short of his pacing and turned a hopeful face on Nicholas.

"I could send a scout forward," he began. Nicholas looked distressed.

"And?"

"I am to make for the crossroads, to come up from the south and surround Dellandore's army. But what if Dellandore has shortened its patrol of the main road? They would only be worried for the road into Rogadon or beyond into Adalonia, but what would they care for anything south of the forest? I could shorten my trip immensely," His large arms spread wide, as a grin turned up his grizzled cheeks. Nicholas smiled back.

"You are smarter than you look, good sir!"

Sir Galland grabbed the nearest mounted knight, a Sir Don, and sent him along the southern edge of the forest, to scout for patrols, urging him to move quickly but to remain undetected. Once he was on his way, Sir Nicholas crossed the narrow bridge over the icy blue water, leading Galland's thousand foot soldiers across the tiny bridge, in three tightly packed rows as Galland circled back towards the Green mountain falls, to insure they had remained unnoticed thus far.

....

"I hate this! Why can't we just charge in! We could take em!" Sir David was nearly growling with his angst, earning him a nod of approval from the riotous Sir Franklin. Jiden grinned and shook his head. They had been camped for two days, freezing, living off deer and rabbit in hopes of stretching their rations of figs, dried pork and cheese. Small fires were allowed, under large canopies, where the men gathered to warm themselves against the bitter cold. In the shelter of the evergreens, snow fall was light, and the wind was buffered. Jiden was grateful for the rest, though he spent most of his time worrying; he worried for his father and mother, for Nicholas and Galland, for Renk, Miala and even *Erik*, and the four thousand innocent men whose very lives depended on the solidity of his strategy. Callana was never very far from his immediate thoughts. Everything in nature seemed to remind him of her; the shimmering white snow, so like her gloriously pale skin, against the deep dark of the tree bark, nearly the same shade as her beautiful eyes. He missed her. Her face, her hair, her laugh, and the way she used to make him feel; like he was amazing, brilliant, and desired. He felt like he could meet her anywhere, any place, and she could make it feel like home to him. So why *were* they fighting each other?

Jiden frowned suddenly with a wrenching thought. He tossed his head over his shoulder to get the attention of his royal guard, gathered near a cauldron where they were melting snow for drinking water. Sir Lashend caught Jiden's look and motioned to the others. The men circled around Jiden's modest fire under a small canopy and knelt with the obviously troubled prince.

"What is it my lord?" Sir Franklin asked, hoping in earnest they were going to attack.

"In my seemingly, inept attempt to formulate a plan, I have disregarded a very key contingency," Jiden began; looking up to find a very confused circle of grimaced faces, save for Sir Gracien. After a silent moment, the supremely intelligent young knight shook a light brown head of hair as he interpreted for the group; gesturing with his hands.

"What the prince is saying is that he did not plan for *every thing* that *could* happen," Sir Gracien finished; inciting a round of ah's and nods.

"You were saying, your majesty?" Gracien indicated Jiden could continue. Jiden bowed his head in appreciation, than continued grimly.

"I fear I did not plan for my plan to *fail*," he made eye contact to confirm his men were following, than went on.

"As in, what if the other armies do not make it by tomorrow? Or...at all?" Jiden was kneeling, staring into the eyes of his closest friends, desperate for advice. None had experienced war, although all were expertly trained for battle. Sir Gracien was furrowing his brow in thought. Laden was absently smiling, as usual, but there was a slight fear behind his adolescent eyes. Lashend was morose, twisting his red mustache in two fingers as he pondered. Senren and David were uncharacteristically quiet as they both seemed to search through compiled tactics for an answer or a wise word. Finally, Gracien spoke up.

"Well, my lord, if we were to attack, it would not be immediately obvious we had lesser numbers and they would still be surprised," he offered. Jiden nodded with this revelation.

"Aye, but how long could we fight, outnumbered three to one?" Jiden's face turned very sullen with his terrible trail of thought.

"How many would fall?" As he asked, he turned to view the few hundred men he could actually see, aware of hundreds more spread about that he could not. The royal guard hung their heads low, none willing to send so many to death.

"No mention of this to the men. I do not need fear to infect this already naïve army. We will deal with that possibility come night fall tomorrow, if we have to. Dismissed." The guard bowed respectfully, than, followed Jiden to make another of their many rounds; checking for injuries, or issues of any kind, and in general, just giving the youthful many a feeling of belonging to something good, and right. Shaking hands with some familiar and some unknown young men, Jiden was suddenly aware of his affect on them. When he walked into their circles, although insisting they remain at ease to assure them they were all on the same team; Jiden found that many were actually awestruck to see him face to face, shake his hand, and speak with him. He realized he had spent years holding training sessions, forced jaunts, archery lessons and practices with the sword, and in all that time, had remained separate, as their prince, as he was taught to do by his father. These men were willing to *die* for their prince, when they had never even *spoken* to him! The very thought filled Jiden with a sickening shame he had never known. True, his father was a great king; known for his actions of kindness, virtue, courage and wisdom, but, to ask thousands of men to fight, even give over their *lives*? For a *stranger*? Who they had only seen from a distance?

Jiden swelled with a new resolve to know these men as he made his way towards a large group. He wanted to let them know him, and to raise them, from soldiers to heroes. From now on, they would fight for him because they believed as he did; in a united valley, where poor and rich did not exist; only content, steadfast, and courageous people, who would forge their own destinies and make their own peace.

Lena paced her bedchamber, having run out of tears and prayers. Odin's patrols had turned up nothing, which was excellent, but unnerving all the same for the worried mother. If Dellandore was not aware of Adalonia's involvement, that would give Jiden his intended edge, and that was what Lena wanted. But what she *needed* was a message, an assurance of some sort that Jiden was still all right. He had promised to send word and she knew he would but wondered how long to wait before they should be worried about why he hadn't sent word! Callana was dealing with missing Jiden by riding patrols, archery, and even, occasionally, accompanying the guards to the Green mule. Lena knew Callana was worried, and her physical appearance was starting to show her strain. She was paler than usual and she had dropped a considerable amount of weight in these first days of Jiden's absence. But for all of Lena's concerns, Callana had refused to see Lustene and insisted she felt fine. She was just as stubborn as Jiden, Lena felt herself grin with the thought. They were perfect for each other, and Lena could not help but feel the great Lord of all the land would not have brought the two together only to tear them apart with death. Just as she had decided to attempt sleep, Odin barged through the door.

"I have a good feeling about this, my love! I believe Ulei will run in the face of our armies and Rogadon will soon be restored." He rushed to her, wrapping immense arms around her and lifting her for a kiss. Lena kissed her husband, but wiggled out of his amorous embrace.

"What is it my love?" Odin tried to appear innocent, but knew all too well his queen would not be entertaining any sexual fantasies this night, or ever it appeared.

"I already told you," she began but Odin stopped her.

"Lena, please?" Lena burrowed under the covers and faced her back to him. Odin growled, storming to her side of the bed to face her.

"You mean to tell me we will not make love while Jiden is in battle?" His eyes squinted with disbelief at his wife's request.

"That is how it has always been. I never made love while *you* were in battle did I?" She argued. Odin grunted.

"I should hope not!"

"Odin, I refuse to…*indulge*, while my only son is out in this terrible cold fighting that hideous man!" Odin put his hands up in surrender and stood.

"I am sorry, I will stop asking. But I wont have to ask anymore," Odin smiled a sinister smile, causing Lena to sit up in bed.

"Meaning?" She crossed her thin arms over her chest. Odin's dimples creased his cheeks as he started to undress.

"Meaning, you may be tough now, but in a few days time you will not be able to control your desire for me and you will be begging *me* to take *you!*"

"Are you *serious?*" Lena gasped, but Odin only shushed her.

"But, do not worry, my queen, for I will accept your advances as apology for this torment you have forced upon me, because I love you. Good night." Odin leaped into bed, pulling the woolen blankets off his wife in the process as he tugged them up enough to uncover his naked buttock. Lena rolled her eyes and tried to hold her angry composure, but the fire lit sight of her husband's deliberately exposed bottom caused her to giggle. Odin rolled over quickly and grabbed her, and attempted to maneuver her under him. Lena giggled again, but socked him in the arm until he released her. He sighed and flung the covers around them both, content to hold her as they drifted into a restless, but needed sleep.

....

"My lord, King Ulei to see you," the gate guard bowed to his king, than turned and stood to allow the handsome man in.

"King Ulei, how deplorable to see you," the young king smiled disingenuously as he rose to greet Dellandore's prized stallion of a man. Ulei bowed, rising with a smirk on his face as he swaggered towards his unwilling host.

"And how excruciating to see you, good King," Ulei answered.

"Let's keep this to the point." The younger man urged. Ulei smiled wickedly.

"Quick and dirty, just how I like it," Ulei was obviously tickled by a fleeting, lurid memory at his own jest. The youthful king was not impressed.

"As I have heard...now, what in hell do you want?" The now irritated king pushed. Ulei feigned innocence as he shrugged.

"Is it so unbelievable that a man would just want to be in the company of his son?" Ulei asked.

"Do not address me as your *son*! You will call me *King* Elei! I have *earned* that title!" Elei glared at his father, who had stopped short at his son's scathing remark.

"You *are* my son just as you are *king* of Esildad,"

"I did not wish to be your son and if I could turn back the hands of time I would choose to never have been born at all to escape your *polluted* blood line!" Elei and Ulei locked identical golden eyes on each other, as Elei's royal guard anxiously reached for their swords. Ulei raised his hands in surrender and backed further away from the infuriated man.

"I repeat; what do you want?" Elei's voice boomed through his lavish reception hall. Ulei felt his virility drain as he worked to form an acceptable sentence.

"I could use your assistance in a certain acquisition of..." Ulei was interrupted by his impatient son.

"No! Let me tell you what you want; you want *my* army to defeat some one *else's* army because *yours* is insufficient due to the fact that Dellandore's king spends his time cavorting instead of training! Correct?" Elei demanded.

"As usual, sire, you are most eloquently correct." Ulei bowed his head.

"Why did you even bother to come here? I have no enemies, I reign in peace, and we have all we need in commerce. Why would I sacrifice men for *your* glory?" Elei was genuinely curious now. Ulei's eyes twinkled with a new purpose.

"I wage war on Rogadon," Ulei was only half lying, but, judging by Elei's pained expression, it would be enough.

"We ride at dawn," Elei announced. Ulei nearly danced with his excitement having discovered the perfect ruse to elicit a reluctant but powerful ally.

....

Callana could not help but cringe this morning at the thought of breakfast. Her stomach knotted with anxiety as she tried and failed to sneak past the ever watchful eyes of the queen.

"Where do you think you are going?" Lena was standing, prim and pressed, in the candlelit doorway of the formal hall. Callana sighed and shrugged her exhausted shoulders.

"I am sorry, my queen. I could not stand even the smell of *food* this morning," Callana came to kneel at the queen's delicate feet. Lena motioned with a slender hand for Callana to rise than grabbed her in a clenching hug. Callana was surprised, but returned the affection.

"Oh Callana, I worry for him too. It has been over a week with no word, from either army. But, the king assures me there is nothing to worry about so, we should try...to not....not worry," Lena's face contorted into a pained smile as she turned the shoulders of the young red head towards the long, planked table and forced her to eat. Moments later, Callana was rushing for the stables and a prancing purple horse.

"Morning all. Lets not dilly dally," Odin sniped as his royal guard joined him on the rise of the village path. They seemed as shocked as Callana was by the uncharacteristically terse tone of the usually good-humored man. She was certain his agitation was attributed to his worry for his son and decided to ignore it. The rest of the guard seemed to do the same.

Dashend and Lashend and Callana were sent east, Graven and Reinhold west, Keiton and Paul south and the king and Kern headed north and west; all were to meet up at the forest line west of the icy Ceruleana in a few hours, than they would give morning report before heading for the falls with the new, doubled guard for the exchange. Callana was happy to be involved, and even more than happy to be with the cheerful red headed cousins on patrol, but still felt a gnawing irritation. Something was wrong or off or...something. She had never thought of herself as intuitive, but she did know she was not completely out of touch with her environment. There was a force at work today she could not describe but did not like in the least. She suddenly felt the need to be with Jiden; not a missing her lover feeling but a fiery intensity to come to his rescue. She glanced over her shoulder towards the departing guards and the western edge of the shadow's forest, than back at the giant, nearly identical men on horse back in lead of her. She felt desperate, depraved, like a crazed, kept animal in search of an escape. She jerked George's large head and turned him west, urging him hard as she did. *"Get up George! Get up!"* Callana let her grip on the leather reins loosen and the gelding broke into a fervent gallop; stretching and curling long, dark legs as he reached for an unseen finish line. Lashend and Dashend called after her, catching the attention of the western bound Graven and Reinhold, who turned their mounts towards the young girl.

Callana huffed with the effort of standing in her stirrups, her thighs on fire, her stomach churning, and her head spinning. What was she doing? Graven and Reinhold would surely stop her from heading into the woods and even if she did make it passed them, the commotion she would cause if the royal guard were to pursue, would give away Jiden's location! Hot tears rolled down her frozen cheeks as she fought to gain control over her driving, irrational urge to see her prince. As she rounded the lakes edge, something caught her eye, causing her to turn towards the flicker of movement amidst the white mounds of snow in the half dead forest. Odin bellowed from her right, heading back towards her from his northern route, having not even reached the castle yet. Callana jerked her head towards the king, then back towards the fast approaching woods, as she realized suddenly that it was an archer she had seen!

The crouched figure had loaded a purple feathered arrow and was pulled back, perfectly aligned with Odin, readying for his unknowing victim to come into range. Callana felt her throat tighten with panic, but instinctively reached for her bow, knotting and dropping her reins as she plucked an arrow from her quiver and aimed in. She sucked in a deep breath and released while her chest was swollen with oxygen, terrified to wait for her exhale. As her arrow struck the archer's arm, he cried out, releasing his own arrow slightly too high. The whistling arrow sailed wide above its intended prey, but the significance hit the big man just as sharply. This was an attempted assassination by Dellandore. The guard closed in on the stunned Callana and her now writhing quarry. The closest and therefore first to arrive was Graven and Reinhold, who nearly leaped off their mounts to subdue and bind the king slayer. Callana sat gaping on her frothy mount.

"Callana! You saved the king!" The approaching guard called out.
"Callana the savior of Adalonia!"
Odin pulled his enormous black big hoofed horse to a stop and dismounted, coming quickly to kneel at Callana's dangling foot. Callana burst into tears as the shock wore off and the magnitude of what had happened set in.
"Callana, I owe you my life!" The sight of the bent frame of the large, regal man shook Callana's last hold on her emotions. She crumpled, nearly collapsing out of the saddle to fall to the ground, wrapping her arms around the big man's neck. Her sobbing shook them both as she cried into his curly blonde hair.
"Oh, your majesty! I was …If you would have died…" Odin was holding her now, softly talking against her forehead.
"Callana please do not cry…" he tried to soothe her but she was spiraling now, having cracked the damn of pent emotions, she could not stop the flood of tears.
"Jiden needs you, Lena needs you….if you.…if someone took you.…I could not live!" Callana squeezed him, and Odin held her tight, flashing a look to Sir Paul, who in turn silently signaled the men to mount and search the nearby forest as he loaded a struggling prisoner on to George's back. When Callana had finally run dry of tears, Odin gently slung her slack form over his shoulder mounted his horse, and carried her gently back to the castle where the receiving guards and a very worried queen helped him put her to bed where she lay unconscious for hours.

....

"Do you think it means Dellandore *knows* of our involvement?" Nona beseeched the frazzled Odin. Corrin turned to confront his fellow council member.
"Well what *else* could it mean? There has not been an assassination attempt on this kingdom for a hundred years! Why *else* now?" The council erupted into frantic chattering. Odin rubbed his eyes and stood to silence the room.
"My council, I assure you, I will collect answers from the prisoner by any means possible," Odin's voice was grim. Lena closed her eyes to pray silently for her husband's soul, fully aware he would torture this man to assure his son's tenuous safety if need be. Odin put a heavy hand on her thin shoulders, causing her to turn her eyes up to him. He could read her so easily after nearly two decades of marriage, and he knew she did not condone what he was about to do.
"My wife, I must ask you for your advice now, for I did not wish to make an enemy in my own house," Lena nodded solemnly and reached for her husband's hand.

"I feel that the secrecy of Jiden's plan is *the* most crucial aspect, therefore, I feel it is...necessary....to *extract* the information, in....any way possible, my lord." Odin nodded bleakly before turning to the council. Before he could ask, the council was nodding their agreement.

"Aye, my lord,"

"Aye, your majesty,"

"*Any* way possible."

"It must be done."

Odin closed his eyes and exhaled slowly. He had never had to use torture against anyone before, and *dreaded* it. When he reached the prisoner's cell however, he found it would not be necessary after all.

....

"Sir Galland, the south is clear. It seems Dellandore is only sending guards as far south as the forest's edge...north of Windt." Sir Don was haggard, but alert enough after a hard two day's ride. He was ready for collapse as he reached the tented fire where Galland stood in wait for him, who was more than pleased, having enough time to arrive and meet Jiden in battle now that he did not have to travel to the crossroads. He and Nicholas would part ways tomorrow as the big man would head straight west to meet the road and turn north and the young prince would slant westward through the forest, only crossing the road as he made for Rogadon.

"You have served well, sir Don. Take your rest immediately after you have eaten, for we ride with dawn." Sir Don bowed gratefully before heading for a nearby soldiers' tent for venison stew and fresh boiled water. Galland took a quick jaunt to the look out tent to check in and assure the four young men were alert. Learning there was nothing to report, he headed back to the farthest end of camp, stopping on the way to wind a path through his men's camps; making conversation, collecting advice, and quelling any doubts. Galland found Nicholas laughing with a rather large group of knights who had ingeniously attached many smaller hides to make one large top, holding forty men, including Nicholas. Galland pulled the younger man aside.

"Sire, the men are secure...and..." Galland began but Nicholas stopped him.

"Galland, I have known you since I was not ten years old. I have you to thank for any and all knowledge of archery and swordsmanship I have. But above all, you are my *friend*," Nicholas reached out and put his hand on the big man's mighty shoulder. Galland softened, smiling wide as he returned the gesture.

"I merely address you as sire, young Nicholas, but I still think of you as a little prig," Galland laughed, earning him a clout in the arm.

"I do have good news; Dellandore only holds the forest. They are not sending scouts south of the tree line."

"Brilliant! Than we should be meeting Jiden, nightfall tomorrow, as planned." Nicholas suddenly frowned.

"What is it?" Galland was puzzled.

"I hope Sir Renk and Erik have had as good of luck as we," Nicholas grimaced.

"Miala will be fine. She is in good company," Galland assured his long time underling.

"I suppose you are right, friend. Miala is not the warrior she wants to portray, but she is determined." Nicholas seemed to be talking himself out of worrying. Galland sighed.

"We will be there to protect her, I swear on my honor, I will not let anything happen to her," Galland put a hand over his heart. Nicholas smiled.

"I know you won't," Nicholas returned the older knight's crooked salute before turning and ducking out of the tent. The young man had no way of knowing what his beloved was heading into, and was regretting allowing her to go. He shook his head with the thought. *Allowing* her go? He could not have stopped her any more than he could have stopped the sun rise! She was the most stubborn woman he had ever met, and oh, how he loved her.

....

"Renk, do you remember it being much farther?" Miala asked her sweating friend. Hours had turned into days since they had entered the suffocating caves, and although the nights were much warmer underground, Renk was starting to miss the blistering cold air he had so eagerly left behind. He turned a weary face towards the small, olive skinned maiden.

"Sorry my dear, it is hard for me to say, for this time I am not fleeing for my life," Renk grinned apologetically.

"Oh...I am sorry I keep asking. Strange, I cannot put a word to my fears, but there is something terrible about this tunnel. I have never felt so...so..."

"*Buried alive?*" Erik was suddenly next to her. She froze with the terrifying possibility.

"We won't be right? These have been...stable...I mean....they have been *open* for ages right? I mean..." Miala was trembling. Renk shot Erik a squinted contentious look.

"He is only trying to unnerve you. We will be fine," Renk assured her. Erik laughed out loud.

"Shut up! You will cause a collapse!" Miala scathed. As if in answer to her worst fears, the ground started to tremble under her feet. She turned a horrified look on Renk, who stared back at her with worry in his eyes. Their torches flickered with the push and pull of the air as it waved in and out around them. The walls made a cracking sound, as centuries old rock groaned and splintered with the shaking of the ground. Miala grabbed for Renk and held his arm. Erik dashed back towards the army, desperate to get as many out of the cave as possible, though he knew they would never make it. Then, as quickly as the tremors had started, they stopped. Erik heaved a sigh of relief as he reached towards the nearest terrified soldier and clasped a hand around his neck. The dust settled around Miala and Renk as the two finally inhaled tentative breaths. Erik started towards them with a stupid grin on his face.

"Tha…" Erik started but was quickly silenced by Miala's tiny hand covering his mouth.

"You will not *speak* until we see daylight, *understood?*" Miala's voice was quiet but stern; teeth clenched with glaring eyes in the torch's light. A very surprised Erik moved his lips to defend himself against the acts of nature.

"SHHHHHH!" Miala hissed, than turned back towards the dark knight, already climbing further into the cave. Erik stood, quietly chagrined, waiting for hours as hundreds of men passed him by, joining the last of the thousand at the end.

....

"She is not injured, but she is not well," Lustene was closely examining Callana when her eyes popped open and she struggled to sit. Lena soothed her, running her gentle hands through the tangled red lengths and patting her trembling arm.

"I asked Lustene to look in on you my dear. You have been asleep for half a day. How do you feel?" Lena had kept a fire burning in Callana's bed chamber, and the warmth was magnificent, but sickening all at the same time. Callana felt her head start to spin again.

"I do not feel hungry, but I think I am," Callana mumbled, the motion of talking making her head pound.

"I will bring something; a caraway and chamomile tea also and I have already summoned the kitchen girls to bring up a hot olive oil bath, love." Lena rose to bring back the promised food, leaving Callana and Lustene alone.

"Am I *sick*, Lustene?"

The grey haired surgeon peered down at her over his basket.

"Just a bit over stressed I think. How do you feel?" Lustene stopped his searching as he tried to asses her health again.

"I…just feel tired I, I think. Caraway is for sour stomach, is it not?" She asked. Lustene nodded.

"Your mother has taught you well, young crusader. The queen is just worried for your loss of appetite of late."

"But she knows more than anyone how worried we all are for Jiden…that is all that it is. I am sure of it! I do not wish to be treated like an invalid when there are things to do!" Callana struggled to free herself from the woolen blankets, and wriggled her way out of bed. Lustene stood between her and the door, dumping his medicines in an effort to stop her leaving, but she collapsed at his feet.

"My dear, you are in no condition to get out of bed!"

"I must!"

"Let your body recuperate young Callana. What is there that cannot be done tomorrow?"

"Lustene, I am frightened!" Callana locked arms with her friend, facing him, her dark eyes shimmering with her rising fear.

"What is it my dear?" Lustene frowned with concern; bracing Callana as she shook with the effort of standing.

"I am afraid that someone will be out there and I won't!" Callana shrank back to the safety of the bed and cried. Lustene came to stand by her.

"You are afraid that Jiden will not have *you* to save him," He assessed. Callana nodded, sobbing quietly. Lustene sat beside her, gently holding her shoulders as he pulled her to him.

"My dear, we all fear for our prince. But do not let it *rule* you. Only God knows when it is our time and living your whole life fearing for the inevitable is not living at all, is it?" Lustene's voice was calm and soothing, easing Callana's sobbing. She raised her head to look up into the intelligent blue eyes of her kind friend.

"You are right, I know. It is irrational. It is strange, Lustene." Callana started.

"What is dear?" Lustene stood and began collecting his basket's contents as he listened.

"I never knew *fear* until I knew *peace*." Callana's eyes were far away, lost in memories Lustene did not know.

"You lived in Windt your whole life. Was it not peaceful?" Lustene asked her.

"I lived in *ignorance*, not peace. I did not know true peace, and I will never know it again, for I will always fear war. I was never afraid to lose someone, until I lost my father and now that I love Jiden so much; I fear losing him. I could live without Jiden, but I would never know a world without him now that he is my world! Oh Lustene! How do people *live* with such fears?" Callana's eyes implored him, begged him for an answer that would stay her fears and slow her pounding heart. Lustene smiled tenderly down on her as he spoke carefully.

"Callana, we all must die, some day; it is the *only* certainty we have in life and the only thing every living thing has in common. Every story must end, so it can be told. All we have is our story; neither you nor I nor anyone else can choose how we begin or end, but we decide what fills the pages; You just have to decide what kind of a book you wish to be," Lustene leaned in and kissed Callana's forehead as Lena ushered in a blustering group of girls with buckets.

"I will leave you to your bath, my dear," Lustene slowly stood to leave but Callana reached for his arm.

"Lustene,"

"Yes?" he asked, turning to her.

"You will be a magnificent story," Callana grinned. Lustene bowed his head and was gone, leaving Callana to reluctantly eat, before dipping down into a luxurious oil bath while graciously sipping her prescribed tea.

....

"Gather the men; I must speak with them." Jiden commanded, grudgingly. Sir David nodded, and solemnly passed the word to the other royal guard members, who began spreading the news, one soldier at a time. Soon, groups of hundreds became one large mass of a thousand men. Once the men were assembled, Jiden cleared his throat to speak; climbing a fallen tree to be sure he was seen by all.

"Men, I stand here before you, not as your prince, but as your comrade at arms. I hold the same hopes as you, as well as the same fears. Time has come for action. As we lay in wait for our armies, Ulei starves Rogadon, for he is a coward, who chooses to torment innocent people to win battles he is too arrogant to show up to fight! We are in this together, united, as brothers, Adalonia and Rogadon, under the same banner of peace. We ride to battle at dawn, with or without our allies, and with or without our allies, we will not show our fear, but instead inflict it upon the soldiers of Dellandore! We will not bow out in the face of our enemies' superior numbers for we have superior strength! If we fall, we will be remembered as heroes, while Dellandore is forgotten. When you sleep tonight, dream of your victory tomorrow, and when you wake, remember your dreams. Let this be your last night as soldiers, for tomorrow you become legends!" Jiden raised his fist, signaling for a silent acknowledgement from his troops and a throng of black gloved fists thrust into the sky at once, all eager to show their pride and dedication for their kingdom, their prince, and all that was right. Jiden remained composed, though his heart swelled with veneration for these valiant men. Tonight, they would dine on cold rations and warm drinking water and sleep on the cold ground. Jiden knew they deserved better, and prayed fervently before he closed his eyes that this icy night would not be their last night.

....

"My lord," the dark haired man knelt in his cell as a confused Odin entered the dimly lit chamber below the eastern end of his castle. Sir Kern shrugged his wide shoulders at his king's furrowed brow.

"You *bow* to me in honor not hours after you attempted to *assassinate* me?" Odin crossed his arms over his burly chest as he waited, admittedly curious to hear this man's reasoning. The large man stood slowly, first slouching to be eye to eye with Odin, than straightening to nearly a half foot taller. Odin was taken aback by the incredible girth of this man. He was powerfully built, not unlike Odin himself, but had more mass by far.

"I can only ask that you would forgive my actions, good king, for they were of pure intentions," when the large man spoke, though his voice was hardly more than a whisper his words resonated off the stone walls; booming through the room. Odin cocked his head, now more baffled than before.

"Am I perceived to be so vicious in Dellandore that you consider killing me a *pure* intention?" The big man immediately balked with this accusation.

"I am not *from* that city of sinners! You were to *believe* I was from Dellandore; hence the stolen uniform and arrows," The prisoner shrugged off the purple cape with obvious disdain. Odin half grinned around at his circle of knights.

"I would think you mad for the manner of which you speak in these irritating circles," Odin began but the larger man spoke up.

"I am not mad, sire, only just, for my entire village starves as you sit unaffected in your limestone palace!" The man's dark eyes burned through Odin as he seemed to come upon a slight light of understanding.

"You are from *Rogadon*? Is that it? And you wish to enlist my army to protect you from Dellandore who is cutting off your food supply and holding you prisoner inside your own city walls?" Odin's revelation brought a simultaneous burst of comprehension to his royal guard and a jaw drop to his immense captive.

"Yes...yes, your majesty," even as he spoke, the big man seemed awestruck.

"Done!" Odin clapped his hands together once than turned with raised brows to his scowling inmate.

"You make light of our suffering!" Two massive hands grabbed for the bars as Dashend and Earnest quickly stepped between the cell and their king.

"I make no jest! I tell the truth. My only son and nearly half my army march on the Dellandore squatters as we speak for we were informed of Ulei's intentions by one of your own soldiers." Odin's indigo eyes were earnest and dark as he spoke of his son. The man seemed to slump slightly with the news.

"I see. Well, I may hang for my treacherous behavior but I will die with honor knowing my city will surely be saved!" The large man pledged. Odin laughed out loud, the noise ricocheting around the small prison cell.

"What is your name, brave and giant *fool?*" Odin asked. The large man bowed his head and answered.

"Carr of Rogadon, your majesty," Carr bowed again before meeting the king's scrutinizing stare. There was something the king could not single out about this huge man, but it seemed as though they had met before. Odin immediately shook the notion out of his head, fully assured he would have remembered a man of this size. It was his eyes though; dark, nearly black eyes, so familiar, so forthcoming.

"Pleasure, Carr of Rogadon. Would I know you from somewhere?" Odin pried, desperate to quell his suddenly overwhelming curiosity. Carr seemed surprised by the king's question, but obliged, seeing as how his life had been spared by this jovial man.

"My family is Rogadon born. I am the only child of Cassen, son of Cale, and Ralla, daughter of Relan, of Rogadon." Carr spoke proudly of his family, but Odin only seemed to become more inquisitive.

"What is your family trade?"

"Stables, mostly sire, and some wood work, my lord," Carr responded cautiously, unsure of the king's peculiar probing. Odin nodded thoughtfully, than shrugged his dismissal.

"It will come to me, but for now, you are free to go. Release him." Odin turned to a stunned Sir Paul, who though perplexed, obeyed without question, turning the oversized key into the rusty tumblers, freeing the lock and popping open the squealing cell door. Carr stepped through, coming face to face with the large Sir Keiton, Graven and Reinhold, who had no intentions of allowing him any where near their king. When Carr reached the outer door, he turned to his liberator, surrounded by a mystified crew of protectors, then dropped to a knee.

"My lord, I owe you an enormous debt; for you have spared my life when I had been so desperate to take yours. Please sire, make use of me in your army," Odin parted his royal guard to come to stand near Carr's bent frame.

"Rise, Carr, and list your abilities that I might exploit in battle," Odin commanded. Carr stood and eagerly countered.

"I have only one ability sire, but I assure you, it is enough. I am a very capable archer," Carr stood straight and proud as he laid his claim. Odin found himself growing quite fond of the big man.

"As was the honorary knight who thwarted your attempt," Odin boasted himself. Carr's pale skin tinted red as he glanced at his punctured right shoulder.

"Aye," voiced Sir Kern.

"Point taken," Carr grinned, pointing to his shoulder to accentuate his jest, rousing a round of chortles from the guard.

"First things first; if you are to fight for me, you must be well. Sir Graven, Reinhold, take him to Lustene then bring him to dine in the royal hall where he shall meet his would be vanquisher."

....

Silvio's prayer of protection hummed behind Jiden's thoughts, leaving no room for feelings.

Almighty Lord in Heaven above, please watch over these men as they march into righteous battle....

Jiden surveyed the land before him, though he knew the shadow's forest by route. As a child he had accompanied his father on countless hunting and fishing trips as well as watch patrols throughout these massive woods; the moss covered evergreens, spiky shrubs and constant covering of crispy fallen leaves had been intriguing, even welcoming to him then. But now, on this morning, the morning of battle, Jiden found the forest tense around him. Stillness and quiet so severe it was deafening.

Give them strength over their enemies and all enemies of peace, great Lord.

It was as if the trees themselves held their breath in anticipation. Jiden was numb, but not from the biting cold. His eyes were scanning the woods while his mind plotted attack.

If any should fall in battle defending those who are weak, deliver them unto your kingdom, merciful Lord. In your name Amen,

He was not tired, though could not remember ever actually falling asleep the night before. He recognized a deep relief that rose steadily with the dawn, for they would finally start this fight he had been dreading for too long. He took a deep breath and readied to make his assignments. His royal guard gathered as the last of the gear was loaded onto the wagons and the soldiers turned frost bit faces towards their prince.
Much to Jiden's surprise, he did not see a thousand fearful youths before him but instead a force. He saw men standing tall where boys trembled only a day before. These were men who had spent their restless night summoning reasons to fight and now held them high as inspiration. These were men with something to lose. Jiden filled with pride in his soldiers, his kingdom and the great Della Verde valley. He ordered his remaining royal guard to pair up, each set with their own section of men and sent Sir Ellis home with their declaration of war. Each detachment set out, making sure to observe a level of stealth to maintain the notion of surprise. As over two thousand feet crunched through ice crusted snow, Jiden's heart rhythmically pounded out the marching beat; an overwhelming eagerness gleaming in his eyes.

....

Nicholas rushed towards the crisp white of the unused road, glancing over his shoulder towards Galland. The painfully slow crossing had set them nearly a day behind. Dawn was rising, signaling the battle's beginning, whether reinforcements were there or not. Nicholas silently cursed his self for offering his own cousin up as sacrifice. The sole heir to the throne of Adalonia should not be the *first* to fight. Galland spurred his impressive armored palomino up to Nicholas's prancing mount and leaned in to speak.

"He can hold them until we arrive," he assured his smaller friend. Nicholas nodded and signaled for the soldiers to move ahead. Being seen on the road now would be of little consequence if Jiden had already engaged, but Galland would scout ahead anyways. The fastest he could move his men without wearing them down was a quick march, just shy of running, and even with that they would just be getting to Rogadon by dusk with the winter's shortened days. Nicholas swore again than kicked his chestnut into a gallop to the rear to check for stragglers or injuries after giving the command to pick up the pace. At once, the five row heads bolted forward into a long, stretching stride and the rest followed suite. Soon the snow packed road had been worn down to slushy brown mud by the crushing of two thousand men.

....

King Elei fidgeted in his saddle as he sat waiting for his royal guard to finish checking over nearly two thousand men. His father had seemed sure that Elei's entire army would be necessary but Elei was leaving a thousand behind. He could not shake the terrible feeling the dawn had brought. He had worried through the darkness of the night before, only to wake with his angst like a hard rock in the pit of his stomach. There was a raw edge to his nerves that furrowed his brow and tightened his diaphragm, making his breathing harsh. He would lose men, and for what? Revenge against Bromell? It would not bring back his mother, even if he killed that wretched man. His black war horse tossed his mighty head with his rider's quick tug of the reins. Stomach unsettled but mind determined to stand behind his word, Elei lead his battle tested knights towards Rogadon and his father's trap.

....

"I hear water," Erik mumbled. Miala glared at him.

"I thought you were not to talk?" She reprimanded. The knight's face dimpled in a huge grin.

"I could scream," he antagonized. Miala shook her head vigorously. Erik tossed shaggy brown hair to expose his ear as he leaned towards the darkness to his left. Renk nodded, his dark eyes nearly glowing in the fire's light. They had chosen to camp, igniting Miala's vehement condemnation, to give the soldiers a night to rest so they would be fierce in battle. Miala glanced around at the closest men; some sleeping, some staring blankly into the red ceiling above, some eating and talking. She turned to Renk.

"Should you say something to them? Some of them are very young," Miala's hazel eyes were slightly pleading, and her words struck a soft spot in the haggard knight behind her. Erik jumped to his feet and strode to the nearest circle of men.

"Gather the men," He commanded to the young blonde knight at his feet. The youth nodded and immediately leapt to his task. Erik turned to Miala and Renk.

"I will do the honors if you do not mind, Sir Renk?" Erik asked. Renk solemnly nodded. He had few words of encouragement at this point in their journey. He had spent the last day of marching dwelling on thoughts of his son and his beloved wife. He had no absolute way of knowing if Dakin had made it to Windt, and today the worry was eating him alive. He turned a furrowed brow on Miala.

"Once inside the courtyard, do not waste time. Ranik will take you inside the castle and you will start your investigating. Erik and I will handle everything else. By my estimation, it will be dawn soon, and Jiden will be launching his assault with Nicholas and Galland bringing in the flanks. We need to get our thousand in place to be of use as soon as possible. Do you understand?" Renk had taken on an uncharacteristically serious tone, and it was unnerving.

"I understand. Renk?" Miala was shivering with her worry over her assignment, or failing her assignment.

"What is it?" Renk was mulling over strategy in his mind while he worked to untangle mud caked boot ties. Before Miala could speak, the troops had filled into the large cavern just below the castle. Renk and Miala stood as Erik climbed a small out crop in the back wall of the cave where he could stand and be seen by all.

"Hear me soldiers of Adalonia." Miala's eyes darted around the expanse, following the reverberation of his words shooting past, behind and above her. "I stand here in awe of the tremendous bravery displayed before me. Here I am, a stranger to your kingdom, asking you to follow me into battle, and in your loyalty to your prince, you obey. You do your great kingdom justice and it fills me with pride to fight side by side with such men. We fight to defend people who have no defense; we fight for those who starve, at the mercy of a terrible man; we fight to bring Rogadon back into the Della Verde where she *will* be rebuilt. Those are the noble demands of your prince, who honorably fights along with his men. At dawn, we *will* break free of this cave, and we *will* charge out of that courtyard as a thousand hell hounds and we *will* strike fear into the hearts of our cowardly enemies!" with his last resounding word,

Erik took his right fist and pounded it to his heart. Miala and Renk stood in baffled admiration as a thousand fists beat back.

....

"He rides to battle *alone*?" Lena turned her pleading eyes on her husband. Sir Ellis bowed his head shamefully.

"Sorry, my lady," He bowed low for both king and queen.

"You have no apologies owed here, good Sir. You may take your night's supper and rest before heading back. I will have a message of my own for my impetuous son." Odin nodded his head as he spoke. Sir Ellis bowed again and gratefully led his exhausted mount to the stables before his meal. Lena felt a sting of anger mixing in with her frustration and worry. Odin took her delicate shoulders in his hands.

"My queen…" Lena shook free.

"Do not *calm* me! My worst fears have come to pass!"

"Wife, he will not be al…" Odin's soothing voice was cut short again.

"He was not to commit to battle until he was met with reinforcements! Is that *not* the plan he proposed to council? Is that not the plan that was voted into action in our very own hall?" Lena was gesturing towards the door behind her now and shaking visibly with her boiling fury.

"He changed his strategy, it would seem," Odin felt his patience fading. He was just as worried as she, but no message could be delivered by now that would stop Jiden. It would have taken Ellis a day to get here, and it would take him a day to get back. Jiden was on his own.

"Send more men!" Lena nearly barked.

"Leaving the castle open for attack is not the answer!" Odin raised his voice as his temper raged up his throat.

"Stalling here is not the answer either!" Lena locked squinted eyes with her husband before they both caught a glimpse of Callana. They turned to her, tempers subsiding at the disheveled sight of her. Her tangled hair hung in a fuzzy mess over her shoulder and her pale skin had purpled under swollen red lidded eyes. She was trembling, sending small waves of lemon tea splashing out of the goblet she clenched in both hands. Lena felt ashamed of herself suddenly. Here she stood, a queen, a lady, fighting like a child in front of a frightened girl! Lena turned apologetic eyes on her husband before coming to Callana's side.

"How are you my dear?" She asked inconspicuously but it was too late. Callana had heard enough to know something had gone wrong.

"What has happened to him?" Callana's hoarse voice nearly croaked out the words. Odin grimaced.

"Jiden has begun his charge on Rogadon," He began. Callana shook her head furiously.

"I already know that! Today is the fifth day, that's what he told council, that's not why you two are fighting and I know it!" Callana was tearing up, dark eyes threatened to spill over as she glared up at Odin. The big king sighed.

"He fights alone," Odin stated plainly.

"No...why? What could have kept the other armies?" Callana looked from Lena to Odin in confusion. It was not possible! Neither Galland nor Nicholas would allow Jiden to stand outnumbered three to one!

"We do not know why the others have not arrived, but can only assume they would be there if they could," Odin's mind was already running through possible reasons for the missing reinforcements as Callana suddenly brightened.

"My lord! Could we not just send in more men?" Odin sighed, pretending not to notice his wife's posturing behind Callana.

"It is not as easy at that, Callana. Ulei will know by now we are involved and may try to infiltrate our kingdom if we let our defenses down," Odin explained. Callana sagged visibly then brightened again.

"Archers! We can send a team of archers!" She nearly squealed with excitement. Lena considered this idea.

"That's perfect! We shall send a hundred archers," The queen agreed.

"Through the caves!" Callana joined.

"Yes! It is the fastest way!" Lena added.

"I will spread the word!" Callana was out the door before Odin could compose himself long enough to interject. Lena was breathing heavily with her excitement when she turned to Odin. Although he was feeling left out of the decision, he had no complaints about the idea. Lena smiled apologetically as her husband grinned down at her.

"I am sorry, my love," Lena began but Odin stopped her.

"Well done, my queen," Odin bent and kissed his wife as the two walked through the heavy wooden doors to drop the new proposal on an eagerly waiting council.

....

"What are we waiting for?" Nodden demanded, flailing his arms and purple cape about wildly. Salen shook his head in irritation of his comrade's impatience.

"We was told to sit so we sit! Is it so difficult to *sit*? From the looks of your back side I'd say you would be an expert!" Salen smirked with the last. Jiden watched from the far end of small snow bank only a hundred paces away from the quarreling couple. His pulse raced with the anticipation of what was to happen. His men were now safely in place, near by, undetected thanks to a light but steady rainfall that started not long after sunrise, concealing their crunching footsteps and the denseness of the pine groves and spiny thickets that delimited Rogadon. Jiden could easily hear the two guards' gruff conversation.

"We need half the army to *sit* on a castle gate?" Nodden persisted.

"That is the assignment, dolt!"

"It's a fool's errand and you know it," grumbled the reddening and wholly soaked Nodden.

"Rogadon hasn't had forces for years. We stand guard against cotters and stinking peasants! He wastes *our* battalion while he is to stay home, dry and warm. Who do *you* wager will take the claim for Rogadon?" Now Salen had lost his patience and stood, angrily gesturing towards the three thousand soldiers milling about around make shift fire pits and hide tents near the castle gates nearly two hundred paces away.

"Once those *stinking* peasants either die or surrender, *Dellandore* will claim Rogadon! Me, you, all under the purple standard!" Nodden seemed to consider this before continuing.

"We'll be heroes you think?" Nodden asked. Salen nodded to his daft friend.

"Rogadon means nothing to anyone; who is to stop us?"

Jiden had heard enough. From his prone position, he rolled onto his left side freeing his right hand to pull back and release a green feathered arrow, signaling the charge. As the sharpened point thwacked into a tree to Nodden's side, Jiden rushed the stupefied army from the east with two and a half hundred men; David and Gracien and their detachment barreled in from the North, shrieking like savages; Laden and Lashend quietly but deftly raced in from the west, near the rear of the castle walls, with their men trailing not long behind their swift captains; Slowest but loudest to come was Senren and a howling mad Franklin, with his contagious vigor echoing in their roaring troops. The stunned guards Nodden and Salen were cut down, before they could remember how to swing their long unused blades. Clinging steel, and men crying out, coordinated with the pounding in Jiden's ears like cadence, as rainfall and blood turned white snow into red mud.

....

Galland slowed his snorting mount to a trot. He reached down to pet the rain soaked neck of his golden horse. She was old for a war horse, nearly seven, but she was solid, in every way. She could not be spooked or agitated, much like Galland himself. She would follow him anywhere, even to death. Galland cherished her, and she huffed under the protective armor that proved it. "Easy Baby," He soothed her. She bobbed her head in response rolling into an easy canter as they headed south down the main road, back to Nicholas with nothing to report. Galland shrugged off a wave of nerves, desperate to keep his thoughts positive for his young prince.
"The men will do their job," Galland informed Baby, inciting another head bobbing. Galland heard before he could see his battalion, as they came into view over the slight rise in the road. He quickly noted Nicholas had yet to return to his post in the lead and spurred Baby to the closest squadron leader.
"The prince, he has not returned from his ride around?" Galland kept out of the way of the marching lines, keeping next to a young knight named Sir Torn.
"He has not, Sir Galland," the puffing youth answered. Galland nodded. "Take your rest, in the forest, until I return," Galland commanded. It had been nearly half a day now at their grueling pace, and Sir Torn gratefully raised a fist, signaling a halt. As squad leaders set about breaking out food rations and building fires for melting snow, Baby leapt into a full run, sensing her rider's anxiety. Once passed the rear foot soldiers, Galland discovered his missing prince.

....

"This is most unusual, Sir Reinhold," Lustene was most unsettled to be expected to treat the very man who had attempted to assassinate his king. But, Odin had been adamant that this rather colossal man was a threat no longer. Graven and Reinhold smirked at the aged surgeon. The graying man took a worried glance towards his separate sleeping room where young Gant lay resting.
"Do not worry, old Lustene," The bulky, brown haired Graven laughed. His lean companion snickered.

"Aye, we'll protect you," Reinhold flexed a long, sinewy bicep to prove his strength. Carr rolled his large, dark eyes.

"I am no enemy, good surgeon. I assure you," Carr swore. Lustene only sighed.

"Well, let us have a look at you then; on the table, tunic off," the aged man ordered. Grudgingly, Carr pulled his bloodied tunic over his head, wincing with the fiery pain that burned through his damaged shoulder.

"I will need to boil some water; you are rather fortunate soldier of Rogadon," Lustene commented gruffly. Carr furrowed a bushy brow.

"For being spared by the king?" He asked. Lustene shrugged heavy shoulders as he turned back to tending his medicinal soup.

"That too," The old man commented.

"But I meant fortunate she did not *kill* you," Lustene grinned to himself, fully enjoying the look of horror on the big man's pale face.

"*She*? She as in a *woman*?" Carr was dumbfounded. Had the king not mentioned his assailant as an honorary knight? That was no *woman's* title.

"Actually, it is *she* as in a young *girl*," now Reinhold and Graven were cackling like jackals as Carr sat slack jawed, staring wide eyed at the three men.

"I was shot by a *girl*? How is this possible? Girls are no archers!" Carr demanded.

"Than your defeat is doubly humiliating, is it not?" Lustene chuckled as he neared his patient with a thick, dirty yellow paste on a leather square. Carr flinched back, holding his nose.

"What is that?"

"Garlic and Fenugreek seeds, for inflammation and infection," Lustene applied the paste as Carr shook his head in disbelief.

"I have been bested by a young girl," he mumbled to himself.

"Aye, along with the best archers from the entire Della Verde Valley and beyond," Graven boasted about his friend as Reinhold nodded reverently.

"This is true? She is tournament *champion*? Your kingdom retains the title once more?" Carr asked, burning with his determination to meet this girl face to face; if only to prove to his chauvinistic mind that she truly existed.

"Not my kingdom," Lustene smiled now at the befuddled man sitting on his examination table.

"Yours," he winked.

"Rogadon sent no one; we did not have the entry fees…this *champion* of yours is false!" Carr nearly leapt from the table, landing hands width from two gleaming blade tips. Reinhold and Graven stood at the ready; their earlier jovial smiles now vanished. Carr wavered, putting his hands up and lowering himself back down to the table. Lustene sighed again, than set about finishing up his work on the now agitated soldier.

"Callana came to us in an effort of uniting Rogadon with Adalonia; the very mission you yourself are on." Lustene's voice was low and soft as he spoke in awe of his dear friend.

"Where you thought to *assassinate* royalty to save Rogadon, she thought to *impersonate* it. She has proven herself to be anything but *false* and you would be wise to remember, *friend*," Lustene made eye contact with Carr as he finished talking, noting the familiarity he saw in those dark eyes. He seemed to be waiting for a sign of Carr's acceptance. Carr nodded solemnly before slowly rising.

"I am sorry for any offense to your, knight, friend, ah, Callana," he gestured towards Reinhold and Graven's swords.

"I spoke only of what we had been told by our king. I would very much like to meet this champion." Graven nodded and the two guards lowered their weapons. Reinhold glanced down at the torn and stained tunic Carr was reaching for.

"Aye, but not lookin like that; she's still a lady," the tall knight smirked. Lustene began boiling another cauldron of water, filling his wooden tub with two cauldrons of cold and two of hot before adding a generous helping of olive oil. Being careful to keep the newly bandaged right shoulder dry, Carr sank gratefully into the tub, scrubbing his pale skin pink with a pumice stone. Rolling onto his left side, Carr dunked his filthy hair and face, rising to receive a shave by Lustene. The older man could not belay the rising sense of connection when he looked at this man. His skin was all but white it was so pale, with dark brown eyes, nearly black in their depths. His size was definitely nothing the surgeon had ever seen before. Even Sir Galland had met his match with this Rogadon soldier. Still, something tugged in the back of Lustene's busy mind. He left Carr to soak and stepped out into the brisk January cold, passing Reinhold and Graven outside in the frosted white world on his way to Galland's home, not fifty paces down the snow covered village path. He quickly returned with a fur lined grey tunic and black trousers.

"You are truly a great surgeon!" A very naked Carr was standing now, mouth open in awe as he slowly rotated his right arm; too busy marveling at the speed of Lustene's poultice to retain his modesty. Lustene quickly cast his eyes down, thrusting the new wear and a soft sheepskin towel in Carr's direction. Carr's cheeks flushed a deep red when he realized he was nude in front of another man as he gratefully accepted the clothes. Lustene busied himself with the cleaning up of his examination table and materials while Carr dressed. After a moment, Carr turned, clearing his throat to signal he was done. Lustene turned and smiled brightly. It was an enormous improvement!

"Splendid! Let us dine than," He donned his long, fur lined green tunic for dinner in the castle. Lustene gestured for the door and he and Carr joined the chilled guards in a short, but brisk walk to the great hall.

Carr was immediately overwhelmed with the savory smell of sage, churned butter and fresh brown bread as he entered the dinning hall. Lena and Odin stood at the far end of the solid cedar table, along with the royal guard. Odin took Lena's hand delicately, as she reluctantly curtsied for the giant assassin. When she rose, Carr noticed she had a cold look in her stunning green eyes, and a small, forced smile on soft pink lips. He was struck by her beauty, forcing him self to close his mouth and bow properly when he caught a hard glare from Odin. Of course he would be jealous of such a woman as this, Carr thought as he bowed low. He himself had spent his life in Rogadon, watching beautiful woman marry other men, as he convinced himself year after year he was not interested in marriage. Now at four years shy of forty, he felt a pang of remorse that such love would never be his.

"I cannot say I am *pleased* to meet you, *Carr* is it?" Lena squinted as she hissed out his name. Carr hung his head as he spoke.

"I understand, your majesty. Please accept my most humble apologies...It was a terrible thing..." Carr stumbled through his explanation without taking his eyes off the stone floor. Odin came to his side and slapped him hard on the back.

"Your reasons were noble enough, just bad planning is all!" Odin grinned at his tiny wife who had one elegant eyebrow raised as she glared at her king. Carr tried to return the king's smile but felt the burning of Lena's angry stare on the side of his face. He tightened his jaw and gulped, remembering now how terrifying woman were and exactly *why* he had remained single.

Once everyone was seated, Odin glanced around the table.

"Callana is on her way; she has been organizing the archers we will be sending into Rogadon to aid my son. I was actually wondering if you yourself would be int..."

"I would be honored, my lord," Carr interrupted, noting the small queen's arms crossing over her shimmering green satin dress.

"You would send your charge with this man you hardly know?" Lena was all but foaming at the mouth. Odin smiled pleasantly at his wife.

"My dear, he has done nothing out of noble character for me to question..."

"He tried to *kill* you this morning!" Lena snapped.

"True, my love, but he had a very good reason," Odin grinned, rousing a round of stifled chuckles from his royal guard. Lena silenced them immediately with a fiery look. Carr felt his stomach nearly swallow itself with the anxious energy that swiftly filled the silence in the great room. As if to end his suffering, the large wooden doors were pushed open by two guards as a red haired girl came in. She seemed nervous, most likely told she would have to dine with the man she had meant to murder today. Her small hands were clasped together in front of her and her eyes were cast down as she subtly bowed for the royal guard who rose as she entered. Carr noted her glowing skin, pale as linen, against her marvelous red hair, nearly putting the roaring fire to shame with its radiance. She came to Odin and Lena, kissing each on the cheek, than Odin stood and lead her to Carr. The large man stood as well, trying desperately to look worthy to be in these fine clothes in this fine room.

"Callana of Windt, meet-" Callana had finally, unwillingly looked up, only to flush with fear. She grasped at her chest, and put her hand on Odin's arm as she gaped at the now bewildered Carr.

"*Father?*" she whispered; collapsing into a purple velvet puddle.

....

Jiden pulled his blade free of another Dellandore soldier before turning to quickly survey the gruesome scene playing out around him. His thousand men stood nearly unscathed, ankle deep in snow, red with the blood of the larger detachment of their enemies that had stood guard around the castle gates. Jiden felt something was amiss. This had been far too easy. David and Gracien seemed to have come to the same conclusion only now as well as they joined their prince.

"This is not what I expected," Jiden scowled, his brow wrinkled in thought.

"Just thinking the same thing, my lord," David nodded with his agreement. Soon they were joined by Lashend, Laden, Franklin and Senren.

"We have defeated Dellandore...in half a day?" Franklin seemed as puzzled as the rest. Jiden made a quick decision.

"Senren, announce our presence to the villagers trapped in the court and organize a hunt, for those people have not eaten in a week. But no one is to leave the castle as we do not know if more Dellandore soldiers are coming,"

"Aye, my lord!" Senren was off, choosing and gathering men for the hunt as he bolted for the castle gate. Jiden turned to David.

"David, gather caldrons and build fires to melt snow," David nodded and set out quickly with a small detachment to make drinking water for the parched Rogadon constituents. Jiden felt slightly more at ease now that the people would soon be taken care of, but he could not stifle the dread that climbed into the back of his mind.

"What is it Sire?" An uncharacteristically concerned Laden asked. Jiden shook his head, than rubbed his aching right arm.

"He meant to starve them until they surrendered or died, than walk into the castle and claim Rogadon," Jiden was deep in thought.

"Aye," Lashend chimed in, jogging up to join them.

"And you planned us to catch them unaware as we did, my lord," Laden added.

"I...I guess, but, did it not seem...*easy*?" Jiden couldn't shake something was not as it should be.

"Could it not just be attributed to our training, sire?" Franklin offered.

"That is just it, Franklin, it was as if these men had *no* training...at *all*," Jiden seemed to come to a conclusion.

"These are soldiers, but not knights! We were out numbered three to one but they had no training! Ulei is still safe in Dellandore with his royal knights while he sent these men to hold innocent commoners inside their own city as prisoners and as soon as they send word of surrender Ulei rides in with his royal knights to lay claim! " Jiden smiled, having talked himself out of his foreboding dismay.

"He sincerely did expect *no* opposition," David added.

"If word is never sent, he will come to investigate, will he not?" Gracien asked.

"Most definitely, only we do not know how long he intends to wait for word," Jiden answered.

"We need to send a party to search for Nicholas and Galland, for they may run into Ulei first," Jiden glanced to Lashend. The tall youth nodded a grimy red head and fled to Silvio's wagon and canopy where they had left their horses. Laden turned to Jiden for silent permission to follow and Jiden nodded.

"Take twenty men," Jiden called after the long knight, who smiled, turning to tap James on the shoulder. The twin was quickly informed of their new mission and with the help of his identical brother Jeremiah, he rounded up the allotted men and set about to ready for the journey; replenishing water bladders, and having a quick ration of dried figs and salted pork before they headed south. Jiden allowed himself a small break; bringing Leviathon to camp along with Silvio and his wagon.

"Silvio, offer your services to the villagers and any who need them," Jiden called out. The young surgeon took his fully equipped medical wagon through the now open city gates. Villagers were rushing water caldrons back and forth, as knights of Adalonia buried Dellandore soldiers in shallow graves deep inside the forest and dead Rogadon peasants in the Rogadon graveyard just north of the outer castle walls.

Jiden took his fill of warm water as he walked purposefully through the dilapidated, stinking city; meeting grateful villagers, and taking a mental stock of the work to be done to restore this once great kingdom.

Everything he had imagined for Rogadon, in all his many visits as a young man with his father was possible now. The very thought sent a tingling excitement rushing through the young prince's very veins. All Rogadon needed was a leader; a lion hearted champion; fearless and honorable; to rebuild anew this kingdom. As if in answer, the heavy hidden trap doors in the city's center crashed open and spewed out a roaring dark knight and his thunderous band of unnecessary heroes.

"Callana? My dear? Are you well?" Lustene leaned over his young friend with concern wrinkling his forehead. Callana shook her head, than nodded absently.

"I am...my father...I dreamt I saw my father," she mumbled. Lena was pacing behind the surgeon with her small hands worrying together at her waist. Lustene helped Callana to sit up.

"Callana, do you recall what happened?" Lena asked patiently. Just as she did, Odin stepped into the small room, followed by a large, familiar figure. Callana gasped.

"This cannot be! You are *dead*! Nearly seven years passed!" Callana leapt to her feet and pointed to Carr, who stumbled backwards with shock.

"What is this Callana? How do you know Carr?" Odin demanded now completely lost in the whole situation.

"*Carr*?" Callana blinked, turning sorrowful eyes to the pale man.

"You are not *Cai*? My *father*? But you must be! You are identical!" Callana's huge brown eyes filled with tears that slowly ran down flushed cheeks.

"I am sorry, young maiden, but I do not know this Cai you speak of. I have no family left, no children," Carr spoke gently, sensing the girl's deep grief for her father.

"I do not understand...you are his exact image...how..." Callana wept into her hands as Lena rushed to her side to hold her, glaring at Carr as she shushed the frazzled girl.

"That explains one thing," Lustene said almost inaudibly. Odin nodded as he met the surgeons gaze.

"The eyes," Both men answered in unison, than nodded in agreement. Lena glanced at the two, than at Carr and back to Callana.

"It *is* true! Those dark, dark eyes...and her mistaking you for her father. You *must* be relatives of a sort," Lena offered. Carr seemed thoughtful about this.

"You said you were the only son of Cassen, son of Cale?" Odin asked.

"*Cale*!?" Lena and Callana spurt out in harmony.

"Cale is *my* grandfather!" Callana continued.

Odin turned to look at the women as if they were insane. Lena bolted from the room, turning back with one command.

"Stay!"

Moments later, Carr was reading a letter his very own royal grandmother had written to his grandfather, exposing their forbidden relationship and resulting child; his father, Cassen. Carr read with a pained look on his face.

"As a child, I had memories of someone, close to me, but I was told he was a friend who had left. I knew stories of my father's royal blood, but my aunt

Kiera had warned me not to speak of such things, lest my parents fate become my own. If your father's father was Cale, than Cai must have been...my twin brother," Carr's eyes had a far off look as he attempted to make the connection. The very thought of having a brother he could not remember and would never see again twisted his stomach. Callana slowly came to him, gently reaching out to take his large hand. Tears spilled out of her eyes as she held it to her.

"You are my *uncle*?" She smiled up to him. Carr took her cheek in one hand. "I never thought I would have...family...a niece...*who shot me*?" Carr smiled down at her.

"Actually, you have *five* nieces," Callana made a face. Carr laughed out loud, a deep, resonating laugh, so much like her father's.

"Leave it to a brother of mine to make five *girls*!" Carr embraced Callana tightly.

"You were raised by Kiera? Therefore Granlund was your adopted father?" Lena probed, trying to put this together. Carr nodded slowly.

"They were murdered during a robbery...their attackers were never found," Carr added solemnly.

"They were admirable people; I am deeply sorry for your loss," Odin offered. Carr grinned faintly.

"Aye, they were. My heart broke for Rogala, for she was only a child. I was old enough to cope with such pain, but I could not comfort the princess for that terrible king Bromell forbid me to see her," Carr furrowed his brow.

"Aye, I would imagine," Odin contemplated. Callana was confused.

"*Why* would Bromell harbor ill feeling towards Carr?" She asked, forcing herself to stop gawking at her father's look a like brother.

"Bromell had to assume Carr knew of his royal line; he hardly waited two weeks out of respect to claim the throne when his own brother died..." Lena stopped, than gasped.

"A might convenient death; for with them died the secret and any obstacles for Bromell to take Rogadon. *It has been in plain sight for nearly twenty years and we did not see it*!" Odin exclaimed, finishing his wife's thought.

"You are saying Bromell...had his own brother *murdered* to assure his place as king?" Callana grasped her stomach with sudden sickening comprehension.

"My family was *murdered* by the very king I *served*?" Carr fumed where he stood as he clenched and unclenched his fists.

"He is a *coward*, he could not have accomplished such things with out aid," Lena was working herself into a frenzy. Someone out there still walked free in the aftermath of such horrible acts. But who would align with such a man? Callana turned to Lena suddenly.

"We need not look any further than the very man who allied with Bromell against *me*; Ulei." She proclaimed. Odin seemed to have already come to the very same conclusion as he turned and paced.

"He may have been involved with Granlund's murder, but as far back as your father? For what end? If he had wanted Rogadon he would have killed Bromell years ago; why is he waiting?" Odin was furiously trying to put ends together but he was coming up short of a feasible answer.

"Perhaps he only takes Rogadon now because he no longer has any use for his old ally," Lustene suggested. Odin stopped pacing .

"Quite possible, but the time gets away from us; The council has requested a two day's waiting period to allow the other detachments time to meet Jiden. Callana, you and your archers are ready?" Odin grimaced. Callana nodded vigorously.

"Carr, you will ride with us?" Callana clapped. She could feel a kinship with this large man, whether it was due to his incredible likeness to her father or his endearing personality, she did not know.

"Aye," Carr nodded; suddenly pulsing with energy.

"Jiden will be in battle, so there is no more need for secrecy; follow Sir Ellis and take the main road. If you ride hard, it will take only a day," Odin's excitement to join the rescue party was so that he could hardly suppress it.

Callana and Carr spent their two days completely absorbed with each other; telling stories and catching up on a lifetime of memories and making plans to save their city.

....

"So this is where I find you?" Galland grinned brightly as he dismounted to clasp hands and slap his young friend on the back. Nicholas was next to a hastily made fire with King Elei and his resting army; laughing and joking like boys.

"Sorry, old friend, I went back for a perimeter sweep and who do I find sneaking around but these scoundrels!" Nicholas jabbed a nearby soldier of Esildad, Sir Falen, one of Elei's own royal guards. Galland remembered the tournament archer well, exchanging hearty welcomes with the entire lot.

"What brings you and your army out in the winter's snow?" Galland asked a ruefully smiling Elei.

"Actually, the same thing that has brought you, as I gathered," he shook his head with confusion.

"What interest would you have in timber?" Galland probed, knowing full well Rogadon was good for little else.

"I did not ride for myself, but for my…father, Ulei," Elei's face twisted painfully. Nicholas and Galland looked bemused.

"Your *father*?" Nicholas finally broke the awkward silence.

"Shamefully, it is true; I was raised by my uncle, King Colius, but only as a convenience; my father only wanted a blood *heir*, not a son," Elei finished.
"All the better he did not raise you in his *likeness*, ey?" Galland huffed. Elei smiled.
"I hate to interrupt this *emotional* moment but do we not have an outnumbered prince to get to? Nicholas chided.
"Aye that you do. What do you say to us un-evening those odds a bit?" Elei grinned viciously. Galland rushed ahead north to rouse his resting army while Elei briefed his men on the change of venue. Hours later, four thousand blood thirsty troops were redundant and very disappointed.

....

"Rogala how is the stew coming love?" Hellena asked as she busied herself with the boiling water and olive oil for soaking clothes. Rogala smiled brightly, stirring an immense cauldron of venison, potato, basil, fennel, for colds and milk production, and sturdy winter grown carrots; back down to her original petite size.
"If smell indicates taste, it will be a masterwork of vegetables and herbs!" Rogala laughed out loud at her own jest. Hellena giggled. Nia was laughing, sitting on a hide in the sand near a small fire, holding a bundled infant; determined to shove pudgy handfuls of salty sand into his mouth. Hellena winked at her friend; Nia made a wonderful grandmother for one who had never raised a child of her own. Their little pieced together family had learned how to thrive quite melodically here by the sea. Christopher had used a small carving blade to make a few wooden animals for the spoiled baby, and a miniature sail boat bobbed just off shore; tethered to a huge rock. Crystalline and Christopher had converted the carriage into their own personal quarters; mostly due to the lack of sleeping room in the cottage, but more so, admittedly, for privacy. They were a marvelous couple, and Hellena could not be happier with their intense consideration for each other, and their contributions to the living arrangements. The new couple handled the trips to market, and they personally saw to all the fire wood needs. Dakin and Cylan were nearly inseparable now as well, but it was still a hands-off relationship. Cylan was old enough for a wedding proposal, nearly twenty one, and though Dakin was a bit younger, at eighteen, he was old enough as well, and Hellena was all but convinced a proposal was inevitable. Caran was, as always, the sweetest girl Hellena had ever imagined could exist and it broke the loving mother's heart that her nearly twenty year old daughter was still without a match. Caran spent most her evenings the same, as she was right now; going from person to person, offering her assistance, and when none was needed,

she tidies, or gardens, or day dreams near the water's edge. Hellena made to join her, but noticed Cella was about to do the same. Hellena sighed. *There* was a girl she wanted to beat about the head when it came to such matters as love. Braden was all but devoted to her, although she had given him little notice in the past ten years. Hellena smiled, remembering when they were only children, Braden and Cella had been so close, until Cai had died. It was as if Cella *feared* love; as she might hurt so badly if she lost him, as Hellena had hurt for Cai. Hellena closed her eyes and forced herself to remember Cai alive, pushing her tears back and urging herself to be grateful for the time she had with her beloved husband. Nia could see the pained look in Hellena's pale face, and knew exactly how her friend was feeling.

Nia signaled for the all but dancing Caran to come watch the still nameless little man then moved to sit on the hard log near the fire pit and next to her red haired friend. Hellena put a smile on her face but Nia only shook her head.

"I know you a little better than that, love," Nia smiled, but it was a hollow smile. The kind of expression you save for your children when you do not want them to know that you and father are cross with each other or that the family dog died. Hellena sighed and stared out at the grey rolling ocean.

"I sit here feeling sorry for *Hellena*, when my girl is out there somewhere in need..." Hellena allowed a single tear to escape before smearing it off her cheek.

"Love, Callana is surrounded by an army, the most powerful army of all; Do not misunderstand me, I know it is not possible to *not* worry about them, but it is *you* I am worried for," Nia held her friend's shoulders and pulled her closer. Hellena sighed, and then burst into laughter as tears fell down her face.

"Is it fair that I want to be loved? I mean, is it fair that I had true love once and I wish for it again? Cai and I used to bicker a lot, you know; the house is too cold; the girls are too skinny; the stew has too much basil! With all the war and sickness that plagues the lands...starving children...senseless violence...am I the only loon who spends her time *wishing* to *bicker* again?" Hellena shook with her emotional out burst, gaining a few troubled stares from her conjoined family. Nia quickly waved off the advancing girls and everyone returned to pretending they were busy. Nia held her friend and kissed her cheek.

"You *deserved* Cai, do you know that? He loved you with all that he was as I gather it from your girls. That woman that Cai adored, she is still intact, is she not?" Hellena sniffled and nodded.

"The Hellena I see is absolutely wonderful with a brilliant wit and marvelous breasts!" Nia provoked a small laugh out of her friend.

"You still *deserve* love, and Cai would want you to love again if he truly cared for you. All right?" Nia prodded. Hellena had stopped sobbing and was smiling weakly at her friend.

"You as well, you know that?" Hellena raised puffy eye brows at her small friend.

"No *one* man deserves so much woman!" Nia primped her hair and shook her perky chest, igniting a round of laughter from everyone at camp. The two friends laughed and swapped expectations of a perfect man; with big muscles, a wide smile and generous heart, until it was time to sleep and dream where the men they would always love would forever live on.

....

"King Elei!" A very dirty, unshaved but enthusiastic Jiden nearly leapt to greet his old acquaintance.

"Ah, prince Jiden; the ugly half of Galland's charge!" Elei laughed. The two took arms veraciously before turning back to the warmth of the large fire. Now that this somewhat surprising battle was over, Jiden was giving his men free reign, and the eager youths had taken to building a massive fire in the city's center; spit roasting deer for those who had not seen a warm night in over a week.

"I was told you would be dangerously outnumbered and on the verge of death but I see you just wanted an excuse to throw a party without parental supervision!" Elei taunted.

"And what help would you have been old man?" Jiden joked at his older friend. Elei feigned deafness. Jiden grinned and laughed out loud, before embracing his long lost captain and cousin.

"Ey ey! Elei and I are nearly the same age!" Galland was offended.

"*Please*, I think your addition is off!" Elei laughed. Jiden shook his head.

"Actually, we *were* dreadfully outnumbered, but by men I am sure had absolutely no training at all," Jiden was still smiling but had a very serious note to his words. Elei was shocked.

"I am getting more and more confused with this entire ordeal," he shook his sweaty blonde hair.

"Speaking of *confused*, what brings you here?" Jiden gestured for the now returned Lashend to have men bring water and stew for the exhausted army of Esildad.

"To be blunt, king Ulei told me I was to battle Rogadon," Elei started. Jiden scoffed.

"He sent you and your army to battle a soldier-less city? What a toss off! Why would you do as *he* suggest anyways?" Jiden laughed until he noticed Elei was not.

"Because he is my father for starters," Elei started, causing Jiden to choke on his stew for a moment.

"It is true my lord," Galland looked at Jiden with a slight disposition

"I am truly sorry…I had no idea a great man as yourself could be tied to…*not* a man like yourself," Jiden stammered. Now Elei had to laugh.

"Do *not* apologize; we do not have the same relationship as most fathers and sons; not like Odin and you. We do not even speak," Elei announced solemnly.

"Why did you come if not to glorify him?" Jiden pressed. Elei looked down at his stew, swallowing hard before continuing.

"Bromell killed my mother, Renna, as well as my aunt Ralla. Ulei was only able to spare me. I came to seek my revenge," Elei stared at Jiden now who slowly nodded with understanding.

"I had no idea; I am very sorry to hear of your family's misfortune. I had always assumed Colius was your father. It is a terrible treachery indeed. Well, Bromell will be *disappointed* in the least; one of Dellandore's own knights helped me to free Callana from prison,"

"*Callana*? The tournament champion? Why was she in prison?" Elei asked incredulously. Jiden looked surprised.

"You did not hear? Erik, who is now a knight of Adalonia, turned Callana in to Ulei for impersonating a princess, and Ulei sentenced her to death at Bromell's request for impersonating the Rogadon princess, Rogala." Jiden looked at Elei for a sign he was still following.

"Go on," The young king motioned.

"Erik felt remorse for her sentence and helped me to free her from prison and take her back to Adalonia," Jiden grinned again, obviously happy about his prize.

"You made this Erik a knight after he *betrayed* her?" Elei was scowling.

"He said he was sorry, and all," Galland smiled. Nicholas and Jiden laughed out loud.

"I do not understand; my father said I was to battle Rogadon, enticing me with retribution against my greatest enemy, knowing I would have arrived to find Bromell *absent* from his own kingdom? And if he had known about your presence he would have mentioned Adalonia's involvement. What was the purpose of enlisting *my* army?" Elei was extremely thrown by this turn of events and weary from his day of travel. Jiden noted his exhaustion.

"I have no answers for you friend, but rest. I have two patrols making rounds and every two hours I receive report. You are safe here." Elei smiled and stood.

 "As always, prince Jiden, you are a true gentleman," Elei retired with unanswered harassing questions tumbling around his fatigued mind.

"Cousin," Jiden said. Nicholas furrowed a brow, much too busy stuffing his gut to speak.

"Someone is in the castle tower for the night," Jiden's wicked grin slowly spread as he turned his eyes towards Renk who was watching a dancing Erik corner a beautiful peasant to flail about in front of her.

"And it seems her escorts are not with her at the moment…" Jiden had barely finished his sentence before comprehension struck Nicholas, who nearly tripped as he fled towards the open courtyard doors. Jiden sighed, than settled in for a few hours of sure to be interrupted sleep. It was strange, however; he expected to overwhelm a massive army of Dellandore's best with his many forces coming from all directions, only to face and destroy superior numbers with only one detachment? And why would Ulei send Elei if he suspected no opposition at the gates? Something was wrong, off, and it nagged at the back of Jiden's mind until it wore him down and he slipped into a heavy, albeit brief sleep.

....

"What of the peasants?" Ulei was in an uncharacteristically chipper temper this morning. His royal guard stood rigid; more than uncomfortable by their king's odd swing of mood. The captain of the guard, a rather bulky man named Sir Runnel answered warily.
"Still no word of surrender, my lord," He choked out, fearful of invoking his king's wrath. Ulei only grinned maliciously.
"Make ready the men," Ulei commanded and turned towards his bedchamber.
"We ride for battle, sire?" Runnel frowned in confusion. Ulei flashed a bright white smile.
"*For our prize*, Sir Runnel," he nearly glowed with his enthusiasm while Runnel grimaced.
"But, Rogadon…they have not yet surrendered, sire," Runnel nearly stammered. Ulei shook his head slightly and winked.
"I have no interest in Rogadon," his golden eyes lit up from behind with his malevolence. Runnel was all but lost now and timidly stepped forward to catch the departing king.
"If we do not ride for Rogadon, what prize do we ride to claim, my lord?" Runnel furrowed bushy eyebrows in uncertainty. Ulei's exhilaration finally spilled out, filling the air around him with its sinister energy.
"Esildad," Ulei crowed, turning to leave his royal guard in their stupor.

....

The evening brought another round of subtle but cheerful celebration. Erik, Laden, and David were manning roasting spicks with wild pig and deer, while women from the city of Rogadon had joined several long, wooden planked tables and festooned them with varied venison stews, and sausage and herb dishes. Vegetables were still scarce as during the winter Rogadon relied heavily on market for potatoes and sturdy winter grown carrots, but Jiden had promised a future escort to his village vendors of about four thousand marching men. Jiden could hardly wait to return home. He would hold his tournament for Rogadon, but unfairly held high hopes Renk would be victorious. His worries had been forced back by his unrelenting desire to stand before the council and declare Rogadon's restoration to the Della Verde. He sighed with his satisfaction, sitting around one of many large fire circles strewn about in front of the castle Rogadon. Promise colored this city's citizens tonight. Lovers now sang and celebrated happily only days after fearing for their end; Parents now held hope for their children's futures, once believed to be bleak and destitute. Elders eased, filled with relief after seeing their own countrymen suffer years of poverty, living on the brink of starvation; now under the prosperous hand of Adalonia's great prince they had already begun to flourish again. Jiden felt his breathing deepen, as his whole body relaxed gratefully against a sticky pine, lazily watching the merriment unfold around his camp. Elei was across the fire, focused on Erik's embellished conquests, as *everyone* usually was. Nicholas and Miala had reported in hours earlier, still chaste, to Nicholas's slight dismay, but nonetheless in love. They had taken a very small detachment, ten Rogadon, ten Adalonia men to search the castle for any viable evidence to Callana's claim to the throne.

Jiden's eyes slowly took in the entire circle of comrades around him, being sure to smile when he made eye contact. Renk was settled, but Jiden could see the longing behind the dark man's expressive eyes. He wanted to be with his family, and he deserved as much. Jiden made a decision; waiting patiently for Erik's latest adventure to come to an end.

"Rogadon's standard boasts a red lion in honor of the mythical beast whose very name struck fear into the hearts of men," He finished, bringing a round of 'awes' and clapping approval. Jiden clapped as well; slightly perturbed he had missed that story.

"You there, dark knight, you must prepare to take leave. I want you gone come dawn tomorrow," Jiden commanded, his serious tone arresting the jovial mood of the evening. Erik frowned.

"Sire? Do I not deserve to be here?" Renk questioned, slightly put off. Jiden shook his head.

"No, you do not. You have shown yourself to be courageous, serving a prince you hardly knew. You *deserve* to be on the beach with your wife and child," Renk's eyes brightened and a wide smile dimpled his bristled brown face.

"Under one condition," Jiden continued. Renk frowned again.

"Yes, my lord," Renk waited.

"You will give me your word you will return for the tournament, and test for ruler of Rogadon," the prince smiled, inspiring applause for the great knight. Renk saluted before rushing to gather and replenish supplies.

Jiden laughed before turning back to his newly formed Rogadon council.
"This will take time, we have to be prepared for that," he began, his posture changing, deepening his voice, as his presence solidified for all to see.
"I want this to be a Della Verde objective, as well as any...worthy kingdoms willing to donate good men to the cause," Jiden motioned towards Elei as he addressed the circle. The handsome king allowed a crooked smile as he stood to acknowledge the offer.
"Esildad would be honored to be a part of this undertaking, prince Jiden. How does a thousand sound?" The young king bowed, and was answered by a round of cheers.
"I had a feeling," Jiden laughed. "I will need to confer with my father, and our council, but I feel confident Adalonia can give two thousand. That will give Rogadon a fighting force as large as Esildad itself. We will begin recruitment and training immediately. In a few years time, Rogadon should be competently outfitted to man the city and we will withdraw." Jiden spoke so assured, the entire assembly was satisfied with his proposal.
"I propose a monthly council to meet here, in the city, to oversee progress personally. Restoring trade is first and foremost if Rogadon is to grow and maintain. Any suggestions?" Jiden opened the conversation, eager to include all opinions.
"I remember as a child, raw timber was in demand, and Rogadon craftsmanship was second to none," Elei started.
"The main road as well as the forest, has been long seen as dangerous, even, at times, deadly to travel." Elei continued; bowing his head as his thoughts drifted to his mother.
"Security along the road would make for easier commerce, even if only to ease people's fears," Elei concluded.
"I agree," Jiden added. Erik spoke up.
"Guard stations would be easy enough to erect," he offered. Galland stood now.
"Rogadon could make rounds through the forest as Adalonia does the valley," Galland presented. Nods and mumblings of approval sounded throughout their small committee. Jiden was excited again, as he had been before battle.
"If there was a designated area, could it not be cleared for farming?" David proposed. Gracien leapt to his feet.
"Brilliant! Clear enough wood for a season of commerce, than plant!" He proposed. David was standing now to add.
"Winter timber; summer crops? It would be at least six seasons or so before the new trees would be tall enough to interfere with growing, then a new section could be cleared and planted."
"Near the river," Lashend interjected.
"Aye, onion, carrots, potatoes...those are sturdy crops, we should start with those," Senren added.

"Plant after the last flood of the season, in April, when the soil will be movable and healthiest," Franklin offered. Talks of Rogadon's come back went late into the night. Plans were solidified, hands were clasped in agreement, and worried minds rested easier. The coming days in Rogadon showed potential; now held by a newly formed pledge.

....

"This is the queen's chambers; untouched since her death," a young Rogadon soldier lead Miala and Nicholas to a heavy, solid oak wood door. The weary couple was desperate for good news after their disappointing search of the ruined library. The rusty lock of the bed chamber was stubborn at first, but finally released its hold and fell to the floor. Miala took a deep breath before stepping over the threshold; her booted foot leaving a print in the thick dust blanketing the stone floor. Nicholas was shocked at the modesty of the room. She had been a queen, but the chamber boasted no gold, no purple linens, no marble carvings or jeweled ornaments. The drapes were thick wool, dyed blood red. The bed was enormous, but unadorned and of simple design with austere linen and a white wool blanket thrown over the foot board. Miala ran her hand along the top of a dusty dresser where a small mirror leaned unceremoniously against the stone wall behind. Nicholas turned to their attendant.

"Camden was a *queen*, but she had no *wealth*?" He asked incredulously.

"She was not wealthy herself, my lord, for she kept no wealth *for* herself." The small man answered, beaming with pride. Nicholas grimaced.

"You are saying she gave everything away?" He persisted.

"No, my lord, she never *acquired* any wealth. Queen Camden welcomed commerce in her city, but turned away gifts, as she considered herself one of us, sire," The young man stated haughtily. Nicholas could see the affection this man felt for a woman he had only heard of. Her legacy of humility was great indeed.

"There is no window here, why a curtain?" Miala pointed at an enormous, wall length curtain directly across from the foot of the bed. The soldier shrugged, before walking towards the thick curtain to tug it open. The room fell silent, as a wave of dust settled with the dropping velvet to reveal a life size painting.

"This is *Camden*?" Miala gasped. The red clad soldier nodded slowly, still in awe of the brilliance of contrasting colors in the meticulous painting he had apparently never laid eyes on before.

Nicholas was stunned silent. The middle aged woman looking down from her higher place on the wall had bronze skin, with glowing indigo eyes, peering over her delicate shoulder as she posed near the window. Her blonde curls cascaded down her narrow back to a petite waist. She had a slight resemblance to Callana, but that was not what caught the young prince's attention.

"Who is *that?*" Nicholas asked. The young escort shook his head puzzled.

"I do not know, my lady," he answered, ashamed. Nicholas stared hard at the man in brushed paint before him. He was an enormous man, younger than Camden, near but not touching the elegant queen. He had large, brown eyes so dark they were almost black, with a small nose, and pale white skin.

"It is like looking at Callana!" Miala breathed.

"She is the perfect match, save for Hellena's red hair," Nicholas agreed.

"We need to show prince Jiden," with that, Miala rushed out of the room, determined to get a confirmation out of that prince and in turn, the council, one way or another. Nicholas lingered, staring intently at the poignant lovers; captured together on canvas, forever apart.

....

Morning found Jiden rested, and eagerly jumping out of bed with the sun. The air had warmed under the grey cloud cover that had rolled in over night. The clouds were not dark or threatening, however, and the mild breeze blowing from the north brought warmth, and promise of sun as it ever so gently encouraged the clouds south. He casually strolled into the forest; reaching the river, he knelt to fill a cauldron, then plunged his face and hands into the frigid water; slinging back a wet, curly mop as he shook himself fully awake. Elei was there when he opened his eyes.

"Did you just put your *head* in that frozen water?" Elei asked unimpressed. Jiden laughed at his friend's disdain.

"Fastest way to wake up," he smiled through blue lips. Elei frowned.

"*Cold* water on a *cold* morning? Ha! Only a lunatic would..."

"Nothing to report, sire!" before Elei could finish, a very naked Erik rushed passed. Erik saluted before throwing himself into the deep, slow moving river, thoroughly soaking both men with his splash. Jiden gasped in surprise than burst into laughter at the sight of the aghast King Elei.

Elei shook his head and flashed Erik a seething look.

"As I was saying; only a lunatic!" He turned sharply and stomped back to the safety of his roaring fire. Jiden put his hands on his narrow hips as he turned to the grinning knight.

"There is something wrong you, you do know that?" Jiden asked.

"So I have heard," Erik agreed, before climbing out onto the hard packed bank and back into his nearby discarded clothes. The chilled and bright eyed knight turned to leave but Jiden called him back.

"Sir Erik?" he appealed. Erik threw a questioning look over his shivering shoulder.

"Yes? Prince Jiden?" the older man was shoving his legs into his pants. Jiden cleared his throat, averting his eyes and staring at his feet. Erik cocked his head in confusion.

"Jiden?" He asked. Jiden shook his head.

"I...I just wanted to ask for some advice...if you had a moment..." Jiden stammered over his words; his anxious fretting bringing a smile to the prickly knight's lips.

"Come now! Could I be that intimidating? You just saw me completely *naked*!" Erik chuckled. Jiden looked down at the soft earth below as he formed his words. When he looked back at Erik, his features were stern.

"Am I going about this...*right?*" Jiden swallowed hard after his vague question. Erik grimaced slightly, un-sure of the prince's reason for concern.

"I thought your battle plan was *clever*...we have secured Rogadon, have we not?" Erik shrugged his shoulders.

"Aye," Jiden conceded, a might embarrassed at his moment of doubt.

"Jiden, I have been in many battles. Some were small skirmishes, some were large scale; all in the name of *land,*" Erik began, but Jiden interrupted him.

"I do not wish to *have* Rogadon, but *free* it!"

"If I did not *believe* that, I would not be here, nor would your men," Erik reassured the agitated prince. Jiden calmed, nodding his head.

"Aye, ah...I am grateful for all you have done," Jiden smiled timidly and Erik grinned back like a mad jackal.

"Yes, you are," The dark haired knight answered, before swinging around to bounce back to his fire, plucking the bread out of Lashend's hand as he passed. Jiden sighed, feeling more confident now, setting out to attend to his breakfast as his mind buzzed with the promise of a new, perfect Rogadon.

....

Cella tended to the roasted pig on a long spick over the fire. She slowly emptied the contents of a wooden bowl over the searing meat, adding her own combination of basil, dill, garlic, parsley and sage. The intoxicating smell was wafting around their camp, enticing the forged family to the fire pit to watch. Cella had to grin. Cylan giggled at her younger sister.

"I thought food was the way to a man's heart!" she tittered, inviting a giggle out of Caran. Dakin smiled, careful to avoid Cella's piercing stare.

"*And* sister? Just what are you getting at?" Cella demanded, a hand going to her protruding hip. Caran giggled again.

"Only that...well....if that were true, you would be crawling with men, instead of...." Cylan shook her head, intent to clear the laugh out of her throat before continuing.

"*Instead of what?*" Cella was gritting her teeth with irritation. Cylan covered her face with her hands in an attempt to hide her giggling. Caran spoke up.

"Making them cry?" Caran offered timidly.

"Or scream," Crystalline added, more than happy to stir her younger sister's rage.

"Oh really? Dakin?" Cella pointed her finger towards the now blushing young man.

"Am I frightening to you?" She demanded.

"You threatened to tie me up the first day we met!" Dakin flinched. Cylan laughed hysterically now as Cella huffed in exasperation.

"*For good cause!*" Cella tried, but Dakin shivered with the memory, sending Rogala and Nia into wild cackling laughter. Hellena walked over to her middle girl and attempted to pat her back for comfort but Cella turned on her, growling.

"I am not mean for no *reason*! There is always a *reason!*" she snapped.

"Yes my angel," Hellena nodded her head and spoke reassuringly, thoroughly invoking Cella's pent frustration.

"Stop talking to me like that! I am not a *child!*" Cella threw her empty wooden bowl at her mother's feet as she stormed off towards the village. The girls erupted into fits again, Hellena burst into sniggering, though she fought to contain it. Through her laughter she called out.

"Cella please, we meant no harm! Come back!" But Cella disappeared over the rise in the village road. Hellena turned to Crystalline.

"It is too cold for her to be off like that, go and fetch her Crystal!" Crystalline wiped tears from hard laughter away.

"Oh mother, she will be fine! It is warming up anyway. We are only weeks from spring...look at the trees!" Crystalline pointed towards the lone oak growing between the evergreen pines and cedars in the far off forest. It was true, there were a few green leaves fighting to open in the filtered afternoon sun. Hellena sighed, looking after Cella. She knew these villagers well enough to know they would never harm, and even adored Hellena's family, but a mother always worries. Although, Hellena could not tell who she was more worried for; Cella or the innocent person who dared speak to her!

....

Rogala woke with a start. It was deep into the night, not near enough to morning for any light to touch the sky. She hurried to her son's small bed, relieved to see him sleeping soundly. Something was keeping her from sleep tonight, but she did not wish to infect the others. She crept down the stairs and out to the now nearly burned out fire and began stoking it. She added split pieces of pine, heavy with pitch to get it sizzling hot and added a thick round of oak to sustain it. Crystalline and Christopher had pulled the carriage closer to the fire. With the dissipating cloud cover, the nights and mornings would be slightly colder for a while. Rogala could smell spring on the brisk night air, and she relished the thought. Her mind was full of Renk; how was he faring in this ridiculous war? How was Adalonia faring for that matter? Dellandore's army was impressive, from what stories told, but so was the fair green city's. She longed to kiss her husband, longed to be near him tonight. It had been weeks, far longer than she had ever gone without him before. She thought of Callana, and smiled. What a tremendous friend she was; taking such a burden on herself as saving a kingdom she did not know, for a silly imitation princess she only just met. Rogala frowned, for as her own friend had sacrificed her life for her, she herself sat here, impotently unable to return the favor.

A snapping twig in the distant woods pulled her attention away from herself. Rogala was only half sure she had actually heard something and now it was silent again. She stood and watched; fully alert and completely unaware she was being scrutinized from afar.

Renk's mind was full, his heart aching with anticipation. He could see the cottage now, with a petite blonde tending a crackling fire. It was his Rogala! Waves of flowing golden hair warmly reflecting the fire's orange light, in her white linen cape; standing so still, so attentive. Renk could contain his excitement no longer. He spurred his old bay carriage horse into a run!

Rogala faltered. Her eyes must be playing tricks on her now, for she saw a figure on horse back bouncing out of the forest and heading right for the cottage! Her throat tightened with fear and she felt her heartbeat race. Should see scream? Warn the others? Wait...in the moonlight, he appeared to be wearing...green? And waving! He was waving! The war was over; this had to be a courier carrying this very message! She waved back, noticing the man was also wearing gleaming chainmail. Why would Jiden enlist a *knight* to deliver a *message*? She heard him calling out just paces from her now. "Rogala!" Rogala's heart flittered in her chest. She knew that voice! She surged into a run, her bare feet slinging sand as she barreled towards him. "Renk? Renk!" She called. She heard him chuckling joyfully and nearly fell with her sudden burst of emotion. The two collided as he nearly dove out of his saddle; he lifted her in his arms as she pulled her legs up and around his waist. They kissed fervently, unable to speak though their tearful reunion.

Finally, Rogala lowered her feet to the ground and the two started the short walk back to the fire, their eyes locked on one another.

"I want to tell you I have missed you, but it is not enough," Rogala breathed.

"I missed you enough to tell you we will never be apart again, my love!" Renk grinned. Rogala jumped up to kiss his lips again.

"Why are you here? Is the war over? May we see Callana? Is she Camden's heir? When..." Rogala was rattling on excitedly but Renk stopped her with a finger.

"I will answer all your questions later. There is something more important for now," Renk smiled down at her. Rogala puckered her brow.

"*More* important? Like what?" She pouted. Renk stopped and pulled her to him. He kissed her hard on the mouth as he lowered her to the warm sand next to the fire. Rogala smiled between kisses.

"This *is* the most important thing I have wanted to do for weeks, my love," Renk kissed her again and under the cover of his green cape they greedily made love.

....

Dawn rose, spilling streams of sunshine through wide slits in the breaking gray cloud cover that had closed in on the Della Verde Valley for months now. Inside his small, canvas tent, Jiden could feel a slight warming as night's chilled hold on the very air around him gave way. Jiden sighed, silently thanking God for an end to a bleak, terrible winter.

"Prince Jiden?" Laden did not hide his surprise to find the prince still in bed.

"Coming...on the way, I mean..." Jiden grimaced at his own fumbling response as he dressed and flung himself out of the tent flap, tripping on his unlaced boots and falling at Laden's feet. Laden was standing at attention, turning red with the effort of staying his laughter. Jiden bent to tie his boot strings.

"Let's have it Laden," Jiden commanded in his deepest voice. Laden cleared his throat and began.

"Sire, the perimeter of the city is clear, as is the main road from Adalonia to Windt, my lord," Laden announced.

"Good, well done, find some breakfast and we will gather the men for another hunt," Jiden turned on his heel and set off towards the castle. Nicholas and Miala had spent two nights inside, and they were sure to have something by now. He was met at the main door by a very excited Miala.

"Oh! You are here! You need to see something! Wait!" Miala was tugging on Jiden's sleeve before dropping it and putting her hands on her narrow hips.

"Wait for wh-..." Jiden was cut short by Miala's tiny frame shoving passed him and rushing towards the river. The confused prince turned to find his grinning cousin leaning casually against a stone column.

"What?" Jiden asked. Nicholas shrugged.

"I was just wondering what it's like living in sin." He winked. Jiden cocked his head pensively.

"Animalistic..." He answered nonchalantly. Nicholas punched him in the arm.

"All right," Nicholas huffed.

"Gratifying," Jiden continued.

"Fine! Now shut it!"

"Sweaty," Jiden grinned.

"Enough! I get it," Nicholas growled.

"Not yet you don't" Jiden teased.

"Maybe I am more of a noble man," Nicholas shot back smugly.

"*Maybe* I am more of a man," Jiden boasted.

"Whore,"

"Depraved jackal," Jiden smiled. Nicholas sagged, turning blue eyes to the ground in shame.

"This is true," he admitted. Jiden sighed.

"Come now, truth be told, we have not...*sinned*, since Dellandore. When I left we were hardly speaking," Jiden admitted. Nicholas perked.

"Really?" he allowed himself a small smirk. Jiden grimaced.

"Aye, between my father and...we are straying off the subject. Now what am I here to see?" Jiden finally conceded. Nicholas laughed and shook his head.

"Not until we have Miala. She is off to fetch escorts Camden's bed chamber is sort of off limits so we will do it all at once," Nicholas explained.

"Then I pray for beautiful escorts...get it? You said do it all at once..."Jiden simpered. Nicholas rolled tired eyes. Miala returned with a Rogadon guard.

"Ready?" Jiden asked Nicholas cheerfully.

"Up the stairs," Nicholas had reached the end of his resistance to Jiden's teasing as well as Miala's fickle tendencies. They seemed to begin consensually but it was always Miala that ended it abruptly. In his angst, it was easier to believe Miala was just cruel rather than face the truth that she was a young virgin with severe anxieties about men; Nicholas almost hated how much power his desire lent this adorably oblivious tiny maiden. Seeing the thoroughly irritated look on Nicholas's face in harsh contrast to the vapid contentedness on Miala's struck Jiden; he quickly made a mental note to leave the subject of sex alone for now.

At the top of the stairs, Jiden turned to Nicholas, who pointed him left. Two guards parted for the party to enter the room. Inside, Jiden noted the stark, plainness immediately. Miala and Nicholas stood silent, eager to see if Jiden would notice the resemblances as they had. Jiden stopped in front of the vivid portrait and suddenly stilled. After a moment of staring, Jiden finally whispered.

"Rogadon has an heir."

....

Morning brought a joyous, albeit tearful reunion for the little family of Frellis. Renk tried to hug each and every beloved member at least once, even giving Christopher and Dakin a firm squeeze. Hellena received a generous kiss and Nia was lifted off the ground in an exuberant embrace. She was, after all, the only mother he had left. Renk was aching to hold his son, and nearly squealed when the little man finally announced he was awake. After spending nearly every second together during his mother's recuperation, the baby boy was beyond excited to see his long lost father again.

"Look who s here, my angel boy," Rogala had tenderly wrapped the squirming blue eyed boy, lifting him out of his bed and into the first rays of sunshine he had ever seen. His tiny face was filled with wonder, and his eyes squinted in the new brightness. He cooed and reached for the light with his fat little hands as his mother placed him in his father's familiar arms. Renk beamed down at his creation, his smile replicated by his adorable look a like.

"Hello little man. Do you still remember me?" Renk asked. The baby kicked chubby legs and gurgled in response. Renk kissed him on his soft brown forehead and looked at his beautiful wife.

"Thank you," he said. Rogala winked.

"I have been thinking about him, about his family story..." Renk began. Rogala looked puzzled.

"Yes?" She prodded. Renk looked down at his son and smiled wide.

"May we call him Granlund?" Renk hardly needed to ask; Rogala and Nia both clasped trembling hands to their faces as tears sprang into their eyes.

"He was such a good man...and I want our son to be a good man..." Renk started again but Rogala came to him and silenced him with a kiss. Hellena held Nia's hand as she softly cried. Crystalline, Christopher, Caran, Cella, Dakin and Cylan came to encircle the trio; mother, father and son in their tremendous moment. Cella was the first to break off from the group.

"I will go to the market for fresh meat and potatoes for a hearty breakfast!" She announced as she marched towards the village; the rest reluctantly set about their usual chores, Renk now included in their newly formed rituals. He and Rogala boiled fresh creek water and let it cool for father and son to get a much needed wash. Hellena and Nia boiled water for mint and fennel tea and Caran and Cylan waited their turn to boil water for washing linens and cloth dressings for Granlund. Dakin pressed on with his repair work to the worn carriage and Christopher tended both horses over grown hooves. Everyone bustled about in the fiery glow of an early February day; the air was full of the smell of fresh growth in the forest and the spraying salt of the sea. Cella returned and immediately prepared the meat for roasting; she used salt water for boiling her potatoes and a strong, thick apple glaze on the pork that she roasted in a cast iron pot to keep it tender. In an hour it was ready. "Everyone ready to eat?" she asked as she began handing out stone dishware. The morning had warmed, and the sky was a filtered blue behind white, non threatening clouds. As the family hungrily devoured the delicious meal, Dakin cleared his throat.

"Well, if Rogadon is secure, then so is Windt and the main road..." He started timidly, turning a worried look on Cylan. She smiled faintly, but quickly turned glistening orange eyes away. She knew he would be leaving now; he had no reason to stay and the thought made her heart sink in her chest.

"Aye," Renk answered, stuffing another fork full of pork greedily into his mouth. Dakin glanced at Hellena.

"Than I should be off...I imagine; with your permission, of course," His hazel eyes were gleaming with a strange excitement that puzzled Hellena. She cocked her head to respond, noticing a smile playing across Christopher's lips as he continued to eat.

"My *permission*? To leave?" she questioned. Dakin nodded and gestured towards the oblivious Cylan.

"Well I can't very well take her home with me without your blessing now can I?" Dakin grinned. Cylan's head popped up and she gawked at him.

"I had better hear a proposal if you plan to take one of *my* red heads anywhere!" Renk growled. Rogala giggled as Caran and Crystalline sucked in a huge breath in giddy anticipation. Nia shushed a gurgling Granlund, desperate to hear. Hellena gasped and turned to face her daughter, who was standing now, shaking and teary eyed. Dakin walked to her and kneeled before her.

"Cylan? I love you and-"

"Yes!" Cylan chirped, interrupting him. Dakin grinned than suddenly furrowed dark eyebrows.

"You are saying yes to *marrying* me, right?" He confirmed. Cylan nodded fervently and dropped to her knees to kiss him. Rogala and Nia rushed to hold the crying Hellena; Crystalline gave Christopher a wink. Cella huffed.

"So...is Caran and I the only ones returning to our *duties* back at Stone's throw?" She set her hands on her hips crossly.

"Cella! Be happy for your sisters!" Hellena laughed. "Just because you do not want to be in love..." Cella cut her short.

"*Who* says I do not want to be in love?" She nearly barked. The happily chattering camp abruptly silenced and turned disbelieving faces on Cella.

"Cella..." Hellena started but was cut off.

"When men show *interest* you seem to get...*angry*," Caran shrugged sympathetically, trying to put it gently.

"Aye, not to mention violent," Dakin offered.

"And scary," Christopher added, ducking his head when Cella flashed a furious face on him. She was indignant now.

"Dolts!" She cursed. Hellena came to hug her daughter but was rejected.

"I wish to marry...someday! It s not as if I would not know how to be *nice* to a nice man, if there were any! You can not just marry *anyone*! Husbands do not just appear out of thin air!"

"Cella!" a familiar voice called out, interrupting the agitated little woman. She huffed and turned around, caught short by the sudden elation she felt to see him and was immediately enraged by her own emotional betrayal. She turned back to face her expanded family, all smirking at the irony of Braden's sudden appearance, and she held her hands up in surrender.

"I will be *nice*...but it still won't work!" she barked before spinning around to face her childhood playmate with a large, forced smile on her face.

"Braden! So good to see you!" She called out, exuberantly out of character. Braden flinched, his face apprehensive at her unexpected affability. Christopher turned to Crystalline and whispered.

"I think Cella *nice* is scarier than Cella *scary*," Crystalline nodded in agreement. Hellena shushed them. Braden approached timidly, keeping his eyes on Cella as he came to Hellena.

"Please forgive the intrusion, Hellena, but I have terrible news," Braden began, warily eyeing Cella as he spoke. She continued to smile eerily at him but her eyes were uneasy. Hellena rose and nodded her head.

"It is all right, go on," she encouraged. Braden shook his head before continuing.

"Dellandore marches south, on Esildad," he started. Renk stood at once.

"*What*? I thought Ulei was after Rogadon?" the dark knight asked angrily.

"You saw the purple army pass?" Hellena asked. Braden nodded wearily.

"Yes, mum, and I heard one of the soldiers say as... as much," Braden sagged.

"You were close enough to hear them and you *escaped*?" Hellena prodded.

"For the most part," Braden chuckled softly before collapsing to the ground at her feet. It was only then they noticed the seeping wound in his back. Cella's fake smile gave way to a horrified gasp as the circle erupted in anxious movement.

"As always, Prince Jiden, it was a pleasure," Elei grasped Jiden's elbow as the two locked arms. Jiden mirrored the young king's genuine smile and slapped him on the shoulder with his free hand.

"More so for you than me, I imagine," Jiden teased. His spirits were so high with the unfolding of events in the last week he could not help but force his unceasing playfulness on everyone around him. Elei shook his head.

"Of course," Elei smiled and turned to mount up. He noticed Jiden and his royal guard had mounted as well.

"What is this now?" He laughed. Galland waved him on.

"It is an escort, you royal ass, now off!" Elei's royal guard snickered at the large man's jest, as well as Elei himself. Jiden had already set up guard patrols for the next few days so he could see his old friend home, as well as training sessions with his squadron leaders. Twins Jeremiah and James were dual commanders for the course of the Prince's absence and Jiden was pleased with how well they had taken to their shared appointment. Elei nodded to his combined army's squadron leaders and six thousand feet thundered into motion on command. Elei led the way, along with Jiden, Nicholas and the slightly shaking Miala; who still had not mastered riding. Elei's royal guard headed off to scout ahead and secure the southern road while Jiden's royal guard circled around to follow the foot soldiers and secure the rear. Half a day would pass at their comfortably brisk pace before their first break. Spring shone through today in all of her golden glory. The last of the snow clung to mountain tops and slushy piles in the forest; the melting had already raised the river. Jiden smiled, the contentment of the moment bringing to mind he had yet to make a formal proposal to the council and Callana, again. First to arrange for the council to view the painting; it should prove, if nothing else, Callana was linked to Camden and her servant. The resemblances were so strong; there was no denying it as far as Jiden could see. He could justify marrying Callana to unite Rogadon and Adalonia and finally be able to marry for love *and* his kingdom and nothing meant more to him. Jiden sighed as the sun sprang into full view over the eastern horizon and gleamed through the dark forest.

....

Braden's eyelids flickered than burst open as he thrust upright, the motion causing his head to spin slightly. Cella was there beside him in the small cottage's large bed. She shushed him still.

"Ey, move slowly. You have not eaten in days and you lost a lot of blood," She spoke gently, atypically so, and Braden found himself staring dumbfounded into her soft sunset colored eyes.

"Cella? Are you ill?" He asked, suddenly worried her kindness was brought on by some sort of affliction. Cella rolled her eyes and sighed.

"I give up! Being nice is too confusing for men, ey?" She started to rise but Braden grabbed her arm.

"Sorry! I was...surprised is all. Stay a moment?" He pleaded. Cella nodded slowly and sat back down.

"Did someone set off to warn Adalonia?" Braden asked. Cella nodded again.

"Aye, Dakin rode for the camp at Rogadon, but Renk fears Elei may be riding for home already," Cella looked concerned. She turned a wrinkled brow towards Braden as he spoke.

"I should have gone there first, but I wanted to tell you and your family about the inn," he began.

"Go on," Cella urged, concern spiking in her voice.

"Dellandore burned it to the ground...along with our entire village..." Braden continued. Cella shook her head.

"There was nothing you could have done...it is a good thing you fled..." Cella stated simply.

"*Fled*?" Braden was cross.

"Aye, that is why you were shot in the back, right?" Cella shrugged. Braden forced himself to stand now, an angry scowl contorting his usually open face.

"I did not *flee*, Cella," Braden began but Cella started for the door.

"No need to get tense. People get scared; it is expected," She left then. Braden stood for a moment fuming, before making his way out and down the steps to join Renk as he left for a morning fishing trip.

Cella watched him limp towards the shore. He threw a last, hardened stare over his shoulder at her before climbing into Renk's small wooden boat. Cella shrugged off the nagging feeling she had done something wrong and set about to make the mid day meal, as had become her assignment due to her adept cooking abilities. Hellena came to her side.

"What was that about? I have never seen Braden cross," She asked, hands on generous hips. Cella yawned and turned towards the garden.

"His pride is hurt, that's all. Men...ha!" She chortled with her own jab at the opposite sex.

"I do not know what he would have to be ashamed of; he saved our entire village," Hellena announced. Cella spun around.

"What do you mean?" Cella was intently glaring at Hellena now, causing the older woman to flinch slightly.

"I mean word has come from Stephen; Anna came all the way from Windt to spread the word of Braden's bravery daughter," Hellena was cocking her head to one side to gauge her daughter's reaction to this news.

"A Dellandore soldier shot him in the back as he pulled one of the elders from his burning home *after* he had sounded the warning bell! He is a hero!" she continued.

"Well I had no way of knowing! I had to *assume* he was shot in the back as a fleeing *coward!*" Cella stuck her nose in the air as she turned to collect carrots and potatoes. Hellena reached for her arm, yanking her around. "You called him a *coward?*"

"Not in those words, I merely said it was normal to be afraid, that's all," Cella was desperate now, realizing but unwilling to admit to her misjudgment.

"Cella! I am ashamed of you! That man has loved you as far back as I can remember and you have never given him any reason to hope you would one day return those feelings..." Hellena was closing in on Cella as she backed away.

"What are you talking..." Cella tried but Hellena barked over her.

"But to sit on high and judge a man you have only barely decided to pay any attention to? How could you be so callous?" Hellena held Cella still, forcing her to make eye contact. Cella's hard glare finally softened and she fell into tears.

"Mother, I am sorry, I...I had to believe he was a coward..." Cella cried.

"Why?" Hellena demanded.

"Because *I am!*" Cella snapped. By now Nia and Rogala had overheard and stood behind Hellena now, pity welling in their eyes for the crying girl.

"You? A coward? Ha! You have never been afraid of anything!" Hellena huffed. Cella shook her head.

"You do not understand..." Cella hung her head as Rogala came to her, reaching out to lift Cella's chin.

"I do...I know...."she said. Cella sniffled slightly as she followed the smaller woman's blue gaze.

"You see that ocean?" Rogala pointed towards the rolling waves with the white tipped crests. Cella nodded.

"I was so afraid of it when Renk brought me here. Endless...deep...terrifying," Rogala closed her eyes as she remembered.

"And the unceasing rising and falling... used to make me so sick...but once I forced myself to follow him in...my heartbeat finally slowed, my head stopped spinning, and when I opened my eyes... I realized that being there with *him* was safe..." Rogala opened her eyes again and looked at Cella. "You just need to learn how to swim," Rogala winked and smiled at her friend and Cella smiled back bashfully. Nia grinned at Hellena.

"Aye, there's a lesson I could use again myself!" The small blonde poked her friend and the two fell into cackling laughter.

"*Mother!*" Cella and Rogala chided in unison and rolled their eyes.

....

"I must say I am...*happy* to know Jiden was successful, but I feel a bit foolish," Callana sighed after she was briefed on the prince's quick disposal of the larger, yet apparently unskilled army. Their tentative respite on Jiden's last day in Adalonia had built Callana's hopes high for reconciliation upon her arrival. According to James he had left only hours earlier to escort Elei to Esildad. She sighed again. Carr laughed nervously.

"Do not be troubled, uncle, the king will be so glad to hear of Jiden's conquest..." Callana tried but Carr cut his niece short.

"He will simply *dismiss* the unnecessary forced march of two hundred archers?" The large man laughed again, causing Callana to swallow hard.

"Aye, this was a bit of a...a"

"Enormous waste of resources?" Jeremiah helped. Callana swallowed again. By now many of the familiar knights of Adalonia had gathered around the princess archer to welcome her to the make shift camp. Carr was in awe of the progress made in such short a time.

"You are making repairs on the city?" Carr had dismounted and started walking towards the worn stone of the outer barriers. Ellis, James, Jeremiah and Jerrik eagerly led the big man on a small tour of the work being done. Rogadon villagers and Adalonia knights were busy, building side by side on the castle. Callana smiled at the nearby knight, Sir Ren.

"He adores this city," she said. Ren nodded a shaggy red agreement. The squat, burly knight, Nevens was nodding as well.

"For all the loyalty her patrons show, you would think this place was paradise," he stated, causing Callana to frown.

"Bromell is solely to blame for the state of affairs here. Rogadon needs a great king to raise her again," the circle bobbed heads in agreement, all eyes focused on the large man admiring a wall.

....

"Mount up!" Elei called, his excitement for home nearly boiling over inside. Riding out for nothing more than a reunion with old friends was not the worst thing he could have been doing for the past few days but he was grateful to get back to his beloved kingdom. Jiden could see the middle aged man's demeanor change the closer they got to Esildad's borders. He had a commanding presence at all times, but with it now was a barely concealed, youthful happiness. Jiden knew what it was to love your home, and he was envious he was days off from his own return.

The border of Esildad was a small, fast moving river called Crystal, for the light blue clarity of her deep waters. The village of Windt fell in the flatlands between the rise of the Shadow's forest and the slope of Esildad beyond; the distant mountains of Roan between the small village and the sea city of Frellis.

The red earth of the hard road contrasted with the fresh green sprouts of spring's first grasses, fighting for patches of sunlight the filling canopy allowed through. In the dense of the forest, snow drops and yellow crocus flowers, once thriving in winter's chill, now shriveled, giving way to blue bells and hardy, pink hellebore. Along the road where the sun had already started to dry out the red clay, long stemmed daisies in yellows and white gleamed in the warmth of the late day.

The band of friends along with three thousand foot soldiers shaded by the spiny branches of the forest pines, spruce, and leafy oaks emerged into the brilliant brightness of the full sunshine of the Rogadon valley's southernmost edge. Verdant fields rose and fell around them with an uncountable army of tiny white clover blooms. The excitement was contagious and it spread through the company like fire.

"What do you say we sprint the rest of the way home?" Elei grinned over his shoulder, inspiring a round of cheers from his homesick men as they picked up their grueling pace.

....

"My lord!" Sir Falen called out, rushing back from scouting ahead. Elei spurred out to meet him.

"What is it?" he asked the breathless knight.

"The village of Windt...at the crossroads...it is gone!" He nearly coughed out the words. Elei furrowed his brow.

"*Gone*? How is that possible?" he asked incredulously. Falen was downing the contents of his water bladder and shaking his sweaty head.

"Sire," he breathed. "It has been burnt! To the ground...there is no one, nothing left!" he exclaimed. Elei turned to the confused Jiden. Galland and the rest of the prince's royal guard had halted the men and were now riding up to see what had stalled the king. Jiden urged Leviathon closer.

"What has happened friend?" he tentatively asked, wary of the crazed look on his long time comrade's face. Elei seemed to be searching his mind for something lost or out of reach. Jiden waited a moment. Elei's golden eyes flashed back and forth, thoughts reeling; he was making cognitive connections one by one until he finally snapped his head towards a Jiden. Clarification had come and Elei felt himself boil with rage.

"How could I be this dim witted?" he exclaimed. Jiden looked around to assure his outburst had not caught any of his troops' attentions before coming closer.

"My lord?" Jiden asked. Elei glared at him, fury rising up to harden the young king's jaw.

"He never wanted *Rogadon*! He sent me on a fool's errand and *usurps* me in my absence!" Elei was trembling now.

"Windt has been destroyed..." Falen tried to fill in the missing pieces for Jiden who finally put the story together.

"How many did you leave on guard?" Jiden's mind raced. It would take a day to ride back and gather men and another two to ride back again to Esildad. Elei only had two thousand here; Ulei had three, maybe more.

"I only left a thousand...the guard stations will sound the warning, but they will be greatly outnumbered," Elei stated, his mind already putting a plan of action together.

"I will help, but my men will take days," Jiden started.

"Too long...if I force march my foot soldiers we will be there tonight, but exhausted...." Elei was counseling himself so Jiden kept quiet.

"I will need to get in, undetected, with a small detachment..." Elei continued. Jiden glanced over his shoulder, catching the attention of his ever watchful captain, signaling him over. Galland spurred Baby into a plodding gallop, pulling up to Jiden's side as the prince hurried to fill him in.

"King Elei suspects Ulei sent him to Rogadon to claim Esildad in his absence," Jiden began. Galland furrowed his bushy eyebrows in thought.

"Windt has been burnt down," Jiden continued. Galland winced with this news.

"It will take days to get our forces here," Galland started but Elei interrupted.

"He will starve my city as he did Rogadon. I will not allow this," the agitated king growled. Jiden clapped a hand on the young man's shoulders.

"I will help you in any way, I swear it!" he promised. Elei nodded.

"I know you will, good prince. We must form a small council and inform my men. We ride out tonight," with that Elei yanked his mount around to gather his royal guard. Hours later, one rider raced north for Rogadon while six others thundered south.

"That was brilliant! Could you show me?" a rather excitable group of farm boys had become taken by the skill of the friendly archer and one reached anxiously for Carr's bow. The big man laughed.

"Here, let me get you your own; this was my father's," he traced the name Cassen inscribed in the bow's intricate handle than turned to retrieve a smaller bow from his quiver. The skinny youth held the bow as tenderly as he would a baby, turning it side to side to watch it gleam in spring's early morning sun light. Callana was returning from washing at the frigid river when she came upon her uncle and his brood. Carr was demonstrating the hold and release, allowing each a turn with the smaller bow. Callana grinned at the peaceful giant, with his slow, gentle movements, captivating his audience with his modest acceptance of an accomplished mastery of his skill. Callana had perched on a fallen log paces behind her uncle, lost in his demonstrated knowledge. Galland would be impressed, even for all of his skill and patience; Carr was incredibly gifted at teaching. This is what Rogadon needed, she thought; a competent, humble leader, with a tremendous love for his country and countrymen. Hours would pass before Callana's day dreaming would be interrupted.

"Jeremiah! James!" a frantic rider vaulted from his horse and dashed for the twin commanders.

"What is it Henry?" the look a likes answered in accord.

"Windt has been burnt to the ground! It is feared Ulei has taken Esildad!" Sir Henry announced, loud enough to catch most of the camps' attentions. Callana gasped.

"You are sure of this? Windt is...*gone*?" she collapsed to the dust below, desperately trying to catch her breath as Carr rushed to her side.

"I am sorry my lady," Henry bowed.

"Prince Jiden, Prince Nicholas and their royal guard set out last night with King Elei for the crystal river. I am to muster the troops," Henry finished his report with a pitiful look towards Callana.

"We will make ready the majority of the men," Jeremiah began.

"Leaving a crew for rebuilding behind," James finished.

"We must send Sir Ellis to Adalonia with word of this," Jeremiah started.

"Our involvement with Esildad will be decided by the council," James finished his brother's thought again. Both turned to Callana who was burrowed in her uncle's chest and sobbing. She shook her head, teary red eyes peering out of muffled hair as she spoke.

"That will take *days*!" she pleaded. James nodded as Jeremiah responded.

"We are sorry my lady," he tried but Callana jumped forward.

"Our prince rides out, we must follow!" she demanded, but both twins shook their heads remorsefully.

"It must be decided by council, the prince knows as much. We will be ready on the councils' command to action." James answered before turning to find Sir Ellis. Callana huffed than suddenly brightened.

"Wait!" she called. James and Jeremiah turned to face her.

"The council *did* assign two hundred archers to assist the prince!" She turned to the stunned Sir Henry.

"We leave at dark!" She announced before flailing around to gather her detachment. Carr watched her leave than turned to face the three gawking faces she left behind.

"She has a point," He shrugged, pivoting around to hastily retreat before anyone could object.

....

"Did you catch them?" Renk and Braden nearly smothered the exhausted Dakin upon his thundering arrival back to Sea Fair. Dakin caught his breath long enough to answer.

"Left last morning for Esildad...I warned the knight on perimeter watch, Sir Henry...we must ride for Esildad," Dakin pulled his water bladder out and downed the entire contents. He had rode hard for an entire day without stopping to get back and was desperately dehydrated. Renk cursed than glanced over his shoulder at his now distressed wife.

"Sorry my love," Renk apologized for his language but Rogala could care less.

"You still try to hide the world from me husband?" she scolded. Renk came to face her, seriousness darkening his eyes.

"Dakin could not catch them," He began but Rogala finished.

"They will be riding to their *death*! Spend these last moments with your son; I shall make ready your supplies." Rogala handed a squirming Granlund to his father as she set about saddling and packing her husband's bay horse. Cylan brought left over breakfast and more water for a very grateful Dakin, leaving him to eat while she watered and fed his frothy horse. Caran, Nia and Hellena set about helping as much as they could, and Cella made ready and began serving the mid day meal. Crystalline kissed Christopher, pulling him out of his hardened staring. She knew he wanted to go; if for nothing more than to prove himself.

"What are you waiting for love?" She asked. Christopher smiled and grabbed her hand.

"I do not deserve you," he confessed. Crystalline grinned brightly.

"I know," she said. Christopher stood with new determination, and walked over to talk to the three men, deep in strategy.

"I wish to go with you," he announced. Renk, Dakin and Braden jerked heads towards him in surprise.

"Wish granted; we had no intention of leaving you behind!" Renk laughed. Cella was busying herself dishing out large wooden bowls of savory lamb stew when her mother came nagging, pulling her guilty eyes off Braden.

"Cella," Hellena whispered.

"What is it mother?" Cella hissed.

"Braden has not been served," Hellena smiled brightly, relishing the terrified look on her daughter's face.

"No mother, you do it!" Cella demanded, shoving the bowl with its steaming contents back at Hellena, who in turn pushed it back, slopping stew down the front of Cella's simple linen dress. Everyone seemed to gasp at the same time. Christopher slugged Braden in the arm.

"You won't even need a spoon!" The lanky man jested. Laughter spurted out around the awkwardly blushing Braden and the now irate Cella. She grabbed the long handled ladle and refilled the wooden bowl and pushed it into Braden's trembling hands. He looked up at her from his sitting position on the sand, the scathing look in her eyes sending a shiver down his spine.

"Thhhank you, Cella, *miss* Cella," Braden stammered out the words, allowing a timid smile to turn up his mouth. Cella's eyes twinkled as she glared down at him and grinned maliciously.

"Sure thing love," she gestured towards her stew covered chest, noting with some delight that Braden's eyes followed.

"Let me know if you want seconds," and with that she turned and swished away, leaving a breathless Braden gaping.

....

"Ulei has released Rogadon, we are rid of him!" Corrin announced, angrily pounding his fist into the enormous council table. Nona shook her head in disagreement.

"He has become more than just a slovenly excuse for a king; he is a disease on this land and he is spreading!" She nearly growled; her piercing blue eyes locking with every member of the council. Kan, a stoic older member stood to speak, his gravely voice rolling out from behind a long, white beard.

"We have claimed Rogadon, is that not what we set out to do? This is Esildad's problem to solve. Our mission is and always has been to secure peace in the Della Verde Valley, as King Triden commanded. Why would we veer from this now? If Ulei is to take Esildad, so be it," Kan sat with the last, unaffected by the anger infecting the rest of the council. The members turned to their queen as Corrin bowed to her.

"Noble Queen, what say you?"

Lena, who had sat quietly through the entire discussion, glanced longingly at her husband's empty chair. Odin had left two days before for mountain guard with the false knowledge that Callana had reached Rogadon to find all was secure, so it fell to Lena to make this tremendous decision based on the laws of Adalonia and its continuing peace. She did not want to be responsible for war. Lena breathed deeply and slowly stood.

"The Della Verde valley has since it's beginning been governed by laws put in place by King Triden and Queen Sarana," as Lena spoke, she circled the seated members; her gentle voice filling the quiet room.

"However, Triden did not rule alone, but instead chose to share his reign with his brothers Nyden, Boden, Ryden and sister Camden. It is in this tradition of family rule that I am asking the council to allow me the council of the descendant rulers of our valley. I have sent for *my* family."

The council hushed with this news. Lena was more than anxious to have their agreement but determined to move without it. The council silently nodded their approval; Nona rose to speak.

"My Queen, we approve this decision," the older woman nodded.

"We will convene in three days time then," Lena bowed her dismissal than rushed quickly from the room. *Three days* to wait in agony to make a decision to aid her son. He was a day ahead of her already and would be in Esildad before the new meeting took place. He had King Elei's thousands of soldiers, hundreds of archers, and a brilliant royal guard. She had nothing to worry about, or so she tried to convince herself. Lost in her thoughts, Lena had not noticed Nona's calling.

"My queen, my queen, a word?" Nona finally snapped the queen from her fretted thoughts and she bowed to her respected friend.

"Forgive me council woman Nona," Lena apologized. Nona turned towards the two constant guards as she spoke.

"A word...in private?" She asked. Lena nodded and dismissed Reinhold and Graven who bowed and left the outer chamber. Lena nodded towards the large entry doors and the two pushed their way into a warm, afternoon sun that illuminated the white limestone steps, nearly blinding in its brilliance.

"What troubles you my dear?" Lena turned to Nona, wrinkling her brow as she reached for the older woman's hand. Nona smiled kindly.

"You," she stated. Lena stopped their descent to face her friend.

"I am healthy, you have no cause for alarm for your queen my dear," Lena offered.

"Lena," addressing her common brought the intended affect and Nona grimaced under Lena's concerned stare.

"What is it?" Lena implored her friend, desperate to help.

"I adore you Lena! Even deep in worry for your son you agonize for *me*?" Lena's eyes began to shine with tears but shook them clear.

"I feel helpless! I am leaving him to fight his own battle, even if it kills me to do so... But it is not *my* life in peril, it is *his*! If only the roles were reversed; I would die a hundred times to save Jiden!" Lena clutched her friend's long hands, shivering with the effort of holding back sobs. Nona nodded as she looked down on her smaller friend.

"I know; I have six of those!" She laughed with that, stirring a small smile out of her companion.

"I do not wish for war, especially without the entire council's approval..." Lena began, but Nona interrupted.

"Even a queen as great as yourself will meet opposition in her own ranks without a king to collaborate. If the rulers of the Valley stand with you, so will your council." Nona guaranteed.

Hours later Lena scribbled furiously through draft after draft, desperate to find the words to send reluctant kingdoms into the war that could end all wars.

....

"Illiam, please make ready your parchment and ink and be in the council hall by mid day," Lena ordered as she rushed passed the round little scribe on her way to Gillian's galley for tasting of the council's spread. Lena placed herself at the head of the table, in Odin's chair, desperate to make known her intent to be seen as the authority of the coming proceedings. She waited for what seemed like an eternity until finally her much welcomed guests nearly burst through the doors.

"Sister!" Lunette's tiny frame pushed passed Sir Keiton before the massive blonde guard could clear a path. Lena clutched her younger sister tight, pressing into her all the fondness she could. It had been the better part of a year since they had seen each other at Jiden's birthday ball. Long letters sent frequently could inform but could not replace the warmth of one, brief embrace. Lunette was almost in tears.

"I have missed you terribly! How is my beloved son?" Lunette blushed with the mention of her youngest child. Lena's brow creased slightly.

"He is, as usual, along with Jiden... on the way to *Esildad*," Lena began slowly.

"Esildad? Whatever for?" Lunette frowned at her sister's worried expression.

"I promise to explain everything, dear sister," Lena smiled reassuringly before moving to greet her quiet nephew.

"Nathan!" she gasped as she closed in on him. He had been standing bashfully at the back of the room. Though he was next in line for his father's throne of Tasladad and boasted the same generous good looks of his younger brother, Nathan did not possess Nicholas's out going charms but instead abounded in shy sweetness.

"You are a dream come true! Why are you not betrothed as of yet?" Lena pressed, further terrifying the handsome young prince. He bowed his head, his cheeks deep red as he smiled sheepishly. His father entered the room in time to hear the dreaded question and slapped his son on the back.

"Forgive him, dearest Lena, he does not possess his brother's...angst...but he will one day *soon* have to choose from his many adoring devotees!" Rasden laughed heartily at his own part jest. The quiet humble nature of Nathan lured more young girls than Nicholas's daring charm and then some. Rasden took his sister-in-law's delicate hand and kissed it.

"And how is my favorite cousin's beautiful wife?" Rasden teased. His twinkling deep, blue eyes sparkling with a devilish quality, so like Odin's, Lena could not help but blush.

"I am surviving, and you? Are you fairing well?" She turned to lead him to his place next to hers at the large table. Rasden shrugged mighty shoulders and sighed.

"A beautiful wife, a thriving kingdom, and two healthy boys...I will manage," He grinned brightly, winking at Lunette. Lena felt her heart break with the knowledge she had terrible news to depart upon such a happy family. She kissed his cheek and turned to greet her oldest brother, just now arriving. Leonard walked in, the spitting image of her father; tall, lean, with the hardened facial features of a man with an entire kingdom constantly on his mind. He had dark shoulder length hair, straight as a plank and slightly thinner than the last time she had seen him. He had a grimness to his smile, having immediately read Lena's nervous body language all too well. He hastily gripped his younger sister's thin shoulders.

"You look fit. I trust your *king* is treating you agreeably?" Leonard forced a smile but Lena knew all too well of her brother's dislike for her choice in a husband. Before their marriage, Odin's genial family history did little to out weigh his own fighting reputation. Leonard had long harbored fears Lena would invoke some hidden malicious tendencies and even after seventeen years it was the first question he always asked her. Lena sighed and rolled her green eyes.

"He treats me like a queen, dear brother, as he always has," Lena scolded. Leonard bowed stiffly. Lena returned the gesture before facing her brother's adorable wife.

"Camela how is life in Maulen treating you my love?" She held her tightly for a moment before releasing her to speak. Camela was the exact opposite of Lena. She was docile, quiet as a church mouse, and had almost no interest in matters other than their daughters, both named after great women.

"I am well Lena...Anna and Sara send their love...they cannot wait for Jiden's wedding!" she piped, glancing towards her husband when she spoke. Leonard smiled down at her and shook his head.

"No need to be so timid my love, she will not bite," he grinned. Camela blushed.

"Of course, my lord," she bowed.

"I do miss those beautiful faces! Thank God they took after their mother, aye brother?" Lena provoked.

"Indeed," Leonard looked down at his wife again who blushed deep under his scrutinizing gaze. She was very beautiful; golden skin, golden hair, and the lightest brown eyes. She was like a bronze statue and Leonard treasured her as such. He was fierce and she was delicate; they made the perfect pair.

Lena turned to the last and the most dreaded guest. Dressed in Felonia's bright blue and white, and looking irate, Felonin stalked into the room. He was Odin's youngest cousin and only family member to despise Lena. He did not approve of women who saw themselves as any more than a bearer of children; much like his own wife, Melanie, who walked behind him and did not speak without verbal permission from her husband and had, at her young age of only twenty two, already given birth to four sons. Lena had her doubts but Camela had assured the queen her baby sister had never been hurt by her strict husband. Lena held her breath as she pulled herself up and met him face to face.

"Lena, how inappropriate of you, *as usual*, to send for *my* council full knowing your King could not attend," Felonin shared his brother's size but not the deep blue eyes of Rasden and Odin, but instead had crystal light eyes making his pupils contrast like small black holes in a clear sky.

"My *husband* and I share the same values for our kingdom and valley as you do, King Felonin," Lena declared. Felonin studied her for a moment through narrowed eyes.

"You speak for him?" He asked incredulously.

"I speak for *Adalonia*," She stated with a hard glare sharpening her features. Felonin sighed, bored.

"Very well, proceed," he nodded and strode away to seat himself. Melanie bowed her head as she passed the stiff queen. Lena took a deep breath as she prepared to address the room that had suddenly become cold. Shuddering momentarily, she strode purposefully to the front of the room as the council filed in. Once everyone was still, Lena nodded for Sir Keiton and Sir Kern to close the outer doors. In the quiet of the enormous stone hall, Lena began.

"Our noble Kingdoms have stood united under the banner of peace for three generations. Through great efforts on the part of our grand parents and parents and ourselves; the Della Verde valley has become the measure of the highest value for all other kingdoms. We are all aware that Rogadon had all but separated from our valley with the deaths of King Granlund and Queen Kiera. I can testify without doubt that Adalonia has secured the lost forest kingdom once more," Lena allowed the room to take in the news. Appraising nods and murmuring traveled the table. All but the council rejoiced.

"However," She grimly continued.

"Through some *appalling* turn of events, it has come to us that as Rogadon was rescued, Esildad is feared taken." As Lena expected, Felonin was first to make his feelings known.

"This is why we were brought here?" He snorted. "You waste my time, *Queen*! What care should we have for *Esildad*?" He sneered. Leonard stood and faced his fellow king.

"You would do well to hold your contempt in the queen's own hall!" He boomed. Felonin jumped to his feet.

"I refuse to be lectured by a *woman* who plays at ruling in the absence of her King!" Felonin barked. Gracien and Reinhold placed anxious hands on their sword hilts and moved forward to stand on either side of Lena. Leonard was fully enraged as he threw aside his yellow velvet cape to draw his sword.

"Your cousin's absence gives your tongue courage! Let me remove it!" Leonard leaped towards Felonin who made to draw his sword. Lena's anger boiled over.

"Enough!" The word rang out and reverberated off the stone walls. All eyes turned to Lena in disbelief.

"There will be no fighting here! Good brother, you needn't protect me, no matter how honorably, and as for you, King Felonin," Lena stormed over to stand face to chest with the large man.

"I *am* the Queen of Adalonia! It is *my* troops, *my* husband and *my* son who secure this valley; that includes *your* home! You will remember that or remove yourself from my hall!" Lena waited only a moment for Felonin to nod a red faced acceptance before she turned back to the rest of the room.

"I stand here before you talking of *decades* of peace and we are together only *moments* and bickering over *rank*? Unacceptable!" The tiny queen slammed a fist into the table, punctuating her words. Leonard and Felonin sat shamed, still flustered and huffing. The room sat in awe of the queen's complete control of the situation. All eyes were on Lena as she calmly began to speak again.

"Prince Jiden was met with nearly no resistance at Rogadon's gates but in the mean time King Elei had been sent by King Ulei to take Rogadon in the name of Dellandore, but altered his allegiance." Lena waited for the room to take in this information. She was not surprised to see a look of confusion throughout. Rasden was first to break the silence.

"Why would King Elei abide such a man as Ulei?" Rasden's question provoked a round of murmurs. Lena sighed heavily.

"King Ulei is his father," She started. The room stilled. Elei had been a part of every Della Verde event since he became fast friends with Jiden and Nicholas at a Christmas ball nearly ten years ago.

"This is for certain?" Felonin asked. Lena nodded and explained as best she could.

"The murder of King Granlund and Queen Kiera has long been believed to be the result of a violent robbery, but new knowledge suggests Bromell himself committed the murders, as well as the murders of two innocent women three decades ago," Lena stopped to allow the shock to hit her audience. Leonard shook his head.

"Bromell murdered his own *brother*? For the throne? But why the other murders?" He asked.

"For the very same reason; you see, Adalonia has recently welcomed Carr, one of the twin sons of the woman named Ralla, one of Bromell's victims. Ralla was wife to Cassen; Cassen was the...secret son of a stable boy named Cale and the queen...Camden," Lena paused again. This time the room was filled with energy. Everyone was hanging on her every word, engaged in a history they had never known they were a part of and desperate to hear.

"*Camden had an heir*?" Felonin gasped. Nona interrupted subtly.

"This is yet to be proven, but we have good reason to believe it is a valid claim," She nodded to Lena who went on.

"Ralla's sister Renna is the mother of Elei. She was a prostitute who became pregnant, and we *suspect* she was murdered for being witness to Ralla's death and privy to the knowledge of Camden's furtive lineage. Ulei managed to save Elei but sent him to his cousin Colius. Cassen was able to separate and hide the twins so they would never be found. Triden's own wife, Sarana and Granlund's wife Kiera took them in and raised them as household staff, but Carr was well aware of his heritage and the danger involved if he was to speak of it, and therefore did not, until now." Lena took a moment to allow for questions. Lunette spoke up.

"This *Carr*, is the rightful heir to Rogadon? What of your son's marriage to Rogala?" Lunette brought up a point Lena hoped to avoid, but now realized it was eminent.

"Rogala is in hiding, she was the product an affair between a common servant and King Granlund, who noble as he was, was not blood royalty but in fact had inherited Rogadon through Camden's bequeathing her kingdom to Kiera. Rogala's lineage was not that of Rogadon royalty therefore....when we learned the woman sent to us was in fact an imposter, it made no significant difference. The wedding was called off,"

"The wedding is off? How do we intend to unite our valley once again with Rogadon? Will this Carr marry in? The only one here with daughters is King Leonard and Queen Camela but the girls are only children! You speak of a man nearly forty years old!" Lunette stated, causing a new round of murmurs and confusion.

"That solution has presented itself," Lena started, waiting for everyone's attention.

"Carr's twin brother had children, five daughters in fact," She was interrupted by an outraged Leonard.

"You will marry a man to his niece? These are desperate times sister, but not that desperate!" He exclaimed. Lena held up her hands.

"I am suggesting no such thing! Prince Jiden intends to return home to re-instate his marriage plans to the young girl who came to us last summer," she announced. Camela was trying to catch up.

"The *imposter*?"

"Aye, the imposter...Callana..." Lena tried.

"You would *allow* this? She infiltrated as a false princess of Rogadon and you reward her with your *son*?" Rasden was snarling now and Lena held her hands up again to gain the attention of the room.

"Callana came to us as a *false* princess to Rogadon but is in fact a *true* princess of Rogadon!" Lena proclaimed, this time Felonin interrupted.

"You talk in riddles! Out with it!" He growled, inspiring a few ayes of agreement. Lena nodded.

"I tell you she is the daughter of Cai, Carr's twin brother, son of Cassen, son of Cale and Camden. Callana is a blood heir of Camden herself!" Lena looked around the room to make sure all heard her loud and clear. This would solve the problem of uniting Rogadon so now she had to move on to the business of saving Esildad.

"We have saved Rogadon and have plans to bring it back into the valley for good, so I ask you, now that you see Rogadon and Esildad's family lines are quite one in the same, do we stand by and let Esildad fall? Our *ally*? Our *family*?" She pleaded with the room now and each member seemed to fall silent in thought. Lunette was first to stand.

"Tasladad will fight for Esildad," she proclaimed.

"As will Maulen," Leonard stood as well.

"The council agrees...we save Esildad," Nona stood to speak.

"For Esildad," Felonin finally answered. Lena exhaled a breath she felt she had held for days. With the support of the valley, she could save Esildad and her son.

....

"If we ride south, between the east face of Mount Roan and the shoreline, we can turn in and follow the crystal river into Esildad..." Renk used a stick to draw a basic map in the sand. Christopher, Dakin and Braden all watched intently; a building excitement was infecting their small band. Renk was much older than all three, his age bringing to mind the experience of war; cold fear, heated rage, and the shallow victory killing brought, usually swallowed by intense guilt. His conscience told him it was not something to put these boys through, but his wisdom reminded him it was only a matter of time for all of them. In the world of men, war was the only negotiating tactic understood by all. Land was bought by battle; boundaries were pushed in the name of greed. Kings marched honorable men into war under the colors of their kingdom, to inspire them to fight for their home or die trying. But did they not *all believe* they were *right?* Renk did not *know* if he was always right, but he *believed* he was. God help us, he silently prayed; make us right.

The four set out with dusk, keeping their farewells short. Lost in their own thoughts, they rode south; the shimmering ocean their gleaming beacon to follow.

....

Traveling under the cover of night, though necessary, was proving to be more agonizing than Callana could have possibly imagined; eager to get to Jiden, but having no visible land marks or recognizable scenery to gauge your speed or location made their pace maddeningly slow. The archers were on foot, so Callana had taken a position in lead, holding George to a long striding walk, while Carr had fallen to the rear to keep everyone together. The entire night of marching would pass before the pink of dawn illuminated the road enough for Callana to see the crossroads sign of her once beloved home. She held her hand up to silently halt the exhausted troops. She dismounted slowly, leading the way east through the forest to the closest curve of the dwindling Shadow's river.

"Make camp. Get fresh water, we eat rations today, no fires," Callana commanded.

"Aye," a very tired Sir Ron, first rank squadron leader answered and turned to commence setting camp. Callana took a deep breath before slowly turning south. She was desperate to see, to verify with her own eyes that Windt was really *gone*; though the smell of burnt wood, and ash, wet with spring morning dew was infiltrating her senses and destroying the last of her clinging hope. Her stomach twisted and clenched with tortuous anxiety. Her leather shoes crunched over pine needles, the sound echoing through her ears as her mind forced out all thought. The forest edge was near; soon, memory told her, the land would slope slightly down, flattening near her village before rising upwards again to climb slightly towards Haven, nearly half days ride from here. Dawn's bright glare had turned from soft pink to a luminous yellow now; its warmth creating tiny mists, steaming off each new green leaf near the top of the canopy. Long shadows from ancient trees stretched west as Callana stepped through the last of the pine perimeter and into full view of the crossroad valley bellow, where her hope could hold no longer.

....

"We must make camp here, where we are still out of sight, and God willing out of reach of Ulei's patrols," Renk dismounted a very frothy bay and led him towards the tantalizing river they had followed for the last several hours. His three companions did the same, all groaning with the effort of standing again after an entire night of riding hard. Each unsaddled their mounts and prepared a make shift camp in the deep crevice of a large pile of enormous boulders. They would have full cover from the castle here and at the same time complete view of its impressive eastern towers and gate.

"Sir Renk?" Christopher stiffly walked over to his shorter, heftier leader; his knee joints painfully popping with protest. Renk smiled and shook his head.

"*Renk*, Christopher," he corrected. Christopher grinned down at his boots before speaking again.

"Renk, what do we do now?"

"There is not much we can do in the broad light of day, young friend. The tower guard will see us coming long away. We will sleep until nightfall," Renk talked as he led all four watered horses to the grove of trees and bush that had grown up in the river's year round run off. Braden and Dakin joined their long-limbed friend in gaping at their designated leader. Renk finished lashing the still bridled horses to a broken branch than turned towards his crew. He furrowed his brows and shrugged wide shoulders.

"What is it?" He glanced towards the oblivious castle and then back to the bewildered faces before him.

"Well...it is only that....we still do not have a plan to get in..."Braden began.

"And once we get in how do we defeat an army?" Christopher worried. Dakin piped up suddenly, anxious to be heard.

"And I am starving!" he scowled. Renk laughed out loud, almost cackling at the boyish rudeness of the young mail carrier.

"Men, we may *eat*! Then we sleep, wake up and by then I will have a plan. Agreed?" Renk gestured towards the trio; each looking to the other and back again.

"Aye," Christopher spoke for all as the other two nodded. Dakin dashed to his saddle bags for dark breads, cheeses and dried pork and handed out equal portions. An hour later, with full bellies and scrambling thoughts, the four stretched out in the now bright sun of mid morning to finally fall into an aching and dreamless sleep.

....

"Morning is coming my lord, we must find cover," Galland warned. Elei, Nicholas and Jiden nodded compliantly before the young king called for a halt. The flat land village of Haven was within view of the castle Esildad, and less than an hour's ride. If they could hide out for the day, then sneaking in at night would be a simple matter of surprise. Their plot was easy enough; they would take the small barge up the river towards the castle, leaving the horses behind, than climb up the bank and approach from the rear of the city. Once Elei had killed his father, Dellandore would have to fall back. Sir David and Senren set off on weary horses to scout the village of Haven for a willing patron who would house the party. Senren suddenly turned his mount and rushed back towards the men.

"Wait, how many is we asking to hide? Hold still.One...two..." Senren began counting.

"Six," Erik raised his hand. Senren turned red.

"Fourteen," Franklin helped, causing Senren to growl under his breath.

"Eleven," Gracien answered solemnly. Senren finally burst.

"Shut it! I can count if you prigs were quiet! One. Two..." he tried again. Gracien shrugged.

"I was being serious Senren," he offered but the agitated red head stomped a short leg.

"Ahhh! One...two..." this time each raised their hand as Senren pointed at them; Galland, Laden, David, Franklin, Gracien, Nicholas, Jiden,

Lashend, Erik, and finally Elei; who reluctantly raised his hand for this absurd roll call.

"Ha! Ten! See who don't know how to count!" Senren grinned, crossing his arms smugly as he glared at his fellow royal guardsman. Gracien rubbed his forehead and sighed.

"You have to count yourself, for pity's sake," he stated. Senren froze, glancing sideways at his prince who apathetically nodded a confirmation. Elei shook his head.

"Oh...yes... I would have...ready David?" the stout guard quickly yanked his sleeping horse around and rode off for the nearest home. David shrugged again and turned to follow. Elei smirked sideways at Jiden who covered quickly.

"He is a brilliant knight...very brave..." he tried but Elei only laughed.

"Aye, who needs to count when you can kill, ey?" he snorted. Soon David was waving them in from the front door of a weathered cottage. A frail woman was standing in the center of the room with head bowed, as the entire rescue party entered her modest home.

"Your king appreciates this greatly, good woman, you will be rewarded," Elei bowed as he spoke. The woman raised her head to look upon the young man and started to shake. Elei came to her but she fell to the floor and started to cry.

"Please forgive me my lord!" Three guards emerged from the only bedroom, escorting two children at knife point. The children ran to their rocking mother and she held them as the three openly sobbed. Elei recognized the trap too late as he watched out of dirty windows, Dellandore soldiers spilling out of the surrounding cottages, creating a wall of purple capes that blocked out the bright mid morning sun. Jiden swallowed hard as he flashed a knowing look at his captain of the guard.

"We have been waiting for you, *Elei,*" One of the three guards inside the cottage snarled his greeting. Galland stepped between the three men and his young royals.

"That is *King* Elei to you, *scrap*!" He boomed. The three moved in unison, swords unsheathed as they charged towards the big man. Jiden's royal guard surrounded Nicholas, Elei and himself in an impenetrable blockade of protection; the clinging of swords ringing out as the small woman and her children ran for the feeble safety of the bedroom. The cottage doors burst open as the windows were smashed in, shards spitting in on the cornered unit. Dellandore forces filled the room, crowding in on the circle of fighting men, pushing them out side.

"Enough!" A familiar voice boomed. Elei turned, unwilling to face his father as Jiden seethed with his hatred for the maliciously grinning king. Ulei winked at the young prince before his eyes locked on his son's.

"So predictable," Ulei sighed. Elei grimaced.

"Forgive me, I am not as versed at sabotage as you," Elei sniped. Ulei nodded towards the guard at Elei's side who immediately thumped the young man square in the ribs with the hard wooden handle of his sword. The sound of cracking bone was audible as Elei sucked in his breath and fell to his knees clasping his side. Jiden reached for his friend but was stopped by a soldier's blade to his throat. Galland tried to get to his prince but Ulei called him off.

"Move and he dies!" The wicked king ordered. Galland froze reluctantly, a fear swallowing his heart. Ulei waved his hand and his guards prodded the small band into movement. Elei was sweating with his intense pain as he ambled slowly towards his home and soon to be prison. Jiden propped his shoulder under his friend's arm.

Jiden was panicked; searching his mind desperately for an escape when he noticed Ulei, staring down at him. The older man seemed to be contemplating as well, before he suddenly started to brighten; a terrible smile spreading across his face, bearing his teeth. Jiden knew in that moment that he would be tortured, perhaps to a slow, painful death, and he was filled with a fear so intense he forgot to breath; gasping slightly as his body reminded him. Jiden could see Galland ahead of him, head hung down in shame, and it pained him; for in all his selfish worries, Jiden knew Galland worried for he and Nicholas far more than himself. So this is how I discover I am a *coward*? Jiden thought. Well, I may have been but no more, he silently pledged. I will die, but I will *not* die in fear!

"Miala!" The exhausted maiden nearly fell off the back of her escort's horse. She ran to Hellena and Nia and allowed herself to collapse in their embrace. They rushed her to the fire pit where Cella was stirring breakfast. She quickly began serving the two knights and her friend. Miala chugged a full water bladder before attempting to explain. Intently listening, Hellena, Nia, Crystalline, Cylan, Rogala, Cella and Caran kneeled down beside the small brunette.

"They will be in Haven today, where they plan to hide out until nightfall," she finished. Hellena was confused.

"Why did they not bring the entire army? They cannot hope to overcome Ulei's men alone?" she chided.

"They hope to surprise Ulei, and Elei is sure if he can defeat his father, the troops will have no choice but to retreat," Miala explained.

"If Elei kills his father, than he will take the throne of Dellandore by default, right?" Nia deduced, having spent most of her young life in and around castle goings-on. Miala nodded.

"That's what Elei says," she gasped between delicious bites.

"Cella, you are amazing!" she nearly cheered. The accompanying knights nodded, very grateful for such delectable nourishment.

"Oh, thank you, but what of the army? Will they come eventually?" Cella prodded.

"Aye, but all decisions are decided by council," a dark knight next to Miala spoke up.

"Even if your *prince* is in danger?" Hellena grimaced. He nodded.

"Aye, my lady," he answered before shoving a heaping spoonful in his mouth than looking piteously at Cella for more.

"Of course," she stood, quickly taking his bowl, filling it then rushing back to sit and listen.

"This is Sir Vern and Sir Joel," Miala introduced the two. The dark knight and the largest, Sir Joel, stood and bowed, slapping his comrade on the back of the head for not doing the same. Sir Vern leapt to his feet and bowed before turning to Cella.

"My lady, may I?" he looked expectantly at the empty bowl in his hands.

"Of course," Cella stood to rush and fill it; smiling politely. Hellena turned her attention to Sir Joel.

"Good knight, what do you know of Callana's whereabouts?" she pried. Miala tipped her empty bowl towards Cella.

"Of course," she said; Cella rose to fill it and bring it back before sitting at Sir Joel's feet and leaning in for an answer. Miala shot a confused look at the uncharacteristically accommodating Cella then Hellena.

"I told her to try to be *nice*," Hellena shrugged.

"Oh," Miala nodded before turning to Sir Joel.

"My lady, I know Callana is safe in Adalonia, or was last I saw her, not two weeks ago," Sir Joel assured. Hellena sighed.

"Well that is good news! I was afraid she had found a way to tag along to war!" Hellena laughed. Nia smiled at her friend.

"Our girls are all safe," her smile faded and a sad look filled her eyes.

"Now we only have to worry for our boys, ey friend?" she bowed her head to look into the blue eyes of her grandson. Hellena tickled the baby's feet and he kicked in response.

"Renk is strong," she promised. Nia nodded vigorously, turning to look over her shoulder at her daughter who had returned to the beach; staring down the shoreline after her husband, long gone.

"Dakin, Christopher and Braden, they are good men, and with Renk as their captain, they will be fine," Hellena forced a smile as she met the eyes of three terrified young wives to be; even if one was still in denial.

"One thing is for sure," Miala chirped happily.

"What is that my dear?" Hellena smiled.

"Your daughters are blood heirs to the throne of Rogadon..." she sang, grinning from ear to ear.

"And I have seen the painting that *proves* it!"

....

"Uncle, you should be resting," Callana urged the big man. Carr grinned down at her.

"As should you, my little niece," he laughed. They had both taken positions near the road to watch for any movement towards Esildad at all, but had seen nothing. Carr turned around to look out over two hundred sleeping archers, undoubtedly still throbbing from their march. They had witnessed two guard patrols of Dellandore soldiers, both of which had come fairly close, nearly fifty yards, but were not able to spot their camp for its elevated location.

"What are we fighting for? I mean, what do you remember of Rogadon as a child? Was it always so...*stricken*?" Callana tried to force strategy or lack of out of her tired mind, hoping ignoring their predicament would bring a fresh solution. She waved the watchman from his position, seeing as how she had no intentions of sleeping for a while

"I remember working in the forest with the other boys from the city. We left out early, eager to take advantage of the full day's sun. We fell every other tree in sections; the biggest trees only. We made our wages per tree, but Bromell never paid much. I worked the entire day just to keep from starving. My uncle forced me to work, though I had been raised in the castle with

Kiera. Once she died, I was thrown out to fend for myself. I was lucky though, had only me to worry for; other children my age were trying to feed ailing families or widows of war. If you had a healthy father who made his own living, you would not waste your time on such spoils as chopping trees," as Carr spoke, Callana sank into his memories, closing her eyes to see what he had seen, and feel as he had felt. Carr was lost in remembering, speaking out loud his reminiscences as they played out in his mind.

"My friends, Landon and Donald, and me, would work in the same section every day. We used to get so excited when the first big tree would fall and the sun would pour in through the new opening. The Shadow's forest is so dark, so cold, and wet all year round...but for the first few weeks after we fell our sections, the forest was brilliant! Flowers popped up through rotted leaves; great blossoms of blues, purples, and reds, and yellow. It was as if the whole forest were celebrating as much as we for the sun's glorious light!" Carr laughed at this, the happy faces of his friends coming to the forefront of his mind. Callana looked at him then, a sadness weighing down her heart.

"I am sorry you had no family," she reached for his hand and he kissed hers.

"But I did," he grinned. Callana looked puzzled.

"My friends were like brothers and their families took me in...I was never alone or forgotten...I was lucky, I told you, but not as lucky as my brother I am guessing!" He winked at her. Callana smiled faintly. Carr winced.

"I do not mean to make you sad," he apologized. Callana shook her head.

"Thinking of him does not make me sad, only regretful," she admitted. Carr was puzzled now.

"Why would you regret?" he asked. Callana sighed, a tear rolling down her cheek as she spoke.

"I regret not telling him how much he was to me, because I did not know he was everything until he was gone...I know that sounds absurd."

"Not at all, love. I feel the same way about Granlund and Kiera," Carr put his arm around Callana's shoulders and squeezed her.

"Want to remember him for me?" He asked. She laughed, putting her head against his chest as she closed her eyes.

"My father was so much bigger than his personality...do you understand what I mean? He was quiet, kind, and gentle...but he was also brave and honorable and he loved us with all of his giant heart. My mother says that when I was very small, I would pace when my father left to work. I would pace in front of the window, for hours, and she would have to make me stop for fear I would worry a hole in my stomach! And when he would return, I would push my way to be first person kissed!" she laughed out loud and Carr chuckled.

"I spent every moment I could with him when he was home. So much so that my mother decided I was the son he never had and gave up training me in household duties. My father taught me all about horses and tack and he let me learn to ride on his war horse, George," Callana pointed at the sleeping purple gelding as she spoke.

"My father rode George into battle one morning; a land dispute between Haven and Dellandore. A few days after, George came back...alone," Callana started to cry as she filled with the sorrow of that day. Carr hugged her as she wept until she had worn herself down and fallen asleep. He held her there against a sticky pine for a while, keeping watch. When Callana woke, he was sleeping soundly, slumped against the tree. She covered him with her Adalonia cape and woke a knight for watch. She came to Carr's side, kissing his cheek.

"I lost my father...I will not lose you too," she whispered. She left him there with her sleeping horse's reins tied to his tree.

....

"Sir, sir, the Dellandore guard is approaching!" the guard shook Carr awake, his voice was little more than a harsh whisper.

"How many?" Carr leapt to his feet, sword drawn. The guard pointed towards the tree line.

"Only six," he counted. Carr nodded.

"We need not give away all; follow my lead," Carr instructed. From a crouched position, Carr slowly pulled out his bow and plucked one arrow from his quiver. The knight did the same. Carr leaned towards his fellow archer.

"I will hit the captain, there in front; that will stop them coming closer. You cover me but do not follow," before receiving confirmation from the young knight, Carr fired, the striking force of the arrow thwacking solidly into the man's neck and thrusting him off his horse. The confused patrol spun their horses in circles, unable to get a visual of their attacker. Carr moved out of the tree line, unnoticed in the commotion. With arrow at the ready he sidled closer until one bewildered knight finally spotted Carr's red cape.

"You there! Halt! Halt or we fire!" even as he spoke it his knights were still struggling to pull out their bows. Carr grinned.

"Fire and you all die...you are covered by my men." He gestured towards the tree line. The Dellandore knight held up his hand, and his fellow knights dropped their bows.

"You kill us, old man, and prince Jiden dies!" the purple knight proclaimed. Carr flinched slightly.

"How is that?" The big man still held his bow ready. The mounted man laughed and pointed towards Esildad.

"Go and see for yourself!" The man barked. Carr turned his gaze briefly towards the castle but could only just see the court gates were open.

"What am I to see from here, dolt?" Carr criticized, coming nearer to the smaller man and aiming his arrow at the now frowning face.

"Prince Jiden of Adalonia, your new stand in ruler, has been captured, just this morning," the man gloated slightly as if single handedly responsible. "King Ulei kills the prince at first sign of an army, and a missing guard patrol will be considered a good sign indeed," the knight openly smiled now, knowing full well Rogadon was under Adalonia's control as of recent, and wanted it that way. Carr kept his arrow on the knight.

"You may live but do not expect me to stand here and be killed! You may go, arrogant prig," Carr gestured towards the castle.

"*You* may live, but take that message to your new friends in Adalonia," the guard sneered then all but fled back to more than likely gather reinforcements and return. Carr had to move the men and he had to do it now. He waited until the patrol was no more than a purple line on the far horizon before dashing back to camp. He was busy rousing the men when it occurred to him Callana was no where to be seen. He rushed back to where he had fallen asleep beside her to see her prancing horse tied to a tree. He untied him furiously; now aware she had left without him in an effort to save his life. He handed the reins to the nearest archer.

"Here! Ride him to Adalonia, warn the king that any army to come to Esildad's aid sentences the prince to death!" Carr commanded. The young man nodded and hurriedly mounted and fled down the main road.

"If anything happens to her I'll *kill* her," He growled as he moved two hundred men across the main road and up the treacherous back of Mount Lisia where no patrol would find them. Whatever he did now, Ulei could not even suspect, or Carr would render Adalonia without an heir.

....

"Captain, we have something for the king!" A knight called out, waking Jiden into painful consciousness. From his terrible perch in the middle of the courtyard, he could see and hear all that conspired around him. His hands and feet had been tied behind him around a large stake on a square wooden stand. His eyes were swollen nearly shut , he was sure his feet and hand bones were broken and his entire core was riddled with swollen lacerations and black bruises from the severe beating Ulei's royal guard had enjoyed at his expense upon arrival. These were not the worst things being done to him; the worst was watching these things happening to Nicholas and Elei on either side of him. Or maybe the worst was having to know that at any given moment, Ulei was going to light the pile of wood under Elei and set it on fire, slowly burning him to death. Or maybe the worst was that the cellar prison had one small barred hole that looked out at the courtyard where Galland

and his guard could see all that was happening, and do nothing to stop it. For Jiden, it was hard to decide which was more excruciating.

Jiden watched Ulei approach the patrol as the captain climbed down to heave a green bundle off his horse's back. The form thumped hard to the stone court yard floor; evoking an eruption of laughter from his fellow patrol. Jiden squinted, desperate to focus on the small shape. Ulei glared at the group of men until the captain yanked lose one end of green fabric and pulled, releasing their spoils. Jiden could just make out green clad legs, and a mass of long, red hair and his blood turned cold.

"Callana!!!!" He screamed. His voice harsh strained as his knees gave in his despair. His mind roared with anguish! His true love was *dead*! It had happened; all he thought he could prevent was coming to pass. His Callana lay dead!

"Jiden..." the tortured voice of his cousin snapped his attention back from the brink of insanity

"She lives cousin...she lives," Nicholas croaked. Jiden watched as she slowly rocked back and forth and his heart lifted. As she was tugged to her feet Jiden saw her bloodied side and he pulled against his restraints. Callana saw him then; his face swollen, almost beyond recognition. She stumbled towards him, her pain twisting her face as she fell at the bottom of his pyre. She clasped her hands to her mouth and screamed.

"*Jiden*! What has he done to you?" She cried as Ulei watched on, reveling in the lover's painful reunion. Callana forced herself to look at Nicholas, and screamed again.

"Nicholas! Oh God! Oh God!" she shrieked as Ulei strolled over to grab her pale arm; flailing her around to face Elei, who looked down on her, his pain so evident in his eyes Callana could not bear it.

"Meet my son, Elei....Elei this is Callana; the undoing of Prince Jiden," he laughed aloud, inciting a round of snickering from his surrounding guards. Elei looked away, unable to watch this young girl weep at his horrific state. Callana's head started to spin as the blood drained from her face. The last thing she felt was the cold, hard stone as her knees buckled. As Jiden watched in horror, two guards drug her limp body into the castle and a fate unknown and he knew in that moment *that* was the worst thing.

....

"What are you saying?" James began, his question finished quickly by his brother.

"The prince is hostage?" Jeremiah halted the two thousand men he had just assembled for battle against Ulei.

"Aye, sir. If Ulei sees or suspects any army he will kill him, and he holds Prince Nicholas and King Elei as well." Sir Peter reported.

"This information was given to Carr?" Jeremiah prodded.

"I heard it as well, and he sent me to spread the word but he keeps the other archers on Mount Lisia in waiting." Peter explained.

"He hopes for an opportunity," James thought out loud.

"We will move the troops back to Rogadon and send Sir Ellis to warn King Odin," Jeremiah concluded as the twins set about turning their forces back for base camp at Rogadon, both admittedly disappointed they could do nothing for their prince. Sir Ellis was sent off immediately. Everyone was so ready to do something and unable to do anything. Worry and angst began to spread throughout the army and no one wished to be in Sir Ellis's boots that night.

....

"The moon is bright tonight, we will be spotted if we are not careful," Renk warned. Three heads bobbed acknowledgement as the small band set out. None knew of Jiden's predicament or of Nicholas's or Elei's for that matter. They only knew Ulei was squatting inside a castle he did not belong in and that was enough. Renk had come up with a good plan and each knew their part. Christopher was nervous but could not fight the excitement building to emerge a great hero, returning home to sweep his Crystalline off her feet as an honorable man of war. Dakin was hyper with the rush of masculinity this mission brought out in him. He felt alive! Incredibly virile and more than anything he felt like he deserved the life he had always wanted but never thought would come; a beautiful wife, many children, and a knight's title; all of which would surely come if he was successful tonight. Renk was calm and collected, only fearing any harm coming to his new found comrades at arms. Braden was afraid of everything going wrong, or even worse, everything going right; for then he would have to man up and go back to Sea Fair a champion, and finally demand Cella marry him. He shivered at the thought. The castle Esildad glowed in the moon's eerie blue light as the four moved towards it. They followed the river and crossed at the rear of the castle to avoid gate guards. Renk had been right to surmise the guard would be absent from the rear wall gangway due to it being the tallest, and therefore the most unlikely to be scaled. Until tonight, that is.

Each man pulled out two broken arrows, just enough wooden stick to get a hand on, and with quivers slung across their back, they began climbing; plunging their tips into the mortar between the stones in the outer wall and slowly moving up. The noise was inaudible over the roar of the river behind them as Renk also predicted and though it was physically demanding; hours later would find them at the top.

....

Lena sat rigid, staring into the fire of her entrance hall. She had been sitting there for hours, since she had received Sir Ellis and his terrible news. Her kingdom was safe, her army was secure, and her husband on his mountain, her sister and brother in their kingdoms were oblivious but out of harm's way; and yet her world was ending all around her, while she could do nothing to stop it. Anything she attempted could bring death to her only child, even if Ulei *suspected* an attack, isn't that what Sir Ellis had said? Her chest was seized; constricted, even strangling her as she sat there frozen in terror. This was her worst nightmares come true and she could confide in no one. The council would demand a response she did not have and her family would demand action. Tears would not even fall to alleviate her gripping anguish. Dread had taken her over, heart and soul, leaving little room for hope. She could do nothing, nothing but stare at a fire and pray.

"Please God, hear my prayer, please spare my son, he is a good boy, please God hear my prayer, please do not take my only son, he is a good boy, please God..."

....

"My dear? Are you able to sit?" a delicate, singly voice woke Callana from a dark, dreary place her subconscious mind had taken her. She could feel the burning wound in her side now more than before and she scowled with the effort of trying to sit. A small, aged woman with a kindly face was standing beside her, holding her arm with warm, pudgy fingers. Callana felt lost, dreamy, almost as if she may have slipped away altogether and was now in a new, pain ridden half world. The events of the day sloshed around in her mind; mixing around and swirling together until finally settling into their appropriate order. Sneaking away from her uncle, foolishly thinking alone she could go undetected, only to be hunted down by the evening patrol. Seeing Jiden there, bleeding, swollen, bound like a criminal to a spike riddled pole for all to see! That image haunted her, and she ached to save him, to save them all. Lost in thought, she had almost forgotten she was still in a mess of her own. She turned her head slowly, the action rousing her queasiness. Callana stared at the little woman, unable to speak, but desperate to ask so many questions. Finally, under the soft woman's persuasive glare, Callana cleared her throat.

"Where am I?" she asked. The graying woman smiled sympathetically at the pale, terrified young face before her.

"This is my room, inside the castle Esildad love," she answered. Callana frowned.

"I am Kila," she continued. Callana shook her head, the motion making her dizzy.

"I am a *friend*, love. Loyal to Elei, as you are to Jiden," she smiled and rolled light brown eyes.

"Well, maybe not *quite* as you are to Jiden...but I would be if he'd have me!" she laughed out loud; the sound light and melodic. Callana blushed heavily.

"Of course," she smiled softly before craning her neck to take in the tiny room.

"Oh, speak freely my dear, Ulei has no intentions of coming in here," Kila huffed before pointing towards the window facing the courtyard. Callana turned, horrified to see Jiden, Nicholas and Elei still bound to poles, under constant vigil, now by yellow lantern light. Callana could see the temporary tent under heavy guard in the court yard.

"He will not chance their escape...not this close to his victory," Kila nearly hissed as she spoke of Ulei. Callana was confused.

"*Victory*? He has already taken the city, what is left?"

"He...he means....he means to...*kill* Elei, *my* Elei, at dawn..." as Kila spoke, tears sprang into her weary eyes and her body shook with restricted sobs. Callana gasped.

"Adalonia will not stand by and allow him to..." Callana began, but Kila placed a hand over her mouth.

"Adalonia must not come, or all three will burn!" Kila pulled her hand away and turned to her boiling cauldron to attend to Callana's poultice.

"How is this happening Kila?" Callana trembled against the cold of the evening and the painful realization of what was coming.

"Adalonia has been warned; if they so much as approach, Jiden and Nicholas will die. Ulei knows he would soon after be captured but Odin's love for his family out weighs his pity for Elei." Kila ran her plump fingers through long, silver hair; quickly de-tangling it and braiding it to one side to keep it out of her way. Callana could not keep her eyes off Jiden's motionless silhouette out side the tiny square window. How did it come to this? Callana took a ragged breath, slightly whimpering with the terrible flaring in her lower ribs.

"You were born in Adalonia love?" Kila asked as she carefully helped Callana lay down again. She gently turned Callana onto her left side and lifted her tunic so she could have unobstructed access to her right side; the gash was deep, and had purpled around the slit. Her muscle was cut, but only shallowly, and she had not lost too much blood. Callana was wincing in pain, forgetting the question as Kila placed a hot cloth directly on the split in

Callana's skin and used her hand to press down, forcing the medicine into the wound. Callana gasped for breath.

"Hmmm? Were you born in Adalonia?" Kila asked impatiently. Callana's eyes rolled around, searching for something she could not recall. Kila took her free hand and held Callana's chin.

"Look here, look at me...talk to me dear," Kila demanded. Callana sucked in her breath as the fiery pain spread through her. She shook her head vigorously.

"Nooo, nooo...Windt....I was born in Windt!" she growled through gritted teeth. Kila held her hand firm against the wound as she nodded unsympathetically while Callana writhed in agony.

"What brought you to Adalonia?" Kila's tone was so nonchalant; Callana was starting to think one of them may be crazy! How can this woman be so calm while Callana herself felt as if she was burning from the inside out!

"I was to marry Jiden!" she snarled her response but it did not phase Kila a bit. She kept right on with her interrogation.

"Really? A girl from Windt to marry a prince? How..."

"Owwweeee!" Callana screeched. Kila raised her eyebrows than continued.

"How did you arrange such a thing?" Callana cried now, tears streaming down her dirty face as she allowed her body to unclench; her spine sinking into the table and her shoulder blades falling back. She took in and blew out a deep breath.

"I met the princess Rogala in the forest and I took her place," Callana breathed in and out again, in and out in and out. Her side started to cool, and her pain started to ease.

"Yarrow, fenugreek, lemon balm and garlic?" Callana asked. Kila smiled brightly.

"Very good love, except I prefer Valerian to yarrow for pain," Kila winked.

"You must have spent some time with Lustene," Kila turned to wash the poultice cloth out and prepare another. Callana tilted her head.

"You know of Lustene?" she asked. Kila shrugged her shoulders and turned around to apply the new poultice. This time the pain was blazing but brief.

"I...spent some time with Lustene," Kila said, trying to sound casual but Callana noted a sparkle in the older woman's beautiful eyes as she seemed to stumble upon an old memory.

"He taught you medicine?" Callana pried. Kila blushed as she held her hand on Callana's side.

"Well, he taught me *something*, but it wasn't medicine," she grinned devilishly. Callana's cheeks turned pink.

"I see..." she said.

"That was a long time ago; I was...built different then!" Kila smoothed a hand over her ample hips as she spoke and Callana shook her head.

"You are a beautiful woman Kila," she argued. Kila shrugged. Callana's smile faded.

"What can be done? There must be something," Callana had sat up again; her eyes searched the room and courtyard for something to catch her attention and give her an idea.

"Well, I have been thinking about that love, but the only way to over power an entire army is with a bigger army," Kila started.

"Aye, but we cannot chance that," Callana finished. Both sagged in disappointment as they wracked tired minds for a shred of hope for the situation. A pounding on the door startled them as Kila swirled around to answer it. It was one of Ulei's royal guard, Callana recognized him from the group standing watch over center court. He sneered at Callana and she shuddered.

"King Ulei says you will make supper...cook is sick. Move out!" The beastly man thrust his sword towards Kila but she hardly flinched.

"I will move out when I am ready. Tell your king supper will be ready in an hour," she slammed the door in his face and angrily turned to face Callana.

"The nerve of that arrogant man! I have half a mind to give him rotten meat and..." Suddenly Kila stilled.

"Callana," she started but Callana shook her head.

"Meats good, but fly mushrooms are better," she grinned wickedly. Kila clapped her hands together.

"Oh I knew I liked you! I have enough; we grind them and sprinkle them around the walls as ant poison," Kila drug a large barrel out from under her table and began piling red topped mushrooms into a mixing bowl. Callana used a wooden pressing tool to mash them into a smooth, powdery consistency. When the bowl was packed, Kila emptied the contents into a jar, adding garlic to disguise it as seasonings, than re-filled the bowl with mushrooms. In moments, the two were ready, armed with a simple plan and three large jars of pounded redemption.

....

"Cousin? Cousin?" A croaking whisper to the left of Jiden woke him from what he could only assume must have been sleep. He cocked his head slightly towards Nicholas, only to wince from the pain it caused.

"Nicholas? You live?" Jiden recoiled as the most recent stabbing spike in his thigh tore slightly, releasing a new round of searing agony and fresh, hot blood. Nicholas chortled; a low, terrible sucking sound of someone with a collapsed lung, or at least Jiden suspected as much. Nicholas froze, only slightly visible by the dim lantern lights ten yards away.

"If you can call this living," he answered. Jiden felt a dread grip his very soul. He felt the end coming for them. He was too afraid to fear anymore and too miserable to weep. Nicholas seemed to be forcing himself to find humor, even now, and Jiden was having a difficult time deciding if he admired that about him or hated it. Nicholas's cracked voice broke his train of thought.

"And Elei? Does he live?" he asked, blood trickling out of his mouth as he spoke. Jiden slowly turned his head to his right and strained to distinguish Elei's face through the crusted shell of blood soaked hair that had dried over his head. Elei tried to shrug.

"Uh," he groaned. His jaw hung slack, causing his words to slur and spit to drool from his mouth. Jiden watched Elei's head droop farther down as another flush of pain overtook his friend and sent him into merciful forgetfulness again.

"Do not worry for him too much, young prince," the thick, swaggering voice of Ulei took Jiden by surprise. He had been standing in the dark nothingness to the far side of Elei, assuredly reveling in the trio's tremendous suffering. Jiden held his tongue, not sure his body would withstand another *confrontation*. Ulei stepped closer; stopping in front of Elei to look him slowly up and down. Jiden's resolve to keep quiet snapped.

"You torture your own *son*?" he snarled through gritted teeth. Ulei shrugged nonchalantly.

"I will *kill* my own son come dawn, as I *killed* his mother and aunt before him." Ulei started to laugh with this as Jiden raged against his bindings.

"*Why?*" He seethed, desperate to break free and strangle the disgusting man at his son's bloody feet. Ulei came to stand next to Jiden, a sneer curling his lips; an eerie lantern light illuminated the gesture, while darkening his eyes, giving him a horrifying, soulless appearance.

"For the same reason I killed Bromell; for being in my way," he turned to pace, his hands behind his back and stomping his boots.

"Renna was a slave; Elei would never hold the throne if the public knew his mother was not royal. I needed him to secure Esildad for me. Her sister, however, was a different story in deed. Ralla was part of the long line of whores attempting to usurp the throne of Rogadon, all the way back to the original whore, Camden!" Ulei was growing increasingly agitated as he paced. Jiden was starting to put pieces together in his exhausted mind now. It was the history he had been hoping to discover himself to exalt Callana, only now it seemed it would doom them all.

"Cassen was the result of an affair between the precious Della Verde Valley's only original queen and her stable boy! For God's sake, *a stable boy!* She hid him away, or so she thought, but some of us knew! She wore black as in mourning for her dead king all the while having her little affair! She was a *whore!* Cale raised him as a peasant but my father knew, everyone knew, and he told me they were dirty blood and he was right! I was born of royal blood! My father, my mother, their fathers and mothers, they were all of *pure royal* blood and this *dirty* queen and her *dirty* stable boy make this *dirty* child and he grew up to make *dirty* children with a *dirty* slave! They defiled their valley! When I found Renna and Ralla to be sisters, I told my father and he and I rid Rogadon and Dellandore of the foul blooded frauds! Kiera hid Cassen's child in Rogadon, Bromell told me! Getting rid of her was easy enough but I never found the boy. But when he surfaces, I will get rid of him as well. Then Rogadon and Esildad will be pure kingdoms, as pure as mine!"

"You are mad Ulei!" Jiden growled. Ulei laughed out loud; a cackling laugh that betrayed his frayed nerves.

"Spoken by the *prince* engaged to a *prostitute*! Ha! You will do the same as your predecessors if I do not put an end to it!" Ulei was openly smiling now with a secret Jiden feared he already knew.

"You can kill me, but she is an innocent girl..." Jiden began but Ulei jumped back to face him.

"Innocent? Innocent? She was a prostitute by *birth*!"

"She was never a prostitute! You are wrong, she left home before," Jiden tried.

"Before running into that false princess Rogala and rushing in to marry herself into royalty!" Ulei glared, Jiden shook his head.

"No! She never wanted royalty, only to spare Rogadon's fall," Jiden was desperate now.

"Fall? Rogadon has been garbage since it was stained by Camden," Ulei waved Jiden off.

"Ulei! I beg you, do not kill her, *please*, I will do anything!" Ulei glared at the broken man before him and shook his head in disgust.

"For a *girl*?" He nearly spit the word out. Jiden nodded.

"For *this* girl, anything," he pleaded. Ulei sighed.

"I suggest a deal then, prince. I release you and your cousin at dawn, and keep Callana here, alive, as collateral that Adalonia will stay any future attempts to regain Rogadon or Esildad," he held his hands out at his sides. Jiden sank slowly.

"What of Elei?" Jiden begged. Ulei only smirked.

"Not part of the bargain," he grinned.

"She will be safe?" Jiden conceded. Ulei nodded.

"Of, course. She will be...kept close," Ulei grinned with this, flicking his eyebrows in a vulgar display. Jiden closed his eyes and felt his stomach swirl. He was condemning her to a life with this terrible man just to give her life at all. Ulei relished the chance to add a little more anguish to the arrangement.

"Besides, the second time is always better than the first," he casually looked away, goading Jiden to bite. Jiden flared with nauseous anger as Ulei shrugged.

"Forgive me prince, I assumed you two had *consummated* your engagement in my very own city; or was *I* her *first*?" Ulei stared at Jiden, waiting for understanding to hit.

"You were...*with* Callana?" Jiden numbed as he asked the question out loud and nearly buckled at the sinister look on Ulei's face.

"*Me... Bromell...*"

"You lie!" Jiden barked but Ulei nearly danced with joy.

"Rejoice young prince! She will be in *good* hands, as you wanted!" With that, the king turned merrily back towards his tent to leave the pitiful prince with the terrible image trapped in his mind.

....

"What is it?" A giant of a man peeled his lips back in disgust at the sloppy contents in the large cauldrons before him. Kila rolled her eyes.

"Food! You want some or not?" She raised an eyebrow and glared at the filthy knight before he finally nodded.

"Aye," He growled. Kila gladly heaped a steaming ladle full into his wooden bowl. The big man leaned down to bring his face closer to Kila's; his rancid breath blowing directly into her nostrils.

"Hold your tongue *woman*, or you will be serving my men in more ways than one," he snickered as he turned around to stride away. Kila grinned and batted her eyes.

"Just let me know if would like seconds, love!" she called. Callana giggled at the innocent look she flashed the grumbling guard. Bowl after bowl, cauldron after cauldron emptied until an entire army had been fed. Purple capes filed in the large dinning hall and back out again with greedy hands full of a concoction like they had never known. Within hours, the first few hundred knights had already begun to show signs; slight delirium, dizziness while standing, and extreme drowsiness. Ulei, who had yet to eat, was starting to notice.

"Drunk *idiots*!" He raged; kicking the nearest barrel of ale, its sides splitting as it fell over sending dark liquid splashing out onto the stone court. Callana could not help but grin at her new ally.

"You there, replace the tower guard so they can eat, and sober up!" Ulei pointed out a group of knights who had slumped up against the stone wall of the inner court. Perfect, thought Callana, that covers all but Ulei. She looked to the three still forms in the center court and felt herself sigh with relief.

"Soon, my love," she whispered. Kila looked over at her with a soft knowing in her eyes and nodded.

"You! Take some to the prisoners," a nearby knight pointed angrily at Callana who bowed her head and complied, easily lifting the near empty cauldron and taking it to the dungeon where she found the guards had not yet eaten. She eagerly rushed to serve them.

"Supper, good knights," She smiled brightly at the two dull looking watchmen who stopped their card game to reach for the wooden bowls. Callana bowed and turned towards the cell.

"Callana?" Galland whispered. She rushed to the door and reached through to grab the giant man and pull him to her. She hugged tightly while pressing her lips to his ear.

"Poison," was all she said. Galland looked startled, than smiled; a light twinkling in his worried eyes. Watching his three friends tortured was enough to kill him where he stood and he had done nothing but beg to take their place since his imprisonment. He turned to Erik, David, Gracien, Lashend, Laden, Franklin and Senren and made a slicing motion across his neck. They nodded an understanding. Callana sighed and handed them their bowls.

"Most kind of you, maiden," Erik bowed before turning to dump his bowl along with the others in the corner and cover it with the straw they were to urinate in. Callana bowed in response and turned to check on the progress. The outer guards were still awake, but had begun to waver and stare intently at their own hands. Callana winked back at Galland.

"I will be back in a moment to collect your dishes, good sirs," She happily swung away leaving Galland and his fellow guardsmen to play a very short waiting game.

....

Renk, Christopher, Dakin and Braden obediently allowed the new shift of night watch to take their places. With their borrowed helmets and capes, they merely nodded and walked by unnoticed and met up in the stairwell.

"We must remain undetected; there are those who may notice we are not one of them." Renk whispered as he turned to lead them out into the dimly lit courtyard and through to the dinning hall. Inside, a small, older woman with a silver braid waved them over.

"Supper knights, supper!" Kila grinned.

"Thank you, good woman," Renk bowed. Kila felt a sting of remorse for what he would go through. Though they had not intended to *kill* the army, only put it to sleep, there was always a risk of not waking when consuming the red mushroom. Kila hesitated before handing him a bowl. Renk looked confused than nervous. Had she recognized him as false? Just as she made to hand him his bowl, Callana appeared from the rear of the room where a spiral stair case led directly to the underground prison. She hurried to Kila's side, barely glancing towards the gaping group of men. She did a double take before clapping her hands over her mouth.

"Callana?" Renk came to her, lifting her up and spinning her around. She kissed his helmet.

"Renk...how did you....wait!" just as realization hit, Dakin had bent to take a bowl from the thoroughly confused Kila.

"NO!" Callana squealed before smacking the bowl out of his hands. Renk timidly placed his bowl back on the table.

"Ey, what gives? I am starving!" Dakin whined.

"You know them Callana?" Kila asked. Callana looked around the room and found a door to a chamber off the main hall.

"Come, we will talk in private," She whispered before rushing the band of rescuers into the small kitchen storage where she quickly explained their poisoned soup and the soon to be freed royal guard. With a new plan formed, Renk and his band stayed hidden in the storage room while Kila went back to her serving station. Callana had a mission of her own and merrily rushed off to serve a toxic dish to a venomous king.

....

"I feel like I may go crazy!" Cella screamed, causing Miala and Rogala to jump.

"Cella!" Hellena scolded. Cella shook her head.

"I am tired of sitting here! Can we do *nothing*?" Cella flailed her arms as she spoke, causing the nervous Sir Vern to flinch. Nia sighed and came to place her hand on Cella's shoulders.

"Love, we all want to do *something*, but what is there to do?" her voice was soothing as she attempted to calm the agitated red head, but to no avail. Cella twirled around and stormed towards town.

"Where are you going?" Crystalline called. Cella yelled over her shoulder, "Town," but never slowed down. Crystalline sighed.

"Mother, maybe we should follow? Who knows what she will do and to whom she will do it?" Crystalline warned. Hellena knew her girls well enough to see that worry was eating them alive. They felt helpless here; so far from their sister and now their men. Hellena had to admit she was feeling the strain far more than she had been willing to let on. She nodded to Crystalline and Cylan, who was holding a sleeping Granlund.

"Aye, we should go with her," Hellena conceded and they trudged up the rise towards town; following the trail her angry daughter blazed through the greening field ahead. Miala was with Rogala; standing shoulder to shoulder and staring down the weaving southern coast line.

"Ro?" Miala asked. Rogala pulled her eyes off the shimmering ocean to face her friend.

"Yes love?" she feigned a smile, but it did not reach her circled eyes. She was hardly sleeping, and when she did, she dreamed terrible dreams. Miala reached out and pulled her towards her in a strong embrace. Rogala giggled into Miala's curls.

"What was that for?" She held Miala's face with both hands and forced her to look in her eyes.

"I just, want to be *useful*, but I do not know how!" she started to tear up but Rogala shushed her.

"You have been a good friend; in times such as these, could there be anything more *useful* than that?" the pretty blonde smiled and kissed Miala's forehead. Miala finally grinned.

"Ro, do you think it would help if Callana's family could see the painting?" The young girl was beaming now. Rogala seemed to consider this, then glanced at the two royal escorts.

"Rogadon is no where near Esildad, so we could not hurt anything; I think it's a brilliant idea Mi!" she laughed out loud, clasping Miala's hand in hers as they rushed up the shore to their fire pit where Caran had reluctantly taken over stirring for the absent Cella.

"Caran, where did your mother and sisters go?" Miala asked. Caran shrugged and pointed.

"I believe preventing mayhem by following Cella on a rampage through town," She said, sarcastically rolling her eyes at her sister's behavioral problems. It was very uncharacteristic of the sweet natured Caran to be so...annoyed. Rogala stifled a giggle.

"Would you be interested in going to Rogadon to see the painting of..." Miala had not finished her sentence when Caran dropped her wooden spoon; that quickly vanished in the deep cauldron.

"Oh Miala! I would love to! May we *please, please please* go?" Caran begged. Miala turned and looked at Sir Joel who was eyeing them suspiciously now. She looked at Caran and winked.

"If you can convince Joel," she teased. Caran blushed, but ran her fingers through silky red hair, pulling it lose of the ribbon that held it back. She untied her tunic at the neck and allowed one corner to dip, exposing a shimmering pale shoulder. Joel was watching intently now, aware this was some sort of ploy, but not willing to look away. Caran brought two bowls of stew to the knights, perched on a fallen log next to the evening fire. The unsuspecting Vern eagerly reached for his bowl but Caran tipped it to spill on his leg.

"Ah!" Vern jumped as the contents bathed his thigh in steaming hot beef and gravy. Caran feigned embarrassment.

"Oh my! Oh dear...Miala? Dear would you take Sir Vern to wash up please?" Caran pouted slightly at the disgruntled knight. Vern couldn't help but gawk at Caran's exposed skin as Miala led him away from the fire and Caran was all too aware Joel was doing the same. She sank down beside him on the log and handed him his supper. Joel carefully took it, never taking his eyes off Caran's shoulder. She smiled politely.

"Sir Joel, you will have to forgive my clumsiness; I did not mean to hurt your friend," She apologized. Joel's eyes were climbing slowly up Caran's creamy white neck, and red, shining hair until they stopped on full pink lips. Caran smiled again.

"Oh...no...Do not worry, my lady, I am sure he will be good, my lady," he stuttered slightly, finally making eye contact.

"And you, sir knight? Are you...*good*?" she leaned in slightly, aware her tunic hung open just enough to be alluring.

"Aye, I am, I mean, I am not injured, my lady, so I am good, good," he stumbled through his answer. Caran decided to feel him out.

"You must have someone at home who longs to see you?" she pried, innocently batting long lashes. Joel nodded.

"No, my lady, I mean, other than my mum, but no women, I mean my mum is a woman of course," he rolled his eyes with his own fumbling effort to speak to this beautiful girl and Caran couldn't help but giggle.

"Of course," she confirmed. She placed a small hand over his long, thick forearm.

"Do not be nervous, good sir, I mean you no harm," she assured him; her touch sending little shocks into his system. Joel was experienced with women, but none as sweet as this one. She had a way of invoking his better attributes and bringing them to his surface as if he had never been anything but an innocent young man. He smiled a large, wide smile; dimpling deep into his cheeks and lighting up his eyes. Caran smiled back.

"Do you miss your home?" she asked, absently stroking her free hand through her red lengths as she waited for his response.

"I do, or not that I do not enjoy being with *you*, my lady," he corrected quickly. Caran giggled.

"I understand. I miss my home too, but un-like you I can never go back," she answered, sadness filling her beautiful orange eyes.

"I am very sorry, my lady," He bowed his head.

"Thank you, young knight," she smiled.

"*Joel*, my lady," he amended.

"*Caran*," she corrected. Both smiled bashfully at their laps for a few moments. Caran heard her mother returning from town, apparently disappointed in Cella.

"All I am saying is it was not his fault! There *was* a donkey there!" Hellena reproached her daughter.

"I heard *that is a beautiful ass*; what did you expect me to do? Pull up my skirt?" Cella snapped. Hellena huffed.

"Well I did not expect you to break his nose!" she sniped.

"*I* did," Cylan mumbled.

"So did I," Crystalline added.

Caran knew her time to coerce Joel had, sadly, run out but tried one last trick.

"Mother, sisters, I may have some great news!" Caran clapped her hands together as she rushed to stand with her family. Miala and Sir Vern had rejoined the group and Rogala and her now informed mother were sitting by the fire holding Granlund with fingers crossed. Caran turned to face the baffled Joel with her family behind her.

"I was speaking with Sir Joel about how much he misses his mother and I was thinking that he and the brave sir Vern could escort us to Rogadon on their way home to Adalonia!" Caran smiled brightly at Sir Joel as her mother and sisters erupted with excitement behind her.

"Oh, Sir Joel, what a brilliant idea!" Hellena gasped. Sir Joel sat in stunned silence; mentally probing their conversation for such a suggestion.

"Ah, well, orders were to stay..." he started as Sir Vern joined in the celebration.

"We was just to keep them out of Esildad is all," Vern said, suddenly desperate to get home. Sir Joel was gaping. Caran's pleading eyes finally pushed him to a decision.

"Well, as long as you are safe...I mean..." he started. Caran ran to hug him around the neck.

"Oh Joel, you are wonderful!" she cried into his ear. Joel delicately put one arm around her small waist. Hellena turned to Nia.

"We can leave word for the boys," she said. Nia smiled and nodded. Rogala kissed Miala on the cheek.

"You sure picked the right girl for the job; I think Joel was drooling!" she whispered. Miala giggled as she watched Caran and Joel locked in conversation again; almost oblivious to the heated preparations for the morning to come.

"He is not the only one," Miala pointed. Rogala couldn't help but grin at the two.

"Well, well. The seductress becomes the seduced, ey?" Rogala laughed. Granlund gurgled from his snuggled place against his mother's chest as Miala tickled his tiny foot. There was a weight lifted from their camp with the knowledge that come dawn they would finally be involved with the unfolding events they seemed shut out from before and it was blazing through them like fire.

....

"Your supper, King Ulei," Callana bowed her head as she handed the bowl over to the usurping king. She nearly vomited with the sight of seeing him lounging about comfortably in his tent while good men were in torturous pain. He had not noticed his royal guard wavering about, but he did note

Callana's cheerful disposition. Instead of taking his bowl, he rose and quickly rushed out side his tent. He was glowering around when Callana came out behind him. She nervously started to shake, hoping he would not catch on before the prison guards were asleep and Renk could free their anxious reinforcements.

Ulei saw some of his men dancing, some slumped sound asleep against the walls, and others were talking out loud to themselves or inanimate objects. His own royal guard was milling about center court, feeling stones on the ground and asking questions of thin air. Ulei swallowed hard before turning a cold glare to Callana.

"What have you done? *Treacherous whore!*" Ulei snarled as he closed in on her. Callana shook her head vigorously.

"I have done nothing my lord!" her eyes were wide with fear and the high pitch to her voice gave away her insecurity.

"This is not *drunk!* This is *poisoned!*" Ulei's angry outburst snapped Jiden out of yet another unconscious reprieve. He could hear the commotion behind him but not see it. He could, however, see the courtyard was full of spinning or sprawled knights and he had to grin to himself. He started to struggle against his ropes though the pain in his hands and feet threatened to destroy his resolve.

"Poison?" Callana stalled, desperately hoping she would see Galland rushing out of the dinning hall to save her. She realized she had no weapon and her eyes searched the forms around her for a lose sword or dagger. Ulei nearly lurched at her.

"You think you can *fool* me? I am not your ignorant *virgin* prince!" He came at her and she panicked, throwing the wooden bowl in his face before turning to run for the gates of the court yard. Ulei's laughing stopped her in her tracks and she twisted around and froze in terror. He had stopped chasing her to stand next to Jiden's pyre. She could see Jiden in the lantern's glow. His swollen face was strained as he wriggled to get free.

"I don't need an army to kill one man," Ulei grinned.

"Please, do not hurt him. It is me you want," Callana held up her hands and walked slowly towards him, desperate to draw his attention from her love. Ulei chuckled again.

"But I already *have* you, Callana; you were a gift from your prince," he laughed again. Callana cocked her head sideways.

"*What?*" She asked incredulously.

"He goes free, and I keep you; he traded your freedom for his! And you fight for him?" Ulei chuckled. Callana turned her eyes to look up at Jiden but he had closed his eyes against her.

"He should go free...he is *needed*. I am of no importance," She sagged with shame. He really had betrayed her for his own safety...but could she blame him? She had betrayed him as well. So in all of this, he really *had* stopped loving her enough to toss her aside in a desperate moment. Her heart fell in her chest and she knew it had broken.

"Now that I think about it, it was all for not anyway," Ulei put his finger to his chin in feigned contemplation.

"I was never going to *kill* Jiden or Nicholas for that matter; killing them would bring down the wrath of Odin for sure...no...I was holding them as collateral to keep Adalonia out of this, but I could not hold them forever. Your prince actually solved my problem for me, quite brilliantly I might say, by suggesting I keep *you* instead. Odin will have to sign over Rogadon *and* Esildad if he fears for your safety and something tells me... he does," Ulei glanced up at Jiden as he spoke and Jiden glowered back. Callana felt sadness rush into her very soul. It was all true. Somehow, she knew Ulei wasn't lying but...how? She felt sick to her stomach. She steeled herself against breaking in front of this evil man; straightening her shoulders to speak.

"Well if I am to be bound to you than it is best you know who I really am," Callana stated. Ulei turned patronizing eyes to her.

"The whore from Windt who found a princess and switched places...beyond that *who* could care," Ulei boorishly waved her off. Callana smiled maliciously.

"I am Callana, daughter of Cai, the son of Cassen who was the son of *Cale!*" she announced, noting that Jiden winced. Ulei froze; a hard stare solidifying his features.

"*You* are Camden's heir?" Ulei sneered.

"I am," she beamed. Ulei seemed to shake with anger as he slowly reached for the dagger at his belt. Callana readied herself for a fight.

"Than God has shown me my destiny," Ulei's voice was trembling, and Callana watched his eyes widen and gloss over with his spreading madness. "I am the one to end all *corrupted* royal lines...that is why I have found you all...that is why it has been so easy...it is ordained!" Ulei raised the dagger over his head; looking to Heaven for a confirmation. Callana saw her escape and spun quickly to the nearest stairway, dashing up two steps at a time. She could hear Ulei's frenzied breath behind her and panic spiked her blood. She rushed out onto the gangway landing; the motion tearing her newly scabbed side. A red stain started to soak into her tunic and she gasped with the searing pain. She bolted for the southwest tower with Ulei's boots skidding around the corner behind her as he rounded through the watch tower. Callana was close; so close he could smell the sticky sweetness of her blood and it excited him. The hunter was closing in on his injured prey; Ulei started to pant with climbing elation as he neared her. Callana tripped; spilling across weathered planks. It was the moment Ulei had been waiting for. He came to stand over her, gesturing with the dagger for her to rise.

Callana felt his presence before his hand gripped her shoulder. It was Carr; coming out of the shadows of the east watch tower and into the gleaming white moonlight to stand behind her. Ulei stumbled backwards; the maniacal smile fading as he gaped in terror. Callana filled with a courage she had never known. Tonight, she stood not only with Carr but with Cai, and Cassen and Ralla, Renna, Camden and Cale. They were all around her, surrounding her with their eternal love for her and each other. A love long punished by the cowering man before them. As Callana smiled down at Ulei in that moment she knew he saw them as well.

Ulei stepped back, raising a shaking finger to point at Carr.

"*Cassen? I killed you! You...You are dead! You are dead!*" Ulei's voice was a shrill squeal as he lost his tentative hold on reality. He stumbled backwards in hasty retreat, this time losing his footing; sending him toppling over the rampart. Callana watched him slam into the hard stone of the court yard; his eyes never leaving hers.

Callana crossed the main road; leaving the brilliantly blooming fields of Haven behind and climbed uphill towards Esildad's open court gates. Kila had sent her to replenish the rapidly vanishing comfrey roots, caraway and valerian and Callana was more than happy to get out of the make shift infirmary for a few hours; not to mention getting an overdue visit to Rogala, Renk and Granlund's recently purchased cottage in Haven; where Renk would be close while assisting with Esildad's revitalization. Callana took her fill of kisses and hugs from her favorite little man then reluctantly left.

The sunrise was beautiful today, as it had been for the last dozen days and would be forever, Callana surmised. Counting her blessings had become second nature now. Ulei was gone; an era of suffering was over, and the time for a great healing was evident all around. The grass was greener, flowers more vivid, markets flourished again; people everywhere were rejoicing as news of Ulei's deeds and death spread across the land. Lena and Odin had been to see Jiden, Elei, and Nicholas during their swift recuperation; bringing with them Callana's family after their accidental meeting in Rogadon. The king and queen were more than fond of Hellena's brood and the painting that Callana had yet to view herself. Lena had promised upon arrival in Adalonia she would arrange for the entire council to scrutinize it as well. Callana's sisters, credited to Lena's forewarning, were more prepared for *their* emotional introduction to their uncle who happened to be identical to their lost father. Hellena however had had quite a difficult time with it. She shied away from speaking to him or looking him in the eye; despite his attempts to connect. One person he had bonded quickly with on the other hand was Nia. Hellena seemed happy for her dear friend, but more so relieved that Carr was preoccupied. Callana had yet to corner her mother for an explanation, but she planned to soon. King Odin had been genuinely awed with Callana's accidental defeat of Ulei, also ferociously impressed in her and Sir Renk's devious plots. He left with a strict command that Jiden and Nicholas were not to travel until completely healed, and Esildad's city brought under control. For now, Dellandore's entire army had been escorted home to await their temporary king's orders. Elei would serve as ruler until Dellandore could determine a new leader either by tournament or election. Either way, Elei had been adamant that he himself had no interest in a permanent appointment.
All in all, Esildad's repairs had been minor; however there had been the gruesome discovery of Elei's thousand soldiers left home who had been over come by Ulei's superior forces and locked in an underground chamber that king Colius had ordered closed off due to its inhumane lack of air and light. The majority had been moved to the large dinning hall on donated blankets

from Haven and nursed back to health but unfortunately nearly two hundred had died from oxygen deprivation, malnutrition or by Dellandore hands. Elei had commissioned the carving of marble statues from Tasladad's own quarry to glorify his brave men and buried them in the royal cemetery to the west of the outer walls. Esildad would be great again, everyone knew it; her recovery as assured as that of Rogadon.

Jiden hadn't spoken to her yet, or anyone for that matter. His throat had become badly damaged from his severe dehydration and abuse, and his raspy attempts to communicate weren't only unintelligible but painful for him as well. It was all the same for Callana. Her weary mind had barely processed the events of late, including the bombardment of engagements and tales of heroism her family had to tell; keeping up with her daily chores here to mend Esildad and its king was all she had time for.

"Morning love!" Galland called as he rushed to embrace Callana as she flounced into the court yard. She fell into his arms; never tiring of the amazing comfort it gave her.

"Morning Galland! And where is your counterpart this bright day?" She pried; not having seen Carr and Galland separate since the night Ulei died. Galland had yet to forgive himself for leaving Callana to fight alone, despite her false assurances that she hadn't been frightened in the least.

"Your uncle is a magnificent archer! Even better than you I think," Galland taunted. Callana put her hand on her hip; balancing her basket of roots and herbs.

"Is that so, you enormous tease?" she feigned indignity than laughed.

"Sounds like a challenge to me," she smiled. Galland shook his head.

"He may be as good an archer, but not nearly as charming in the cape," Galland laughed before bowing generously and hopping to mount his massive horse for morning report.

"Did I miss them?" Carr rushed by, with George in tow. Callana laughed.

"Where were *you*?" she peeked around her large uncle to find Nia pretending to arrange a nearby fruit stand.

"Or do I need to ask?" Callana raised her eyebrows, causing Carr to blush bashfully.

"We were just talking," He began but Callana gave him a stern look. He blushed brighter.

"May I borrow him?" Carr nodded towards the agitated purple horse. Callana herself had not been able to go for her morning rides with her duties to Kila, and George had grown quite accustomed to riding morning patrol with Carr. She finally smiled, straining on tip toe to kiss her uncle on the cheek.

"Of course, now get on with it before he starts to whine," She ordered.

"*That's* my favorite red head!" Carr laughed, earning him a few sharp looks from her nearby sisters.

"Ey? That's what you told me Uncle Carr!" Cella chastised. Carr grinned.

"I said one of, *one* of my favorite red heads!" he assured. Callana giggled at her uncle on the prancing purple horse as he clip clopped his way through the stone courtyard to rush down the hill. Callana sighed; eager to get to her duties with her new found work force.

"Sister! Where have you been?" Cella scolded as she threaded a hot needle for a nasty gash in a young soldier's leg. Callana smirked and held up her basket as offering, setting it on a nearby wooden supply table.

"Oh, good, we were needing some things," Cella did her best to assume control of their operation here in Esildad, and Callana could not help but enjoy it.

"So, who can I help?" Callana readily clapped her hands together. Cella motioned with her head.

"He is the *nosiest* today," she said, keeping her eyes on her stitching. Callana turned to start, noting the advanced age of the knight motioning and moaning towards her.

"What can I do for you sir knight?" she asked kindly. He held his jaw and squinted his eyes in pain. Callana nodded.

"I see; gums?" she asked. He nodded vigorously. It had been a common ailment among the older knights to have severe gum pain, as malnutrition led to severe tooth decay and loss and the older men were most likely to have been dealing with that even before their imprisonment.

"I will be back as fast as I can," she rushed out the large doorway and across the sunny court yard to Kila's chambers where all the concoctions were made. She quickly grabbed a wooden bowl and began mixing smashed blackberry, apple balm and coltsfoot for toothaches and inflammation. Kila was busy with her own patients' needs and only had time to give Callana a quick smile in greeting.

"My sisters are in the infirmary and my mother has gone to the market in Haven for fruit; do you need anything else Kila? Anything at all?" Callana asked while she worked her mixture into a paste. Kila shook her head.

"No thank you love; you are all so wonderful!" Kila laughed. Her mood had lightened considerably in the last few days due to her ward's miraculous recovery. Both shins were still broken but had re-set well and Elei's ribs were healing and now only slightly tender to the touch. The most incredible new development was that his eyesight and hearing on his left side had come back! He would never be as he was before, but he was on the mend for sure and the scar from the stitches needed from his blow to the head would be hidden under his hair. His jaw had splintered on the right side, but it would heal. For now he drank his meals to avoid chewing until the bone was strong enough to endure. It would be weeks before he walked, maybe months before he could ride, but Kila was ecstatic in the knowledge that all these were inevitable. Callana was pleased as well, mostly for Nicholas and Miala. The tiny brunette never left his side and treated him just as Hellena had instructed her, in effect saving his life. They were inseparable and Nicholas had even been on brief shuffling walks out side the castle with her assistance. He and Jiden both had suffered broken toes, some foot bones and fingers; due to Ulei's liberal use of a wooden sledge. Jiden had also suffered a cracked cheek and eye bone on his left side; both just needed time and pain management to heal. Nicholas's right lung had collapsed under the pressure of the tight bindings but Kila and Hellena had ingeniously used a sharpened reed, shoved just through the muscle, to release the escaped air from his chest. This alleviated most of his pain, and allowed his lung to re-fill on it's own. Now, he only had to keep the small incision covered until it closed and his lung would hopefully sustain.

Every night, Callana and her family prayed for all who were injured; praying and experimenting with new mixtures was the best they could do. Even Kila was discovering ailments she had never seen before, so documentation was key; everything that worked was written down as well as adverse reactions. Every day was so demanding, Callana found herself collapsing late after treatments and clean up was done. She had even forgotten to dream in her exhausted state. The weary princess sighed then snapped herself out of the beginning of another of her delusional Jiden fantasies that had begun surfacing during the day; quickly finishing her mixture and hastening out to attend to her patient with her mind reeling from the rush of emotions her once lover's image caused her. He affected her entire being, yet she seemed to do little more than fill him with pity. Perhaps it was better he could not speak; at least in his silence, she could still pretend there was a future for them. Callana shook her head to free her thoughts of him once more and set her mind to work. She burst through the dinning hall doors and rushed over to the kindly knight. She knelt down and motioned for him to open his mouth.

"Open," she said, he obediently complied.

"We need to cover your gums with this," She said as she used her finger to rub the medicine into his bright red gums. His eyes closed in blessed relief and he sighed. Callana allowed herself a small smile as a reward for getting the blend just right. She took his hand and dipped his finger into the bowl.

"You can put this on whenever you feel pain, all right?" He nodded slowly, the glassy expression in his eyes a testament to his healing. Callana smiled and turned to go but the older man reached out, grasping her arm.

"Yes love?" She asked. He sat up and reached into a leather bag tied at his waste. She could hear coins jingling together and quickly shook her head.

"Oh, no no no you do not pay me love, I am merely an aid," she explained but the older man furrowed his brow and continued searching. Finally he pulled his hand out to expose the treasure he had been looking for. Callana bent to examine the small wooden piece.

"That is extraordinary! Did you make it?" She asked; her eyes focused on the intricate wooden horse; carved out of a smooth, burgundy manzanita branch. Callana shook her head.

"I cannot accept that, it is too much," She insisted but the older man creased a wrinkled forehead and forced the horse into her hand.

"You...the girl with the purple horse," he spoke in a gruff low moaning voice. Callana shivered. She felt as if she had a title; as if she was someone; someone worthy.

"I will keep it, always...it is the most beautiful thing I have ever seen...thank you very much," she held the miniature horse in her hand and pressed it to her heart to express her gratitude. The knight seemed satisfied with the exchange and laid back down, closing weary gray eyes. Callana sighed to herself as she turned to make her rounds through the rapidly improving men; glad to be of use.

Jiden was watching Callana from his spot near the back wall. He found himself watching her a lot, maybe a bit too often. Her strength of character was admirable, she was beautiful, and everyone seemed to adore her; so what was so confusing? Why was his head battling his heart every waking moment of every day? His body was exhausted from his extensive injuries, but he lay awake at night; watching her move from soldier to soldier, duty to duty, and then leaving to sleep in the servants' quarters across the court yard. She did not say good morning, or good night. She did not stare at him incessantly and when she caught him staring, she did not wave or even smile. He was a complete mess inside, but unable to articulate a single word of explanation! It was maddening; knowing she believed he had handed her over to Ulei and not being able to convince her otherwise. Nicholas had tried on his cousin's behalf but Callana had only waved him off in a rush. She was always in a *rush* anymore. Jiden wanted to ask her if she was a mess; was she confused about how she felt for *him*? Was she hurting or angry or devoid of all feelings for him at all? He could not ask; so he watched.

Jiden forced himself to his knees, turning around and slowly walking his bandaged hands up the stone wall until he was bent but standing. His feet had been bandaged tight and he had pushed them snugly into leather boots in his determination to walk today. He stared at the stone wall before him, sweating from his efforts as he slowly rocked back and forth and side to side until he had turned around again.

Jiden took a deep breath and closed his eyes. One foot in front of the other; that was all he had to do. His whole life of taking that for granted flashed before his eyes and he smiled to himself. He sucked in a big breath and opened his eyes to step forward only to find himself looking down on a familiar pair of dark brown eyes.

"What do you think you are doing?" Callana raised one eyebrow at Jiden, who had abruptly forgotten what he was doing.

"You are not to stand without help or walk without a guide," she continued sharply. Jiden's eyes were pleading and he put his hands together to beg. Callana rolled her eyes tiredly.

"All right, just let me tell someone," she turned and hurried away to find Cella. From across the room Jiden could see the squinted eyes of the older sister as she confirmed Callana's alibi than reluctantly nodded. Callana hustled back to Jiden, bracing herself up under his shoulder and the two hobbled out into the golden sunshine of the late morning under the penetrating orange glare of four disapproving sisters.

Callana felt her heart flutter in her chest. Being next to him was more than exhilarating and terrifying all at once. Jiden stopped to rest in the courtyard, sitting down slowly on a wooden bench across from the rear fortification where tables were decorated and set three times a day for meals. Jiden gave Callana an apologetic look and she smiled timidly. Jiden tried to grin but winced with the pain. Callana grimaced and pulled a leather pouch out of her brown linen tunic. She pulled the water bladder off his belt and added some ground yarrow, shaking it to mix before handing it back to him.

"Yarrow, for pain," she informed him. Jiden nodded his thank you and downed the entire contents in a few big gulps. Callana caught herself watching his supple throat move and frowned. The days of spending all their time together in Adalonia, even that incredible night in Dellandore seemed like a lifetime ago now. She sighed heavily.

"Sorry," Jiden croaked humbly, assuming she was growing impatient. Callana cocked her head.

"Do not be sorry, my lord, we can quit if you like," she suggested. Jiden shook his curly head vigorously and shakily stood. He reached for Callana's support again and the two moved slowly in unison towards the dinning hall. Jiden started to tug her slightly north towards the gates with an eager look in his eyes. Callana laughed out loud.

"Are you sure, my lord?" she asked. He nodded anxiously towards the opening. When they had neared the top of the slope towards the Crystal river, Callana hesitated.

"My lord, I am afraid I may drop you," she stiffened, forcing him to stop. Jiden looked at her with a worried furrowed brow, than suddenly grinned mischievously, taking his arm off her shoulder and lowering himself to the ground; stretching out parallel to the river below. Callana realized what he was going to do.

"No! What if you roll in to the river?" she reprimanded but Jiden crossed his arms over his chest and winked before shouldering himself into rolling motion. Callana gasped. He was picking up speed! She dashed after him, pulling up her linen dress to free her legs for a full sprint. Jiden easily used his knee to stop before the river's green bank as Callana frantically tried to reach out for him. She tripped over him; plunging into the chilly water. Jiden got to his knees and crawled for the river as fast as he could, reaching for her as she emerged gasping for air. Jiden pulled her gently to the warm grass, looking down on her with a panicked expression. Callana lay heaving from the shock of the cold water, grateful for the full sun of the day. She looked at

Jiden who was using clumsy, bandaged hands to wipe her hair out of her face. He looked so handsome right then. The sun gleaming down through his golden curls, the wide deep blue eyes studying her intently, even the scar on his dimpled cheek was charming. It made her heart ache to have him so close.

"I am all right, my lord," she assured him. Brushing his hand away and immediately regretting it. He nodded, casting a glance down her clinging clothing and back to her eyes. Did she have any idea what seeing her like this was doing to him? But, she had pushed his hand away; she did not want him to touch her when that was *all* he wanted to do. He started to roll onto his knees to get up and Callana reached for his arm.

"Lay with me?" She asked. Jiden's brow relaxed and he smiled softly, collapsing next to her in the warm sunshine. The sky was bright blue today, contrasting with the deep green tree line of the far off Shadow's forest to the north. A gentle breeze rose and fell around them; bringing the sweet smell of the jasmine vines growing on the western wall of the castle. They slept peacefully for hours together on the hillside in the sun; and for the first time in weeks, they dreamt.

Days went by this way; fewer soldiers to care for by the day, left her more and more time for walks with Jiden. The two sat next to each other at the evening fires after supper and had even taken a few evening rides to view the glorious sun sets over Mount Lisia.

"Oh, I need to rest a minute," Callana nearly moaned as she knelt in the cool grass next to the river after one of their walks. Jiden came to kneel carefully next to her. He had started to pat her back when she lurched forward, vomiting violently. Callana panted for a moment; her head was spinning again; just as it did after every walk. She was starting to think she may need to see Kila about this. She finally sat back, embarrassed about her disgusting display. Jiden's brow was furrowed with deep concern but Callana waved her hand.

"It is nothing, sire," a faint smile played on her pink lips.

"Nothing would be once," He croaked, shaking his head. Callana knew he was right. She had gotten sick every day for the last few days, but she instantly felt better after throwing up. She nodded as she reached for his shoulder and used him to stand.

"I just need to get used to all this sunshine again after such a long winter is all," she argued. Jiden had stood and was crossing his arms over his chest; a scowl scrunched his eyebrows. Callana sighed.

"All right all right, I will talk to Kila tomorrow," she tried to turn but Jiden grabbed her arm.

"Now," he growled. Callana threw her hands up in resignation.

"Fine! If you really want to waste a perfectly good day!" and with that, the two headed for Kila's chambers. She was cleaning up after an early day and eagerly welcomed the two inside.

"Oh come in come in! Look at you two...wait," She stopped in mid hug to examine Callana closely.

"You look terrible love," She worried over Callana; checking her head for fever and noticing how sticky the girl's skin was.

"I spent too long in the sun is all," Callana laughed nervously. Kila tisked.

"*I* will decide what the matter is. Prince Jiden you must go, so I may examine little miss sunshine," she turned on her heel and was boiling water before Jiden had time to kiss Callana's hand and stumble through the door.

....

"Go on without me," Galland called out to the royal guard. Erik looked confused.

"What do you mean, exactly?" He asked. Galland had suddenly become very interested in something up the main road and was fidgeting with his hands. David snorted; glancing around at the rest of the stunned guard.

"I...ah...have something I need to do...just give report without me....*you*...Gracien...you like to talk. You give morning report!" Galland ordered. The thick knight's jaw hung slack.

"*Senren* likes to talk," he corrected even though both were known for their mouths, Senren *was* a bit more excessive in that department. Galland sighed with frustration.

"Fine, Senren, give the morning report," Galland gestured unceremoniously but before he could swing Baby around north, Senren spoke up.

"What kind of a thing to say is that anyway? Who does *not* like to talk? I mean we all like to talk; how else would we say anything?" Senren was rambling. Galland let lose a curse, earning him everyone's undivided attention.

"I have never heard you curse Galland," Senren said in an awed tone.

"Have you ever heard *anything* with all your sputtering?" Galland's outburst set off a blustering round of laughter from the thoroughly bewildered men.

"What is the matter, big man?" Franklin finally asked as the chuckles died off. Galland ran a hand over his face in an attempt to calm down. In the distance, from behind his enormous silhouette, a squeaking wheeled cart appeared with Hellena pulling hard.

"Ohhhh," Gracien, Lashend, Renk, Franklin, David, Senren and Erik seemed to gasp all at once. Laden faltered, then gave Galland the thumbs up as understanding came to him. Then the entire royal guard turned to gallop south for Esildad, leaving Galland to conveniently come to the rescue. Hellena had spotted the group while coming down the hard packed dirt and she was having a hard time admitting to herself that seeing Galland sent shivers up her spine. She tried to appear nonchalant as he approached but she found herself freezing and awkwardly fidgeting with her hands.

"My lady," Galland dismounted and bowed graciously for the blushing Hellena. She shook her head.

"Sir Galland, you may call me Hellena...if you wish, that is....if it is easiest," she concluded uncomfortably, frowning with disappointment in her sudden lack of abilities to speak. Galland grinned down at her; his dimples creasing his unshaved face and narrowed his eyes.

"Hellena, thank you, I was wanting to tell you that," He paused. It had been nearly six years since he had even spoken to a woman he was interested in and his insecurities warned him she may not be as *interested* in him. He decided to take a diplomatic approach.

"I am going to accompany you to the market from now on...prince's orders," Galland lied. Hellena smiled and tilted her head.

"Oh, well if it is an order than how can I say no," she complied. Galland immediately tugged his big hoofed horse over to latch her to the cart before climbing into the saddle. He reached one hand down to lift Hellena up.

"Put your foot in the stirrup and give me your hand love," Galland said sweetly, winking one golden eye. Hellena obeyed; happy to pretend they were just doing their duty and not shamelessly flirting. Riding behind him, she felt a strange comfort; as if he solved some illusive problem that had been plaguing her. Galland was riding along with an enormous grin stretching across his face and reeling with the sensation of being with Hellena; she was the curvy red haired angel he had prayed to have for so long.

....

"How may I be of service, young king?" Lustene bowed low at the gate for Elei who quickly returned the bow for his old friend.

"Lustene? You are a day early, dear friend." Elei hobbled stiffly next to the old surgeon as they made their way for Kila's quarters.

"Yes sire. All is well in Adalonia so I decided to lend my meager services to any who need help here," Lustene offered. Elei pointed towards the dinning hall that was now empty of all injured men.

"Well, my men have healed magnificently due to the efforts of Kila and Callana's family." Elei started, noticing Lustene's surprised expression.

"Do not worry Lustene, I know two princes that could use a good once over and..." Lustene cut Elei short.

"Oh, it is not that sire, I was just startled to hear that Kila is your surgeon. We were...*friends*, long, long ago," Lustene smiled bashfully as Elei laughed out loud.

"You were a wild one weren't you, old dog!" He chuckled again.

"Well, once you have reacquainted yourselves, perhaps you could take a look at my legs," Elei's smile faded. Lustene cocked his head.

"But you have Kila," He started but the young king shook his head.

"She worries too much so I have been avoiding seeing her; besides, she has her hands full with Callana right now," Elei grimaced. Lustene turned to Elei and pointed at the young man's legs.

"I will see your legs *now*, and Kila later," he commanded. Elei sighed and nudged Lustene towards a table inside the dining hall. Once there, Lustene un-bandaged the wooden supports from each shin to find the lacerations had turned green and slimy. Lustene held his nose.

"Oh sire! They are badly infected! Oh, I will get my bag," the older man hurried from the stench of Elei's shins to retrieve his leather bag from his mule, stopping on the way to ask Crystalline to boil salted water in the center fire pit, still burning from breakfast. An hour later, Nicholas and Jiden were sitting on either side of their young friend to assure he stay put in the stinging hot aloe, salt and burdock leaf soak as Lustene rushed off to see to Callana.

....

Lustene knocked on the heavy plank door and waited patiently for a response. Kila came storming to the door in an apparent rage.

"Enough is enough now, I said she will be fine prince..." Kila swung the door open to see an older, familiar face.

"So sorry, good sir, I thought you were Jiden...again," she apologized; afraid Lustene did not remember her.

"You are as beautiful as you were twenty years ago Kila," Lustene gushed. Kila bowed her head bashfully and straightened her ratted braid.

"I did not think you would remember me, Lustene," she said.

"How could I *forget*," Lustene smiled brightly, his blue eyes dancing with a naughty memory. Kila's cheeks burned bright red as the same images ran across her mind.

"I could leave if you would like some privacy?" Callana offered from the back of the room. Kila flushed, snapping herself back into a surgeon frame of mind. Lustene frowned as he entered the room.

"You will do no such thing!" Kila ordered, following Lustene towards her examination table. Callana sighed.

"I feel much better now Lustene, I promise!" she begged but Kila shook her head sternly.

"For the last few days she says she becomes ill after time in the sunshine; I have never heard of such a thing!" Kila was obviously exasperated. Lustene bent to look at the pale, sweating red head.

"Lay down please," he ordered as he stepped forward.

"May I?" he asked as he held his hands over Callana's neck.

"Of course," Callana nodded, nervously twirling her newly strung horse necklace; hoping a quick exam would show her healthy as can be and she would sent on her way. Lustene began by checking for swelling in her neck, then listened to her heart beat. When he placed his hands under her breasts to check if she had swelling in her diaphragm, Callana winced.

"What is it dear?" He stopped and pushed down on the breathing muscle under the bottom ribs. She shook her head.

"Nothing..." Callana was bright red. Lustene smiled sympathetically.

"Your breasts are tender?" He asked. Callana nodded.

"It is all right my dear, I am a physician. Are you due for your menses?" He asked. Callana's eyebrows knit as she thought.

"When was the last time love?" Kila tried to help but Callana seemed confused.

"I...the last time I *remember* was before the tournament, but that was December," she frowned. Lustene's smile faded and he moved his hands down to Callana's abdomen. As he pressed down low, under her belly button and between her hip bones, she squirmed uncomfortably.

"That feels...strange...and I have to pee!" Callana sprang off the table and rushed for the short hall to the chamber pot. When she emerged, Lustene had his hands folded in front of him with a pleasant smile on his face. Kila looked as confused as Callana felt.

"What is it?" Callana asked, suddenly scared.

"May I ask, did you happen to...*experience*...Prince Jiden in Dellandore?" Lustene raised one eyebrow. Callana gasped.

"Lustene! Please, do not tell Lena, or my mother, or my sisters because *they* will tell my mother...or" Callana was running her hands through her hair in her panic. Lustene chuckled and shook his head.

"My dear, I am not going to say anything, except..." He came forward and took Callana's trembling hand.

"Congratulations Callana; you are *pregnant*," he smiled. Callana's eyes closed and she collapsed to the stone floor. Kila rushed over to help Lustene lift her back onto the table. Lustene chuckled at Kila's terrified gasp.

"She will be fine," he assured her. They covered Callana with a linen sheet.

"I am surprised you did not come to that conclusion first, Kila," Lustene smiled at her. Kila smiled back sullenly.

"I would not have known...I have never had children," she said, a sadness lowering her tone.

"That is a pity; you would have been a splendid mother," he bent and kissed her cheek before turning to leave.

"I need to speak to a certain young prince; if she wakes have her eat something," he ordered as he walked out into the warm afternoon sun; blissfully unaware he had anything but wonderful news to share.

....

Today was the first day in the better part of February that Elei's entire army attended formation. The injured were now healed and the weak recuperated. Elei himself had, against Kila's strict forbidding, devised a wooden fitting for his leather boots that would support his shins and absorb most of the punishment of walking. He was desperate to command his army as a man, and not an invalid. His hair had not yet grown over his scar, but other than that, he looked the part. His skin had regained its natural olive color and though he had lost some weight, his tall frame did not appear thin or frail. His blonde hair had a healthy shine and his brilliant gold eyes were gleaming with his eagerness to be back to himself again. Kila was impressed.

"My my my, young man, you are looking miraculous," she put her hands on her hips and leaned forward expectantly. Elei kissed her cheek and stomped across her small quarters.

"Not too bad, can barely feel them," he lied as his shins screamed in protest. Kila shook her silver head.

"I am against this, you know that?" she scolded. Elei nodded, bashfully looking at his feet.

"I know. I love you too mum," he kissed her cheek again and she melted. He had come to Esildad as Colius's motherless ward. Kila had instantly taken to the quiet infant who had grown into a tense but kind young man and they had been inseparable every since. She heaved a sigh as she looked over him. He had not changed much in twenty eight years.

"I know you think you are ready...but this counsel meeting," she tried to argue but his stubborn resolve hardened his features.

"Kila, life has to move on. People need to get back to their *own* kingdoms; they have all sacrificed too much as it is. I am not incapable of rebuilding this city," he stated. Kila hugged him fiercely.

"I know. I believe in you," she smiled up at him and he grinned back.

"That is why I will succeed," he winked and plodded out for his arranged counsel meeting with a new fervor in his mood.

....

"Lustene!" Jiden's entire royal guard sang together as the older man approached. Lustene smiled brightly at his much missed band of ruffians. It was a welcomed sight after so long worrying after them while they had been gone. The grey haired surgeon shook hands with all save for Jiden and Nicholas who grappled him in a welcomed embrace. He was beaming with his joy to see them all still alive and mended after all that had transpired. He turned shinning blue eyes on Jiden.

"My lord, a word with you," Lustene gestured for the open gates of the court yard.

"Is it Callana?" Jiden grumbled, suddenly very concerned knowing full well Lustene had just come from her examination.

"It is about both of you, sire," Lustene grinned, shrugging his shoulders. Jiden stood as quickly as he could and followed Lustene to the dirt path leading out of the front gates and down the rise; glancing over his shoulder towards Kila's quarters and frowning as he left. When he was sure they were out of anyone's ear shot, Lustene took Jiden's hand firmly.

"Now before I give you the news," Lustene was stern when he spoke now, vexing Jiden even more.

"Is there anything you have to tell me of your trip to Dellandore?" Lustene's face had grown so serious Jiden's mind began to fill and jumble with memories. Lustene saw the furrowed brows and decided to be more direct.

"In other words, did you have an...*encounter...* in Dellandore that you have never had before?" Lustene waited patiently for understanding to dawn in the prince's face before both shifted uncomfortably.

"Forgive me sire, I only ask to prepare you for the line of questioning sure to come when your parents arrive this afternoon," Lustene smiled softly. Jiden sighed and nodded.

"Callana and I made love," Jiden stared out across the blue sky northwest over Mount Lisia and grimaced. Lustene was thoroughly confused by this reaction to such a thing as making love to the very woman he confessed to being in love with to Lustene himself.

"My lord?" the older man prodded. Jiden turned a fierce green stare on his old friend and stiffened his jaw.

"So much has happened since then...I did not mean to disgrace Callana; my father did not know of this when he called off the wedding," Jiden's voice grew too raspy and he put his hand to his throat but Lustene had understood enough of what was said.

"I see" He paused.

"Do you love her still?" Lustene pried. Jiden instantly turned away again; searching for his answer in the tall tree line of the Shadow's forest.

"Would you *marry* her?" Lustene pushed. Jiden cleared his throat uneasily.

"If she were royal?" Jiden asked.

"If she were *pregnant*," Lustene prompted. Jiden stilled, his eyes fixed on Lustene's.

"Is she?" Jiden asked. Lustene sagged slightly; obviously disappointed in Jiden's lack of enthusiasm. Jiden put his hands on his hips.

"Lustene, is she?" Jiden was almost pleading for an answer. Lustene huffed slightly then folded his arms.

"Yes," He replied downtrodden. Jiden's face softened, and there was an earnest sadness in his eyes that caused Lustene's spirits to wilt.

"Forgive me, sire, I did not mean to cause you *pain*," the older man bowed and turned to walk away but Jiden rushed to confront him.

"You are cross with me?" he croaked. Lustene stiffened.

"Speak freely!" Jiden demanded. Lustene flushed red but did not raise his voice.

"I must say I am more than unimpressed with your cold lack of love for your own child-"

"It may not be my child!" Jiden barked the words out, determined to validate his hostility towards this situation.

"What are you saying? She was not a *virgin*?" Lustene nearly whispered now. Jiden put his hands in his hair and blew out a long breath.

"I was her first...but in prison...Ulei...*took* her," Jiden explained. Lustene's eyes widened and he wavered. Jiden felt his tiredness all at once. How could this be? Especially when he and Callana had connected again so well in these last few days.

"He *raped* her?" Lustene confirmed. Jiden nodded slowly.

"Sir Erik told me as much the night after Ulei died; Callana does not know *I* know," Jiden explained.

"This is troubling indeed; it will be a hard secret to keep but after the wedding everyone will assume it is your baby whether it is or not," Lustene started but Jiden snapped suddenly.

"I want nothing to do with any *seed* of Ulei's! Not in my own *home*!" Jiden crossed his arms over his chest defiantly. Lustene's patience wore thin as he pointed a finger towards Kila's room.

"You mean to hold this against them? They are *victims*! Not *criminals*!" Lustene argued ferociously but Jiden tensed.

"Enough! This is my decision, mine! And I will make it on my own!" Jiden's voice cracked under the strain of his outburst and he coughed loudly. Lustene was shaking with rage. He felt betrayed by Jiden, as he knew Callana would. He gathered enough composure to give Jiden a curt bow.

"Of course, my lord," he said and hurried away. Jiden immediately regretted his actions yet at the same time could think of anything to say to redeem himself. He let one of his dearest friends walk away before he turned for the courtyard and a dreaded confrontation with another.

....

Kila had just stepped out to fetch Callana's meal when she nearly smashed into Jiden. She bowed low, trying hard to hide her excitement for the couple. Jiden smiled politely and returned the gesture. Kila pushed the door open for him than closed it behind him; merrily prepared to take a very long time to return.

Callana was sitting with her back to the door. She had a sheet puddled around her waist and draped over her legs and nothing else. Jiden could see the dimples in her milky skin that her back bone made. He could also see the tip of the rippled scar over her left hip bone from a mule's kick when she saved Gant along with the newly sewn gash on her right side where she had been sliced by an arrow coming to his rescue; evidence of so much pain, and here he was about to hurt her *more*. His mind reeled and his heart burned with the thought of losing what they had recovered together. He could not bear fighting with her and saying terrible things as they had before. He tried to form what he would say but she made a sound that stilled his thoughts. She was weeping; her shoulders were shaking visibly now with her soft sobs. He sighed; the noise startling her and she grasp for her sheet, pulling it to cover her body as she turned to see who it was. When she saw Jiden there, she filled with so much love for him at once that it hurt her to hold it in.

"Jiden? I did not hear you come in," she said, wiping tears away with her hand as she slowly maneuvered herself to face him. She was smiling brightly and her dark eyes sparkled. Jiden attempted to talk, but could not decide how to start. His flustering was enough.

"You know, *don't you?*" she asked, her heart immediately sinking with the pity welling in his eyes.

"You are *ashamed* of what we did," Callana assumed. Jiden came closer, shaking his head.

"Of course not," he forced his words out through raw vocal chords. Callana looked away from him, unable to tolerate the sympathetic look on his face.

"You feel sorry for me, is that it? So you do not want any part of this child?" she asked; tears spilled out of her eyes as she glared at him. Jiden tried to reach out and hold her but she moved away. He felt his temper rising; she was going to treat him like the *villain*?

"That is not fair," He started, waiting for his throat to stop throbbing.

"*Fair?*" she growled through clenched teeth.

"We do not even know if it is mine," he finally said. He looked down on her and watched realization come over her. She sagged and hung her head.

"How do you know about that?" she whispered. Jiden shook his head.

"Erik was there...outside the prison in Dellandore," Jiden admitted. Callana fell into sobs again. Jiden felt his mind humming with spinning thoughts and feelings. He reached to hold her again and she slapped his hand away, sitting up straight with a cold look on her face.

"Do not trouble yourself *prince!*" she sneered out the word, infuriating Jiden.

"I can't help how I feel Callana-"Callana leapt off the table, pulling her sheet tight around her. She was looking for clothes and finally found her riding leggings and tunic. She quickly dropped her sheet to dress with a scathing look on her face. Jiden crossed the room, limping from the weakness setting in his exhausted injured feet. He snatched the tunic out of her hands, leaving her standing with just her green leggings on. Jiden forced his eyes off of her breasts but not before Callana caught him staring. She crossed her arms over her chest.

"You can't help the way you *feel* about anything can you?" she chided. Jiden threw the tunic across the room and grabbed her by her shoulders.

"See it from *my* eyes!" he pleaded. She struggled against his grip but he held her tight.

"If you knew it was *his*," Jiden started, his eyes traveling down towards her stomach.

"Would you still *want* it?" he pressed. Callana pushed away from him.

"I want this baby because it is *mine*," she forced passed him to collect her tunic. Jiden sighed heavily.

"But it may not be *mine*? Can you not understand?" he begged. Callana had hardened. Her time for tears was over as she belted her tunic and quickly braided her hair.

"How simple men are," she said flippantly. Jiden seethed at the cold, emotional shut down in her tone.

"And how complicated women are!" he barked. Callana laughed out loud.

"You, men, royal men like you, they speak of duty and service and honor! Ha!" she taunted as she headed for the door. Jiden cut her off, wincing at the tremendous stinging in his toes.

"You are going to walk away?" Jiden snarled.

"Just saving you the trouble, *my lord*!" Callana shouted as she flung the door open and dashed for the front gates. Carr was just returning with George and without a word she pulled her uncle down, mounted and spun her tired mount around and in a moment she was gone. Jiden stood alone in the center of the courtyard and a dozen stares, feeling his pride crumble and his heart break.

....

"King Odin and Queen Lena; I am most grateful for your presence again," Elei began. Both bowed their heads respectfully.

"You look much better, my lord," Lena complimented. Elei blushed slightly over the attention.

"Thank you, beautiful Lena," he bowed. Odin winked at his tiny wife before clearing his throat to speak.

"There is a lot to address from the sound of your letter," he began. Elei nodded as he sat in the grey velvet chair at the head of the large oak table.

"And I am afraid I have to add something to that list," Elei stated, as the large doors pushed open and Lustene entered the room.

"Good afternoon, Sire and my lady; so sorry for the intrusion," Lustene bowed his head for both.

"What is this about?" Odin grumbled as it was not customary for a closed meeting to be interrupted by the physician. Lustene held his hand up apologetically.

"Sire, I can assure you I would not have asked for your council if it were not of extreme importance," Lustene glanced towards Jiden as he spoke and the young man bowed his head dejectedly.

"What has happened Lustene?" Lena's green eyes beseeched her dear friend. Lustene took in a deep breath.

"Callana is pregnant," he blurted out. Elei, who himself had not been told any thing of why Lustene needed to see King Odin, spit out his mouthful of water. Odin and Lena glared at their son.

"Is this true Jiden?" Lena asked heatedly. Jiden nodded his head, his eyes downcast; refusing to see their disappointment in him. Odin slammed his fist into the table.

"You have *disgraced* her! You have disgraced *yourself*!" He stood to glower down on his son. Jiden nodded his head again, forcing himself to look up at his father.

"Forgive-"Jiden started but Lena cut him short.

"Before or after your father called off the wedding?" She demanded. Jiden knew either answer made his actions shameful. He swallowed hard and stood to answer.

"Before...but-"This time Lustene silenced the prince.

"My lord," he interjected, causing Lena and Odin's head to snap towards him. "There is more," He said grimly. The room was still. Lustene sighed heavily than started.

"Prince Jiden may not be the father," he mumbled. Now Lena sat with her hand over her mouth in shock as Odin scowled. Elei grimaced as he glanced sideways at his younger friend, now slumped in shame.

"She was with another?" Lena whispered.

"*Taken* by another," Lustene corrected.

"*Raped?*" Odin clarified. Lustene nodded solemnly.

"By Ulei," he finished. Elei stood.

"*What?*" the fuming young king demanded. Lustene nodded again.

"Dear God," Nicholas sighed.

"But surely we would know when she delivers who the baby belongs to?" Lena offered. Lustene shook his head.

"I am sorry my lady, it is too close to simply count back," Lustene argued.

"How close?" Odin was absently clenching and unclenching his fists. Lustene lowered his head.

"Within a day, sire," he finally answered. Lena gasped and looked to Jiden.

"We will have to re-instate the wedding of duty; the council has agreed the painting and the royal seal prove her line, as well as Ulei's own admission of murder," she started. Odin was nodding.

"This information will never leave this room; the kingdoms will accept the child as royal heir to Adalonia," Odin agreed.

"We will have the wedding soon, before she begins to show and-" Lena started; Jiden stood.

"Mother, father! Do I have no *say* in this?" he shouted hoarsely.

"You have an *objection* my son?" Odin raised his eyebrows. Jiden shook his head.

"No, well yes, but..." Odin stood face to face with his son and lowered his voice to a graveling growl.

"Tomorrow morning at the ceremony you make the announcement or I make it for you but either way you will honor your commitment; understood?" Odin's tone made it clear he was done with this discussion. Jiden felt lowly; cowardly and vile. Everyone saw this to be his responsibility and all he could see was the dishonor. Even Nicholas was disturbed by Jiden's hesitancy. Jiden knew he loved Callana yesterday; why was today any different? His head spun as he bowed low for his father.

"Forgive my *detestable* objections, sire; Of course I will uphold my commitments, father," Jiden rose to look his father in the eye. Odin heard his son's promising words but his defeated eyes told a different story. Lena felt her heart plummet with the sorrow she saw between them. As Lustene turned to leave, Elei continued the once hopeful meeting that had now turned solemn. Plans were made for the coming ceremony, the coming wedding, and the appointments of two cities before Elei and Nicholas escorted the visiting couple to their quarters and Jiden was left alone.

....

Callana brought George to a halt at the western edge of Shadow's forest. She could not stop the tears from falling as she filled with the blended memories of the sweetest and most horrific recent days of her life. She had watched from the western wall of the castle as Lena and Odin and their royal guard had arrived as she hid in cowardice. They would hear of her, *condition*, and they would pity her as Jiden now did. Her own mother and sisters would be hearing from Lustene, as well as Miala and eventually Rogala as all would attend the feast tonight. Jiden's guard as well as Elei's guard, who were out hunting for boar and goose and when they returned they would be informed as well, no doubt. All the while Callana would hide; the scandalous, *would be* whore of Windt; an *erroneous* princess carrying an *unwanted* child. Callana clutched her belly and sobbed. She tried to think of an infant with Jiden's curls and green eyes and Callana's pale skin but Ulei's image took its place and she shook her head to dislodge it. No...This was *her* baby! She would do this alone if she had to. Her family would always love her and she was sure she could find a kingdom somewhere that had never *heard* of her. Dellandore knew her as a false princess; Adalonia would surely remember her as a usurper and nothing more; Esildad will see her as a pitiful, disgraced victim. This valley would unite together as Elei planned to propose, and she would be outcast. She was weeping into her hands on her now sleeping mount when she was interrupted by a familiar voice.

"Callana?" Erik called softly, startling her. She turned in her saddle to see him riding towards her from the castle and she forced a smile on her reddened face.

"What is wrong?" He asked as he neared and could see her tear soaked face. Callana nearly laughed.

"Have you not *heard*?" she asked incredulously. Erik frowned as he thought.

"I heard you are a mother to be and heir to the throne of Rogadon, as well as a wolf killing archery champion who saved Gant's life as well as the King's, and that you killed Ulei just by looking at him," Erik grinned from ear to ear. Callana smiled; her mood lifting.

"You do not *pity* me?" She asked. Erik shook a shaggy head.

"Not at all; I admire you for all you have done," he admitted. His grey eyes darkened with his sincerity.

"You do?" Callana grinned.

"I do; but the question is, what do *you* think of yourself?" he pried. Callana slumped her shoulders. Erik reached out to take her hand.

"It is not what happens to us that makes us who we are. It is how we overcome and endure. Let *your* actions define you; not the actions against you," Erik lifted her hand and kissed it before turning his dappled grey mare around and heading back to the castle. Callana took a big breath in and exhaled slowly. She would never have thought that in her moment of darkness *Erik* would be the light to show her the way. Now that she thought about it however, he had been there for her before in her escape from prison; even as Jiden had turned against her. Callana's scorned heart flittered in her chest with a new hope. Perhaps she really could be *welcomed* somewhere. Callana urged George back towards the castle, unaware that Jiden had been watching from the western tower. His eyes followed her in her bouncing approach as he scolded himself for the physical reaction it caused. Even now he was acting disreputable! He would tell her, no, ask her to marry him, tonight before the announcement in the morning. He steeled himself against the wave of confusion that threatened to break his reserve as he made his way down the stair well. When he emerged into the courtyard, he could smell the celebration dinner Nia, Cella, and Hellena were preparing. Miala and Rogala were chatting away, swinging Granlund gently between them in the stone courtyard with Kila and Lustene. Carr, Renk and Jiden's guard were readying the meat in the overwrought butcher's shop off the main square. Callana rode in and was greeted by four squealing sisters. Hellena and Nia stopped stirring as well to rush in and squeeze the exhausted red head. Elei and Nicholas even made their way over to kiss her cheek in congratulations. Jiden felt his determination falter. Just as he had decided to turn back for the safety of the tower, Galland spotted him.

"You little *devil*!" he pointed, rousing a thunderous cheer from the court. All were ecstatic for the young prince, save for Lustene, Nicholas and Elei who knew better how Jiden himself truly felt. The three of them held back and solemnly watched from afar. It was the reaction he had dreaded most. He needed to mend this, and soon before it got any worse; if anything was worse than to be ostracized by your dearest friends. Jiden made his way to Callana; noting the tight smile she gave him as a courtesy. He pulled her close to whisper in her ear.

"May I speak with you?" He grinned falsely.

She smiled politely for the boisterous crowd's benefit and nodded. Jiden took her hand and the two slowly made their way through the barrage of back slaps and tummy rubs to the gates and out side. Once out of eye sight, Callana yanked her hand away and headed east along the wall and around, leaving Jiden limping to catch her. When he rounded the corner, she was leaned back against the stone wall; arms crossed defiantly over her chest as she eyed him suspiciously. He cocked his head and raised his eyebrows.

"Nice performance," he bowed. Callana glared at him through slotted eyes.

"I was going to say the same to you," she sniped. Jiden sighed, glancing around before speaking.

"Do not worry prince no one is witness if you wish to push me down the hill," she gestured with one hand towards the steep decline and smiled. Jiden's temper spiked.

"Enough Callana," he barked. She rolled her eyes. Jiden could feel it starting; the rude remarks and argumentative postures; the contest to tear each other apart. He came to stand directly in front of her.

"Please? I do not want to fight with you," he was pleading; infuriating her more.

"You want *me* to feel sorry for *you*?" she asked incredulously.

"No! I want you to give me time to think! I only just heard of what Ulei did to you then Lustene discovers you are pregnant, I..." Jiden growled in frustration. Callana turned on Jiden, cutting him short.

"Which bothered you most?" she demanded. The hard look in her eyes bore through him.

"You know very well *which*," his voice was barely more than a scratchy whisper now. His esophagus was protesting nearly as much as his twisting stomach. Callana nodded; her face softening slightly.

"Could you tell me something Jiden?" her voice was suddenly so small and sweet, Jiden ached to hold her. He nodded slowly, swallowing the lump that had formed in his aching throat.

"If there was no doubt that you were the father, would you be *happy*?" she was watching him closely for a reaction. His forehead crinkled as he shuffled his feet. Callana sighed and cleared her throat.

"Never mind...It does not matter," she said, a resignation in her voice that tightened her chest. Jiden watched her set her jaw.

"This is not how either of us wanted it, but I am going to uphold my commitments," Jiden stated firmly.

"What are you saying?" she asked. He took her hand in his.

"I mean to marry you; I make the announcement tomorrow morning," he stated matter of factly. Callana yanked her hand away.

"I will not marry you as your *burden*; your *obligation*!" She shouted but Jiden grabbed her shoulders with a livid look boiling in his eyes that silenced her.

"This can be as miserable or agreeable as we make it Callana but in the end marriage *is* obligation! This obligation is exactly what you rode into Adalonia for, *remember*? You wanted to be a princess, ey? Well now you are; your entire life will be *obligations and burdens*; what is expected of you is what you do from now on, and we are *expected* to marry and I am *expected* to accept that child as my own, and we are *expected* to live our lives in false bliss all the while keeping dark secrets from the world around us!" Jiden's voice was hoarse and his tone scathing. Callana had shrunk back at his outburst in horror as he depicted their coming marriage and life together as a tragic play. She started to cry but he yanked her towards him and wiped her tears away with his sleeve.

"No more tears, love; our audience awaits," he started pulling her back towards the gates of the castle but she tugged against him.

"Jiden...please...wait!" she cried. But Jiden pulled her forward so hard she yelped.

"Sorry princess, no time to *think*, just act," he mocked as he nearly dragged her towards the front gates. She continued to struggle as Jiden suddenly turned to face her.

"Do you want your family and friends to believe you are truly *happy*?" his ragged voice was low. She nodded her head vigorously, shaking lose her disheveled hair. Jiden started to comb his fingers through her tangled lengths as he spoke.

"Me as well; there is no sense for everyone around us to see us any other way, understood?" he had taken on that commanding stance he always had in front of the council. Callana searched his eyes for the same sadness she felt but saw only diplomacy. She took a deep breath and nodded her head.

"I understand," she agreed. As they walked through the gates, they smiled wide and held hands warmly for all to see while inside they ached to be one of the oblivious believers themselves.

....

Morning came too quickly for Callana. She woke, in the beautifully adorned silver room made up for her and her sisters. Hellena and Nia had their own beautiful rooms, although Nia spent the evenings with her daughter and grandson in Haven as often as she could.

Today everyone would hear of their engagement and all will cheer and celebrate and Callana will stand next to the man she loves and he will look adoringly upon her and it will all be an *act*; just as last night was and every night to come. Callana regretted her decision to lend Carr her horse for patrol; morning rides were an escape she greatly missed. She suddenly leapt out of bed with a new purpose burning inside of her. If she was to *marry* royalty, she would reap the advantages of royalty. She stormed out of her room and down the hall to where Jiden slept. The guards bowed and stepped aside as she pushed through his door, slamming it behind her. Jiden was slung across his bed sideways, snoring like a bear, wearing nothing more than his linen pants. She walked up to him and tapped his bare shoulder but it did not rouse him. She huffed and grabbed his blanket with both hands, tugging backwards until the better part of his body was suspended by velvet in the air than she let go. Jiden slammed to the wooden planked floor of his second story accommodations; thudding like a boulder plummeting off a cliff. He floundered about, tangled in his blankets as he struggled to confront his attacker. He kicked his night stand over before he made it to his aching feet; glaring green eyes peered out at her from under his sheet.

"Everything all right my lord?" The guard outside shuffled nervously from all the commotion. Callana smiled and winked before making small moaning noises.

"Ooo, not so rough my love," she groaned. Jiden's mouth fell open as he stood staring at her in disbelief. She was mussing her hands through her hair and moaning softly with a devious smile on her face. Jiden regained his composure long enough to assure the undoubtedly entertained guards.

"Ah...yes...everything is fine..." he moved towards her and she let out a loud groan. Jiden yanked her over to the large armoire and pulled them both inside, closing the door angrily behind them. They stood cramped in the dark for a moment while Jiden slowed his breathing.

"A little early for pretend sex isn't it my love?" he snarled, crossing his arms over his bare chest as he peered through a cut out letter E shape in the door of the mahogany wardrobe. Callana found herself stifling a giggle at the cantankerous expression on his face illuminated by the first rays of dawn slanting into the room now. She cleared her throat.

"Just keeping up appearances love," she batted her lashes playfully and he rubbed his eyes.

"My mother and father are two rooms away!" he growled.

"As if their opinions of me could get any lower," Callana shrugged.

"They do not think badly about you, why would you say that?" Jiden shook his head. Callana elbowed the door open and cried out.

"Oh Jiden!" he quickly pulled the door closed again and cursed under his breath.

"What do you want, *love?*" he asked, tiredly rolling his reddened eyes.

"I was just hoping my *performance* would earn me a *small* favor," she smiled at him. Jiden scrunched his nose.

"Just tell me what to do and I will do it...I have many other *pretend* things to do today," he sniped. Callana clapped.

"Give my uncle a horse! Than I can have George again," she commanded. Jiden watched her eyes dance when she spoke of her purple gelding; as his likeness jingled between her breasts. He let his eyes travel all the way down and back up her dawn lit linen clad shape before his rough voiced answer.

"A horse for a little moaning and groaning? Ha!" he crossed his arms over his chest.

"What would *earn* me a horse than?" Callana frowned. Jiden grinned down at her. Callana found herself squirming against the devouring look in his hungry emerald eyes; unsure of his sincerity. Jiden creased his brow, suddenly very ashamed of himself; forcing his eyes off Callana and to his feet.

"It was only a joke, Callana; Carr shall have his horse before morning patrol," he said sadly. Callana felt terrible about her teasing display; her body was aching to be touched by him, in earnest, but her pride made her fight her desire. She pushed the doors open quickly and stepped out, turning to shake his hand.

"Thank you, Jiden, and..." she stumbled over her own words in her mind and stopped herself short of saying anymore. She turned to go but Jiden called her back.

"Callana," he said, then looked around the room as if in search of something to talk about to keep her from leaving.

"It was good to see you," he said, instantly feeling foolish about it. She smiled awkwardly and hurried out of the room. After she had gone, Jiden slapped his hand to his forehead.

"*It was good to see you?*" he mocked himself before dressing for morning patrol with Callana's provocative display stirring in his mind and weakening his already feeble hold over his shameless desires.

....

"Morning Carr!" Jiden called to his soon to be uncle-in-law. Carr eagerly rushed to shake Jiden's hand.

"Morning, nephew! To be anyway," he laughed heartily, causing Jiden to grin. Carr noticed the gleaming white Clydesdale behind the prince and whistled.

"That is a beautiful war horse sire; you are not giving up Leviathon?" Carr came closer and started examining the mare; running his fingers over her shoulders and spine.

"Who would have that glorified mule?" Jiden laughed out loud. His voice was clearing slightly today he had noticed and it helped ease his mood. Carr turned a puzzled stare on Jiden.

"This is Elei's horse's dame, ey?" He surmised.

"That's incredible, how did you know?" Jiden asked.

"Similarities, is all," Carr shrugged sheepishly.

"Do you like her?" Jiden grinned widely, slapping the shimmering neck as the large mare bobbed her head. Carr nodded as he stroked the silky mane.

"Aye," He said.

"She is yours," Jiden handed him the long black leather reins. Carr took them and blinked.

"Oh, my lord, she deserves someone...more," Carr stammered. Callana watched from the northeastern stairway as her uncle fumbled the reins of the magnificent horse through his fingers. She smiled through teary eyes at the honest gratitude in her uncle's sweet face.

"You are much more than you think, Sir Carr. Please...take her...she is a gift from Callana for your ceremony today." Jiden lied. Carr bowed gratefully with the stunned surprise still on his face. Jiden bowed back but Carr picked him up in a squeezing embrace and laughed out loud.

"Thank you thank you so much, young prince; I guess we are both lucky men, ey?" he laughed again as he mounted the mighty white horse.

"Aye," Jiden nodded and smiled. Once Carr was out of sight Jiden turned back to the stables where he climbed up into Leviathan's saddle for the first time in weeks and led the abandoned George out into the court yard. Callana was there with a deep appreciation softening her eyes.

"That was very kind of you, prince Jiden," she said gently. Jiden smiled down at her as he bent to drop the reigns into her small hands.

He winked before leading his white stallion out of the open city gates to lead his guard around the dawning city on their last tour of duty in Esildad.

"George!" she cried as her snorting friend pushed anxiously at her back with his nose. She mounted quickly and trotted the excited horse out of the gates and opposite the patrol's western route, heading for the rocky base of Mount Roan to watch the sunrise with her oldest friend.

....

Most of Rogadon and Haven had gathered for the ceremony today. In less than an hour, Rogadon would have her king and four worthy men would be knighted. Hellena and her girls would be in charge of tonight's feast as well, and Cella had designed a menu of roasted pig, pheasant and goose, sliced green apples dipped in caramel, dark bread, and boiled potatoes, carrots and figs with garlic and butter. Women from the village had been up late plucking, beheading and removing the gizzards from nearly sixty plump geese and over a hundred good sized pheasant after bleeding out fifty large boars. Twenty spics would rotate and be replenished until all the guests were fed while twenty large cauldrons would be heated and filled with vegetables. Cella, Crystalline, Caran and Cylan were dressed in brilliant grey velvet dresses to represent Esildad as they served wine and bread. Callana, Miala, Rogala and Nia had decorated a dozen long oak tables with silver centerpieces filled with lilacs, pink daisies and tender fern leaves; several silver water pitchers were filled from the Crystal River and spread down the length of each table. Lena came down to collect Callana and stopped to squeeze Hellena.

"Oh my! I can't stop smiling!" Lena squealed as Hellena laughed.

"I know! I keep pinching myself to make sure I am not in a dream!" Hellena laughed, catching Galland's attention.

"Let me know if I can help with that," he grinned devilishly. Lena gasped in surprise as Galland winked at Hellena on his way to formation.

"*Hellena*! I had no idea, you and Galland?" Lena blushed as she asked but Hellena only laughed.

"Lena, are you really so bashful after so many years?" as if on cue, Odin walked out of the dinning hall and towards his queen.

"Afternoon most beautiful Hellena... and my little seductress!" Odin flicked his eyebrows. Lena gasped again and put her hand over her mouth.

"I hope you are not so shy this evening love...the war is over. Seems we have some catching up to do," Odin's large blue eyes smoldered as he ran them over the svelte form of his thoroughly mortified wife. He strode passed and out of the courtyard to line up for the marching formation as Lena caught her breath.

"I swear that man has no shame!" Lena let out a self-conscious laugh. Hellena hugged her again.

"None do love!" She laughed out loud and Lena burst into giggles.

"Come, we need to get Callana ready for the evening," Lena motioned for Hellena to follow. Crystalline was kissing Christopher one last kiss before he had to get in position. He was dressed in the supple grey of Esildad with a large black wolf on his shimmering cape.

"You look incredible," Crystalline complimented. Christopher smiled brightly.

"I love you," he bent to kiss her once more then dashed away. Cella snatched her oldest sister out of her gawking.

"We need to ready our sister and..." Cella was cut short by someone calling her name.

"Cella?" Braden called again. He was also dressed in Esildad's colors and Cella could not help but appreciate the taunt black trousers. He ran up and bowed before her.

"Cella, I was hoping," He stopped; suddenly aware Cella's eyes were locked on him with an expression he had never seen before.

"What is the matter?" He asked, frowning with concern. Cella raised her eyebrows and shook her head.

"Nothing at all," she answered with a silky tone to her voice. Braden's stomach flipped with the anxiousness he felt around her. He glanced at Crystalline than back at Cella.

"Oh, good...I was hoping you would dance with me...later...as...as my gift for becoming a knight...or not *gift* but..." Braden turned red as his attempts faltered and failed. Cella allowed a smile to lift her mouth as she bowed her head.

"I would be honored to be your *gift*, Sir Braden," she took Crystalline's hand and turned to gather her sisters. She threw a glance over her shoulder and caught Braden staring at her back side and turned back around, coming face to face with Braden again. He swallowed hard, fearful she was withdrawing her acceptance. Cella pulled the black ribbon out of her hair, allowing the shimmering lengths to spill loosely down her chest, than slowly lifted her skirt to tie the silken threads around the top of her shapely thigh. Braden's eyes nearly popped out of his head when she finished straightening her skirt and leaned in and kissed him softly.

"Bow on top, ey?" she whispered before swaying away leaving him gawking.

"Cella you are a terrible tease!" Crystalline scolded

"Who says I am teasing?" Cella shrugged as they surrounded Cylan, Caran and Callana and rounded them upstairs to get ready.

....

The ceremony started in late afternoon. The slanted rays of sun spilled through the courtyard and illuminated the brilliant colors on display. Esildad's silver army lined the path from the shimmering Crystal river and around the court square as well as the watch towers and walks. Odin and Jiden's royal guards in rich Adalonia green stood in a long row behind their royal family. Rogadon villagers in luminous red and Haven villagers in their Esildad grey filled the court in wait of the festivities. Finally, the horns sounded as Renk escorted Carr through the front gates in their lush red uniforms. Carr knelt before King Odin and bowed his head. Odin drew his gleaming long sword and tapped the big man on each shoulder.

"As proven blood heir to the throne of Rogadon, by the power of the Della Verde Valley, I dub you King Carr, ruler of the red city; Rise King Carr, of Rogadon," Odin's booming voice echoed off the stone walls of the courtyard. Applause rang out around the mighty man as he bent for Lena to place the silver crown on his blonde head. She bowed to him and him to her than he turned to the crowd as they erupted in cheers again. Carr was then escorted to the back of the court yard by Renk as Dakin, Christopher and Braden filed in. Dakin knelt in front of Odin; he was dressed in plush green Adalonia wear with the crescent moon reflecting sun light from his cape. Christopher and Braden knelt before Elei as Odin stepped forward again with his long sword.

"For your bravery in Esildad's darkest hours, I dub you Sir Dakin. Rise knight of Adalonia," Odin bellowed out again. Cheers sounded out for Dakin and the skinny, hazel eyed youth blushed as he bowed and took his place next to Lashend in formation. Elei pulled out his broadsword and tapped each man before him on both shoulders before speaking.

"For courage and dedication to this city, I dub you Sir Braden, and Sir Christopher; rise honored knights of Esildad!" Elei smiled as the lanky Christopher turned and waved and the stout Braden grinned sheepishly out at the roaring crowd. Then, Jiden stepped forward to make his announcement, clearing his throat.

"It is also on this day of celebration that I make known my intentions for the princess of Rogadon as I have asked her to marry me," Jiden held for the gasps of surprise before continuing.

"And she has accepted; Ladies and gentlemen, I give you the princess of Rogadon, and future queen of Adalonia, Callana of Windt!" Jiden gestured towards the stairwell as the crowd caught their breath at once. Callana was slowly walking towards Jiden in a gleaming white form fitted gown adorned with emerald jewels throughout the skirt that glinted and sparkled in the sun's orange light. Her beautiful scarlet hair was cascading down her back with a delicate silver crown placed gently on her head. She was so beautiful Jiden felt as if he was seeing her for the first time all over again. She glowed from the inside out. With her enormous dark eyes and soft pink lips she was beyond stunning. Jiden was only vaguely aware that everyone was cheering as he took her hand and kissed it before the couple turned to face everyone and bow. Elei raised both hands before shouting.

"Let the celebration begin!" Plates and tables were filled as everyone lined up for the savory meal. Cella was moving from spic to spic basting liberally as some of the Haven villagers started slicing and serving the various tender meats. Jiden, Callana, Odin, Lena, Nicholas and Elei sat at the first table and were served by Miala and Crystalline. Jiden was watching Nicholas's eyes follow Miala around the table.

"Why do you not just ask her?" Jiden leaned in to whisper. Nicholas sighed and shook his head.

"She is too young to consider marriage," He started but Callana stopped him.

"She *has* considered it," she assured him. Nicholas and Jiden both blushed having been caught gossiping like children.

"She has?" Nicholas brightened.

"She has," Callana nodded, smiling brightly.

"So ask," Jiden suggested. Nicholas nodded, his eyes searching out his prey and nearly leaping out of his seat when he found her. Callana and Jiden laughed quietly for a moment before Jiden shifted towards her.

"You and Miala have talked about marriage?" He asked.

"Of course, Jiden, all *poor* girls wish to be married," Callana shrugged nonchalantly. Jiden looked at her and nodded.

"Miala talked of a marriage to *Nicholas?*" He pried. Callana nodded again. "And who did you talk about?" he pushed, staring intently into her eyes. "Please do not be dim-witted tonight," she warned. Jiden shook his head. "I am not being *dim-witted* I want to know," he slid closer to her on the long bench, determined to get a direct answer. Callana gave him a hard stare.

"Are you so conceited that you torment me for answers you already know?" she sniped. Jiden frowned.

"If I were so *conceited* I would not need you to say it," he snapped. Callana huffed and crossed her arms over her chest as Jiden sighed and slid back to his own place on the seat.

"Are you so resolute to *hate* me? Uncross your arms, people are looking over here," he smiled nervously as two villagers from Haven glanced towards Callana. She tossed her hair and glared at him with one raised eyebrow.

"I am too tired to *pretend* tonight, love," she argued sarcastically as Jiden glowered at her.

"We agreed we would get along," he reminded her with a fake smile stretching his face. Callana sighed and smiled widely at him.

"And how will we *get along* after the wedding?" she asked nonchalantly tracing her hand up and down Jiden's arm for the sake of passers by. Jiden moved closer and put his other arm around Callana's middle.

"How do you mean?" Jiden asked catching his mother's watchful eye and leaning in to kiss Callana's cheek.

"I mean your mother will not be in our *bedchamber*," she said quietly. Jiden took her hand and led her to the stair well of the northwest tower where they would not be seen or heard.

"When we are married I intend for us to live as *husband and wife*," Jiden stood with his arms folded over his chest trying his best to look as stern as he sounded. Callana's mouth fell open. Jiden shifted uncomfortably.

"Callana, we are taking a vow, death do us part," he explained. Callana shook her head.

"You mean even if we do not even *like* one another you expect..." Callana's eyes were wide with disbelief.

"You are expecting a life of *celibacy?*" he challenged. Callana flustered.

"Well...no...But I expect to be loved by the man I go to bed with!" Callana snapped.

"And I expect to make love to my wife!" Jiden roared. Callana started to cry.

"I refuse to fight every time we are together Callana! There must be worst things to suffer than *me*," Jiden's temper flared.

"Enough!" He took her hand and pulled her up the stair well and passed the guard to the tower walk way to look out over the village of Haven.

"Look, look!" Jiden pointed to the north. Callana looked towards the forest and wiped her reddened eyes.

"Beyond that forest is my kingdom, *your* kingdom, full of people who live their lives under the protection of *our* army and *our* laws," he explained with his ragged voice. Callana just stared blankly.

"They need to *believe* in us, Callana. They need to see us united and strong; not bitter or bickering. Do you understand?" Jiden gripped his tired throat when he was finished. Callana sniffled, turning to face him with a yielding innocence on her face.

"I understand," she said. Jiden's brow relaxed and he sighed. Callana felt an intense wave of nausea wash over her. She carefully bowed her head and moved passed Jiden towards the eastern wing and her bedchamber.

"Forgive me, my lord, I need to rest," Callana slowly started for the safety of her soft bed. Jiden watched her go before turning back to watch the sun sink leisurely into the top of Mount Lisia. His life was moving in a direction he had never imagined it would and it was terrifying him. Nearly a year ago he had protested his marriage of duty only to fall desperately in love with a false princess who he then, essentially deserted. Now that she was authenticated as a genuine princess, he was forcing *her* into a marriage of duty because he was too prideful to admit he was still in love with the woman who may or not be carrying his enemy's child? It was ridiculous; almost as ridiculous as hiding his feelings until *when*? She gives birth to a baby he cannot deny is his and then he will suddenly smother her with love and expect her to *reciprocate*? He held his temples against the pounding headache he had given himself and made his way to his own room; the muted sound of Callana's weeping filling the quiet hall as he passed.

....

Morning came too quickly; bringing with it a bittersweet departure from Esildad. Not only had Callana come to adore the Crystal river city, but she would be leaving Crystalline, Cella, Caran and Rogala once more. Saying her tearful goodbyes, Callana found comfort in the knowing that they had found where they belonged and they were happy. In a weeks time she would see them all again for her *make-believe* wedding; at least she could look forward to that.

Odin and Lena and their royal guard were first to leave, than Carr and Nia, last would be Jiden and Callana followed by his royal guard including Nicholas and Miala. Callana dropped back and rode next to her small friend the entire trip; eager to avoid Jiden and her latest false identity.

"*So?*" Callana leaned closer to her smiling friend. There was something different about the tiny maiden; a sparkle in her hazel eyes and a glow to her freckled olive skin that was hard to ignore. Miala blushed bashfully as she watched Nicholas spur ahead to talk with his cousin.

"I do not want to tell you! First we have *your* wedding...then *mine*!" Both girls squealed with excitement. Callana knew Miala had been waiting through all that had transpired for such a proposal and she could not be more thrilled for her. Miala deserved happiness.

"Miala! I am so excited for you! I know he loves you...you can see it when he looks at you," Callana grinned brightly.

"Really?" Miala flushed. Callana laughed at the virtuousness of her friend. Though they were only a year apart, Miala still retained her childlike purity and hope and Callana prayed she always would.

"Of course! He is taken with you, heart and soul!" Callana assured. As if in testament, both girls looked ahead to catch Nicholas turned around watching Miala and they squealed again.

"*Talk about taken*! Did you see that look on Prince Jiden's face?" Miala giggled. Callana frowned, glancing ahead to see Jiden's back.

"I did not catch it," she mumbled, thoroughly disappointed she had missed it; then she realized it must have been for appearances sake and it infuriated her. She had gone from a false princess *truly* in love to a true princess *falsely* in love! Her mind was reeling as her friend went on to describe Caran's experience with the apparently adulterous Sir Joel and the shameless flirting Cella was using against the dumbfounded Sir Braden. Callana pushed her selfish problems to the back of her mind and for the first time in days, she enjoyed herself. As she listened, she wondered how much of life had she missed as she wallowed in her own self pity? They laughed and gossiped, just like old days. Miala was having so much fun she nearly forgot she was riding a horse at all! Callana looked ahead to see Nia behind Carr riding next to Hellena behind Galland; the two women were holding hands like girls and smiling incessantly. Callana felt her heart lift. So many of her friends and family were *happy* in this now peaceful valley; she refused to let them be otherwise. If Jiden could put on for everyone, so could she; and it would be the performance of her lifetime, literally.

"Oh my goodness! I forgot to tell you!" Miala leaned closer to whisper, "King Elei danced with Caran all night, I mean as close to dancing as he can in his state," Miala informed. Callana joyously laughed out loud.

"I missed it? Oh I would have loved to see that. Do you think he is serious about her?" Callana tingled with the possibility of the two of them together.

"Well I can not say but I can attest that several men tried to cut in and were adamantly turned away by the king himself!" Miala giggled with delight.

"I feel as if I have wandered into a fairy tale! My own sister? With a *King*?" Callana was smiling brightly when she saw Jiden throw a glance towards her over his shoulder. She decided to play along and answered his sweet smile with a phony one of her own. Jiden's brow furrowed at her obvious display. She rolled her eyes and went back to listening to her friend; ignoring the now deeply annoyed expression on Jiden's face. What did he expect? She was holding up her end of their bargain right? What more could he want?

The forest started to open up as they rounded the western edge of Lake Ceruleana. Jiden sighed; he could not express how much he had missed this glorious place. Odin and Lena and their guard sprinted ahead, save for Dashend and Earnest who rode on either side of Lashend; shoving him playfully between father and uncle. David and Franklin socked each other in the arm over and over again to see who could take it the longest before yelping in pain; Gracien and Galland were laughing with each other about the crew of misfits that had somehow survived through all that had happened; Laden was smiling contentedly as usual next to Senren who was uncharacteristically quiet as they passed the lake. Nicholas hurried his rambunctious chestnut back to collect Miala and the two cantered merrily up the winding path through the village. Callana slowed George to a halt as Jiden slowly brought his gleaming white stallion to rest beside her.

"Do you remember that spot?" He asked, with a biting tone.

"Of course I *remember*," she snipped back.

"Do you remember being that *sweet*? Or was that the counterfeit you?" He frowned down at her. Callana shook her head in confusion.

"What are you so angry about?" she asked with wide, dark eyes.

"Oh *what am I so angry about*? Brilliant performance back there," Jiden flared gesturing towards the dim forest road where they had just left Nia and Carr behind in Rogadon. Callana squinted irritably.

"You as well, prince *hypocrite*!" she kicked her sleeping horse to move forward but Jiden reached out and jerked the reins out of her hands, turning George around and bringing Callana to face him.

"It was not an act!" He barked through his scratchy throat. Callana held her hand out.

"Ha! Give me back my reins!" She demanded. Jiden shook his head.

"You won't allow me to be nice to you, fine!" He slapped the leather reins into her palm.

"I do not have to be," He warned, as he swung Leviathon around again. Callana suddenly felt panic ripple through her hardened façade.

"What...What do you mean?" she stammered timidly. Jiden grinned maliciously.

"All royalty are not like me; the show must go on, ey? I will play the hard prince and you can play the docile, obedient princess. From now on, we do it *my* way, understood?" Jiden's tone was cold and spiteful; Callana opened her mouth to object but Jiden silenced her.

"Mouth closed eyes forward; you will not speak, eat or sleep without my permission or I tell everyone you carry a dead king's bastard child! Are we clear?" Jiden was glaring at her, apparently expecting her to have a response for such an outburst. She was gaping at him in shock; aggravating him further.

"This must be what you *want* because I try to be polite and you are rude; I try to be friendly and you are sarcastic and cold; so this is all that is left, Callana. Congratulations you have turned me into my uncle!" he spurred Leviathon and glared at Callana motioning for her to move. Callana sat in stunned silence, finally shaking her head.

"I don't want this Jiden," She tried meekly but Jiden only gritted his teeth.

"What you *want* is irrelevant now; this is *my* kingdom, *my* home and *my* threat is very real," Jiden condescended. Callana finally nodded; there was little else she could manage. She felt suffocated; her chest was constricted and her throat was burning. *What had she done*? She had played her part, had she not? Suddenly he is angry and nothing else will appease him other than this wretched arrangement? They rode in silence until they reached the small rise in the path where they were in full view of the villagers. Jiden leaned over to speak to her.

"Ride to the stables, wipe those tears off your face!" he ordered. Callana bowed her head and used her sleeves to wipe her face. Jiden scrutinized her for a moment before nodding his head.

"Now smile for God's sake," he commanded. Callana nodded quickly.

"Yes, my lord," she watched his profile soften as he forced himself to smile and she mimicked him. They wound slowly up towards the stables where Edward eagerly rushed to embrace the dismounting Callana.

"Oh princess! You have been sorely missed!" He held her tight. Callana hugged him back as hard as she could; noticing Jiden was glaring at her again. She stopped abruptly and pulled herself away, bowing her head towards the now confused stable boy.

"Good to see you, Edward," she said awkwardly; glancing at Jiden for approval. He nodded as Edward looked his way.

"Ah, of course, my lady, forgive me manners; it is a pleasure to see you home safe my lord," he bowed low for Jiden. Jiden smiled but it did not touch his eyes. He bowed his head curtly before turning to exit.

"Thank you, Edward, come princess; they will be waiting for us in the dining hall." Jiden called nonchalantly over his shoulder. Callana turned an apologetic look to her troubled friend before rushing after Jiden.

"Yes, sire," she followed him out onto the village path.

"Here," he said, pointing his finger to the ground at his side. Callana hurried up and paced herself next to him.

"Yes, sire," she huffed as she stretched to keep up with his grueling strides. Jiden was feeling his power now; enjoying the escape from callous arguments and nasty looks. He sighed with his satisfaction. When they reached the front doors, Jiden turned to her. He straightened her riding clothes than shook his head.

"This wont do; change into appropriate dinner wear once we are inside, understood?" he ordered.

"Yes, sire," She nodded compliantly. The door guards, Sir Ellis and Sir Jerrik exchanged puzzled glances but snapped back to attention when Jiden noticed their concern. Once inside, Callana dashed to her room and slammed her door falling back against the limestone wall of her sanctuary; grateful for the brief reprieve from the new tyrannical Jiden. She had finally slowed her breathing when there was a knock at the door. She gasped and rushed across the room to her wardrobe. She frantically pulled out a pink satin over tunic when Jiden opened the door.

"I am wearing black, dress to match me," He demanded snidely. She huffed; running over to slam the door, cutting off his exit.

"Jiden, I cannot do this!" her eyes were pleading; her hands clasped in front of her as she begged for mercy. Jiden's stone façade remained as he shook his head.

"How should we break the news then? Formal announcement?" he asked contritely. Callana fell to her knees and cried.

"Please? I can hardly breathe...I..."Jiden pulled her up by her arms and slammed her against the door.

"This is how it is! Get used to it princess! Now get dressed!" He pushed her away as he left, slamming the door behind him. Callana's sobbing was interrupted by a knock on the door. Callana frantically tore through her dresses in search of a black dress.

"Coming, my lord," she called.

"What is the matter my dear?" Odin asked gently. Callana spun around and rushed to hug the enormous man.

"Oh, sire, it is you! I was just..." she stopped short of explanation when Jiden's warning filled her ears again. Odin may already know of her rape by Ulei, but the kingdom did not. She backed away and bowed for him.

"Forgive my display, sire. I will be dressed momentarily," she promised. Odin's eyes widened in disbelief but he bowed politely, assuming it was the hormonal ravages of pregnancy in action. Suddenly he remembered why he had come to her door and he handed her something.

"My son said you would be in need of something to wear," he said kindly. Callana took the black satin dress out of his hands and held it out in front of her with tears in her eyes.

"Oh, black! Thank you sire! Thank you!" she turned to dress as Odin shut the door and walked slowly towards the dinning room. That was quite a dramatic reaction to a simple dress in deed. He mentally reminded himself to talk to his wife about the young princess later and brushed it aside. Tonight, he swore to get drunk and forget the last few weeks.

Callana stood before the full length mirror in her room and turned side to side. The dress was backless, so she should braid her hair, maybe to one side? Or let it fall? Up on top of her head? She felt as if she were spiraling. She was even second guessing her own hair style! She was shivering slightly with her stomach swirling when she made her way to the dining hall. As she entered, Lena put her hands to her delicate face.

"Oh Callana, you are stunning! Just stunning!" she cried, rushing to kiss her cheeks. Callana checked Jiden for consent; he nodded so she kissed Lena back and smiled brightly. Though it was hardly a movement, it did not go unnoticed. Odin looked at his son who shrugged casually. Something was going on but Odin reminded himself he did not want to know tonight, and brushed it aside.

"Thank you, my queen," she replied sweetly. Jiden pulled Callana's chair out for her and she thanked him. Than Gillian served dinner and she thanked her. Odin asked for wine and when it was poured Callana thanked him. Odin was starting to want to strangle the thanks right out of her! She was completely silent if she was not saying 'thank you' or 'yes sire' and she had that phony smile stuck to her face all through dinner, and Odin *swore* she had looked to Jiden for consent to eat! Something was going on, but he promised he would drink until he forgot and brushed it aside. It had been over a month since he had taken his wife to bed and discussing anything that even sounded like a problem to be solved would ruin his chances for tonight as well. Once dinner had ended, Odin stood and excused himself and his wife and rushed her to their room leaving Jiden and Callana alone at the table. Callana rose and bowed her head.

"I wish to retire for the evening if you have no objections, sire," she said politely. Jiden stared at her for a moment; he had to admit he missed having actual conversations with Callana but he feared if he was to surrender his hold on her, they would only bicker again. Callana was looking at him expectantly.

"We need to talk," He shook his head and pointed at her chair. Callana sat obediently but her face was distressed. He sat up to be closer to her as he spoke quietly to be sure they were not heard.

"About the wedding," he started. Callana froze; a cold fear climbing up her spine. She turned beseeching eyes to him.

"*Please* do not call it off Jiden! I mean your majesty! I will do better, I promise!" she begged. Jiden looked around to see if anyone had heard her than took his sleeve to wipe a tear off her cheek.

"Callana, I am not calling it off; calm down before someone hears you!" he whispered. Callana slowly nodded as one last sniffle escaped. Jiden felt a sting of remorse for what he was doing to her. He stood suddenly and led her down the hall. Once they were inside her bedchamber he led her to the bed and sat next to her. Callana was terrified. Her large brown eyes; like a doe's, staring at him in fear.

"What is so frightening my love?" Jiden tilted his head as he asked; gently running his fingers over her jaw and neck. She was trembling visibly, but she shook her head and forced a fake smile.

"Nothing sire, nothing," she assured him. Jiden sighed heavily.

"What would you say to me right now if I had not forced you into this agreement?" his voice was soft and kind. Callana felt her head spin with her confusion.

"I do not have anything to say sire..." she tried but Jiden cut her short.

"Jiden," he corrected. Callana was irritated now.

"I have nothing to say, Jiden?" she tested. Jiden ran his hands through his hair and cursed.

"I am asking you to be yourself, do you not understand anything?" Jiden stood to stoke the slow burning fire, built to ward off a particularly cold February night. Callana took one of her pillows and stood; slapping Jiden across the face with it.

"No! I don't understand anything because you are confusing me!" She paced back and forth and mocked him.

"*Shut your mouth and smile*! Now you want me to speak freely and say *what*? Something to make you mad and then you tell everyone about me?" she came to stand in front of him and slapped him in the face with her pillow again. Jiden stood wide eyed with his jaw slack. Suddenly Callana stopped pacing and turned on him with accusing eyes.

"I know what you are doing!" she said, pointing her pillow at him than her bed.

"You think if you are sweet to me for a few moments we will make love and than you will get up tomorrow morning and be cruel all over again, well no thank you! I still have a few days before this body belongs to you and until than forget it!" she turned towards the door, swinging it open and gesturing for him to go. Jiden walked dejectedly into the hallway as the door slammed shut behind him.

"That went well," he murmured as he ambled towards his room. She could not have been further from the truth, but it was just as well he hadn't weakened. It was obvious that given her *own* will, Callana was content to squabble and Jiden could not have that. His new persona was exhausting, however and it upset Callana; he decided that if they both lived to see their wedding day, he would take back his threat; hopefully winning back his *true* Callana.

....

"Something is going on," Lena was pacing the floor of her bedroom while Odin watched on with dwindling patience.

"Love; there is nothing to worry about! Callana is...is....finding herself....trying to be a princess and all," Odin tried, patting the bed and smiling.

"Come here beautiful," he winked, exasperating his wife even further.

"Odin! I know you see it! He is....controlling her, or something...like your cousin!" she accused coming to an abrupt conclusion.

"Lena, *wife*, if truth be told he could be a fairy wood sprite right now and I could care less," Odin sighed. Lena gasped.

"She is *pregnant*! Do you not see the stress she is under? This could affect her baby!" she stomped her foot. Odin shook his head.

"Again, cannot care right now," he started undressing as Lena watched on in horror.

"Is this about *sex*?" she demanded. Odin stood naked on the opposite side of their large feather bed and grinned.

"Aye; lots and lots of sex," he flicked his eyebrows and jumped into bed. Lena crossed her arms and raised one eyebrow.

"I am not in the mood," she looked away casually to avoid her husband's naked form crawling across the bed towards her.

"Lena, you will feel much better if you take off that itchy dress," Odin pouted as he pulled himself onto his knees, reaching out to turn her around to unlace her dress. Lena felt herself smiling despite her mood. It *had* been a long time and Odin was unbearable when he was deprived. She dipped one shoulder than the other, letting her silky pink gown drop to the floor before turning to face her husband. She reached up and plucked the pin that held her hair, letting her light brown lengths fall down her back. Odin pulled her closer and kissed her softly on the lips as his hands slid down her trim waste and over her hips. He lifted her up, one leg at a time and entered her slowly. They made love for hours that night and with mornings light they made love again. When they finished the last time Odin rolled onto his side and propped his head on his hand.

"Now, what were you saying about Jiden?" He sighed. Lena giggled and pushed him backwards off the bed.

"Fix it!" She demanded as she rolled out of bed and began dressing for morning council. Odin saluted as she left the room then dressed in his chainmail. He would accompany Jiden on morning patrols until the wedding; after which Jiden would be in charge of defenses again. Odin dreaded prying into his son's relationship no matter how peculiar it was; but for Lena, he would walk through the fires of hell. If only Jiden were as easy.

Outside, the brisk morning was already starting to lighten as crimson dawn chased the deep sapphire of night out of the sky. He could see Jiden was already mounted and waiting and it gave him hope. At least he knows where he is supposed to be, Odin thought. When he reached the stables, Edward had already saddled the king's giant black horse and was holding the reins out for the king with his head bowed.

"Good morning y y your majesty," Edward stuttered nervously. Odin frowned.

"Good morning, Edward. Is something the matter?" he asked. Edward shook his down turned head.

"No sire, your majesty, my lord," Edward answered. Now the stable boy was crazy, the big king decided.

"Edward, look at me," Odin ordered. Edward looked up timidly. Odin bent to look him over.

"Are you *sick?*" He asked. Edward shook his head vigorously.

"Have you gone mad?" He asked. Edward shook his head again. Odin sighed.

"Thank you Edward, that is all," Odin bowed his head and mounted up, eager to get out of this uncomfortable meeting. *What was going on?* He had known Edward's father before there was an *Edward* and in all that time he had never patronized the boy; surely there was no need to suddenly put on airs. Odin's mighty mount clopped down the path to meet up with his and Jiden's guard.

"Morning sire," they shouted in unison. Odin smiled.

"Thank God you are not all insane as well," Odin muttered. Galland chuckled, then socked Senren in the arm.

"You sure about that?" Galland challenged. Sir Kern laughed out loud as the stout red head blustered angrily.

"You are absolutely irritating when you're in love, you know that?" Senren shook his head. Galland laughed even harder. Odin noticed everyone seemed to be in joyful spirits today, save for Jiden. He watched his son's eyes scan the dim horizon as Callana and George thundered into view then they squinted contemptuously. Odin made his assignments quickly.

"Galland, Kern, Dashend, Lashend and Earnest; East," He commanded.

"Aye!" they answered and galloped off towards Green mountain falls.

"Franklin, Senren, David, Graven and Reinhold; West," he continued.

"Aye!" they answered, spurring eager mounts towards the distant opening of the caves.

"Erik, Laden, Gracien, Paul and Keiton; the road," Odin called.

"Aye!" they rushed out for the newest leg of the patrol. Odin than turned to his agitated son.

"Father, that leaves just the two of us," Jiden condescended. Now Odin knew something was wrong and looked him over grimly.

"Come my son, let us talk," Odin motioned north and Jiden rolled his eyes.

"*Please;* Callana is pregnant, I think it is a little late for this," Jiden snarled. Odin halted in place and stared at his son in shock.

"You speak lightly of fatherhood? So you assume yourself an expert?" Odin chastised as he urged his horse next to Jiden's. The angry prince shrugged.

"What could be so difficult? I will take him hunting once in a while, have Galland teach him archery and the sword and then I will leave for war and break his heart. Besides, it is probably not even mine," Jiden waved his hand nonchalantly; thoroughly enraging his father.

"What ever is making you an antagonistic little whelp do not take it out on me! I did not *choose* to march into war and leave my family! I am the king! I make decisions for my *kingdom* not *myself!*" Odin bellowed. Jiden turned to him with his head tilted and a sarcastic smirk.

"Well if *you* can do it than how difficult could it be?" he glared at his father with red eyes. Odin had reached his limit; he struck out, punching Jiden square in the jaw with enough force to knock him off his horse. Jiden fell hard but recovered quickly; jumping to ram into the dismounting Odin, taking him to the ground. The two rolled around snarling and muttering until the returning patrols had spotted them and rushed to pull them apart.

"My lord!" Galland yanked Jiden back by both elbows as Kern and Keiton grappled Odin and held him back. Jiden kicked with all his might, shattering his freshly healed foot as it met with Galland's thick shin bone. Jiden cursed. "Let me go Galland! Now!" he was struggling hard but Galland was too strong.

"Calm down, my lord, he is your *father!*" Galland held strong until Jiden had stopped wiggling. Odin was mortified by his own actions. He reached for Jiden and hugged him tightly. Jiden did not fight; he fell into his father's chest and held there as the flabbergasted guard looked on.

"What if it is not *mine*? What if it is not *mine*?" Jiden's muffled voice kept repeating the same thing over and over again. Odin gave Galland a look and the big knight nodded and waved his hand to clear out the rest of the guard. Odin did not think of morning report or patrol; he did not notice the sun rising over Mount Andoria warning that he would miss morning council; he could think of nothing more than holding his sobbing son and doing whatever it took to ease his pain.

....

"Where is the king?" Lena asked. Kern scratched his unruly blonde head and furrowed untamed eyebrows.

"Ah, he and the prince, they were..." Kern searched his mind for an appropriate word as his hands gestured about.

"They was hugging, your majesties," Senren offered, smiling wide for Lena and Callana's benefit. Both women exchanged glances before Lena spoke.

"*Hugging?*" she clarified. Senren nodded.

"Hugging," Laden nodded happily. Galland slapped his hand to his forehead then smiled at the queen.

"We have some training to do, my lady, my *ladies* that is; if you do not mind?" Galland bowed and turned to usher his idiot patrol out of the room. Sir Kern was waiting for Lena to discharge him, as she was the other half of his responsibilities.

"That will be all, Sir Kern," Lena bowed her head gracefully and the group backed out of the room slowly as if she might change her mind. As they turned to walk through the open doors of the hall Graven flashed a smile.

"Hugging," he nodded. Lena smiled back and nodded.

"Yes, thank you Sir Graven," she called. When she turned to face Callana they both fell into riotous laughter.

"Barring none, that was the oddest report I have ever received! Come I have something to show you," Lena nearly skipped out of the room. On her way she had Sir Nevens take a message to Corrin that morning council would be moved to this evening. She took Callana's hand and rushed her to the large library where a long, semi flat package lay on the table. Callana laughed at Lena's excited giggle.

"What is it my lady?" Callana asked.

"Oh enough of that; honestly you were more of a princess when you didn't know you were one!" Lena laughed. Callana released a ragged breath in relief. At last, *someone* wants her to be herself.

"Thank you Lena; this has been..." she stopped, suddenly aware she had almost gave away her and Jiden's secret pact.

"What my dear?" Lena asked as she handed Callana the package.

"Nothing," Callana smiled and carefully pulled the top off to find a shimmering, wedding dress made of the softest velvet in the most luxurious shade of daisy yellow Callana had ever seen. She caressed the fabric gently and held it to her face.

"Oh Lena! It is wonderful!" she exclaimed as tears streamed down her face. Lena shushed her.

"None of that!" Lena scolded. Callana sniffled and laughed softly.

"I thought, seeing as how Dellandore *hated* me..." she started. Lena shook her head.

"Actually, the carrier that brought that brought a note from Talera herself that expressed her fondness for you and how much you deserved this dress!" Lena smiled brightly and kissed Callana's forehead.

"And it is true," she added.

"Now, I know your mother and sisters will be eager but no one can see you in it until the wedding day, understood? It is bad luck to be seen early," she warned. Callana nodded fervently and spun around holding the dress to her. When she stopped, Lena was standing in front of her with something clutched in her hands.

"What is it?" Callana asked. Lena opened her hands, revealing a gleaming necklace. The emeralds and sapphires were clustered in the shape of an oval hanging off a delicate silver chain. It was magnificent.

"This was my mother's and I was to pass it down to my..." Lena did not finish and she did not have to. Callana took the necklace in her hand and grabbed Lena in a fierce embrace.

"Lena, I would be honored to wear it as I am honored to be your daughter, if you will have me?" Callana cried. Tears streamed down Lena's cheeks as she kissed Callana on each eye lid.

"You are a wonderful daughter and you will be a wonderful wife and mother," she said as she patted Callana's still flat tummy. Lena put her hands on her small hips and sniffed.

"Do you smell sausage?" She asked. Callana laughed out loud.

"I thought I was just imagining that!" she giggled. Lena took her arm and marched her back to the dining hall.

"If its Gillian's sausage gravy we'd better hurry before Odin gets back from *hugging* or it will be gone!"

....

"You know if it *is* your child or not is up to *you?*" Odin posed to his son as they rode easily through the western plains of their kingdom. Jiden looked puzzled.

"How so?" he asked. Odin looked at him for a moment before answering.

"He will be born to you; he will know no other father than you; your family, your friends, your entire kingdom will see him as your son," he explained. Jiden seemed to brighten a little and he smiled.

"That is true, isn't it?" the youth sighed. Odin felt his own worries for his son lift with the satisfaction in that sigh. He slapped him on the back.

"That was a good hit; almost killed the old man!" Odin chuckled as Jiden ran a hand over his own sore jaw line.

"Serves you well, *old man!*" Jiden laughed. Odin's grin faded as he turned serious eyes to his son.

"Just so I can tell your mother that we talked...perhaps you could ease up on Callana?" Odin raised both his dark bushy eyebrows after he spoke; Jiden grimaced.

"Oh, you noticed that did you?" Jiden felt a terrible guilt fill him suddenly. It was terrible he had struck such a deal with her in the first place but to treat her badly enough as to be evident to everyone was absolutely shameful. Jiden cleared his throat in an attempt to explain the cruel arrangement but was saved by his father's own summation.

"You must allow her to be the princess she *wishes* to be; if she is forced into her role, she will be miserable and believe me when I tell you that a miserable wife means no..." Odin stopped abruptly to rephrase.

"No *bedroom* play," He continued; ominously deepening his voice and frowning. Jiden laughed out loud with this.

"I see, so that is why you are so desperate to solve my petty problems, ey?" He grinned devilishly. Odin shook his head.

"Not entirely, but it is the greatest motivator," he wiggled his eyebrows and smiled, causing Jiden to cackle wildly. As they neared the stables, Jiden could see Callana coming down the winding path and entering from the northern end. Odin saw her as well and turned to wink at his son. They dismounted together and Odin tossed his reins flamboyantly over his shoulder for Jiden to catch.

"Take care of my horse, boy," He teased and strode away towards the castle.

"Ah yes, your majesty," Jiden shook his head and sighed and entered the stable with both horses in tow. Callana was bent and picking out George's hoof when from her upside down view point she saw Jiden come in. She stood quickly and nervously started to fidget with her hair. Jiden led Leviathon into his pen and his father's giant black horse into his own before walking slowly over towards Callana.

"I have not seen you," He started quietly. Callana did not answer; she was still braiding and unbraiding her hair fretfully.

"I have been thinking," he began. Callana immediately jumped and turned to face him, bowing her head graciously.

"Yes, my lord?" she asked. Jiden's temper spiked suddenly, as it seemed to around this new, demeaned Callana. He sighed heavily.

"Callana, I have been thinking about calling this ridiculous thing off-" Jiden did not finish before Callana burst into tears.

"No! Please, sire...I have done everything you've asked! I beg you do not break your word please? I will do better!" she was sobbing now as she begged and Jiden realized his mistake in phrasing.

"I only meant I will not-"Callana cut Jiden short again; horrified to hear him cancel their wedding.

"We have only one more day, your majesty! I...I...I will go...yes! I will leave for the entire day as to not upset you or bring shame to my station, my lord! Please..." she backed away slowly; pulling the bridled George towards the northern door. Jiden threw his arms up in exasperation as she left; evidently to ride bare back, until the sun went down. He kicked some straw with his stinging foot and inadvertently sent a clod or manure sailing across the stable and smacking right into the chest of a petrified Edward.

"Where did you come from?" Jiden snarled as the clod unstuck and fell with a loud plop to the ground at Edward's feet. The young man looked to his feet ashamed.

"So sorry, my lord...I...did not mean to be eavesdropping...been mucking the whole time, my lord," he mumbled and turned back to his dirty work as Jiden rubbed his exhausted eyes.

"Look, Edward; please forgive my behavior," he started but Edward shook his filthy head.

"Oh my lord, no need to be asking me for forgivin my lord," Edward insisted. Jiden stepped towards him and the young boy stiffened and braced for what he apparently thought was an inevitable attack. Jiden gritted his teeth as he reached out to take Edwards rigid forearm in a handclasp.

"It was unacceptable and I am asking you to forgive me," Jiden clarified but Edward only looked more befuddled.

"But you are the prince, prince Jiden; I should not be forgiving anything you do," Edward explained. Jiden sighed and nodded his head.

"Yes, I *am* the prince that is precisely why it was *unacceptable* and you should *not* forgive me," Jiden said slowly. Edward sat agape for a moment than started to nod, smiling crookedly as understanding came to him. He yanked his hand away and crossed his arms with a raised eyebrow.

"Fine! Then I don't forgive you," He announced; smugly turning his head to avoid Jiden's gawking expression.

"*Please*, forgive me Edward?" Jiden finally asked. Edward waved his hand and laughed.

"Of course I forgive you my lord!" He snorted and shook his head as he went back to mucking and Jiden left the stable convinced Edward no longer remembered what to forgive Jiden for.

....

"Thank you Gillian, most kind," Jiden grumbled as the hefty cook replenished his third bowl of mutton soup and his sixth goblet of red wine. Gillian bowed and turned to leave as Jiden reached out and slapped her on her generous behind.

"Leave the bottle, beautiful!" he commanded offhandedly as he leaned back in his father's throne in the cavernous, empty hall; propping his feet up on the long cedar table and stretching back to stare blankly into the fire. The entire day had passed and true to her word, Callana had kept out of his sight. Out of anyone's sight for that matter and he knew why. His churlish demands had her so insecure she did not know how to behave around everyone so she chose not to be around anyone at all. He had tried to tell her to be herself, that he had had enough of this game and she had ruined that attempt and who could blame her? Even he could see how she had made the mistaken assumption that he was canceling their wedding. Tomorrow they would stand before their families and friends; six kingdoms would be in attendance, all to see a shivering creature scared in her own skin pledge her devotion to a shameful prince. His aunts and uncles, and cousins would be meeting her for the first time and save for his uncle Felonin, all would be appalled by her quaking mannerisms. They would no doubt have heard the stories of her great heroism and would stand before her and think them counterfeit! He wanted them to know the fiery red headed beauty who saved a boy, killed a wolf, took an archery tournament and ended the reign of Ulei; the woman who shot her own uncle to save his father, and bravely came to his own rescue after he had so easily turned on her in her time of need in Dellandore. The woman he had come to know and admire.

Heated by two bottles of wine and a burning purpose, Jiden swaggered down the hall to Callana's room.

....

Callana felt cold, though the fire in her room blazed against tonight's dreadful chill. She stood in front of the intricately stained window, praying for strength. Her self prescribed chamomile and mint tea steamed in wait as she held her hands together in front of her and begged God to see her through this charade; even for her lifetime. She silently promised to be a true wife, a good princess and the finest mother she could be, if God would hold Jiden's tongue about the circumstances surrounding her pregnancy.

"Amen," she said quietly as she leaned onto the cold stone ledge to look out over the moonlit path winding through the sleeping village and around the shimmering lake before disappearing all together into the dark of the forest.

Lost in thought, she did not notice the gentle tap on her door or that Jiden had walked into her room. He stood for a moment; entranced by the sheer white of her night gown, gleaming in the ashen moon beams and the desolate look in her beautiful dark eyes. He closed the door, startling her out of her deep contemplations and she whirled towards him with widened eyes.

"Sorry," he grimaced. She sighed and bowed her head.

"Of course, my lord," she offered tiredly. Jiden walked over and stood his now empty bottle on the end table nearest the fire and opposite the side of the bed where Callana stood. He scrunched his eyebrows and scratched his chin in deliberation than threw his hands up.

"No, this wont do! I must alter the deal," He proclaimed. Callana sagged visibly but obediently came to stand in front of him and bow politely.

"Yes, my lord," she answered dejectedly.

"I will play Jiden and you will play Callana," he began but Callana tilted her head with a wrinkled brow.

"I *am* playing Callana," she insisted but he shook his head.

"I want you to be the Callana from before," he suggested. She stood frowning still so Jiden clarified.

"The Callana who had just come from a very bizarre meeting with a fugitive princess bride to be and was on her way to meet...*me*; I will play the Jiden that was dead set against my duty to marry said princess and felt my whole world would end...and then... I saw you," his theatrical voice softened as he took both her hands and held them.

"You were innocent and beautiful; and completely taken with me on sight, of course, as you peered out around your...great, noble steed," he embellished with his hands and raised his voice. Callana smiled gently; Jiden could see her soften and it relaxed him.

"*That* is the Callana I want tonight; *that* is the Callana I want to marry tomorrow," He brought her hand up and kissed it.

"Now tell me...what Jiden you want me to be," he stared intently into her eyes, almost pleading with her. She felt the tentative hold on her emotions start to break.

"I don't know," she looked down and shook her head. Jiden lifted her chin and forced her to look at him as a single tear ran down her cheek.

"Please tell me?" he asked earnestly. Callana seemed to release the breath she had been holding for days as tears spilled out of her eyes.

"I wish you were the Jiden you were before you were *ashamed* of me! Before you knew me to be a liar, and a fake! Before you knew about Ulei..." she did not finish. She covered her face with her hands as tears wracked her body. Jiden felt his heart breaking for all she had endured only to have him use it against her. He wrapped his arms around her and pulled her to him; stroking her hair gently as she cried. As he held her there, he closed his eyes. He remembered her timid smile on the day they met; her beaming with pride after her first dead center arrow; the sweet innocence of her face when they made love; the hardened determination the night she defeated Ulei. All of the things he admired in her came to the front of his mind at once and he knew without a doubt that he loved her, wanted her and needed her in his life, forever.

When she had quieted, Jiden pulled away, lifting her and putting her on her bed. He collected her tea from the mantle and brought it to her, blowing it off as he walked.

"Here," he said handing her the cup as he propped her pillows behind her. Callana drank eagerly; never taking her swollen lidded eyes off Jiden. He was watching her with a small smile on his face. She leaned over to set her tea on the table as Jiden sat at the foot of her bed.

"What would you have this Callana and Jiden do now?" she asked. Jiden's smile faded as he stood to undress. Callana watched; her eyes covering every inch of his fire lit form openly. The smoldering look on his face made a tingle rush through her and it took her breath away. He moved across the bed to cover her with his body. Looking down on her, he traced her entire face with his eyes before kissing her lips tenderly.

"You will say I want you Jiden," he commanded in a husky voice.

"I want you Jiden," she complied; her voice breathy and soft.

"Then you say, I love you Jiden," he said.

"I love you Jiden," she said. Jiden kissed her hard, running his hand down her body; outlining her shape until he reached her thigh where he tugged her night gown up to push himself inside her. He watched her as he entered; desperate to see acceptance in her eyes. She was so beautiful underneath him; her expression pure and engaging. She clung to him as he wrapped his arms around her, tightly holding her to him as they surged together. Months of separation and pain were erased and the two were one again; their need for the other more powerful than ever. Her kisses moved from his mouth to his neck, to his mouth again; causing him to groan. They rose to orgasm together; the ecstasy so intense it was nearly agonizing. Jiden collapsed beside her; turning her to face him as he caressed her cheek.

"I love you, Callana," he whispered before he pulled her to him and held her there as they dreamed.

....

Callana woke before dawn and sighed. She knew Jiden would be gone by now, as he was not supposed to see her before the wedding. She rolled onto her side and watched the dancing fire; an indication he had only just left. Perhaps that is what woke her. She stretched for a moment, lazily swinging her legs over the side of the bed to stand and walk over to open the window. The sun's light had yet to breach the deep blue of the night's sky to the east but the moon had already begun to sink and fade, leaving the kingdom a light grey. There was a mist rising off Lake Ceruleana; white wafting clouds spiraling around and twisting together as they lifted towards the warming sky. The Shadow's forest was a dark, unearthly green fortress; now home to her dear uncle and his bride to be. The village path snaked passed dark homes with grey, puffing chimneys, warming the sleeping people bellow. She could smell pine pitch from their smoke, mingling with the dewy wet smell of hay and horses. She smiled, thinking of George down there, impatiently awaiting his daily outing. Callana dressed quickly, and rushed down to ride; careful not to collide with morning patrol and her husband to be. As she saddled and bridled her purple mount, she tingled with the nearly uncontainable excitement she held for this day. She tried not to, but it was hard not to fear that Jiden's inebriated reprisal could be temporary and by the light of dawn would insist on her absolute obedience again. But last night had been so real, as wholly together as they had not been since Dellandore. When she thought of the way his eyes devoured her or the way he touched her and was affected by her, she could not believe it had been anything but honest intimacy. George found his own way down their old familiar path towards the lush green of the farmlands to the east and the rushing Green Mountain falls. As they reached the sloping shore of the lake, she encouraged him into an easy cantering loop around. She settled into the saddle; leaving the steering to George so she could unwind her jumbled thoughts.

Less than a year ago, she had set out with the same uncertainties about herself as she wrestled with today, and yet this was new. She no longer feared the unknown of her destiny, for it stretched out clearly before her as far as she could see. She would marry today, and this time, she would stand before Jiden as a verified princess of Rogadon; not the false runaway she had been the day they met. In so many ways she was exactly the same girl; even in her deception, she had remained true to herself. Truth be told the only thing about her that had changed was the validity of her title but not the title itself. She was stronger, harder, and even wiser than she had been, but the frightened child was still inside. Jiden had fallen for the same girl, had he not? He was not in love with her position after all, he was in love with *her*; so why did she doubt? He had already assured her they would wed today; but could she be assured he would love her if this baby proved to be Ulei's? Would that end his love for her? Or worse, his love for this baby? Callana saddened with the thought. Children did not *choose* their fathers; and in Callana's case, she did not *choose* the father either. Could Jiden harbor ill will towards an innocent baby for who his father might be? Callana could feel the anxiety threatening to strangle the peace she had only just recovered last night. George stretched into a loping gallop, suddenly excited about something; jerking Callana's attention back to where she was. Then she saw what he had seen; there off the main road came a giant white mare carrying a large red caped man! Callana gasped and urged George even faster. The long horse compliantly switched lead legs and burst forward. As Carr drew closer, Callana pulled George to a stop and leapt off his back; rushing to hug her enormous uncle.

"Carr!" She cried. Carr laughed out loud and spun her around.

"I know, I know, I am early, but I wanted to see you first; I have a wedding gift, but Odin will have to agree to it," Carr said, placing her gently back on her feet. Callana cocked her head.

"Why would *Odin* get to decide what *I* receive on *my* wedding day?" she smiled playfully. Carr looked sheepishly down at his feet.

"I will show you," he said bashfully. Callana giggled at his childish expression as he walked back to retrieve something out of a large leather bag attached to his saddle. When he came back to her, he pulled a burlap sack off to reveal a glossy wooden carving. Callana covered her mouth with her hands and started to cry.

"Now, remember it has been years since I worked with wood," Carr warned, assuming she was disappointed.

"Oh, uncle, it is the most beautiful thing I have ever seen!" she gasped. Carr had carved a large crescent moon, representing Adalonia, with the widest part of the sliver being nearly as wide as a grown man's thigh. Carved along the top of the smallest tip of the crescent was the eclipse of moon over sun representing Tasladad, than below that was the side view of an eagle in flight representing Maulen, under which was a roaring lion of Rogadon, and under that, where the wood was thickest, was the flying horse of Dellandore, under which was the large wolf of Esildad, and under that was the rearing horse of Felonia. Callana was overwhelmed with the intricacy of each figure.

"King Elei has proposed to stretch the Della Verde to incorporate Dellandore and Esildad now, and this is my design for the new Royal seal and seeing as how the original ruler was Triden, I made the crescent of Adalonia the base on which all others were carved. I used Manzanita because it's curvy," Carr explained proudly.

"I love it!" she exclaimed, jumping to kiss his cheek.

"Honestly?" Carr asked. Callana nodded vigorously and hugged him tightly.

"It is the most incredible thing I could imagine to represent the new valley; you must show it to him at once!" She insisted. Carr grinned widely than turned to look towards the main road.

"Oh forgot to tell you, there was this unruly band of red heads following me all the way here," he teased as he pointed out the familiar old carriage being driven by Renk and Rogala. Callana clapped excitedly, whirling around to mount George.

"Let's see how fast that old girl can run, ey?" Callana challenged. Carr stepped easily into the stirrup and swung aboard the mighty horse and turned her around to chase after Callana. When they reached the carriage, Granlund was squealing with delight as was his mother who climbed down with baby in hand to embrace her dear friend.

"Look at you! You are stunning!" Rogala pulled back to look her friend over.

"Pregnancy looks dazzling on you," Renk winked as Rogala nodded.

"It really is flattering!" she grinned. Callana led the way to the stable where Edward rushed to take care of the horses and unload the exhausted family inside.

"You all came together? This is wonderful!" Callana exclaimed as her mother, Nia and all four sisters spilled out of the tiny carriage to smother their youngest member with all the love they could smash into her in one big embrace.

"What are you doing outside? What if the prince see s you?" Hellena scolded and the rambunctious squad ran for the front door and the shelter of Callana's bed chamber where Miala had already prepared her bath. As Callana soaked and allowed Crystalline and Cella to scrub her raw and detangle her hair, the woman took turns telling their stories. They shared their newest experiences; in every hilarious, romantic, ridiculous aspect until they were rolling with laughter than crying tears with joy. Lena joined them when it was time for breakfast and tea and had them served in the room. She brought in the dress and Hellena cried when Callana put it on. It was form fitted, and brilliantly flattering. The lush yellow velvet held tightly from her neck to her hips before spilling loosely out around her legs and into a magnificent train in the back; the shimmering dress a marvelous backdrop for the beautiful sapphire and emerald necklace that clung to Callana's collar bone. Nia and Rogala left only to collect fresh daisies for Callana's hair as the entire morning passed with each woman having a hand in the bride's striking materialization. She had been transformed from a beautiful young girl to a remarkably striking woman, ready for marriage and motherhood. Nia and Lena cried as they held Hellena as she sobbed. Cylan, Crystalline, Cella and Caran held hands and the tears poured as Rogala placed the delicate crown on Callana's elegant red head. As the room stood in silent awe, Callana stared gaping at the stranger in the mirror before her. She was running her hands up and down her dress, her hair and her face in disbelief of all she would become in less than an hour.

There was a soft knock on the door but when Miala opened it a crack, there was no one there, only a note folded on the stone floor. She picked it up and handed it to Callana. With shaky hands, Callana slowly unfolded it and read;

Our last act,
You will be the Callana you have always been
I will play the Jiden I should have always been
Who loves you and our child and can not wait
To marry you and never pretend again.
Yours, Jiden

When she finished reading, Callana held the note to her chest and sighed deeply. The feeling of completion, of totality sank in and she reeled with the enormous lifting she felt knowing there was no doubting or fear left to hold; just the eternal devotion of the man she loved. She nodded to her mother. "I am ready," she sighed. Hellena nodded with tears in her eyes. "My princess," she cried softly.

Callana made her way to the hallway, where her Uncle met her and took her arm. Carr placed her trembling hand in Jiden's open palm and then kissed her cheek. Everyone was awestruck with her, but none as much as Jiden. He stared at her, with sincerity and admiration all over his face. She was more than the most incredible thing he had ever seen, she was *his*; forever. There on the glimmering limestone steps of the great white castle, in view of the Lord above and the kingdoms of Felonia, Maulen, Rogadon, Tasladad and Esildad; Jiden took Callana as his wife and she took him as her husband. With loyalty and love as their guides they swore to uphold each other, their child and the great new Della Verde Valley.

THE END